WOLFE'S BANE

Jessica Hepburn

Dedicated to my dad.

Who will forever live on in the hearts of

those who loved him so dearly.

Table of Contents

Prologue

24 years ago, Eastern Louisiana, Silvertooth Territory

The packhouse looked deserted and resembled a sentry, resolute and solemn, as it stood guard over its empty realm. Though the curtains were thrown wide, not one light flickered within the dark interior. There were no sounds. No movement, either. Vehicles sat parked along the circular driveway in the unsettling quiet, abandoned. A thin layer of frost blanketed the landscape, glittering under the pale light of the full moon just reaching its peak in the star-speckled sky.

Tucked in the back corner of the property, a massive pavilion stood hushed near the edge of the dark, dense forest. The thick poles lined the edge of the platform wrapped in string lights, still twinkling merrily. They coiled high into the exposed beams crisscrossed throughout the ceiling, swooping elegantly from one side of the space to the other. In the center of the smooth plank floor, a sunken fire pit of polished river stones sat beneath the ventilated opening in the roof. The acrid, soured stench of char, still heavy in the air, was the only indication of a raging fire that had long died out.

The warm glow of the lights cast a long, formidable shadow across the lawn of Mordecai Wolfe, Alpha of the neighboring pack lands, Crescent Ridge. His keen green eyes assessed the scene before him, taking in the smallest of details as he slowly meandered around the edge of the structure. His breaths condensed in the cold, crisp air, and he buried his hands in his coat's pockets. The Alpha noted the stillness of the forest, the trees, and its underbrush as he walked along its border. It was empty. Deserted. Just like the packhouse. Even the stench of rotting food, blood, and decay had not enticed the scavengers to venture near the horrific scene.

'*No tracks.*' his inner beast, Dolf, rumbled in his mind, '*No scent.*' Giving the air a ginger sniff, he realized the wolf was correct. Nothing remained except the pungent odor of death and char. Mordecai dragged his gaze from the pavilion and peered at the dark packhouse in the distance. Every so often shadows briefly darkened the bare windows. Several of his warriors swept the large mansion in pairs, clearing each floor with quick efficiency. A voice crackled over the radio hooked on his belt, relaying the team's findings, or lack thereof, to Mordecai's Beta.

"Confirmed. Search it top to bottom," the other man commanded into a handheld radio, authority radiating in his voice. Two quick chirps informed them the message was received.

Beta Alaric Leal, who also happened to be his brother-in-law, stepped up beside him taking in what lay before them. The carnage was brutal, unlike anything either man had ever seen. Impossible to discern where one victim ended and another began. A mishmash of bodies tangled across the plank flooring of the pavilion, their blood soaking into the wood, staining it various shades of red and brown. Men, women, and children, all mutilated beyond recognition.

It had been nearly a week since Alpha Desmond Reeves of the Silvertooth Pack had missed their annual meeting. Until the alliance with Crescent Ridge over a decade ago, Desmond had been hellbent on expanding his pack lands by any means. Though the Silvertooth Alpha had conquered two small packs during his raids, he often failed in his endeavors. As steward of Louisiana, it was Mordecai's responsibility to ensure the safety of, not only the humans that lived in and visited the state but the supernaturals that lived within its borders as well. So, he had presented Desmond with a choice; Maintain the safety of the locals and tourists in New Orleans and Baton Rouge from Youngling Vampires and Rogues, and in return, he would expand the pack lands and assist in the training of its warriors. Or Desmond could go before the council and receive a judgment that would result in exile or execution. The Silvertooth Alpha chose the former.

A glint of metal shone in the pale light on the far side of the sunken fire pit, catching Mordecai's attention. Rounding the structure, he stepped onto the platform and knelt down next to the remains. Finding purchase on one of the thick poles, he reached across the slaughter and turned the hand. He was only mildly surprised when the appendage detached at the wrist, lifting free from its body. Carefully angling the hand, his heart sank as he examined the ring on the dark-skinned finger. A coat of arms featuring a shield and two scythes crossing behind a snarling wolf head. It was Alpha Desmond Reeves. Returning the hand, Mordecai carefully looked over the mangled corpse, taking note of the savagery inflicted on the man. The wounds on his torso no longer oozed blood but were deep and, more noticeably, fatal. The Alpha's entrails had slithered out of the multiple lacerations to his abdomen, and his head tilted at an extreme angle from being nearly decapitated. It was a gruesome and horrific way to die.

Desmond had been an imposing man, stacked with muscle beneath his dark complexion, and intense brown eyes that reminded Mordecai of polished onyx. Being one of the more authoritarian Alphas, Desmond had ruled his pack with restrained brutality and was notorious for dealing out punishments for the simplest of rules broken.

The members of Silvertooth themselves had been a motley crew to say the least, each of them having a history of law-breaking in some form or another. Mordecai might have feared the man in another life with his domineering, and at times, volatile personality. When he couldn't reach him or anyone in the pack for several days, his instinct took over.

"What d'you suppose did this?" Alaric asked loudly from across the pavilion. No doubt the Beta had already noticed the lack of tracks – or any evidence, for that matter.

"Well, based on some of the wounds I've seen, I can tell you it was Wolves," Mordecai said, making his way back around the structure. "You ever seen victims neatly corralled in a single area like this?" he asked, stopping beside Alaric. The bodies were all within the perimeter of the pavilion. Not one had stepped from the platform to fight or escape their fate.

"Never." From the corner of his eye, Mordecai caught the familiar movement of his brother-in-law rubbing the side of his forefinger under his bottom lip, and he could practically hear the Beta's mind working.

"Desmond was a hell of a fighter, man or wolf. I just don't see him and his entire pack being reduced to…*this*, corralled or not. His warriors alone were a force to be reckoned with. You and Alora trained them," Alaric stated, mirroring Mordecai's thoughts.

"I was thinking the same thing. If it *was* Rogues, they weren't workin' alone. They couldn't have been." Mordecai rubbed the back of his neck, and said, "Not speakin' ill of the dead, but his pack members weren't exactly the most upstanding. Hell, I wouldn't be surprised if this were an–" the radio came to life, squawking loudly.

"Sir, you're gonna want to see this. Comin' up."

"Copy that, Ridley. Meet y'all up front." Sharing a look as Alaric clipped the radio back onto his belt, the men trudged across the lawn towards the front of the estate. Aside from the forest rolling around them in all directions, the property was almost completely devoid of trees or plant life. Several homes dotted the far side of the expansive clearing, with some in the beginning stages of construction. A few businesses had been set up since Mordecai's last visit, including a barber shop, grocery store, and a bar. The pack had finally found their footing and started to thrive, to make a real home for themselves. Something that Desmond had been proud of, even if he refused to openly admit it.

As they rounded the corner of the packhouse, they spotted one of their Delta Team Leaders, Ridley Bronson, standing on the front porch, talking with one of his team members.

"D.T.L. Bronson. You got somethin' you wanted us to see?" Mordecai called out as they neared the two men.

Ridley turned to the Alpha and gave a nod in respect as he and a team member stepped apart, revealing a child that could not be more than ten years old.

"Found 'im hidin' in a crawl space in the basement," a Delta, Michael Dalton said, and Mordecai looked at the small boy, surprised at how he survived. His clothes were filthy, coated with dirt, and his hair had become matted with cobwebs. Kneeling, he waved the boy over with a soft smile.

"What's your name, son?" asked Mordecai, and he quickly realized that the child's hair was not covered in dust and webs, but instead it was pure white on the ends and jet black at the roots.

'*Strange,*' Dolf gruffed from the edge of his mind.

"Cormac." His voice was small, almost weak.

"Where are your parents?" The question was gentle, soft. Fearing that the boy may have lost his parents in the massacre, the Alpha did not want to cause more trauma to him by demanding answers.

"My mother's dead, and my father ran into the woods to try to get help from the neighboring pack. He told me to wait in the basement and lock the door. That I could only come out if I had to for food, or to pee."

"How old are you, Cormac?" Alaric asked as they looked down at the child who seemed to speak far too well for his age.

"Nine." Came his one-word response after a moment.

"I have a son about your age." Mordecai smiled softly, his chest expanding with pride at the thought of his only child. The boy remained quiet and still, his eyes a bit vacant as he stared at Mordecai. He wondered if the child had witnessed the events that led to such carnage. Wondered if the boy was possibly in a state of shock.

"Alpha." Mordecai looked up at Ridley, hearing the tension in his voice, and noticed him looking over their heads.

Peering over his shoulder, Mordecai stood to face the long driveway leading to the packhouse. Headlights emerged in the distance and grew brighter as the vehicle sped towards them. Ushering Cormac inside, he sat him on the couch, telling the boy to wait until one of the men told him it was safe to come out. He gave a slight nod to show he understood. Mordecai considered the child for a long moment, almost unnerved by his stoic indifference. Cormac did not move or look around at his surroundings. He sat and he stared at a solitary spot across the room.

Scratching his head at the unusual behavior, Mordecai rejoined his men on the porch, drew his sidearm, and readied himself for the potential threat barreling down the lane. Double-checking the magazine of his pistol, he suppressed the grimace that threatened to pull his lips into a frown. Wolves using silver on each other was frowned upon, but they needed any potential suspects subdued, not dead. Unfortunately, silver-laced bullets were the best option. Enough to hurt like hell, but not enough of the metal to kill even an Omega.

The Delta's stood alert, eyes focused on the rapidly approaching vehicle. Weapon safety's clicked off one by one as the men spread out along the expansive porch, finding clear, tactical positions in an instant as they sighted down their barrels.

"Thoughts?" Alaric asked, remaining by his side, the pistol hanging cradled in his hands.

"Worst case or best?" Mordecai gave his brother-in-law a crooked grin.

"Best case." The Beta answered, amusement lacing his words.

"They're deliverin' pizza." Alaric nodded with a chuckle, and the warriors agreed, their amusement easing some of the tension. The headlights were blinding as the car flew up the driveway to the mansion, narrowly missing several parked cars as it slid to a screeching stop. The wheels had barely stopped rolling when a man flung open the driver side door and jumped from the seat. Twelve firearms lifted, all trained on the stranger as a cacophony of shouts rang out, ordering the man to halt and identify himself.

"I'm Apollo Daughtry. This was my pack." The man spoke loudly, hands raised to show he was unarmed. "I ran into the forest to the neighboring pack to get help. I–I left my son here. Told him to stay in the basement and lock the door. He wasn't supposed to leave unless he needed food or to use the bathroom." explained Apollo breathlessly, his eyes wide and wild.

"Stand down." said Mordecai, and another series of clicks sounded as the Delta Team returned their weapons to safety, though they did not holster them.

"Have you seen my son? His name is Cormac." Hands still raised he leaned to the side, trying to peer around the two men that were standing in front of the entryway.

"You can lower your hands, Mister Daughtry." said Alaric as he turned and poked his head through the doorway. "C'mon out, kid." He said gruffly, and a moment later the boy shuffled out of the house and down the steps towards his father.

Mordecai kept his expression neutral while he observed the father son duo. There was no rejoicing, no hugs or tears of relief. No, instead of an overjoyed father reuniting with his son after days apart, Apollo stood rigidly on the front lawn, barely even casting a glance at his young son. Mordecai noted the shift in body language, and the way the boy seemed to cower, his small body trembling.

"D.T.L. Ridley, call in the medical team. Have them transport these two to the pack hospital." Mordecai said, assessing the man as he descended the steps. Apollo looked like your typical Omega, with a high forehead, thick angular brows, and sky-blue eyes. Strong but still the weakest in the pack hierarchy. His hair was jet black and in a state of disarray. He had a strong broad nose and thin lips. A fair amount of scruff covered his face and his black clothes were dirty and torn in multiple places. He seemed to have lost his shoes as well. When the Medivan arrived a minute later, Cormac was quickly loaded into the back and wrapped in a thick blanket.

"I'm Alpha Kai of Crescent Ridge, and this is Beta Leal," he said, addressing their new acquaintance as he clambered into the van with his son. Alaric nodded to Apollo with his introduction but offered no greeting to the man. "Mister Daughtry, I–"

"Call me Apollo," the Omega said, cutting Mordecai off. Alaric bristled at the disrespect shown to his Alpha. Though this man was technically not bound by pack laws at the moment, it was still common practice to show respect to an Alpha and higher-ranking wolves when speaking to them - specifically by not cutting them off.

"All right. Apollo, I'd like to ask you a few questions," Mordecai stated and the man nodded hesitantly. "Can you tell me what happened here?"

A tense silence hung in the air as the man lifted a hand to scrub across his stubbled chin. Mordecai rested his forearm against the door frame and placed the other hand on his hip, waiting for the Omega to speak.

"Everything happened so fast. It was hard to keep up with it all." Apollo offered up, clearly trying to buy a little time to collect his thoughts.

"I understand this has been difficult, but if there's anything you can tell me about what happened here, it would help us in trackin' those responsible." Mordecai kept his tone calm and understanding.

"We were celebrating the Winter Solstice. Alpha Reeves hosted a gala like he does every year. Everyone in the pack had shown up and was having a great time. Drinking, dancing." He looked down at his hands, balling them into fists when he noticed them tremble. "I was trying to keep to the outer edges of the party. Large gatherings make me a bit nervous. I should have sensed them. I should have done *more*. They came from the forest, hundreds of them just spilled from the treeline surrounding the whole pack and attacked. Goddess damned Rogues. No one made it off the pavilion." Apollo's eyes snapped up to look at the Alpha standing opposite to him. Something about the man's testimony set off warning bells in Mordecai's head. The words felt almost slimy like a drum of warm oil had been poured over him. He held up a hand to halt the man's next words. His eyes flitted to Cormac momentarily, before fixing Apollo with a hard stare.

"Until this matter is fully investigated by the Council, you and your son will have a temporary home within my pack on one condition." Mordecai knew this was a terrible idea as a growl rumbled through his mind. However, given the man had a child, he could not turn them away. His conscience would not allow it.

"You'll tell me everything about the attack once you've been released from the hospital, and cooperate fully with the Elder Council in the comin' investigation. You'll be under surveillance until the matter is settled. That understood?" Authority permeated his words, and Apollo was forced to bow his head in submission.

"Yes, Alpha," Apollo ground out the words through clenched teeth, obviously despising the uncontrollable reaction. With a curt nod, Mordecai pushed away from the Medivan, and slammed the doors shut, bumping a fist on the metal to signal the driver. Propping his hands on his hips, he took a step back as the transport pulled away. He expelled a heavy breath, his cheeks puffing out with the force, as Alaric stepped up beside him. They both watched the vehicle until it disappeared in the distance, heading to the pack hospital.

"D'you really think it's wise to bring that man into the pack, Kai?" Alaric was one of the few who could get away with questioning the decisions Mordecai made as

Alpha. While every member of the pack was free to come to him for answers or guidance, very few were permitted the freedom to question his decisions as leader of Crescent Ridge. Most decisions were made in meetings with his council but there had not been time in this situation. He knew that the majority would have agreed with him. Probably.

"Don't start with me, Ric. The investigation'll take months, and by then both father and son would've become Rogues if they hadn't found another pack. I did what I could in a shit situation." He did not even glance in his Beta's direction as they strode across the lawn and through the front gate. They had known each other since childhood, been best friends for nearly forty years, and Alaric had been his brother-in-law for almost half of that. He knew what his friend was going to say. Knew the concerns he would voice since he had them too, and he knew, without a doubt, that Alaric felt the whole thing reeked foul.

"He's got a young son. What if that were Declan and I?" He knew his friend only wanted to keep him and the pack safe. "It was the right thing to do." Mordecai clapped his brother-in-law on the shoulder.

Alaric grunted in response but did not argue. "Right or wrong, Kai, let's hope it doesn't get *us* killed in the process." Mordecai scoffed, a half grin on his face but only nodded as they climbed into the SUV they arrived in earlier that night. Recalling the strange similarities between Cormac's and his father's stories, Mordecai voiced his concerns.

"You think it was rehearsed?" Alaric said, glancing in his direction as he turned over the engine and pulled away from the high gate bordering the property.

"I can't say that it didn't sound that way," he admitted. The father and son had relayed almost the same explanation, word for word, with Cormac using words that no nine-year-old would think to say unless instructed to.

"Their reunion was weird, too," Alaric said, his tone contemplative.

"Somethin' isn't right with all of this." Mordecai rubbed the back of his neck trying to ease his tense muscles. "Whatever's goin' on, we have to report this to the Council and petition for a formal investigation tomorrow."

"Do I have to make the call?" Alaric asked, warily eyeing the Alpha.

"I should have you call them just for the laughs I'll get seein' you deal with them, but no. I'll make the call in the mornin'." Mordecai chuckled at the relief that washed over his friend's face. He knew the Beta hated dealing with the Council on a good day, and often made popcorn for the times he was available to enjoy to show.

"You're a cruel man sometimes, Wolfe." Alaric chuckled just as his phone began to ring. "Alaric." He tapped a button on the phone and Ridley's voice rumbled from the speaker.

"We just wrapped up the inspection of the car Apollo showed up in. Thought it was strange for a man that said he left on foot." There was a beat of silence on the other end of the line, "Turns out, it's stolen from a dealership in New Orleans. It has the spec printout on the back window, paper floor mats, and there was a business card in the glovebox." The Delta informed them over the sound of an engine roaring to life in the background.

"Well, that's not suspicious at all." Mordecai's brows pulled together, thoughts careening through every possible scenario that could lead to Apollo stealing a car that was well out of the way of where he said he was going. Crescent Ridge was the only neighboring wolfpack to Silvertooth, and with secondary packhouses dotted along their borders, Apollo should have been able to get help rather quickly.

"Nice job, Ridley. Take care of the car. Return it if you can. I want a report on my desk tomorrow evening." Alaric disconnected the call, dropping the phone into the center console. "Yeah, somethin's not addin' up here."

A heavy feeling of dread settled deep into Mordecai's chest as he leaned his head back against the seat, lost in his thoughts. The little information they had gathered only left them with more questions. He knew that going to the Elder Council and leaving the matter to them was the right move. Their resources far outweighed those of Crescent Ridge, and not to mention, was required by their laws that an attack of this magnitude and severity be reported immediately. They would investigate and eradicate without prejudice. He could only hope that they found those responsible sooner rather than later. *Before* it was too late.

*   *   *

22 years after the Silvertooth Massacre
Southwestern Louisiana, Crescent Ridge Territory

There was a charge in the humid mid-June air as the members of the Crescent Ridge pack hustled around the massive estate. Echoes of excited chatter drifted from all corners of the house and up from the lawn far below the window despite the stifling heat. The myriad of indistinct conversations was a distant hum through the open office door as Mordecai stared, unseeing, at the activity below. Members were busy readying for the Alpha Ceremony later that night. Lights were hung around a large patio, delicious food prepared down in the kitchen, and champagne chilled in the large walk-in wine cellar nestled in the basement. Several Omegas were currently setting up an elevated platform that would serve as the stage for the night's auction and ceremony.

However, the Alpha's mind was lost to ghosts of the past, and a familiar sense of dread settled deep in his bones. What should have been a time to celebrate had turned into an anxiety-filled day of constantly looking over the shoulders of his people. Why the pack council had decided to hold the Summer Solstice Gala and the Alpha Ceremony on the same day, Mordecai did not know. He had tried to voice his concerns and convince them of the possible threat, but it had fallen on deaf ears. Now, the entirety of the pack would be congregated at the main packhouse, leaving them all at risk.

A familiar knock sounded on the doorframe; two firm raps in quick succession. The sudden noise pulled Mordecai from his thoughts, though he did not need to turn to see who the visitor was.

"C'mon in, son." His gaze finally focused on the flurry down below, "I thought you were trainin' this mornin'."

"Yes, sir," Declan said as he crossed the office, "just droppin' off the latest Delta report then I'm headin' out."

"How're they lookin'?" Mordecai asked as he took the thin stack of papers held out to him, flipping through the pages.

"Mostly in top form. The D.T.L. prospects are on the last page," Declan reported as he leaned against the large oak desk behind him, folding his arms across his chest.

"*Mostly*?" he echoed, raising his brows as he flipped to the list of potential Delta Team Leaders. "Let me guess. It's Cormac."

"Yes, sir. Hasn't been showin' up for trainin' the last week, and he barely put any effort in for this evaluation." Mordecai noted the annoyance in his son's tone. He had appointed Declan to Training Master years before, and the decision had resulted in some of the finest warriors in the pack's history. Though trying to teach and discipline an Omega was something that neither of them had any experience in, and it had been a frustrating journey.

"Well, we can only hope that he's realized he's not actually cut out for it. I respect his drive and ambition, but the fact is Omegas are not built to be warriors." He turned, placing the stack on his desk.

"Tell him I've issued a demotion notice. He wanted this. Slackin' off now he's got it, isn't how he's gonna keep it. He's got two weeks," Mordecai stated, leaving no room for argument.

"Yes sir. I'll let him know when I see him at the arena." Declan assured him, giving a quick nod.

"Good. I will not allow him to become a liability to the safety of this pack," Mordecai stated, hoping that was not already a reality they could not escape. A sense of foreboding settled heavily in his stomach as he glanced at Declan, clearing his throat.

"Listen, if *anything* should ever happen to me and Uncle Ric, check on the ole girl, all right?" Declan's brow furrowed, but he nodded in understanding.

"Dad, what's goin' on?" his son looked at him with concern, straightening from his relaxed position against the desk.

"We'll discuss it tonight at the lake house, so try not to worry until then," he said, placing his hand on his son's shoulder, squeezing firmly. "Now, you have some last-minute trainin' to get to, and I've got a few things I need to finish up here. So– get out." Mordecai jerked his head in the direction of the doorway, chuckling and Declan gave him a crooked grin and nodded.

"Yes, sir."

Chapter 01

Declan pulled the door closed behind him, brow creasing as his father's words echoed in his ears. Something was bothering him. Then again, something was always bothering the old man. For as long as he could remember, every Summer and Winter Solstice, his father had become increasingly anxious until the festivities had passed. They never had a problem but as the years went on, his father had come to dread these events more and more. He knew some of the reasons, having heard about the Silvertooth massacre, and the investigation by the Elder Council that had followed. Nothing substantial had been found and the case was still considered unsolved. His father had never been able to let it go, but if the carnage was anything like Declan had heard it described, he could understand why. Out of one hundred and fourteen pack members, only two had survived the attack.

Apollo Daughtry and his son, Cormac.

'Worry later, Dec,' his wolf gruffed in his head as Declan quickly made his way down the staircase near his father's office and strode down the carpeted hallway to his bedroom. As he drew closer, he caught a faint scent that caused a low rumbling growl from the beast within. Rolling his eyes, Declan twisted the knob

roughly and shoved open the door, the force bouncing it off the doorstop on the floor.

"Hello, *Alpha*," a sultry voice crooned from the direction of his bed as he stepped over the threshold. Declan knew, without having to glance her way, who lay on his bed. He also knew that she would be naked. His wolf snarled violently, nearly breaking to the surface in his attempt to run off the intruder.

"Ananasi, get out. Now." Declan stopped near the foot of the bed, body rigid with fury, his eyes flashing crimson.

"But I want to play, Declan." She brushed her hands over her breasts, the words coming out in a seductive moan.

Declan had to stop himself from physically cringing at the sight of her theatrics. Ananasi was far from ugly, in fact, she was gorgeous with tanned skin, straight brown hair, and round blue eyes. Her body was near perfection with a flat stomach, long legs, and toned muscles. It was her wretched personality, though, that made her hideous. He had caught her numerous times bullying other female pack members, trying to provoke the Deltas into drunken fights, and seducing any male who glanced too long in her direction. He had made the mistake of sleeping with her one time and she had been a thorn in his side ever since. She had been convenient and willing, and he had stupidly taken advantage of that. Now it had become a common sight to find her lounging in *his* bed like she owned it. The woman had turned into the biggest regret of his life.

'Told you..' his wolf chided while Declan eyed her warily as she crawled to the edge of the bed and reached out for him. He took a quick step back, her fingertips skimming over the front of his loose muscle shirt.

'Persistent little parasite,' his beast gnashed out. Declan could not help agreeing since he knew that she hoped he would give in to her seductions. Knew that she had the insane notion that they would be together as chosen mates and lead the pack. The day she had called herself the 'future Luna of Crescent Ridge', Declan had laughed in her face at the absurdity. Though it had grazed her ego, it had only made her more determined to win him over.

"Does it look like I'm remotely interested in *playing* with you, Ana?" Declan felt a hint of satisfaction when her eyes flicked to the front of his joggers and realization seemed to smack her in the head. However, burning irritation quickly replaced his momentary triumph as Ananasi looked up at him with renewed determination. She changed her position and laid back languidly on the mattress again. Propping her feet on the edge of the bed, she let her legs fall open, exposing herself as she slipped a hand between her legs.

"Well, we can fix that–"

"ENOUGH!" Declan roared, rage and disgust making his hands fist at his sides. Ananasi instantly clamped her legs together and slid down to the floor at his feet, head bowed in submission.

"Get. Out. *NOW!* Do not come back," Declan commanded, and stepped back as she quickly scrambled across the floor, gathered her clothes from a nearby chair, and stumbled towards the door. He breathed a heavy sigh as she fled from the room without a backward glance.

Anger coursed through him as he stalked over to his closet and snatched his bag from the floor. Slinging the rucksack over his shoulders, Declan made his way down the stairs, and out of the packhouse. He took off at a jog toward the training arena situated about a mile into the forest behind the sprawling mansion. The more he thought about Ananasi's blatant disobedience and her never-ending advances, the faster he ran. Declan clenched his teeth until the muscles in his jaw ached. She was a problem and always had been. He considered sending her to another pack once he had taken over as Alpha but knew the pack council would never agree to such a thing without a valid reason.

'Is harassment not valid enough?' his beast gruffed angrily. While he did agree, Declan could not bring himself to, literally, throw another unsuspecting pack to the wolves. He would figure it out. As the arena

appeared, Declan felt calm and his rage dulled significantly as he slowed to a jog. The prospect of a fight, whether training or a full-on brawl, always brought out the savage within. It was a side of him not many knew he possessed.

On the outside, he was the typical heir of an Alpha, trained from birth in the ways of combat, weapons, and politics. His body hardened from years of relentless training, and muscle bulged at his shoulders, and on his upper arms. His abdomen was well-defined and tapered into the hard ridges that traveled over his hips, and powerful, defined legs were currently covered by the fabric of his gray joggers. He had a mop of unruly dark brown hair that hung shaggily halfway down his forehead and settled near the collar of his muscle shirt. Eyes the color of dark chocolate, a straight Roman nose, high cheekbones, and full lips that were slightly downturned. A layer of black scruff covered his angular cheeks and square jawline.

Overall, Declan was the definition of a rugged Alpha in appearance and training, but there was a darkness in him that he had yet to fully understand. A vengeful, merciless side that he tried to keep on a tight leash. A side that thrived in a fight, relishing in bloody knuckles and the pain that came with it. He knew he was a bomb waiting to be set off, unstoppable once the fuse was lit, and damn near impossible to control.

Yanking open a side metal door, Declan ambled into the coolness of the arena and dropped his bag onto a bleacher. He flipped open the canvas flap, digging around for a moment before he began giving instructions on how this training session was going to go.

"All right, Cor, I want to run over defensive maneuvers. You'll pair with–" Declan trailed off as he looked up from where he had settled his rucksack, eyes scanning the cavernous room. He appeared to be the only one there. Waiting several moments, he straightened and ambled out onto the tumbling floor. Reaching into his pocket to grab his cell phone, his ears picked up on the faint thumping of an erratic heartbeat. Someone was trying to sneak up on him.

Declan kept his attention on the screen in his palm, feigning that he was typing out a text message when the sound of a soft footfall came from behind him. Cocking a sideways grin, he ducked down suddenly and spun his body with supernatural speed, sweeping his leg out.

"*Motherf-*" was all the would-be attacker managed to get out before his feet were knocked out from under him, the air forced from his lungs as he landed hard on his back. Declan leaned over Cormac, his hands braced on his knees as he stared down at him, amusement dancing in his dark eyes.

"Better luck next time, brother." Declan held out his hand and hefted the Omega to his feet. Clapping his friend on the shoulder, he looked in the direction of his cousin, the future Beta, when his voice rang out in the cavernous space.

"Oh, that was gold!" Wyatt said as he stepped from behind a stack of tumbling mats, laughter punctuating his words. He was grinning from ear to ear as he walked over to them, mischievous delight glittering in his dark brown eyes. Wyatt was notorious for filming, having collected hours of videos of fights, drunken antics, misadventures, and embarrassing moments.

"You better delete that, asshole." Cormac took a step toward Wyatt, and his cousin raised his hands, palms out. The amusement never left his eyes as he gave a rational, though completely bullshit reason to hold on to the video.

"Consider it trainin' material for how *not* to sneak up on your Alpha. I'm willin' to bet the trainee's master it by the end of the week," Wyatt said, pocketing his phone.

"Cormac," Declan said, interrupting the incoming remark. "The Alpha issued a demotion notice. You've got two weeks." Relaying his father's order, he watched as Cormac's eyes shifted from hazel to a sickly pale green and his face contorted in anger. Before he could say anything else, his friend turned on his heel and strode across the building.

'*Trouble, that one,*' Declan's wolf grumbled in his head, and he had to admit the beast was not wrong. If he considered himself a time bomb, then Cormac was the definition of a loose cannon.

"Check this out, Dec," Wyatt said quietly, retrieving his phone and tapping the play button on the screen. The takedown was clean and precise but could have been executed much sooner. Cormac had nearly reached him before the sound of his footsteps alerted him.

Irritation prickled at the base of his skull at the lack of awareness of his surroundings. The most dangerous attacks were those within the comfort of pack borders when guards were down. Movement in his peripheral caught his attention and he looked up from the screen to see Cormac striding back over to them with long, angry strides. Something in his body language set off a warning bell and his wolf bristled in anticipation.

"Done with your temper tantrum, princess?" he asked, eyeing him warily.

"Fuck you, Wolfe." Cormac spat in his direction, slinging out his arm. Wyatt made an attempt to snatch the projectile midair but was a second too late and Declan felt the solid thump against his shoulder, followed by a deep, searing pain. He looked down to see the hilt of a thin blade protruding from the hollow just below his collarbone. The beast within him let loose a vicious snarl, pushing violently in his mind as he tried to lunge at the man's throat.

"Have you lost your fuckin' mind?" Declan asked through gritted teeth, his voice low and lethal. He grasped the blade and yanked it from his body, allowing the wound to knit back together.

"You won't take this away from me," Cormac growled, eyes shining bright.

"So, your first thought was to stab me to keep your Delta rank?" his voice rose as anger boiled up in him at the irrationality of it all.

"What the fuck, Cor?" Wyatt demanded angrily, stepping forward and placing a hand firmly against the Omega's chest. All the humor had disappeared from the Beta's eyes, the irises fading quickly into an icy blue.

"You won't take this away from me!" Cormac repeated, and this time, he lunged. Wyatt threw his hands up momentarily and backed away from the raging Omega.

Declan's fist shot out, striking Cormac mid-lunge. Bone and cartilage crunched beneath his knuckles, blood spurting from the man's broken nose. A vicious kick to the abdomen sent him sprawling to the mat, gasping for air. Glaring as his attacker healed, Declan's eyes shifted crimson while his beast writhed just beneath the surface.

'*Kill him.* Kill. Him,' the wolf in him snarled mercilessly. He shook his head, resisting the overwhelming urge to slit the man's throat.

"Yield, Cormac. Walk away," Declan said, trying to reason with him. Although he had worked his ass off to become a Delta, he was still the weakest out of them all. Still just an Omega.

"Fuck you, Wolfe!" he screamed once the bones had knit back together, blood dribbling down his chin. Cormac advanced, guard up and Declan rolled his eyes, tossing the blade to Wyatt, who caught it by the hilt midair. Blocking an attempted sucker punch, he locked his arm around the Omega's and yanked him forward. His forehead smashed into Cormac's nose, shattering it again. As the man's head snapped back, Declan gripped him around the throat, silencing his yell of pain, and hefted him into the air. Fingers dug into the flesh as the Alpha slammed his former friend back down to the mat. The impact reverberated beneath Declan's feet, echoing around the open space. Air whooshed from Cormac's lungs with a strained grunt, and he fought to drag in a breath.

"It'd be wise to walk away, Cor," Wyatt said, twirling the blade deftly between his fingers. Declan circled his adversary, silently willing him to get back up as the rage he felt boiled over. The Omega finally gasped loudly, barking coughs skinning along the back of his throat as he drew air into his lungs.

"I'll kill you both," Cormac rasped out once he could speak, and he struggled to his knees. The statement pulled a menacing growl from Declan's chest and he grabbed a handful of that oddly contrasting hair. Jackknifing his knee, he snatched Cormac's head down, shattering his cheekbone. Declan struck from below, landing a haymaker under his chin, knuckles splitting open. His arm shot out a final time, fist balled tight. The devastating right hook slammed into the other side of Cormac's face. Bone cracked under Declan's fist and the Omega dropped into a heap at his feet. Kneeling in front of his battered opponent, he pulled the man up by his hair once again, forcing him to straighten and look at him.

"Better luck next time, *brother*," Declan spoke the last word with contempt, spitting on the floor.

Without warning, Cormac's hand shot out and wrapped around his throat, squeezing tightly. Declan never flinched, gaze piercing into the Omega as he calmly reached up to wrap his hand around the man's forearm. A wicked smile pulled up the corners of his mouth. There was no time to react as razor-sharp claws erupted from Declan's nail beds and plunged deep into Cormac's skin. Blood squelched from around his fingertips, as a snarl ripped from the man in front of him.

"Come near me or my family again and I'll kill you, Cormac." With a violent twist of his wrist, bones and tendons snapped. His smile only broadened as Cormac's agonized scream bounced off the walls around them, feeding the darkness that swirled within. Claws receding, he released his hold and shoved the broken arm roughly against Cormac's chest. Blood dripped from the ends of his fingers as he stood and walked away. Snatching up his rucksack, he shoved open the arena door and strode out into the humid Louisiana heat.

'Should have killed him,' his wolf gruffed. Shaking his head, Declan disagreed with the statement. No matter how irrational Cormac's reaction might have been, the right call was made. Without a formal challenge issued, Declan could have faced severe punishment or even exile from the pack had Cormac died by his hand.

'The blade in your shoulder was not a challenge enough?' his wolf growled before slinking off into the corner of his mind, clearly upset that Declan had not removed the Omega's head from his shoulders.

"What the fuck was that?" Wyatt asked as he caught up several minutes later, falling into step beside him. Declan glanced at his cousin but did not say anything as they rounded a bend in the trail. He was not ready to tell him about the darkness he harbored, not yet.

'Jealousy,' whispered his wolf from the shadows. Declan knew Wyatt was not talking about Cormac, and the beast huffed at his thought. Wyatt did not ask any more questions as they traipsed through the forest. The two of them had grown up together with Declan only being a year older. The man probably knew him better than he knew himself sometimes. As he glanced over at his cousin again, guilt dropped heavily in the pit of his stomach.

"Hey," Wyatt said, the back of his large hand thumping against Declan's shoulder as they trudged across the lawn of the estate. "What's goin' on with you?" When Declan again said nothing, and instead glared at the scuffed toes of his sneakers, his cousin sighed.

"All right, well, I gotta go find dad, but I'm here if ya need to talk, cousin. I'll even braid your hair, and we'll do makeovers." Wyatt fluttered his lashes jokingly, earning an amused scoff from him. "See ya at the ceremony, yeah?"

"Yeah, see ya." Guilt gnawed away at his gut as he watched his cousin amble off towards the Delta barracks. Declan knew that he needed to talk to him about what had happened in the arena. Needed to tell him about the darkness. Still, he hesitated, unsure of how his own family would view him once they knew the truth.

'You are a protector. Vengeful and savage, but you are still a protector. Your heart is good.' The kind but gruff words from his wolf caught him off guard. Declan nodded, working his jaw. His eyes roamed over the forest beyond the grounds before he turned and entered the massive kitchen in the wing at the back of the packhouse.

Weaving through the men and women bustling about the large space, Declan quickly searched the busy crowd. Spotting a lithe woman with her dark brown hair tied into a messy bun on the top of her head, he wove through the staff and placed an arm around her shoulders, squeezing her gently to his side. His mother was currently elbow-deep in dough, and by the looks of the baskets of freshly baked croissants, she had been at it for a while.

Alora Wolfe leaned away from the unexpected affection and turned to look up at him in surprise. Recognizing her assailant immediately, she broke out in a broad smile and wrapped an arm around his waist in a quick hug.

"There's my angel!" his mother said as she wiped the sheen from her brow with the rolled-up sleeve of her blouse. Her dark brown eyes flicked over to the splotch on his shoulder as she turned back to the task at hand and she stilled, expression instantly dark.

"What happened?" she demanded, examining the bloody hole in his shirt.

"Had a fight with Cormac." Her brown eyes snapped to him at the mention of the Omega.

"And he stabbed you?" she asked incredulously.

"Be glad the armory was locked." Declan gave her a pointed look. "He got pissed over Wyatt recordin' a takedown. Tellin' him dad issued a demotion notice didn't help the situation much either." He shrugged and leaned back against the counter.

His mother took a deep steady breath and stared at the countertop for a long moment. She might only be five foot five, but she was a hell of a force to be reckoned with, and all their warriors knew it. She had helped to train the Deltas before the title of Training Master was passed down to Declan. Alora Wolfe had sent many of their finest stumbling to their asses on the arena mat. She was slight, almost willowy, but deceptively strong. She had wavy dark brown hair reaching to the middle of her back, dark brown eyes that shone with kindness, and a button nose over Cupid's bow lips. Declan had never seen an angel, but he imagined his mother gave one a run for their money. At the moment, however, her anger made her resemble an avenging angel rather than the stereotypical being with white robes and a halo.

"I'm surprised he's still alive," she said under her breath, making Declan chuckle. "He'll face punishment, I hope he knows that."

"I'm not too sure he cares, Ma. He's always gotten away with it 'cause it was never serious. Just a hot-headed Omega tryin' to prove his worth." he shrugged, reaching into the breadbasket for a croissant. His mother smacked his hand, effectively making him drop the pastry back onto the pile.

"I'll speak to your father before the ceremony. This can't continue any longer. They need removin' from this pack," she said, her tone leaving no room for argument. Declan knew that it was unwise to contend with his mother. No one ever won when she set her mind to something. Well, except him. Sometimes.

"Don't bother him about this, Ma. I'll talk to him about it tonight. Wyatt and I are supposed to meet Dad and Uncle Ric at the lake house after the ceremony. It'll be fine." She glared up at him. He knew that she just wanted to protect him, but she knew he was not a child anymore, and he had not been for a long time. Huffing softly and nodding her head, she gave in.

Declan gave her another hug and took the moment to snatch up a croissant. Only his mother knew him too well and, without even looking, swatted his hand again. He backed away a step, hands held up in surrender before he dove again for the basket.

"See ya later, Ma." Declan gave her a crooked grin and wiggled the croissant between his pointer finger and thumb as he ducked out of the kitchen. He picked up his pace when he looked over his shoulder and saw her poke her head out, calling him back to her.

"Declan Elijah Wolfe, I swear! Thirty-two years old and you still act like a damn child sometimes!" Amusement laced her voice as she slipped back into the kitchen, shaking her head. Declan climbed a curving staircase down the hall from the kitchen, stuffing the croissant into his mouth as he went.

Strolling into his room, he wrinkled his nose at the lingering odor that Ananasi had left behind. At least he would not have to worry about that anymore. Dropping his rucksack in the chair by his bed, he kicked off his sneakers. He tossed his ruined shirt in the trash can and ambled into the en-suite bathroom. Turning on the tap, he stepped from his joggers and tossed them at the laundry basket, groaning softly when the pants hung on the side for a moment, then slowly flopped to the floor.

Stepping under the showerhead, he closed his eyes and tipped back his head, letting the water run over him for several minutes. The fight replayed over and over again in his mind. The hate and hostility he had seen in Cormac was concerning, to say the least. An uneasy feeling settled deep in his gut. It was not unusual for the man to fly off the handle every once in a while, or take some ribbing a little too seriously, but this was something entirely different. Cormac had attacked him, intent on dealing major bodily harm, which in turn, had brought out his darkness. Enticed Declan to hurt him in return, only worse.

Savage. Vengeful. His wolf's words rang in his head and he heard a faint huff of agreement from the beast. He shook his head, pushing away the thought, and quickly washed the dried blood from his body. Turning off the water, he snatched a towel off the rung just outside the shower stall and wrapped it around his hips. Sauntering over to the sink, he checked his reflection in the mirror. Aside from the scruff he had forgotten to trim up the day before, his skin was clear and flawless. Though he liked the rugged look, he was debating whether he should clean up for the ceremony. He ran a large calloused hand over the lower half of his face before deciding against it.

After tugging on a pair of boxer briefs from the dresser, Declan pulled a garment bag from the crowded clothing rack and padded over to his bed. Once dressed, he stepped up to a full-length mirror and the corners of his mouth angled downward as he nodded his approval. The tailored suit was dark gray, similar to his wolf's fur, paired with a black dress shirt. It fit him well, showing off the lines of his powerful form without being too snug. Adjusting his cuffs, he shook out his arms, settling the layers comfortably over his shoulders. He then released a couple of buttons on his shirt, adding to his cleaned-up rugged appearance. As he left, Declan made sure to lock the door behind him. The last thing he wanted after today was any more unexpected guests lurking around in his room.

Chapter 02

A sharp smack to his cheek jolted Declan from a deep sleep. His eyes snapped open as he tried to lash out at the offender but found that he could not move at all. In fact, he could barely even lift his head. Lolling his head to the side, he peered down his body and noticed thick leather straps tethering him to a gurney. His clothes were now covered in blood, from fine spatters to a massive stain covering one sleeve. Where was his family? The pack?

The questions swirled groggily through his mind. It took him several moments to realize there was a small crowd gathered loosely around him. Peering up at each of them, he noticed they wore robes of white and gold. Colors of the High Council, and each member was staring down at him with varying degrees of contempt, sadness, or fear. Declan tried to recall their names but nothing came to mind. It was then that he caught part of a conversation being held several feet away.

"-the entire pack? How did you say you were able to subdue him, again?" questioned a rich, proper voice.

"A tranquilizer designed for elephants. With some modifications to account for the increased metabolism and genetic makeup of werewolves, of course." There was a pause before Apollo continued. "I assure you,

Elder Caine, they were only made as a precautionary in case of a Rogue attack. We *never* anticipated that we would have to use them on one of our own," The Elder grunted at this statement before stepping over to Declan, sadness etched in his stoic features.

"Declan? Can you hear me, my boy? Do you know why we are here?" Elder Caine asked as he leaned down over him. Declan tried to speak but was unable to get the words to form on his numb tongue. He needed to explain that he did not know what was going on, or how he had come to be strapped down to a gurney. He knew nothing of the tranquilizers that Apollo had mentioned and wondered why the man would lie about something like that.

"I'm afraid the effects of the tranquilizer will last quite a while, Elder Caine," Apollo said, sauntering up when Declan did not answer.

"How long will that be, Mister Daughtry?" Elder Caine lifted his eyes to look around at the group, giving a solemn nod of his head.

"I am not entirely sure. We never tested it. Thought it– inhumane– to *test* the drug on a living subject." Apollo crooned, his voice fading as the gurney was wheeled out of the house by four men wearing black uniforms.

"It'll take us four hours to get to Saint Thaddeus. Do we have enough sedatives for this?" one man asked.

One of the others assured him they did. They bumped and jostled Declan into the back of a modified armored truck. An IV was quickly jabbed into a vein in his forearm, while two of the men conversed back and forth about his vitals and the sedative dosage.

"Shoulda left the bastard to bounce around after what he did here," One man standing outside the truck said to his colleagues as they dropped from the back step and slammed the doors shut. Broken conversation floated through the thick steel wall and the few words Declan could make out, made his blood run cold.

Staring into the inky blackness, he tried to remember the events that led him here. His most recent memory seemed to flicker in and out, and he had some difficulty holding on to it. He had spoken to his father that morning about the D.T.L prospects, ran off Ananasi from his room *again*, and fought with Cormac in the arena. A fight he had lost. His brows furrowed, confused as a growl reverberated faintly in the back of his mind.

'*Not possible,*' the beast snarled feebly, and Declan frowned at the uncharacteristically weak and groggy voice. The diesel engine roared to life before he could contemplate the state of his wolf further, echoing loudly in the bare hollow space. Reality set in alongside the dread gripping his throat in a vice. Declan had heard stories about the place he was being taken to. Saint

Thaddeus – a psychiatric facility built to house supernaturals who were deemed unsafe to society. Those who had no hope of coming back from the clutches of their inner beast. The lost causes. As the driver ground the gears trying to shift, an emotion he had not felt in a long time lanced through his body.

Fear. Cold, unrelenting fear.

Chapter 03

Leaves of red, and orange clung desperately to their branches in the early morning rain. A stark splash of color against the gray gloom hung over the picturesque main street. Those who could no longer remain anchored drifted heavily like colorful snow from overhead to the rain-sodden sidewalks below. A blanket of rain clouds blotted out the sunlight over the small town, threatening another downpour, as Lorelei McCann hurried along the puddle-dappled main street. Her soft boots scuffed every so often against the concrete beneath her feet, while an overstuffed messenger bag bounced heavily against her thigh. Glancing up at the clock tower of the courthouse, she cursed under her breath. She was late for work, and the hot chocolate clutched in each hand was why. A late-night rainstorm had caused an abrupt weather change, turning their usually warm autumn temperatures to cool, and brisk. With the overly chilly morning, everyone in the sleepy town had stopped at Dottie's, the local diner, for a quick warm-up. The line had been nearly out the door when Lorelei arrived. Though seeing as how the diner was the only place in the one-red-light-town to get coffee, she was not all that surprised to see the crowd.

Slipping around an elderly couple that ambled down the sidewalk hand in hand, giggling like teenagers with their heads bent close together, she could not help the soft smile tugging at the corners of her lips – or the pang of jealousy that stabbed her heart. She had always wanted a family of her own. Had daydreamed, like most young girls, about the man she might marry and the children they would have. The reminder of what could have been forced her eyes to drop briefly to the smooth raised scar that marred her right wrist, and she clenched her jaw. Its twin was concealed beneath the sleeve of her cardigan on the left. The only outward evidence of what was violently taken from her all those years ago. The innocence that had been stolen from her. Dreams that had been replaced with fear and anxiety that no one would want her if they knew the truth. Shaking her head roughly, Lorelei refused to give new life to the ghosts of her past and took a deep, steadying breath.

Rounding the corner at the end of the block, the office of Dawson Therapies came into view. It stood amongst a row of vintage storefronts lining the quiet downtown street. As she stepped onto the sidewalk, the owner of the bookshop that was situated next door, gave her a friendly wave and pointed to a stack of books piled on the counter. Giving the woman a broad smile and a nod, Lorelei made a mental note to stop in and see what new books were in stock. With one cup stacked precariously on the lid of the other, she pushed in the ancient door of the office and stepped into the slightly warmer interior. Lorelei greeted the receptionist at the front desk as she sped past, making her way to a small conference room at the end of the hall.

She smiled brightly when she saw the six-year-old boy at the table coloring a picture of a turkey sitting on a pumpkin, his little feet swinging back and forth. His head snapped up, and he cheered as she entered, nearly tumbling from his chair in his haste to throw his arms around her middle. Laughing softly, she carefully set down the two cups she had been carrying and hugged the boy tightly.

"I see you're doin' better this mornin', Mister Tyler." Lorelei knelt in front of him and gently poked his chest. Tyler giggled, suddenly bashful, and quickly returned to his coloring page, glancing curiously at the cups.

"Doctor Lori?" Tyler's voice was small as he addressed her. Lorelei removed her blue cable knit cardigan and hung it on the back of the chair that sat opposite her small client.

"Yes, Mister Tyler?" she asked in a professional tone, sliding into her seat.

"Whatcha got in the cups?" Lorelei fought the smile as she answered his question.

"Hot chocolate?" Tyler echoed, his eyes sparkling as he sat up a little straighter. He looked at one of the cups hopefully, and let out another cheer as Lorelei slid the smaller cup in his direction. She had made sure that the employee preparing their drinks added a couple of pieces of ice to his, knowing Tyler lacked the patience to let it cool down a bit first. Within minutes, he drained the cup and set it down out of the way of his crayons.

"So, Tyler, last week we talked about different copin' skills you can use when you start to feel upset. D'you remember what they are?" she asked, watching as he colored in the turkey's feathers. Lorelei was a psychologist who worked with children who had witnessed, or survived, traumatic events. Primarily, Rogue attacks. Dawson Therapies specialized in supernatural species, and while most of their clients were werewolf children, they never turned anyone away who sought treatment, human or otherwise. Rubbing the scar on her wrist, Lorelei knew just how much therapy could help someone overcome their demons. Or, in her case, learn to live with them.

"Uhm, I can take three deep breaths, count to ten, or groanin'," Tyler said slowly, most of his concentration on his coloring page.

"Very good!" Lorelei chuckled at the words, "But it's called *grounding*, not groaning, kiddo." She made sure to enunciate her words and had Tyler repeat them back to her again. Once he got the pronunciation right, she worked with him over the next forty-five minutes on the techniques of grounding.

"So, three things I can see, two things I can feel, and one thing I can hear? Is that right, Doctor Lori?" Tyler looked up at her questioningly. Lorelei nodded as she held up her hand to give him a high-five.

"Great job today, kiddo." She smiled broadly as Tyler whacked his little hand against hers, and did a happy dance in his chair. There was a soft knock at the door as Tyler's mom poked her head into the room, smiling brightly at them both. Mother and son were equally happy to see each other, and their reunions never failed to make Lorelei smile. She gave Tyler's mother a quick rundown of his progress and went over the techniques with her if he struggled to remember. As she walked them to the front lobby, her boss, Adam Dawson stepped out into the hallway.

"Lorelei, can I talk to you for a minute?" Nodding, she waved goodbye to Tyler and his mom and entered his modest office. Adam nodded at the door, and Lorelei closed it softly behind her before taking a seat across the desk from him. He was tall and in excellent shape with sandy blonde hair, and ocean-blue eyes. His tanned, angular features reminded her of Matt Lanter with a dash of Brad Pitt. Her boss also happened to be a werewolf, an Omega, of the Blue Mountain pack. There were a few territories that surrounded the small mountain town, and Dawson Therapies provided counseling to wolves from each, ranging from children to young adults. With their quaint town being nestled in a valley of the Blue Ridge Mountain range, Rogues were a frequent nuisance and, often, would go on the offensive, attacking during the night.

"All right. So, I wanted to talk to you about a new long-term case I'd like for you to take. Exclusively." Adam leaned back in his chair, his eyes still on the patient file he had pulled up on his computer. "It's a bit . . . unusual but with your skill set, you might be able to provide clarity on this particular patient." Adam finally turned his gaze to Lorelei.

"What's so unusual about the case?" Her interest was piqued, and she leaned forward trying to get a look at his computer screen.

"Well, it's an adult male werewolf." Lorelei lifted her brows expectantly, "Who's bein' kept in a psych facility for supernaturals. He's been there for a little over two years now."

"What's he accused of?" she asked hesitantly, a little shocked. Lorelei only knew of one asylum for supernaturals in the south, and that was Saint Thaddeus in northern Louisiana. The ones sent there were considered hard cases with barely any humanity left in them. The lost causes. Whether from a mental break, consumption by their inner beast, or psychosis in some form or another. Those deemed unfit to remain in society were usually sent there.

"Mass murder." Adam looked away from her now. In fact, he seemed to be having trouble reading his screen at the moment.

"What else, Adam?" Lorelei narrowed her eyes at her boss.

"Rape." Her jaw went slack at his words as she stared at him.

"Are you fuckin' kiddin' me?" she demanded as fear and rage bubbled up inside her, threatening to spill over in a spew of curses and name-calling that were sure to get her fired.

"Unfortunately, not, but there's more." Lorelei took a breath and closed her eyes for a moment, trying to quell the emotions surging to life in her chest.

"Accordin' to the patient, he can't remember anything from that night, and outside sources who were very close to him and his father insist that the man couldn't be responsible." She threw her hands up in the air and flopped back against the chair.

"Of course, their friends would defend them!" Adam held up a hand.

"Lorelei, one of them is High Elder Caine." She gaped at him now, her mind reeling at this information.

"Elders can be biased too, y'know," she countered weakly, crossing her arms over her middle.

Adam sighed softly, standing from his chair, and gestured to the computer, inviting Lorelei to view the file. Raising hesitantly, she stepped around the desk and sat down, glaring at the screen. An open email hovered over the patient file with the official seal of the elder council in the center of the page,

Greetings Dr. Dawson,

I'm writing to you in the hopes that you could help me with a bit of a quandary I find myself in. Two years ago, the son of a close friend was sent to Saint Thaddeus' Asylum for Lost Causes for crimes that, I am now certain, he did not commit. I am well aware that my closeness to the accused and his father has the propensity to make me seem biased. I can assure you that I am not. I say that with confidence due to the fact that I was the figurehead in sending the poor man to Saint Thaddeus in the first place. However, I have had time to reflect on many things since then, including the history of the man I condemned. I believe it deep in my bones that he is innocent.

As for the purpose of my inquiry of you, I am in need of a psychologist who could help me in proving the aforementioned.

With Regards,
High Elder Caine Masters

High Elder Caine,
Please send the patient's file. I may have an associate that could help.
Adam Dawson

Lorelei sat back and stared at the computer screen for several long minutes, biting her bottom lip. What Elder Caine had said was the truth. He truly believed that the man was innocent and needed help proving it to the rest of the council. That was, as Adam liked to call it, her skill set. The gift of insight. An ability to discern truth from lies, reveal hidden spells and see beyond the glamor many supernatural species cloaked themselves with to hide from human society.

Taking a deep breath, she minimized the email window and focused on the patient file next. Her eyes scanned over the screen, and she leaned forward, resting her chin on her palm. Lorelei scrolled past the basic information, affidavits, and witness statements until she reached the charges that were being levied against her potential client. As she read through the list, her stomach churned violently; murder, rape, two counts of parricide, corpse-dismemberment, and several others. Her insight told her that there were lies within the documents, but she could not pinpoint what it was.

Lorelei stood and walked back around the desk, folding her arms across her middle. Her mind was racing as she tried to process the moral dilemma she had just been handed. The woman in her did not want to be within a hundred yards of this man, but the psychologist in her wanted to try to help him badly. The fact that Elder Caine had spoken true about his beliefs, and her insight of the charge sheet, gnawed at her conscience. Could she live with herself if she refused the case, only to find out later she too condemned an innocent man?

"Lorelei, I know this is askin' a lot given your past," Adam's voice pulled her from her chaotic thoughts, "but if this man's truly innocent, we have to at least try. Like I said, with your gifts, you can uncover the truth about this. There's also an incentive bonus, on top of double pay for the duration of your time spent with the patient." Adam returned to his chair, resting his forearms on the desk as he leaned forward.

Glancing back at the computer, she sighed heavily. She had to try. *Needed* to. It was calling to her like a siren's song. She just hoped that she could avoid getting pulled down to her death in the process.

"Fine. But you're personally responsible if somethin' happens to me, Adam," she told him, giving him a pointed look.

"Nothin' is gonna happen to you," he scoffed, "'Sides it's not like you're goin' in there defenseless. You're a *Witch* after all." Her brows raised as she nodded her head in thoughtful consensus, lips slightly pursed. Adam rolled over to his printer and pulled a thin stack of papers from the tray.

"Your first session is scheduled for tomorrow morning," he said, slipping the documents into a manila folder. Adam's words felt like a punch in the stomach and she gaped at him, unsure if he was joking or not.

"What? I can't leave now, I have clients this week, and I have to pack, and-" Lorelei protested when she realized he was completely serious.

"And your clients have been taken care of. Julia and Miranda are goin' to see them for the time bein'. Their parents have already been notified," he said, passing her the folder.

"Did I even have a choice in this?" she asked as she looked up from the file to her boss. Adam refused to meet her gaze as he turned his attention back to his computer and began typing out a message, presumably to Elder Caine. When he stayed silent, she knew the answer to her question. No. She would have been made to take the case whether she wanted to or not. The realization of this made her feel slightly nauseous, and she silently left the office without another word.

"You're not seriously considerin' this, are you?" Wilhelmina McCann inquired from the bedroom doorway. Her grandmother had badgered her with questions from the moment she walked in the back door, curious as to why she was home early. A quick explanation turned into an argument that traveled from the kitchen and up the stairs to her room. The older woman now glared across the space while Lorelei stuffed clothes into a suitcase.

"Nana, it's my job. I have to go," Lorelei said, barely keeping the exasperation from her voice. Even if she *had* been given a choice, she would still be packing to leave for Louisiana.

Curiosity often killed the cat, but the cat never had magic to protect itself with either. Though she was not afraid to meet her new client, she was anxious to see the state of mind he was in. Having been away from his pack for over two years, there was a high possibility that he could be well on his way to turning Feral. Lorelei had only ever met one Werewolf who had lost themselves to their inner beast; a young woman who had survived an attack on her family while they were camping. Disoriented and injured, she became lost and spent nearly a year out in the wilderness alone – slowly losing her humanity without the bond of her pack. Luckily, she had been found before her inner wolf could completely consume her mind. It had taken Lorelei and a team of specialists several months, but they were eventually able to reign in the woman's beast and help her re-assimilate back into society, and her pack.

"Your *job* is to help little wolf children." The sneering statement pulled Lorelei from her thoughts, morphing her irritation into full-blown anger, "Not some psycho at Saint Thaddeus!" It was no secret that the McCann matriarch was not a fan of Werewolves, considering they had run-ins with Rogues nearly every week. Their quaint cabin was situated in the middle of countless acres of forest near the base of the Blue Ridge Mountains, and this meant that, more often than not, traveling Rogues would happen across their home. It also meant they were usually thought to be easy targets. The Rogues were wrong every time.

"Nana, enough," Lorelei said sternly, slamming the suitcase closed. "I get you don't like them, and I know that you hate me workin' with them, but a packless Rogue is not the same as a traumatized *child*."

Wilhelmina huffed audibly from her spot in the doorway as she crossed her aged arms over her torso, drawing the pale green gossamer shawl tight over her slight frame. Crystalline blue eyes glared disapprovingly at Lorelei, a shimmer of magic making the irises dance like the surface of a pond in a rainstorm. She knew her own eyes would be akin to liquid silver, bright with the high emotions and roiling magic she carried within herself. A gentle tinkling from somewhere below them was the only sound to break the tense silence that hung heavy in the air.

"But we're not talkin' about a *child*, Lorelei," her Nana said slowly as if she were talking to a confused toddler.

"No, Wilhelmina, we're not," Lorelei said coolly, dragging the suitcase from the bed, "We're talkin' about a man who may or may not be guilty. A man who has no memories of the crimes he's been accused of. It's my job to find out the truth." Brushing past her grandmother, Lorelei trudged down the stairs, anger swelling in her chest. She loved the old woman but hated that she judged before knowing the whole, or even some, of the picture. Wilhelmina McCann had always been like that, though. Judgmental and self-centered – two traits that Lorelei had thankfully never inherited.

Dropping from the bottom step, she exhaled heavily. The force puffed out her cheeks as she lifted a hand to her brow. The gentle tinkling sound had morphed into metallic clangs, and Lorelei turned toward the source of the noise.

Her mother, Katherine McCann, stood near a large open window, staring out at the dense foliage surrounding the cabin. One hand rested against the frame, slender fingers gripping the wood in a vice while the other fiddled idly with a silverware windchime. Guilt stabbed Lorelei in the heart as she settled her luggage by the front door and ambled over.

"Mama?" she said gently, watching the woman's fingers weave around the utensils.

"Sun's shinin' on the raven," her mother said in a hushed tone, "Rain's comin' for the black."

"Rain's a good thing, Mama. I love you," Lorelei said, tears brimming in her eyes as she kissed the woman's cheek. Taking a deep breath, she retrieved her suitcase and left the cabin.

Chapter 04

It was nearly eight hours from her mountain range home to the parish of Red River where Saint Thaddeus was located. Luckily for her, Adam had taken care of most of the details and booked a room at the local bed and breakfast for the expected duration of her stay in Louisiana. During one of her pitstops, Lorelei checked the distance between her new temporary home and the asylum and found that she would be around twenty minutes away.

As she pulled onto the narrow lane leading to the bed and breakfast, ancient mighty oaks stretched high on either side. Thick, gnarled branches created a natural tunnel continuing beyond the small parking area in the distance. A red brick pathway led up to the old but pristine plantation house where she counted eight columns standing proudly along the front porch and balcony above. Large picture windows framed by dark shutters, their heavy curtains thrown open, shone brightly along the ground floor in the dying light. Lorelei wondered why someone would consider setting up their business, even one as beautiful as this, so close to the institute. Given its infamy and the type of supernaturals it housed, she could only assume that humans owned and operated the inn.

Being the only guest, Lorelei slipped into the first parking spot and stepped from her old Wagoneer. It felt like she had been transported back in time two hundred years as she gazed around the beautifully maintained grounds. The sun was just beginning to set behind the trees, their branches resembling thick spiderwebs silhouetted against the glowing orange ball. Thousands of fireflies twinkled across the lawn and out into the forest beyond while a symphony of crickets and cicadas chirped and buzzed all around her. Lorelei inhaled deeply, her chest tightening with wonder and nostalgia. The latter confused her some since she had never even visited Louisiana before, let alone seen a centuries-old estate like the one sprawling before her.

Hefting her suitcase from the back cargo space, she made her way up the brick path to the solid front steps. The porch was picturesque, featuring two stout wooden swings, one for a single user, and another for couples. The ceiling was painted in traditional Haint Blue, and the pillars, balusters, and railings were bright white in the soft glow of the entryway sconce. Lorelei stood in awe until the sound of the screen door whining open caught her attention.

"You must be Doctor McCann!" a sweet, and *southern,* voice said from the doorway behind her. Lorelei smiled when she turned to see the short plump woman standing beneath the light fixture with one hand resting on the handle of the screen door. Wire frame glasses sat over a cute button nose, and her stern blue-gray eyes shone with kindness. She wore a purple flannel over a navy blue tee shirt and faded straight-legged blue jeans while the house shoes kept her petite feet warm in the cooler evening air.

"Yes, ma'am, but please, call me Lorelei," she said, smiling politely.

"Well, Miss Lorelei, welcome to Tuckered Out Bed and Breakfast. I'm Betty Jones. Come on in and make yourself at home." Missus Betty Jones held open the screen door and they both entered the spacious front room. The small woman had a slight limp as she ambled behind the high desk a few inches taller than her and reached into a low cubby hole for a room key.

"You'll be in room one. There are fresh towels in the cabinet next to the commode, and some soaps and shampoos in the shower stall, if ya need 'em. We've got a small kitchenette down the hall from your room that we keep stocked with snacks. In case you get a hankerin' in the middle of the night," she chuckled softly. "If there's anythin' else you need, just lemme know." Missus Betty nodded her head and tottled off into the belly of the estate.

Lorelei took her time as she looked around at the antiques that filled the front rooms. Pictures dating back over two hundred years lined the walls with original light fixtures dotted along throughout. Finally climbing to the second floor, she noticed a set of French doors on the right opening into a sitting room complete with a pool table, television, a jukebox, and a baby grand piano. Lorelei smiled at the mixture of new and old, her sense of nostalgia only growing as she let herself into her room.

Lifting her suitcase onto a settee, she gazed around at the decor, in awe once again. The carpet was a deep red and unbelievably plush as she padded around the room. Elegant black and white floral wallpaper decorated the walls stretching up to the high ceiling above. Heavy black curtains of crushed velvet framed a stunning bay window with a bench seat that overlooked the well-manicured lawn. Lorelei spied the fireflies still dancing out in the distance, their slow winking patterns almost hypnotic.

Pulling her gaze from the window, she made her way to the bathroom where the walls were a pale bluish gray with stark white wainscot and pearly white tiling covering the floor. There was a large walk-in shower with sliding glass doors, a spacious sink with a white marble top perched on elegant double cabinets, and the commode, complete with wall wall-mounted tank and pull cord.

Sighing almost happily, Lorelei pulled a towel from the wall cabinet and walked over to the shower, turning on the tap. Stepping in front of the sink, she looked in the mirror for the first time since she left the cabin that morning and groaned. Her naturally curly hair tumbled over her shoulders in a frizzy mess, her eyes were tired, there were bright orange cheesy poof stains near the neckline of her pale-yellow t-shirt, and it looked like there was a smear of chocolate on her cheek. Embarrassment warmed her cheeks, and she dropped her head into her hands. All she could do was chuckle, wondering what Missus Betty had thought of the state she arrived in as she disrobed. Kicking her dirty laundry into a pile by the door, Lorelei stepped into the expansive shower stall, moaning in relief as the hot water cascaded over her body.

The tension in her shoulders seemed to wash down the drain as she lathered up her body and hair. She stayed longer than she should have under the spray. Only when her fingers started to resemble raisins, she decided it was time to get out. She dried her thick hair, squeezing out the excess water, and hung the very wet towel over a wrought iron towel bar next to the shower.

She donned an oversized t-shirt and slipped on a pair of clean undies. Snatching up her auburn curls into a messy bun, she grabbed the patient file and flipped it open to the first document, sitting cross-legged on the bay window bench seat. She flipped over the first several pages with her work details and her breath caught in her throat. There was a full-page black and white photo of the man she would be meeting in a few hours. His hair was dark, the waves a bit tousled, like he had just rolled out of bed, and his brows were mildly prominent and perfect over his dark, piercing eyes. Her gaze drifted down a straight Roman nose, and she noted his perfect lips that were not too thin nor too full. His jawline was squared and covered in dark stubble.

Her pulse quickened as she stared at him, unable to look away from the beautiful man who seemed to stare right into her soul. Something tugged at the center of her chest as she laid the photo aside. An invisible string tied around her sternum had suddenly pulled taut. Shaking off the strange feeling, Lorelei shuffled through the small stack of documents until she found her client's basic information.

"Declan Elijah Wolfe, born February fourteenth. A Valentine's baby, huh? Cute." Lorelei caught herself mid-chuckle when she remembered she was looking at the files of a potential mass murderer and rapist, not a dating profile. Clients were off limits, even if he was the most gorgeous man she had ever seen with kissable lips and just-had-sex hair.

Lorelei groaned and facepalmed into the open folder. It had been quite a while since she had slept with anyone, though she had been extremely picky. She glanced involuntarily at the scars on her wrists. The permanent reminder of all she had suffered and survived. Huffing out a breath, she straightened her spine, squared her shoulders, and went back to reading the file like a professional.

"Declan Elijah Wolfe. Born February 14, 1989. The only son to Mordecai and Alora Wolfe, deceased." She bit her lip, recalling the charges of parricide, the murder of a parent, or in this case, both parents. Lorelei stared out the window a moment before she continued reading, "'Reports from surviving pack members state that they saw the accused, Declan Wolfe, sexually assault his mother before crushing her skull, in addition, eyewitnesses state that another seventeen women were raped by Declan Wolfe. Witnesses also state that he 'shredded' his uncle, and removed his father's heart shortly after the murder of his mother. Photographic documentation will be provided upon request, as the scene was too graphic to file publicly.' Goddess.." The more she read, the more anxious she became about meeting Declan Wolfe. She glanced at the photo once again. Despite the brutal statements she just read, her stomach did a little flip and her heart hammered in her chest. What the hell was wrong with her?

"'Eyewitnesses reported that after Declan Wolfe had murdered his parents, he danced around the 'paralyzed' partygoers, murdering them one by one. Among the two-hundred and twenty-eight that were murdered were his parents, Mordecai and Alora Wolfe, his uncle, Alaric Leal, forty-eight children, eight infants, and seventeen pregnant women–'" unable to read anymore, Lorelei snapped the file shut and released a shuddering breath. She stood from her seat by the window and dropped the folder on the nightstand. Bracing her hands on her hips, she stared down at it for a moment, wondering what in the hell she had gotten herself into.

Chapter 05

The guard at the front gate buzzed Lorelei in without so much as a glance at her or the identification she held out to him. He simply waved her through, never looking up from his cell phone. As she waited for the heavy doors to roll open, she peered up at the fences surrounding the property. They were at least fifteen feet high and made of wide vertical slats of steel, topped with rolls of razor wire. Gaze drifting, she took in the expansive manicured lawns and two small parking lots on either side of the front entrance in the distance. There was a large statue of Saint Thaddeus holding a halberd surrounded by what looked like dark, leafy Begonias situated on a narrow strip of grass between the two lots.

Lorelei swung into an empty parking space and looked up at the formidable building, listening to the slow swipe of her windshield wipers. A drizzling rain and occasional lightning were the perfect backdrop, adding to the foreboding she felt in the pit of her stomach. The whole facility was a dirty mottled slate with a thick border of green lichens and algae growth lining the slick stone near the ground. Extensive wings stretched out on either side of the main building with large, caged windows. The anchor points created long trails of rust that had stained the dull walls over the decades, giving the illusion that the building itself was bleeding.

Expelling a heavy sigh, she slid from the Wagoneer and hauled her messenger bag over her shoulder. Crossing her arms tight across her middle, she trudged up the steps to the large door of the front entryway. Quickly realizing that there was no doorknob, Lorelei cast a glance around for a doorbell or call button. She was surprised to see an ancient wrought iron door knocker instead. The embellishment was forged in the guise of a gargoyle with a large, weighted ring held in its toothy jaws. Seeing no other option, she lifted the ring and thumped it three good times. A moment later, a loud buzzer sounded and the door automatically swung inward.

Stepping over the threshold, the bright lights of the fluorescent overhead seemed momentarily blinding compared to the dark, gloomy sky outside. Blinking several times, Lorelei took in her surroundings while her eyes adjusted to the stark white environment. The lobby was sparsely decorated with two rows of uncomfortable-looking chairs in the middle. A large portrait of a rather unsettling man hung over the window of the front desk situated across from the entrance. Gold letters were embossed on a large black nameplate beneath the minimalist frame showcasing the name of the doctor and his licenses.

Doctor Mastan Grimes, PhD, PsyD, M.D.

His dark eyes had been painted in a way that no matter where you were in the room they followed you, giving visitors the sensation of constantly being watched. Suppressing a shiver, Lorelei adjusted the strap of her messenger bag and walked up to the large window. A young woman with short blonde hair sat at a computer just on the other side, her fingers quickly tapping away on the keyboard. Turning her attention to Lorelei as she stepped up to the small counter, the woman smiled politely and lifted her brows in question.

"G'morning, I'm Doctor Lorelei McCann," There was a thickness to her voice and she cleared her throat, "here to see Declan Wolfe."

The woman stared in surprise but remained silent as she held out a hand for Lorelei's identification. Tapping in some details, the receptionist returned the driver's license and then held up a slender finger as she turned to a small machine. Ripping off the name tag from the label printer, the woman slid the slip of paper through the slat at the bottom of the desk window. Sighing softly, Lorelei removed the backing and slapped the sticky side to her chest. The woman gave her a nod and pointed to another door down a side hall that was labeled security.

"Thank you," she said, and again, the woman just nodded with another polite smile.

Curious if she was reading lips, Lorelei asked her if she was deaf in American Sign Language. The woman shook her head gently and made several hand gestures, explaining that her tongue had been cut out. They went back and forth for a few minutes, and Lorelei learned that after witnessing her coven leader practicing dark magic, he had sliced out her tongue to silence her. Expressing her sympathy for the woman's circumstances, the receptionist smiled, signed thank you and good luck, and promptly shooed her away.

Knocking on the door of the security office, Lorelei was greeted by a large woman whose black hair was wrapped up tightly in a smooth bun. Her insight saw past the glamor, revealing the guard was, in fact, an Ogre. She was surprised to see one working amongst other supernaturals since Ogres tended to stay with their kind on farms or out in the marshes. Though the uniform stayed the same, her body expanded considerably. The Orgess' skin changed to a rough clammy gray, and her nose took on a rather lumpy, bulbous shape. Yellowed eyes glared at Lorelei as they glanced up from the computer where her information was being punched in. Despite her rather grotesque physique, her complexion was flawless considering her species. Ogres were not known for their hygiene or grooming habits.

"You have a lovely complexion, Officer-" Lorelei leaned sideways to check her name badge. "Strickland." The Ogress eyed her before a small smile pulled at her blackened lips.

"Thank you, Doctor McCann." Her voice was harsh but feminine. She glanced around her to make sure no one was eavesdropping before leaning closer, "The secret is sheep's gallbladder. It eats the dead skin right off!" Lorelei leaned back in feigned surprise while forcing a smile as she nodded at the whispered admission. Her reaction had nothing to do with the thought of using animal organs for an exfoliant. It was the horrendous smell of her breath that nearly knocked her off her feet. Green and black stained teeth, some of them chipped or broken, shone dully in the overhead lights as Officer Strickland smiled broadly at her.

"I will definitely keep that in mind if I ever need to switch up my skincare routine," Lorelei said, trying not to breathe more than necessary to stay conscious. Officer Strickland was, unfortunately, a chatty woman, and by the time they were finished, Lorelei started feeling lightheaded from the lack of sufficient oxygen.

Now, slowly pacing around a small barren conference room, she noticed an iron coupling welded to the table on the opposite side of where she would be seated. Glancing up at the security camera in the corner, gave her little reassurance, or confidence about her current situation. Taking a deep breath, she tried to calm her nerves, but at that moment, she heard the soft click of the latch as the doorknob turned.

Lorelei stepped around to her side of the table as a muscle-stacked guard walked in, followed a few seconds later by Declan Wolfe. His dark eyes locked on her from the moment he crossed the threshold, an unreadable expression on his handsome face. The muscles of his shoulders tensed, and it felt as if all the air had been sucked out of the too-small room. Sheer, undiluted predatory grace radiated off the man, and Lorelei became momentarily overwhelmed by the fight or flight response. Her heart hammered wildly in her chest, breath stalling in her lungs as she watched him watch her. The man was even more gorgeous in person, and she could feel the heat rising to her cheeks under his inscrutable gaze.

Another burly guard stalked into the room, escorting her client the short distance to the table stationed in the center of the room. Easing down, the chair groaned slightly in protest from the added weight, and Declan lifted his cuffed hands. She noticed the hard tick of his jaw as his dark chocolate gaze continued to burn into her. Notching her chin up a fraction, Lorelei returned his stare. Though it was probably unwise to challenge any Werewolf, it only took her a moment to realize she was unwittingly challenging an Alpha.

However, despite her defiance, she could have sworn that the corner of his mouth lifted in a ghost of a smile at her boldness.

Declan winced as the cuffs were retightened, his lips curling to reveal perfectly straight, white teeth as the metal bit into his flesh. His canines were slightly longer than normal, a trait that was common amongst his species. Brow furrowing at his reaction, Lorelei dropped her gaze to his wrists. The tan skin beneath the metal looked as if it had been burned, and blood seeped from several fissures caused by the bumps and grooves of the handcuffs.

"Mornin' ma'am, I'm Officer Thoreau, and this is Officer Marshall, just let us know if you need any assistance," The first guard said, pulling her attention away before she could really understand what she was looking at. Officer Thoreau was tall with a dark complexion, and his shaved hair accentuated his squared features.

"We'll be just down the hallway, ma'am," Officer Marshall said. He was shorter and rounder than his counterpart with cropped sandy blonde hair. They gave her a stiff nod, glancing at Declan as they left the room.

Her gaze followed them out before sliding back to the man sitting at the table, which now seemed far too cramped for him. The room itself felt as if it had been reduced to half its size ever since he walked in, his presence dominated the space. Clearing her throat softly, Lorelei slid into her chair opposite him and tried to ignore the fact he was still watching her like a predator watches its prey.

"G'mornin' Mister Wolfe. I'm Doctor McCann. At the request of the High Council, I'll be handlin' your psych evaluation in the comin' week, and all of your future therapy sessions." Her tone was calm and professional, but when she offered him her hand, she noticed him lean away slightly.

Declan eyed her warily as her open palm hung in the space between them. Lorelei bit her lips softly and nodded her head at the silent rejection. She lowered her hand, making a mental note of his trust issues. His shoulders relaxed some after she withdrew and adjusted his position, trying to pull his hands down to his lap. The chain snapped taut against the coupling, forcing a soft curse from his lips as he settled his forearms atop the cold metal surface.

"Do those hurt?" she asked quietly. A long moment passed and he said nothing. Lifting her eyes from the cuffs, her heart filled with concern for a man who could be more diabolical than any devil. Declan tilted his head, seeming confused about why she would care.

"They're silver," he stated, his voice was deep and raspy like he had not spoken in some time. Lorelei had to suppress the shiver that threatened to skitter up her spine. A confusing combination with the anger that she felt at his mistreatment. She could understand sedatives and even encouraged them in severe cases, but this was cruel. This was torture. Silver would not kill a Werewolf, but their skin reacted similarly to the way a human would if it came into contact with a corrosive substance. Blisters, peeling, and open wounds. Infection was also a concern since the silver impaired their regenerative abilities, making them easier to kill if there was enough in their system.

Tipping her head in the direction of the security camera, she felt her magic swell and release as she charmed the video feed in the security office. All the guards would see was her and Declan having a normal conversation. However, when she moved to slide her hand across the small space between them, he jerked back, causing the silver to bite into his skin. A string of curses spilled through his gritted teeth as new wounds appeared on his wrists.

"I can help if you let me," Lorelei said softly to him, trying to earn a grain of his trust. She waited several beats before cautiously reaching out again, and though he still eyed her incredulously – this time he did not pull away. His fingers twitched as she lay a soft hand over his. It felt as if electricity crackled beneath her skin where they touched, demanding more concentration than normal. The distinct clicks of the metal teeth sounded far too loud as the bonds loosened. Brows furrowing slightly, she kept her gaze fixed on him as she healed the wounds encircling his wrists. Lorelei tried to ignore the tingling sensation and the warmth of his skin as she pulled away. Declan watched her intently for another moment before staring at his cuffed wrists, turning them over to inspect his healed skin. Clearing her throat again, Lorelei forced herself to look away from him busied herself with the patient file, and opened it to the first page.

"Why?" The question caught her off guard, but the answer was not one she had to think about.

"Because you were in pain, and it was the right thing to do," Lorelei said softly, keeping her eyes on the documents in front of her. She could feel the weight of his gaze on her as she sifted through the papers until she found the one she was looking for.

"Can I have your full name, please?" She leaned back over to the messenger bag and snatched out a pen, shaking out her hand to try to rid herself of the lingering sensation.

"Declan Elijah Wolfe." Lorelei placed a small check next to the entry, desperately trying to ignore his deep southern drawl.

"Birthday?" Another check.

"Who were your parents?" She looked up at him when he did not answer.

"Mordecai and Alora Wolfe." His brow creased with mild confusion but she continued with the preliminary questions.

"Do you know why you're here in Saint Thaddeus, Mister Wolfe?" asked Lorelei, surprised when he shook his head.

"I never could get a straight answer about it. 'Tore up the Alpha Ceremony' is about all I know." She studied him for a long moment, insight telling her it was a half-truth.

"Mister Wolfe, durin' this process, I'm gonna need you to be as candid with me as possible. See, I know when you're not bein' truthful and when you are, so let's just agree to be honest with each other from here on out. Deal?" Her tone bordered on playful as she watched him for the usual surprised look that most clients gave her when she revealed her gift.

"Ah, you have insight," he said, head tilted again as he watched her.

"You're familiar with it?" Lorelei asked, brows lifting in surprise.

"My great-grandmother had the same gift. Made gettin' away with anything *real* difficult for me and my cousin." Declan smirked. Butterflies fluttered wild in her stomach as his features softened, rendering him even more irresistible. She silently cursed the thunderous jackhammering of her heart. His eyes flicked to her throat and she knew he could hear the uptick in her pulse. What she did not expect was the coy, half smile that he gave her when he drew his gaze slowly back up to hers.

"I heard bits after they'd loaded me into the transport. 'Carnage, mutilated, and dead.'" Truth.

"Thank you." She scribbled down some notes in the margin of the document, wishing she had thought to bring her laptop.

"Don't thank me yet, Doc. I don't remember anything about that night." Truth again, and Lorelei nodded, making another note in his patient file. Unusual case, indeed.

"Any trouble sleeping? Insomnia, nightmares?" She wrote quickly as Declan informed her that he had trouble falling asleep most nights, and had woken up yelling or fighting on occasion but could never remember what the nightmares were about or if they occurred every night.

"Do you harbor any guilt, Mister Wolfe?" Lorelei watched him as he thought about her question.

"I can't feel guilty for somethin' I don't remember, but I do feel guilty that I can't remember. Make sense, Doc?" She smiled softly at him and nodded. It made perfect sense, and more importantly, it was the truth.

"How's your appetite? Are you eatin' enough?" She was surprised when he let out a mirthless laugh.

"I'm hungry all the time. They don't feed any supernatural here how they should. A starved patient is a weak patient." Anger roiled through her veins, and she took a deep breath to calm herself, staring down at the metal table, jaw clenching.

"I think that's gonna be all for today, Mister Wolfe. I just realized I have somethin' I need to talk to Doctor Grimes about." Lorelei seethed at the thought of mistreated patients in a place meant to help them. They should not be starved, or tortured.

"Wait, before you go, I wanted to ask, earlier when you asked about my parents. Did you say 'were'?" She nodded with a hard swallow as anguish flashed in his eyes.

"When? Why wasn't I fuckin' told?" he asked angrily.

"They died the night of the attack two years ago. Eyewitnesses state that *you* took the lives of your parents," she told him gently.

"I'd never have killed my parents," he said with a dangerous growl. Lorelei's lips parted slightly, surprised at the conviction in his voice. Truth. Her stomach flipped when Declan's eyes flicked to her mouth briefly.

"I believe you," she stated softly, causing his gaze to snap back to hers. He was silent before another growl rumbled in his chest, and he looked away from her with a scoff.

"Don't patronize me, Doctor," he said angrily, but Lorelei did not take offense. His anger was justified if he had not been told of the events that led him here. Although his sudden change in attitude did piss her off.

"Trust me when I say, I will be the last person to patronize you, Mister Wolfe. I'm tryin' to help you." She bit back as she started packing up her things again.

Declan stared at her so intensely as if piercing her soul, sending goosebumps all over her. Stubborn and unwilling to let the man rattle her, Lorelei stared back. A subtle shadow darkened his gorgeous face and the soft silhouette of his wolf appeared, the chocolate brown of his irises disappearing into orbs of crimson red. Her lips parted, shocked as she watched the color slowly fade back to dark brown. His wolf retreated once again into his mind. She witnessed Declan's gaze dart to her mouth once again and back to her eyes. He shook his head, letting out a contemptuous huff as he adjusted his body in the small chair, leaning onto his forearms.

"*Trust you?!*" he demanded incredulously, "How 'bout this? You lose every-damn-thing in a single night and not have a fuckin' clue as to why. Not know why you were put away, and never have a Goddess damned question answered about it. Dropped off in the bowels of Hell and forgotten. When that happens, Doc, then come talk to me about fuckin' trust." Declan seethed, emotions clashing in his eyes. She opened her mouth to retort that she knew exactly what it was like, but thought better of it. It was none of his business anyways.

"You could have just asked me." Lorelei ground out, enunciating each word. Declan swallowed hard, his Adam's apple bobbing slowly. The anger that had drawn his features tight dissipated ever so slightly, and he gave her a nod.

Withdrawing the folder from her messenger bag once again, she took a moment to steady herself. Lorelei knew the charges, whether true or not, would be a shock for him to hear. It was not uncommon for patients to block out traumatic memories, but Lorelei knew he was unable to remember several hours before, during, and after the incident. Something that was rare for a Werewolf. Deadly Nightshade, though needed in copious amounts, and dark magic were the only two methods that could possibly harm the mind of an Alpha that she knew of. She took a deep breath as she flipped open the file and began to read, her voice soft to try to lessen the blow he was about to receive.

"Murder, two hundred and twenty eight counts. Rape, eighteen counts." The sound of the cuffs rattling suddenly in the coupling made her stop and snap her gaze to him. His jaw was clenched tight, the muscles bulging, and his large hands were balled in white knuckled fists. He took several deep breaths, trying to quell whatever emotions had rumbled to life within him.

"Please," he said, voice strained, and Lorelei was not entirely sure if he was wanting her to continue or begging her to stop. She stayed silent until his dark eyes found hers and he gave a small nod.

"Corpse dismemberment, two hundred and twenty-eight counts. Murder of a sitting Alpha, one count. Murder of a member of the Alpha's council, eleven counts. Razing of an established pack, one count. There were also eyewitness statements identifyin' you as the sole offender."

The sudden slamming of his chained fists on the table caused Lorelei to jerk back in her seat. Over and over he struck the metal, dents forming from the heavy blows as blood began to smear on the cold surface from his busted knuckles. The conference room door burst open with enough force to loosen the hinges. Lorelei jumped up between the guards and Declan, holding out one hand to stop their advance. Even as the man behind her let out a ferocious growl, she did not feel fear. Blinking in surprise, she realized that she wanted to protect him.

"Everything's okay. It's just an emotional outburst." Not a lie but not the whole truth. She released the breath that she had been holding when the guards stopped near the table and eyed Declan warily. Lorelei pulled her magic from the camera, not caring that whoever watched in the security office would know she charmed the feed.

"Maybe, Doc, but time's up," Officer Thoreau gruffed. He and Officer Marshall moved towards Declan, violently pulling away and resisting their attempts to hold him. New wounds opened on his wrists as the silver cuffs dug into his flesh with more blood pooling and smearing on the cold metal table. Lorelei watched in horror as the two men wrestled with her client, threatening and cursing as they struggled to get a hold of him. Officer Thoreau yanked a baton from his belt and landed a stomach-churning blow to the back of Declan's head.

"No!" Lorelei's shout was lost in the sound that was a mixture of man and beast as it ripped from the Alpha's chest. Taking advantage of the momentary pause, the guards slammed Declan's head down onto the tabletop with a resounding bang as they finally managed to pin him. Dark brown eyes locked on hers, holding her in place as Marshall snatched a syringe out of his pants pocket. Swiftly uncapping it with his teeth, he jabbed the needle deep into Declan's neck. Another enraged yell echoed in the small space as he cursed at the two guards restraining him. Seconds later, Declan went limp, and the guards quickly removed the cuffs from the coupling on the table. Without a word, they hooked him under his arms and hauled him out of the small conference room. Lorelei stood there in shock for several moments trying to wrap her mind around what she just witnessed. Smacking her hand down on the file, she snatched it and her messenger bag from the floor before taking off after them.

"Hey! Where're you takin' him? I told you it was just an outburst!" her voice rose angrily, echoing in the deserted hallway. She caught up with the trio as they entered a restricted access area. The iron bars clanged shut just as Lorelei skidded to a halt in front of them. Her anger shifted into boiling rage.

"That was unnecessary, asshole! Me or my client decide when the session's over! Hey!" She rattled the bars angrily, the clanking metal and her yells reverberated loudly after them. Helpless, she watched the guards drag Declan down the corridor, his head lolling with their steps, and into a waiting elevator. When they turned, both guards wiggled their fingers at her, sneering as the doors slid shut with a soft thump.

Fuming, Lorilei shoved the now crinkled folder into her messenger bag and strode back to the main lobby. She marched up to the front desk and rapped her knuckles loudly on the thick glass. The receptionist turned towards the sound, irritation evident as she looked up at Lorelei.

"I want to speak with Doctor Grimes. *Now*," she told her. In the reflection of the window, Lorelei could see that her eyes had shifted from gray to shimmering mercury silver. A common occurrence when she used magic or experienced high emotions. The woman stared wide-eyed up at her and shook her head, signing that the doctor was out at the moment.

"Then you give him a message for me. You tell Doctor Grimes I'll be here in the mornin', same time. And if anyone so much as thinks of mistreatin' my client in or out of my presence, they'll deal with me personally. Am I understood, Miss.." Lorelei looked at her nameplate in the window, "Singer?" Lorelei looked at her expectantly, but Miss Singer did not answer her. Instead, the woman was still watching her, mild fear in her eyes. She slammed her hand down on the ledge of the window, startling the young woman.

"Am I understood, Miss Singer?"

Miss Singer nodded her head quickly and Lorelei spun on her heel, striding angrily from the building. Snatching the driver's door open, she slung her bag onto the bench seat and climbed into the Wagoneer, yanking it shut with unnecessary force. She panted hard in her anger as she gripped the steering wheel tightly, trying to calm her rage.

"What the actual fuck?" she demanded out loud, glaring at the entryway of the asylum.

Chapter 06

The sprawling basement of Saint Thaddeus was in a constant state of dampness, causing mold and algae to grow along the walls in thick, stinking masses. Stale air heavy with the foul odor of decaying earth, sweat, urine, and excrement seemed to cling to everything within the confines of this hellhole. Exposed pipes and thick support beams made the basement resemble a deserted factory instead of the modified torture chamber it had been outfitted into. Situated along the walls, cell after cell lined the interior of the basement, each one designed to contain its occupant without fear of escape. The bars were lined with individual metals like iron or silver, while others were rigged with tiny flame throwers along their perimeter. A living hell for the supernaturals that currently lay within, huddled on pitiful mattresses.

The constant trill of rats squeaking and squealing in the nearby shadows slowly roused Declan from his chemical-induced stupor. Groaning loudly, he squeezed his eyes tight against the pounding in his skull. A side effect of the nasty concoction he had been dosed with. As the sedative began to wear off, clouded memories of that morning drifted back to him.

The witch with auburn hair that fell past her shoulders in loose curls. Her kind gray eyes were full of concern at his pain and unmatched fury over his poor treatment. Her soft fingertips brushed his wrist to heal his wounds, and her irises shimmering like liquid silver as she channeled her magic. His skin had tingled where her hand had laid over his, and the sensation had stirred something deep within him. It had been a long time since he had experienced that level of kindness and despite the lingering sedative, his body reacted swiftly. The speed of his erection caused a low grunt to thump in the back of his throat. Though the reaction confused him, it was not entirely unexpected. Even his wolf had urged him to mate with her from the moment he saw the Witch standing in the conference room. It had been quite a while since he slept with anyone, and the woman was stunningly beautiful. She had the perfect body with plump, full breasts. Her flawless, lightly tanned skin with a light smattering of freckles over her cheeks and the bridge of her button nose could rival a goddess. Full Cupid's bow lips the shade of dusty pink roses, and her voice had been slightly husky with a southern accent that she failed to hide. His shaft throbbed almost painfully at his recollection.

'*Must mate,*' his inner beast huffed, nearly panting at Declan's thought. Pushing the wolf to the back of his mind, the charges Lorelei read off to him that morning floated hazily in and out of the fog in his mind.

Searing pain broke through the dredges of the sedative and Declan lurched upright into a sitting position. He was jarred roughly back again, throwing a hand behind him to keep himself upright. It was then he felt the smooth silver collar encircling his throat and the heavy weight of chains crisscrossing over his torso. Large cuffs had been clamped around his biceps and his thighs. All of them were made from silver and laced through a massive ring anchored to the wall behind his cell. Declan hoped that this time they would forget to chain him. He had lost count of how many times he had been hauled down to the basement of horrors and knew this would not be his last trip.

Murder. Rape. Parricide. The crimes he was supposed to be guilty of rang clearly in his ears now as if Lorelei were whispering them to him herself. His breaths came in rage-filled pants, each becoming more ragged as he remembered each charge. Chest heaving under the crisscrossed links lying across his ribcage, he tried to calm the tsunami of emotions crashing over him while the beast paced in his mind, snarling viciously.

'*Let go!*' his wolf growled and Declan gave a hard shake of his head, his body trembled. If he did, he and his wolf would suffer from the silver chains that were wrapped around him. His flesh would blister and burn, and wounds would open, taking days or weeks to fully heal.

The crimes he had been accused of echoed in his mind again and another crash of white-hot fury coursed through his blood. He was unable to contain the deep guttural scream that pulled his lips back from his teeth and left his chest burning. The sound slowly morphed into a soul-shattering howl that reverberated endlessly around the cavernous basement. Losing his grip on the remnants of his control, the beast surged forward with a ferocity he had never felt before. His eyes blazed crimson, and his hands and feet grew to several times their normal size. Short, deadly claws erupted from his nail beds. The pain was a welcome distraction from the turmoil raging inside him. His hands contorted, pads forming at the base of his fingers and around his palms. He leaned forward bracing them against the cold concrete floor. His jaw lengthened as razor-sharp teeth grew from his maw, snapping together when they fully extended. His limbs began to elongate, the joints popping and shifting beneath his skin. His chest expanded, muscle stacking on muscle, forcing his clothes to rip apart at the seams. Declan grew taller, his heavy body crouching on thick hind legs and he snarled when he felt the bite of the silver chains against his hide. Thick, dark gray fur sprouted, covering his massive body, and he tore at the tattered remains of his clothing. Shaking his head much like a normal wolf, long pointed ears formed and stood straight, swiveling in the direction of the slightest sound.

The beast roared in the confines of his cell as he thrashed, pulling and straining to break free of his silver-lined prison. Declan swiped and kicked at the bars that caged him in. Ragged pants huffed from his snout as he tore into the only thing that he could. The mattress. The ease with which the pathetic thing ripped apart only infuriated him more, and he strained against his chains once again, trying to dislodge the heavy anchor.

Crimson had long stained his torso, blood oozing from the wounds marking his hide, the lacerations wrapping around him like a gruesome infinity symbol. Blood streaked down his skin from the shackles circling his upper arms, their chains rattling with his movements. Every so often a cough would huff from him at the tightness of the collar around his thick neck. Most of the fur had rubbed away, the skin was now raw and bloody. He finally sat back on his haunches and hung his head in defeat, still angry but no longer frothing at the mouth. Slowly, Declan shifted back into his human form while his wolf retreated to the back of his mind and he fell to his knees – exhausted physically and emotionally. Stretching to reach some of the larger remains of his clothes and bits of mattress, he piled them on the floor and sat naked, muscles trembling with fatigue.

"Five, four, three, two…" muttered Declan, canting his head towards the doors on the far side of the room. Right on cue, hinges whined somewhere in the distance, and he listened to the pair of echoing footsteps that approached. Entering through a set of key-coded double doors, Officer Dick and Officer Asshole strode in.

"On your feet, Wolfe," Officer Asshole called out as they neared the cage.

Stumbling slightly under the weight of the heavy chains, Declan stood and steeled his body. He refused to give them the satisfaction of seeing how exhausted he truly was. He made no move to cover himself as the two stepped inside. He was not an oversized monster, but he was proud of the well endowment.

"You gonna play nice?" Officer Dick asked as he reached for the lock on the shackles around his arms. Declan nodded, unsure of the strength of his voice.

"Good." The two guards made quick work removing the shackles and chains, "Shower, dinner, lights out." With that, each man grabbed an arm and escorted him out of the cell and through the double doors.

The trek back up from the basement was a short one, and now Declan stood in one of the communal showers on the ground floor. He hissed at the burn from the heat and soap on his wounds as he scrubbed the basement grime from his skin. Taking a moment, he braced a hand against the cool tile and watched the fresh blood and tiny bits of dead flesh circling the drain between his feet until they disappeared. The showerhead automatically switched off as he traipsed over to the sink ledge, grabbing up his towel. He quickly dried himself and pulled on a clean set of black scrubs, careful to avoid his wounds in the process. Ignoring the hard slide-on sandals on the floor, Declan strolled past the two standing guards and shook the remaining droplets from his hair. Feeling a bit of satisfaction at their disgruntled protests, he left the bathroom and made his way to the cafeteria at the opposite end of the hall.

Declan wove through the dining area to an empty table near the back of the room and sat down. He stared at the goopy slop on his plate and wrinkled his nose, top lip lifting in a disgusted grimace. Using the plastic fork, he prodded at the partially gelatinous substance causing a thick bubble to rise from the center, slowly expanding until it popped silently. The smell was absolutely rancid and he wondered what could possibly produce such a foul stink. He debated on just drinking the bottle of water he had slipped into his pocket, but his stomach rumbled loudly at that moment. Tipping back his head, he prayed to the Lunar Goddess that whatever this was, did not kill him.

The consistency was even worse than it looked. Chunky like cottage cheese with a slimy, thick texture like an oyster. Declan barely stifled the gagging that threatened to bring the goop right back onto the plate in front of him with every bite. When his eyes watered and he was unable to force down anymore, he tore the bottled water from his pocket and twisted off the cap, chugging the contents.

"Let's go, line up!" shouted a guard from the doorway on the other side of the cafeteria. Tossing his trash, Declan fell in with the queue of other supernaturals shuffling to their dorms. A loud buzzer sounded as they approached the ward, and the barred door slid open. Another guard that Declan had not bothered to learn the name of, strolled in behind them ordering them to line up along the wall. The other patients quickly found their rooms and stood next to the doors, awaiting the mandatory pat down. Several had their contraband confiscated before being roughly shoved into their dorm and locked in for the night. When the guard reached Declan, he scoffed up at him before taking in the raw wound around his throat and the blood seeping through his scrub top.

"Wha's dis?" The guard spoke with a thick Creole accent, his ruddy round face shining with sweat. He lifted the bottom of Declan's top to observe the wounds underneath, tsking at the sight. Dropping the hem,

Creole ordered him to turn around and place his palms flat on the wall.

Sighing, Declan complied and gritted his teeth when the guard patted roughly over the lacerations, causing his wolf to snarl. He knew the man was trying to get a reaction out of him. Knew he was looking for any excuse to send him back down below. When Officer Creole finished, he humphed and grabbed Declan by his arm. He was shoved like all the others with the door slamming loudly behind him.

The room was tiny, maybe ten by ten feet, if that, with its sparse furniture heavily bolted to the floor. There was a narrow cot shoved into one corner complete with a threadbare blanket, and a hard, flat pillow. Occupying another corner was a thick, rounded metal slab serving as a very small desk with a chair anchored too close to sit comfortably. The final corner of the space was home to a stainless-steel toilet and matching sink with no soap, and no towels. A single window sat high up on the far wall, encased in iron bars lined with silver.

Padding across the little room, Declan gently tugged the scrub top from his body, wincing as his movements aggravated his wounds. Three steps placed him in front of the small metal sink, and for the next five minutes, he scrubbed the blood from the material. He wrung out the excess water and hung it over the back of the chair to dry. Two steps to his cot and he groaned inwardly, staring down at the rough canvas. The fabric was stained with various-sized splotches of blood and sweat, most of which was from him. Gingerly, he laid down on his side trying to avoid the worst of his wounds, hissing when parts of his raw flesh scrubbed against the cot.

A deafening buzzer jumped to life, reverberating around the small room. The unholy noise jolted Declan awake, making his ears ring. He wished he had something to hurl at the speaker in the ceiling above his cot. Muscles aching and sore, he slowly pushed himself into a sitting position. His wounds protested his movements with some sticking to the canvas beneath him. Looking down at the intersection where the chains had crossed in the middle of his sternum, blood oozed from a dislodged clot. Had the chains not been made of silver, had he been bound by any other material, Declan would have healed in minutes. Now, he was healing at the rate of a human.

Straightening his spine, the vertebrae cracked, and he popped and rolled his neck trying to work out the tension. Shuffling over to retrieve his scrub top, he rumpled the material to try to ease its stiffness just as the door of his room popped open. Slipping it carefully over his head, Declan joined the group of supernaturals congregating at the end of the ward. As they waited for the guards to escort them to breakfast, he absently rubbed at an itch on his chest. His breath hissed through his teeth when his fingers glanced over his wound. When he looked down, he saw that there was blood discoloring his fingertips. For the briefest moment, he wondered what Doctor McCann would think of his treatment.

'*Anger.*' his wolf growled, causing Declan to drop his head, shaking it gently in disagreement. He doubted the Witch cared about his treatment in this place. No one ever did. Healing his wounds yesterday had been a means to an end. To earn his trust. In the back of his mind, the beast huffed with annoyance but remained silent.

Sidling up to the bars, the guards ordered the supernaturals to line up and be quiet. Declan leaned a shoulder against the wall as he waited for the rest of his block mates to form a haphazard line. Satisfied, the guards opened the gate and ordered them all forward. The sound of stiff sandals shuffling across the linoleum was the only disruption to the tense quiet as they wound their way down to the cafeteria.

Seated again at the back table, Declan stared down a similar plate of goop like the one from the night before. His stomach rumbled loudly and he grimaced at the thought of forcing down more of the slop in front of him. Hunger was a constant state here, and had been for the last two years since he arrived. Being a Werewolf meant that his metabolism burned through calories faster than most species, and that was a fact Saint Thaddeus did not know or just refused to care about. He truly believed that they intentionally kept them hungry to keep them weak, only providing the barest of three small "meals" a day that was not even enough to sustain the resident fairy that had been committed a week after him. Uncapping the bottle of water, he was given with his breakfast, he guzzled half of it trying to satisfy his empty stomach.

"Wolfe!" The shout echoed around the cafeteria and the entire room fell silent. Glancing around at the congregation of stares focused on him, Declan finished off the water before tossing his untouched breakfast in the garbage. Every head in the room followed him as he strode toward the guard who called him out. It had never made much sense, but Declan was infamous within the walls of Saint Thaddeus though he had never caused trouble, or fought unless it was self-defense. He never even spoke to anyone unless necessary.

Stopping in front of the security office door, he rapped on the metal twice in quick succession. The whirling from the overhead camera told him it was focusing on him. He tilted his head to look up at the lens. Lifting a hand, he flipped the operator off just as the door buzzed to let him in. Before he could push his way inside, Officer Dick and Officer Asshole emerged. Silver cuffs waiting. He sighed and held out his arms, refusing to react when the bracelets were tightened until they pinched his skin. Without a word, Officer Dick shoved his shoulder in the direction of the conference room, irritation etched across his face.

When they entered the small space, Declan found that the doctor was not there yet. He was surprised to feel a stab of disappointment as he took his seat. Settling his cuffed hands on the metal table, the guards started working to secure the chain through the coupling.

"What in the fuck happened to his throat?" Lorelei's voice demanded angrily from the open doorway. Declan leaned past the guards, and his stomach clenched when he saw the beautiful woman with her blazing silver eyes. She was far more casually dressed today with her hair in a messy bun, a rock band tee shirt hanging loosely over her body, and a pair of black leggings that molded to her long legs. His mouth practically watered at the sight of her. She truly was the most stunning woman he had ever seen.

"Tried to hang himself last night, Doc." Officer Asshole said flatly without missing a beat.

"That's a damn lie," she said vehemently, "You know it and I *definitely* know it." The two men glanced at each other as they continued to shackle him to the table, ignoring her. Declan could feel the fury rolling off of her in waves. Her gaze flickered from the guards to him, and then to the tabletop.

"That won't be necessary. Now get out," she ordered, walking a step further into the room.

"Sorry, Doc. It's protocol," Officer Dick said stiffly and secured the cuffs to the table.

"It's Doctor McCann to you, and you don't have a choice," she stated bluntly, and suddenly the cuffs, the chain, and the coupling all vanished. Declan grinned crookedly up at her, impressed by her skill and, more so, her nerve. The guards sputtered and cursed, demanding that she fix the table or be removed from the premises. Instead of arguing with the two, she simply held out a neatly folded letter, giving them both a languid grin. Officer Dick snatched it from her, quickly reading over its contents. Glancing at one another, Declan was surprised to see them pale slightly as the letter was folded and returned to her.

"Apologies, ma'am. Please let us know if there's anything that you need," Officer Asshole remarked calmly, and he noticed that both of their heads were bowed slightly.

"You can get me that incident report from last night in the next five minutes if he did indeed try to hang himself," she said pointedly as she stepped aside to allow the two men to walk by.

"Actually, you can get me *all* incident reports pertainin' to Mister Wolfe." The revision had Officer Dick and Asshole glancing nervously at each other but they both slightly nodded before retreating down the hallway.

Staring, Declan watched them leave as Lorelei closed the door quietly behind them. Shifting his gaze back to her, he regarded her carefully as she set two cups down on the metal table and slid one toward him. His name was printed on the side in neat, bold letters.

"I can heal that," she offered softly. He watched her for several long moments, calculating the risk of trusting her more before nodding. Lorelei stepped around the table and placed both hands on his shoulders, directly onto the wounds he had there. He jerked away from her, growling at the sudden pain. She snatched the neckline of his shirt back before he could stop her and let out an audible gasp.

"What the fu- shirt off. Now," she commanded, and he froze, unsure if he should laugh or obey. Declan turned to look up at the woman standing behind him. There was no fear, no sign of submission or wariness as she held his gaze defiantly. His beast huffed in admiration, realizing that she was daring him to deny her order. A bit dumbfounded at the reaction of his wolf, Declan stood from his chair and gently tugged the scrub top over his head. He groaned deep in his throat as muscles and injuries alike protested his movements.

There was a sharp intake of breath from Lorelei when she saw the extent of his wounds, and she pulled out her phone, snapping several pictures of the lacerations. Each time he turned for her to take a photo, she cursed under her breath. He could hear her heart thundering in her chest and noticed how her fingers lingered a little too long as she examined his skin. What Declan did not expect was the tears that brimmed in her eyes as she stared at the damage. She cared, but he could not fathom why.

"After you were hauled away, they chained you in silver, didn't they?" She asked quietly, stepping closer to him. Declan nodded as she placed a hand over the intersection marring his chest. He could feel her magic rolling over his skin, helping it knit back together. The energy vibrated gently, leaving a tingling sensation in its wake and a shiver that raced up his spine. As he stood peering down at her, a silent tear trickled down Lorelei's cheek. Before he realized what he was doing, Declan lifted his hand, gently brushing the droplet away with his thumb. An almost imperceptible gasp parted her lips and she lifted her bright silver eyes to his.

'*Must have her. Mate,*' his wolf growled, repeating the words like a mantra in his mind. Ignoring the beast,

Declan pushed the thoughts aside with a gentle shake of his head.

"Thanks, Doc," he said softly as his wounds finished healing.

"You're welcome," she whispered, her fingertips pressing into his sternum. Lorelei seemed to realize that her hand was still against his chest and suddenly stepped back -snatching away as if she had been burned and cleared her throat.

She took her place across the table and busied herself with removing items from her messenger bag. As she set a laptop on the table, the coffee cup she brought for him slid over the metal surface, stopping in front of his chair. Taking the hint, Declan pulled his shirt back on and reclaimed his seat. He tried to ignore the pleasant sensation dancing over his skin. Her warm handprint lingering on his sternum as if she still touched him. Removing the lid, he sniffed the aromatic black liquid before taking a long sip. The coffee was smooth and bold, nearly overwhelming his senses. It was all Declan could do to not moan into the contents of the cup.

"How'd you know I took my coffee black?" he asked, setting the cup down. She looked at him and shrugged as her fingers began flying over the keyboard.

"I didn't. I think I've got enough sugar and creamer in my bag for a whole month." she chuckled softly, glancing back at the screen. She sent the letter sliding over to him as well, her tone taking on a more serious note.

"In case you're wonderin', High Elder Caine has ordered that any requests or demands I have be accommodated immediately. No exceptions." With a final tap on the keys, she lifted her eyes to his and gave him a half smile.

Declan glanced down at the letter, and quickly read the missive that she had just summarized for him. The official seal of the Elder Council stood out in stark contrast to the white paper. Sliding the letter back to Lorelei, he mulled over this new information, realizing that she could either be a great ally or a deadly foe.

"So, you have friends in high places then." he stated, keeping his eyes on her as he took another sip of his coffee.

"Not until yesterday," she admitted as she leaned over and hefted a large paper grocery bag onto the table, unrolling the top. Declan was taken aback. He had not even noticed her bring the large bag into the room. As she pulled out several styrofoam to-go plates and laid them out in front of him, the most delicious aroma filled the tiny space.

"Eat if you're hungry. We won't be bothered again by Thoreau and Marshall," Lorelei said as she opened the top. He paused, and grabbed the box that smelled of sausages, looking up at her curiously once her words registered, lifting his brows in question.

"The guards." She pointed to the door, her head canted to the side as she observed him for a moment longer, "Speakin' of them. I'll be reportin' your abuse to Elder Cain," she stated as she reached for the same box and flipped open the lid. She laughed at his euphoric expression when he saw the round sausage patties piled high on parchment paper. His brain momentarily malfunctioned seeing the amusement light up her face, and he was not sure which he wanted more at that point – the sausages, or Lorelei. She was an absolute vision when she smiled, and the sight and sound of her did things to him. Things he had not experienced before; things he wished he could have experienced elsewhere in different circumstances. Though it was unclear to him if that was a good or bad thing yet.

'*Good*,' his beast gruffed.

"It's not just me. Everyone gets a piece of it, eventually," he said, helping her open the rest of the trays. She sighed heavily and returned to her laptop while Declan filled his belly with pancakes, bacon, sausages, hash browns, and eggs for the next thirty minutes. Lorelei plucked a sausage or piece of bacon from containers every so often while they sat in comfortable silence. When Declan felt as if he could roll over and hibernate for a month, he sat back in his chair and took a long drink of coffee to wash it all down.

"That's the most delicious breakfast I've ever had. Thank you," he said, rubbing a hand over his full belly. Her brilliant smile took his breath away and he could not help the return smile tugging at his lips.

"You're welcome. Now that you're full of good food, I'd like to talk to you about the day of the attack, and what all you remember. If that's all right with you?" Declan nodded as he took another sip of coffee. "Do you mind if I record the audio on my laptop?"

"Go ahead, Doc." He waited patiently until she gave him a nod, signaling that she was recording, "Like I said before though, I don't remember anything. The last memory I have of that day, is fightin' with Cormac in the trainin' arena," he repeated and listened to the soft tapping of her fingers on the keyboard.

"Who's Cormac?" she asked as she adjusted her position in her chair.

"Cormac Daughtry. He's an old friend of mine. Well, he *was* a friend until the fight," he admitted, recalling the blade the bastard had sunk into his chest.

"What did you two fight about? A girl?" He tilted his head at the tone of her voice, and she stared adamantly at her computer screen. The thought of her being jealous prickled something in him that he could not quite place. He grinned and shook his head, hearing how her heart rate kicked up.

"There was no girl, Doctor McCann. I'd met him and my cousin, Wyatt, to train before we had to get ready for the ceremony. Cormac was tryin'a sneak up on me, catch me off guard. It was a normal thing we practiced. Wyatt and I teased him a little after the take down but it wasn't anything unusual, we were close." Declan paused, letting Lorelei make her notes before he continued, "I relayed a demotion order my dad had given, and he just lost his mind over it, I guess. Stormed off and when he came back…" Declan trailed off, lost in the memory. Something about it seemed wrong somehow but he could not figure out what.

"He musta had the blade on him, cause when he came back, he said I wouldn't take his rank from him and stabbed me." He saw Lorelei nodding as she pursed her lips, her brow furrowed slightly as she typed her notes.

"Where did he stab you?" she asked, fingers still on the keyboard in front of her.

"Left shoulder, here." Declan tapped the fleshy hollow between his underarm and collarbone with two fingers.

"What happened after Cormac stabbed you?" Lorelei peered over the laptop at him, and he wondered if she might think he killed the man.

"We fought," he said, lifting his cup, "I lost."

'Not possible.' the beast snarled viciously and Declan sighed inwardly. He and his wolf had argued about this constantly over the last two years. Apparently, it *was* possible for an Alpha to lose to an Omega. Another snarl reverberated in his mind, louder than the last. Ignoring his wolf, Declan held her gaze as she stared at him. Her brows were furrowed, a look of confused concentration on her face.

"I'm not entirely sure that's true, Declan," Lorelei said slowly, eyes roaming his face. His lips parted with his inhale as he struggled to find words. Confusion drew his brows together until Declan was sure his expression mirrored hers.

"How can what I remember not be true?" he asked, trying to wrap his mind around a rational explanation.

"Deadly Nightshade is a possibility. Could you have ingested it the night of the ceremony somehow?" she asked. He realized she still had not looked away from him. Still stared at him with confusion and concern.

"Doc, my last memories of that day are the fight with Cormac that mornin', and bein' woken up strapped to a gurney with the whole fuckin' Council in my house *that night*," Declan said, frustration building, "I don't know what happened for the span of about fourteen hours."

"I know that," Lorelei said softly, "But amnesia can be tricky. You never know what might trigger a memory."

Declan drew in a deep breath, closing his eyes. He knew she was right, and it was hardly fair for her to be the target of his irritation - especially when she was only trying to help him. Sighing heavily, he exhaled and nodded.

"You're right. I'm sorry," he said sincerely, opening his eyes, "This's just startin' to feel more like an interrogation than anything else." With that, Lorelei smiled.

"I can see how it feels that way, but if I don't ask questions, I can't figure out a way to treat the symptoms, let alone find an answer," she explained, and he nodded in understanding. When she broke it down like that, it made perfect sense.

"Goin' back to this memory about the fight. Does anything about it seem off to you?" Lorelei glanced down at her laptop screen, eyes darting back and forth.

"It all seems off. I can't recall anything about the fight beyond him stabbin' me. I just remember that I lost," Declan told her, lacing his hands behind his head. He stared at the ceiling for several long moments, debating how much he should tell her.

'Everything,' his wolf growled, prodding at the edge of his mind.

So, he did.

Chapter 07

Every morning was the same routine. Lorelei would meet Declan at the security office, minus the silver cuffs, and head to the little conference room to have breakfast. Each day, Thoreau and Marshall looked displeased at the changes. Both men would stand behind the counter, arms crossed and scowling. Once, Officer Thoreau had tried to argue that it was against protocol for a prisoner- patient- to be outside of lock up without the proper restraints. He had even admonished her for bringing in food that had not been properly inspected. Lorelei had quickly informed him that he could shove his protocol up his ass. Officer Stickland and Declan openly laughed at this and she thought the vein on Thoreau's forehead might explode when he turned bright red, fuming with resentment.

Today marked a week since she had arrived in Louisiana. Lorelei sat in her usual chair across from Declan as he scarfed down the majority of the breakfast she brought. It seemed that the cafeteria still was not providing adequate, or edible, food for its residents. Two days before, Declan had managed to smuggle in his breakfast from that morning and the sight and smell of the foul substance nearly cost Lorelei her stomach. Even now, the stench of it lingered in the small space.

As the days wore on, Declan opened up to her more about his life at Crescent Ridge, and the nuances of day to day life before he had been brought to Saint Thaddeus. She quickly grew to look forward to their sessions. Even though she was in the process of assessing his mental state per her contract agreement with the Elder Council and Dawson Therapies, she enjoyed her time with him. So far, she had yet to find a logical reason for him to be housed in the asylum.

"Missus Betty sent you some deer jerky this mornin'," Lorelei said, digging in her messenger bag. Declan lifted his gaze to her as she set the overfull baggy of thick cut strips beside his plate.

"Why?" he asked, reaching for his coffee cup.

"I've talked to her a little about the conditions here and she insisted that I bring you something to ease the hunger pains," Lorelei explained, before quickly adding, "She doesn't know about *you*. Your name or anything. Confidentiality and all that." She let loose a soft, nervous laugh seeing the look Declan was giving her. Tension coiled the muscles in his shoulders.

"You talk about me outside of here?" he asked, watching her with that predatory gleam in his eyes.

"A little," she admitted softly, with a one shoulder shrug, "but like I said, nothin' personal. You're known as 'my client' at the bed and breakfast. Missus Betty knows more about the quality of food in this place than anything." He continued to stare at her for another minute. The air growing heavier as the seconds ticked by. Lorelei held his gaze, willing her body not to squirm under its intensity. She was not afraid, no. The fact that he was looking at her like he could devour every inch of her, made heat flood to her core.

Nostrils flaring, he finally averted his gaze, though the tension never left Declan's shoulders. Lorelei released a breath she had not realized she was holding, and cleared her throat.

"I'm not sure what to make of this Cormac guy you talked about last week," Lorelei said, changing the subject.

"No one was, Doc," Declan snorted, casting a quick glance in her direction, "Cormac's educated, well-spoken. But he's angry all the time. A stick of dynamite with a lit fuse. He *always* had somethin' to prove. Great example is houndin' me to join the Delta Team until I gave him a shot."

"What made you change your mind?" she asked, leaning an elbow on the cool metal table top and propping her chin in her palm.

"His persistence," he said, "The drive he had to prove he could make it."

"And did he?" Lorelei inquired, her brows lifting with her question.

"He did. Barely." Declan conceded with a nod, "Cormac had to work ten times harder than the Delta's simply because he's an Omega." Declan paused, seeming to get lost in the past. He worked his jaw side to side as he remained silent for several moments.

"It didn't last though," he continued, "he had been on the Delta Team maybe six months by the time the ceremony rolled around. A week or so before the massacre, Cormac had started slackin' off. Would skip trainin', and put in no effort when he did show up. So, my dad issued an intent to demote order that mornin'."

"Seems a bit odd that he'd work so hard and then throw it all away," Lorelei mused, thoughtful, "What does the Delta Team do, exactly?"

"Well, that all depends on which team you're askin' about on a given day," Declan said, pausing briefly, debating on telling her, "Delta One, usually the Beta and a Delta, accompanies the Alpha. Delta Two runs perimeter. Three's surveillance. Teams Four, Five, and Six patrol the pack border. Though their assignments can vary dependin' on where they're needed." Lorelei did not take notes as she listened to his explanation.

"Cormac was on Team Six," he answered when she opened her mouth. Biting her lips gently, she typed out one short note before closing the laptop. Leaning over her messenger bag, she pulled out a stack of large cards.

"Ever taken an ink blot test?" she asked, holding up one of the blotchy images.

"No, but there's a first time for everything," he said, the corner of his mouth lifting as he canted his head to the side.

Chapter 08

"I'd like to try somethin' with you," Lorelei said one morning. They had been trying for two weeks to trigger a memory but nothing had worked yet. When he raised a flirtatious brow at her she scoffed, and her crooked smile nearly seduced him on the spot. Their mutual attraction was undeniable, though Lorelei had stayed professional with him the entirety of their time together.

"I'd like to see if I can access your lost memories, Mister Wolfe." she gave him a less-than-subtle once-over while she crossed her arms under her breasts. The action brought his gaze momentarily down to her chest, and the vision of all he was tempted to do flashed through his mind.

'You call me a hound,' His wolf mocked, apparently forgetting it was him who had practically begged Declan to *mate* with her for days. Sensing a retort coming, he pushed the beast to the back of his mind, demanding silence.

"How would you do that?" he asked, refocusing his attention a little above her breasts. He was intrigued by the possibility she could do such a thing. Then again, Declan knew little about Witches and the extent of their abilities.

"Well, I'd use my magic to try to repair, or remove, whatever's blockin' them. It's painless, and the worst I've heard is feelin' a bit dizzy after." He considered before nodding his head. The little witch was gaining more of his trust day by day.

'That was quick,' his wolf gruffed with amusement. Completely ignoring the beast now, he focused on the woman in front of him. A force far more powerful – and mesmerizing – than any creature.

Lorelei rose from her chair and walked around to his side of the table, ordering him to face her. Hesitating, he turned, swallowing hard when she stepped between his knees. His heart raced as her legs brushed against him, and even through the fabric, he felt the pleasant tingles dancing on his skin. Her fingertips settled on either side of his head making his scalp prickle. She took a deep breath and looked down at him, eyes shimmering silver. The minutes ticked by but nothing happened. He opened his mouth, intending to let her know he was ready, when a memory suddenly flashed in his mind, making his breathing stall.

At a birthday party, his mother's face, the definition of joy as she helped a five-year-old Declan cut a piece of cake. Another flashed, this time he was a teenager, being flipped over his father's shoulder, and thrown to the arena mat. The next was his first shift when he turned eighteen. Memory after memory flashed in his mind's eye but when the vision of Ananasi's naked body flit passed, anger pulsed through him. Lorelei tensed at the brief image, shifting her weight uncomfortably. Without thinking, Declan placed a large hand against the outside of her thigh, squeezing gently. He would be damned if she believed Ananasi was in any way a part of his life. Relief rushed through him when he felt her subtly press against his palm, easing her tensed body.

Finally, an unfamiliar memory flashed rapidly, blinking in and out of the darkness. A dull ringing started to drone annoyingly in his ears as the images became clearer. In the fragment, Declan stood in his room checking his reflection, wearing a dark grey suit with a crimson pocket square, and a black dress shirt. He realized those were the same garments he had surrendered when he arrived at Saint Thaddeus.

As Lorelei pressed deeper into the darkness, the ringing grew in Declan's ears. The shrill sound quickly grew louder and louder until it suddenly snapped. All at once, a violent stab of pain ripped through his skull like a gunshot. Lorelei cried out as he vaulted to his feet, just as a ghost-like apparition of his wolf leapt from him with a vicious snarl. Instinctively, Declan turned his head away from Lorelei. He wound his arm around her waist, yanking her out of the path of the beast's open maw. The loud snapping of its jaws echoed around the room while a coarse groan of pain ripped from his chest.

His wolf retreated as quickly as he came, leaving him panting heavily as the pain slowly subsided. Hand braced on the tabletop, Lorelei still clutched at his side, Declan was dumbstruck at what had just happened. He looked down at the woman clinging to him, her face turned away.

'I am sorry. I was not trying to hurt her. So much pain,' the beast whimpered before retreating deep into his mind.

"Lorelei," he panted hoarsely, heart hammering in his chest. Instant relief washed over him when she looked up at him uninjured, eyes wide. Her heartbeat pounded in his ears along with his own as they stared at each other for a long moment. Electricity danced along his skin, every nerve attuned to the warmth of her body pressed against him.

"I don't know what that was," Declan said finally, mind still reeling.

"I do," she said quietly, "Your memories are blocked, possibly even altered. The spell used– I've never felt anything like it." Declan stared at her, still trying to process what had happened moments ago.

"What spell?" he demanded gently, his confusion growing more by the second.

"I… I need a minute," she said as she slowly stepped away from him. His fingers flexed against her waist wanting to keep her pressed against him but he nodded and let his arm drop from around her. His body lamented the loss of her warmth the moment she withdrew from his embrace.

Lorelei stepped out into the hallway, and a moment later, he could discern her hushed conversation on the other side of the door. It seemed like a one-sided conversation. She was relaying the incident to whoever was on the other end of the phone. His body tensed as she went into detail about all that she had learned over the last few weeks. He was about to yank the door open and confront her when he heard her address Elder Caine.

'Trust. She is good. Can feel it,' his wolf huffed softly, surprising Declan with the earnest statement but he decided to trust both Lorelei and his beast. For now, at least.

Returning to his chair, he picked at the remaining food and finished off the rest of his coffee just as Lorelei stepped back into the room. Turning his attention to her, he watched her reclaim her seat on the other side of the table.

"I just spoke with Elder Caine. He's gonna call an emergency meetin' with the council." He nodded his head slowly like he had not been eavesdropping.

"So, what's that mean exactly?" he asked, tossing his empty cup into the nearby trash can.

"Well, it'll take some time, since he needs to convince the Council to hear your testimony but they'll meet, discuss what I've told him, and vote. If the majority rules, you'll go before the Council, and plead your case."

"How can I plead my case if I can't remember it?" he asked, a bit frustrated.

"Because I'll be goin' with you." Her statement was simple, matter-of-fact, and he blinked at her in surprise.

"You'd be released into my custody for the hearin'." Declan sat back in his chair, staring at her, not knowing how to respond. Lorelei shifted her attention back to her laptop and they sat in silence for several minutes.

"My wolf said he's sorry. He wasn't tryin' to hurt you," Declan finally said, rubbing the back of his neck.

"It's all right," she said quietly, a soft smile making the corners of her mouth twitch. "You said that's never happened before? Your wolf just–" She mimicked the moment, her hands lifting to the sides of her face and pushing out.

"No, never," he said, chuckling at her animated gestures. Declan was certain it had been the pain that caused the beast to leap from him. It was unlike anything he had ever felt before, and he was sure he would have felt it even in death. Lorelei let out a thoughtful humph, tipping her coffee cup to her lips before tossing it into the trash.

"I felt it too. The pain." Her gaze slid up to his and his brows drew together briefly.

"How?" He leaned his forearms on the tabletop and looked at her curiously. She leaned back and lifted her arms, drawing his gaze to her breasts as she regathered her long curls and twisted them back up into her claw clip. When he heard her heart rate increase, Declan's eyes drifted up to meet hers and saw that she was watching him. Slowly lowering her arms, she readjusted her shirt and cleared her throat. Her cheeks had turned a delectable shade of pink.

"The spell seems to have a defense mechanism built into it. I'm guessin' the pain we both felt was it tryin' to keep us from seein' what it's hidin'," she explained, leaning an elbow onto the table and propping her chin in her hand.

"I saw myself in the same suit I surrendered when I was brought in. From what I remember, I was transported directly from my home that night," he said, relaying the memory fragment he had seen.

"That's what I saw too," she said, "at least now we know for sure that your memories were tampered with. Specifically, your memories of the Alpha Ceremony."

'Sexy and smart. We are in trouble.' Declan already knew that but still was inclined to agree with his beast.

The weeks flew by, and soon, more than a month, with Declan and Lorelei adding to their routine. She would arrive at the same time every morning, two coffees and a mountain of food in hand, and they would sift through the information they had gleaned from the fragments. They managed to recover a large portion of him talking to his cousin outside on the lawn of the packhouse and with his mother in the kitchen about the fight with Cormac. Each new memory they uncovered brought them closer to the truth of what happened that night. It was not much but Declan felt more and more hopeful about the upcoming hearing. He also began to trust her greatly and found himself sharing more details about himself and his life that were unrelated to his case. Lorelei in turn opened up about her life, and he found himself entranced with her animated storytelling. Drinking in even the most mundane details.

Though they were together for hours upon hours every day, Declan never grew tired of her company and looked forward to seeing her, hearing her voice, and stealing glances at her body that made his mouth water. Lorelei remained professional aside from a bit of flirting, but he had heard her heart pounding throughout their sessions. He saw the flush of her cheeks when she was thinking of forbidden things, and caught her eyes wandering over him multiple times. Today was no exception.

Declan glanced up from the breakfast spread to Lorelei, who was sitting with one knee pulled up near her chest. She was scrolling through her laptop, her brow creased as she read whatever was on the screen. She finally gave him the mandatory psych evaluation and was in the process of going over all the results from the last several weeks.

"Good news or bad news first?" she asked, finally looking up at him over the screen. Declan narrowed his eyes and chomped into a piece of bacon when he saw the mischievous glint in her stormy grey eyes.

"Surprise me," he said, giving her a crooked grin.

"Well, the good news is you're completely sane." She feigned disbelief and crossed her arms.

"And the bad news?" He raised a brow.

"The bad news is you're completely sane." She smiled at him as his grin widened at her teasing. "*However*, you have insomnia, and night terrors. Both of which are bein' caused by your blocked memories. We didn't need a psych eval to figure that out, but they'll more than likely continue until we can address the trauma that's been neglected for nearly three years." She took a sip of her coffee just as her phone pinged on the table next to her. Declan watched her as she read over the message, a myriad of emotions passing over her gorgeous features.

"Somethin' wrong?" he asked when she set the phone back down on the table.

"I wouldn't say wrong…" she bit her bottom lip, and the simple action had Declan hardening at the sight. Ever since he had first laid eyes on the Witch, he had been in a constant state of arousal. At first, he had refused to give himself any relief, believing that she would come and go without much thought. But over time, the pressure became too much to bear. It had come to a point where he had caught himself absently rubbing his throbbing length during one of their sessions. Not wanting to feel like an absolute creep, he had stroked himself into a blinding orgasm that night and every night since trying to alleviate the near-painful erections the good doctor gave him daily. The device sliding over to him pulled Declan from his dirty recollections, and he picked it up while she summarized the email he was scrolling down to view.

"Elder Caine has ordered your release into my custody. Effective immediately. The hearin' is tomorrow afternoon in Atlanta." The phone slipped from his hand, clattering to the metal tabletop. Declan stared at her in disbelief, though she refused to meet his eyes. She had busied herself collecting the food and condensing the leftovers into a single tray.

"You're not thrilled about that," Declan concluded as he took in her body language. He was a little confused when she grimaced, pausing as she reached for her laptop.

"It's not that– It's the *not knowin'* that gives me anxiety. Look, Elder Caine is as adamant about your innocence, but you have to understand. While I know when y'all are tellin' the truth or lyin', we still don't have the hard evidence," she said and Declan nodded his head.

"I'm worried too, y'know," he said, and she finally looked up at him, her brows lifting in surprise at the revelation. "I'm puttin' my life in your hands, not knowin' if I'm walkin' into the lion's den or an angel's savin' grace. But I'm willin' to take that chance." Declan watched as her mind worked overtime, considering his words. It stung a bit that she still had concerns regarding his innocence, but he understood. Even though he might not remember what happened that night, he knew for damn sure he would have never hurt his family *or* his pack. That was a hill he was willing to die on.

"Then let's get outta here, Wolfe," she said, canting her head in the direction of the door. When he stood from the too-small chair, Declan adjusted the front of his scrub bottoms before following her out of the room.

After several phone calls to a *very* angry Elder Caine and a pile of paperwork later, they finally stepped from the security office. As Lorelei handed over his discharge papers to the admissions office, he leaned against the cool brick wall near the large window, waiting to reclaim his belongings. Laughter accompanied by a blur of movement caught his attention, and Declan groaned inwardly when he glanced down the long hallway.

Officer Dick and Officer Asshole rounded the corner, grinning like idiots. They both came to a stumbling halt, and Declan could see the vein throbbing in Officer Asshole's forehead even at this distance. Anger and disbelief quickly replaced their obvious good mood and both men quickly made their way through the lobby, ignoring that Lorelei was standing less than ten feet from him.

"What the hell are *you* doin' out here, mutt?" Officer Asshole asked as he advanced, stopping only when they were nose to nose. From the corner of his eye, Declan saw Lorelei bristle as she turned from the counter.

This was the first time since reading the letter from Elder Caine that they had openly approached him. He had been meeting Lorelei at the security office ever since that day. No cuffs, no guards. Just him and the doctor. In fact, he had not been sent back to the basement since Lorelei came to the asylum. Despite being mouthy to some of the other guards, and getting into a fight only a week prior, Declan received the bare minimum of punishments.

"Didn't y'all get the memo? I'm gettin' the hell outta, Dodge," he said, grinning when the men fumed and sputtered. The vein in Asshole's forehead threatened to explode while Dick's face turned a vibrant, splotchy red. Declan would have laughed out loud at the sight of them but he knew that would only make the current situation so much worse.

"You're a psycho, Wolfe. No one in their right mind would let you outta here." Officer Dick spat at him, both men reached out to seize him by the arms. While Declan would have been justified to push back, he refused to make a move on either of them. Not this close to freedom, and certainly not when Lorelei could wind up in the middle of it.

"Thoreau, Marshall! Back the fuck up!" The stern command radiated authority and Declan looked down at Lorelei just as she forced her way into the small gap separating them.

'So much for keeping her out of the middle,' his beast huffed, and Declan had to suppress a groan when her backside brushed firmly against his half-erect shaft. She did not acknowledge the growing bulge, though he felt the infinitesimal tilt of her hips as she shifted against him again. Stifling another groan, he dragged a hand up to her waistline. The hem of her shirt lifted, exposing a sliver of skin, and Declan gripped her hip, fingers digging into her flesh trying to halt her movements.

The two men took a step back, glaring at him when his eyes shifted crimson. Lorelei just reached above their shoulders, squaring up with the men ready to haul him back into the asylum. The woman was protective and he liked it. A lot.

"Well, aren't you cute, Doc?" Asshole said smoothly, "If you like crazy, I can show you a thing or two that'll blow your mind."

A growl ripped from his chest when the man reached for her. Before Declan could introduce the man's face to his fist, a near-invisible burst of magic exploded from Lorelei, the power of it forcing her back against his chest. In front of them, the air warbled softly as both men were gut-punched by two balls of energy, flying backwards down the hall. They crashed into a large soiled linen cart, tangling in a pile of sheets with Goddess knows what staining them.

"How's that for cute, asshole?" she asked dryly, side-stepping around Declan. Slamming her hand down on the sealed bag that was slid onto the counter, Lorelei snatched up his effects and headed for the door. He dragged his gaze from the woman striding for the exit to the guards struggling to escape the oversized cart.

'She is full of surprises,' his wolf mused with a growl.

"C'mon Declan, we're goin' shoppin'," she called, shoving open the front door.

Not far from Saint Thaddeus, Lorelei cruised down the nearly deserted street of a small, shabby town. They pulled into the parking lot of a discount department store and found a spot near the front. In the distance, thunder rumbled as dark clouds drifted slowly across the sky. A streak of lightning flashed overhead as they trudged across the asphalt. Nearing the entrance, Declan felt Lorelei's gaze on him and he slowly swiveled his head to look at her.

"How long have you been barefoot?" she asked, the amusement clear in her voice. Declan looked down at his feet as they entered the building, pausing while she grabbed a shopping cart.

"The slides at Saint Thaddeus are awful. I wore 'em once when I first got there but it was more comfortable goin' without," he shrugged, giving her a lopsided smile.

"All right, so we need," she gave him a onceover, "everything."

"I don't need much. If the hearin' goes sideways, I'll be back in black scrubs before the day's over," he said entering the men's clothing section. She was silent while they browsed but Declan could hear her heart pounding in her chest. When he lifted his gaze to peer at her over the clothing rack, there was a deep crease between her elegant brows.

"What about this?" he asked, pulling a tee shirt from the rack with a graphic of an angry kitten and the words, 'Beast Mode' written beneath. Her face lit up with laughter when she noticed the shirt and the sight made his chest constrict. Goddess, she was a beautiful woman.

"I think it's perfect for you," Lorelei teased him, sifting through another rack filled with sleepwear. He nodded and placed the shirt in the cart, her eyes bounced from the garment to him, shaking her head.

"What? I can use it for a workout shirt if I make it home. I know Wyatt will get a kick out of it," Declan reasoned, checking the tag on a pair of joggers.

"*When,*" she corrected him, "when you make it home." Their eyes met and he gave her a subtle nod, a gentle smile tugging at the corners of his lips.

They spent the next hour and a half browsing through the men's clothing and managed to piece together a presentable outfit for the hearing, along with a few pieces to mix and match. A package of socks and boxer briefs, some necessary toiletries, a decent prepaid cell phone, and a surprisingly comfortable pair of dark brown boots were all piled into the cart. They meandered over to the small travel department and found a decent-sized duffle bag for his new belongings.

"Thank you," Declan said as they left the store, carrying most of the bags. Lorelei smiled while a slight blush colored her cheeks.

"You're welcome, but there's really no need to thank me," she said, unlocking the back gate. When he took the bags from her, his fingers brushed over hers. There was an almost inaudible gasp from Lorelei when their skin came into contact. The tingles he felt radiated up through his palm to his wrist.

"You–" His words were interrupted by a deafening clap of thunder, and both of them ducked away from the sudden noise. Sharing a look of startled amusement, Declan tossed the bags into the back and shut the gate, hurrying around to the passenger side.

Missus Betty had only been mildly surprised when Declan had traipsed onto the porch behind Lorelei, both of them soaking wet from the torrential rain that now flooded the estate grounds. When they started to trudge upstairs, the old woman insisted they come down for some supper. Now, he and Lorelei sat in the warm, cozy kitchen wrapped in fluffy towels while Missus Betty served up two bowls of steaming beef stew.

"Now y'all just leave the dishes in the sink when you're done. There's plenty'a stew there on the stove if y'want more," The elderly woman said, tottling out of the kitchen.

"Yes, ma'am. Thank you," Declan said, grinning as a hand was thrown in the air in acknowledgement, and she disappeared down the hallway. Just as they were about to dig into their meal, Lorelei's phone rang. Elder Caine's name illuminated the screen and she quickly answered the call.

"Hello?" she asked, turning on the speakerphone.

"Doctor McCann, I do hope I find you well this evening?" Elder Caine's proper English accent filled the space around them. For a moment, Declan was dragged back to the night of the massacre when he woke up from the blackout. He remembered how he had struggled to find the words to speak to the Elder, to tell him he had no idea what was going on.

"Yes, sir. We're both just fine," she replied, glancing at Declan. Her head canted to the side gently in silent question, brows knitting together. He shook his head and gave her a soft crooked smile before folding his arms on the tabletop.

"Excellent! I've just phoned to confirm that you know the location of the Elder Council headquarters, my dear," said Elder Caine.

"I know where it is," Declan stated, his voice almost lodging in his throat.

"My Goddess. Declan?" Elder Caine's tone held an edge of sadness.

"It's me, Caine," he replied, trying to clear the lump stuck behind his Adam's apple. The urge to demand answers from the old man was nearly overwhelming and Declan had to remind himself that the hearing was the following day. Pressing his luck with the High Elder was probably unwise.

"We have much to discuss tomorrow, my boy. So much to discuss." Caine bid them safe travels and ended the call.

"I guess tomorrow's judgment day," he said a bit grimly as he stared, unseeing, down at the bowl. He felt so helpless. Standing on the sidelines while everyone around him took the brunt of it all. Declan did not like this feeling one bit.

"Everything will be fine, Declan. I promise," Lorelei said, taking a bite of her stew. His brows drew together briefly, and he gazed at her for a long moment. Lies would taste bad to someone with her gift. He knew this thanks to his great-grandmother but Declan saw no sign of deceit in her. Deciding to trust her word, he grabbed his spoon and took a bite.

Chapter 09

Lorelei could not help but stare as a look of ecstasy fell over Declan's features and his head tipped back. Chewing slowly, he closed his eyes as he reveled in the flavor; Lorelei covered her mouth to stifle a giggle. When he lifted another spoonful, their eyes met and Declan gave her a grin, completely unashamed. A soft grunt of satisfaction rumbled from the man beside her when his lips closed around his second bite. The sound shot straight to her core and Lorelei gave herself a rough mental shake. He was eating for Goddess sake. That should not be a turn-on. Yet here she was, barely able to keep her eyes off of him while he ate beef stew of all things. A sly glance from Declan told her that he was well aware of her inner turmoil. Averting her eyes, she silently willed her thumping heart to calm as the heat burned her cheeks.

They ate in contented silence. Lorelei managed to keep her eyes firmly on the bowl in front of her until she felt his gaze burning on her skin. Glancing in his direction, she found Declan watching her. That predatory gleam flared to life when her eyes found his, and the sight tied her stomach up in knots. Goosebumps erupted, making her hair stand on end, and a shiver threatened to race up her spine. The silence stretched on for what seemed like an eternity, tension so thick you could cut it with a knife. Lorelei averted her gaze from the smoldering fire and reached for her glass of water. Taking a long sip, she hoped to quell the dryness that suddenly had her tongue sticking to the roof of her mouth.

"What?" she asked once she felt like she could speak again. Relieved that her voice did not sound like a drowning frog.

"Just- admirin'," he confessed, pupils dilated. The admission left her stunned for a moment and she blushed, biting her lips gently. Unsure how to respond, Lorelei stood from the table and collected their dirty dishes, trying to find her voice. She silently rinsed the bowls and left them in the sink for whoever to wash in the morning, heeding Missus Betty's instructions. As she dried her hands on a nearby towel, her mind raced. The code of ethics that had been hammered into her memory since college replayed in her mind; *Psychologists Do Not Engage in Sexual Intimacies with Current Clients/Patients.* Even if Declan wanted any kind of relationship with her, which she doubted, the code barred any such involvement with a client until two years after their release from the therapist's care.

Sighing inwardly, Lorelei turned around to head back to the table and stepped into the hard wall that was Declan. Strong fingers caught her shoulders, the touch firm and gentle all at once. She gasped at his sudden appearance and instinctively reached out to steady herself. Her hands flattened on his sides, fingers splayed as tense muscles flexed beneath her touch. She could have sworn she heard him hiss under his breath as if he had been burned. Lips parted in surprise, she lifted her gaze. She never even heard him walking up behind her, and the thought made her shiver. He truly was a predator.

Several seconds crept by until he lifted a large hand to her cheek, and leaned forward. Lorelei closed her eyes at the feeling of his lips pressing softly to her forehead, hungry for the sensation only his touch could create.

"I don't know how I'll ever repay you, but I'm damn sure gonna try." His voice was low and seductive. She found herself wanting to lean into his calloused hand. To feel more of the tingling warmth, prickling along her scalp and around her eyes. However, uncertainty kept her from doing exactly what her body was demanding of her.

Swallowing hard, she gave a small nod as she gazed up into his dark brown eyes, her pulse quickening and her breath hitching. The last month had put her professionalism to the ultimate test. One that she failed every night in the privacy of her bedroom. The man had invaded her dreams, overpowering her senses even when she slept. His powerful body hovered above her, pounding mercilessly until they were both panting and moaning. Hands exploring and caressing every inch of her. Though every time either of them was on the edge of climax, she would jerk awake. Needy for release, she would toss and turn until she slipped a hand into her soaked panties, desperate to relieve the ache. Even now the thought made heat pool between her legs. Above her, Declan closed his eyes, swallowing hard.

"We should probably pack," he said, taking a deliberate step back. Lorelei snapped back to the present, shaking her head a little. Mumbling her agreement, she stepped around his large frame. Gathering up several of the shopping bags, she hurried up the staircase, trying to put a little distance between them. All too soon she would be confined in the small space of her Wagoneer with him for hours. However, a sudden realization hit her as she walked into her–*their*–room. There was one bed and not much else in the way of sleeping arrangements.

"I can sleep on the floor," Declan offered as if reading her mind. He moved to the settee to start removing tags and folding his new clothes into the duffle bag. Lorelei hated the idea of him sleeping on the floor, especially after what he endured in his time at Saint Thaddeus. She opened her mouth and closed it with a huff, shaking her head.

"We can share the bed. It's plenty big for the two of us," she said as she pulled out a change of clothes for the morning and laid them to the side. She packed up the rest of her things, stuffing them roughly into her small suitcase.

"It's no big deal, the carpet here is ten times softer than anything at the asylum," he said, shrugging his broad shoulders. Lorelei scowled, watching him crumple up a bag and toss it in the trash can. Gritting her teeth, she stuffed some dirty clothes into one of the empty shopping bags before walking over to take the pair of pants he currently held.

"Go take a shower. I can finish this up for you," she said, folding the joggers neatly and placing them on the short stack Declan had already made. He did not argue with her as he selected some clean garments from the pile and headed for the bathroom.

"We're sharin' the bed," Lorelei said over her shoulder, finality ringing in her voice. The hair on the back of her neck stood on end as a shiver skittered up her spine. She did not have to look at the man to know that he stopped in his tracks halfway across the room. She could feel his gaze on her skin, branding her. The bathroom door thumped closed after a few moments, and she released the breath she had been holding. Giving orders to an Alpha was not the smartest thing to do, but he had been denied basic comforts long enough.

She refused to let him sleep anywhere but in the bed. If that meant raising the hackles of an Alpha Werewolf by ordering him around, so be it.

Lorelei was acutely aware of the shower turning on and it only took half a second for her professionalism to slip. She glanced over her shoulder towards the bathroom. What she saw nearly caused her to drop the pair of pants she was holding. The thump she had heard was merely the door bumping into the frame. Apparently, the flooding rain and moisture in the air had caused the wood to swell, preventing it from closing all the way. Instead, the door had swung open several inches, giving her a generous view of the man beyond the threshold.

Flat planes, bulging muscles, and the length of a tattoo that spanned over his broad shoulders – the sight drew her in like a moth to a flame. The letters were in the style of old English touting a short phrase in what Lorelei thought might be Latin. She had seen the tattoo weeks ago, but she had been so disgusted by the injuries, so absorbed in documenting his mistreatment, that she had hardly noticed the ink. Her eyes roved over the muscles of his back, admiring how they flexed with his movements. When he disappeared momentarily, Lorelei found herself leaning to keep her eyes on him. She may have seen him shirtless already but Goddess, she could stare at him for days, or longer, and not tire of the sight of him. Declan's silent sudden reappearance made her startle slightly. Steam was beginning to fill the bathroom, making him look like a scene from one of her numerous erotic dreams. However, when he hooked his thumbs in the waistband of his low-slung scrub bottoms, Lorelei tore her gaze away. She enjoyed a good show like anyone else but she was not a total pervert. Cheeks flaming, pulse pounding in her ears, she resumed the task of folding his clothes, knowing full well he could hear her thundering heartbeat.

Moving about the room, she tried to stay busy while Declan took his time in the shower. She had already finished packing up his clothes and cleaned up the few remaining shopping bags littering the floor. After changing into a dry shirt and shorts, Lorelei sat on the edge of the bed and tore into the packaging of Declan's new cell phone. Slipping under the fluffy down comforter, she drew her knees up and began working her way through activating the device.

She was just finishing the set-up when the bathroom door opened wide and Declan stepped out, steam swirling from the doorway. Her breath stalled in her lungs, and her stomach clenched almost painfully with butterflies. His hair was damp, hanging in shaggy waves over his forehead and down his nape. He was wearing a black muscle shirt that showed off his thick biceps while the gaping hole in the side exposed the uppermost ridges of muscle along his ribcage. The pair of grey joggers that clung to him did very little to hide his muscular legs or the thick length between them. Lorelei followed his fluid movements as he came around the corner of the bed, the now-forgotten phone cradled limply in her hands. She was almost hypnotized by the predatory grace of the man in front of her. Tension drew his muscles tight, and she admired the striations that banded over his shoulder. Her gaze drifted down his arm, staring at the shallow valleys and divots dancing beneath his skin as his fingers flexed. It was then she noticed the black scrubs from Saint Thaddeus balled in his hand as he stepped up to the trash can beside the entryway. She stayed silent, barely breathing while Declan glared down at the garments. He let them fall into the bin, the soft rustle of plastic echoing louder than it should have. He drew in a slow, deep breath, chest expanding, and the tension in his shoulders visibly eased. His head swiveled in her direction, the ghost of a smile turning up the corners of his mouth. There was a knowing look in his eyes. His gaze swept over her, the tip of his tongue slipping over his bottom lip.

Goddess, damn her pounding heart.

"It'll take us about nine hours to get to the Council from here," he said casually as if the tension in the room was not stifling, "I think there's a hotel down the street. We could freshen up there. Change clothes." Running a hand through his hair, Declan sat down on the other side of the bed, the mattress sagging under his weight.

"Sounds good to me," she said with a soft nod, amazed that she had even found her voice. Lorelei smiled at him and returned her attention to the cell phone as he stood and turned down the comforter.

"You're sure?" he asked before climbing into the large bed. Nodding, she watched him slip under the covers with a heavy groan.

"Oh hell. I haven't laid in a bed this soft in a long time," Declan said, adjusting his pillow.

"Well, get used to it. We're gonna figure this out one way or another." Lorelei glanced over at him while he remained silent. His eyes were closed already, breathing slowly and evenly. Surprise quickly morphed into amusement as she struggled to stifle a giggle. The smile slowly faded when she realized that she trusted him. She did not know why though since she still had no idea if he was guilty or not. When she really thought about it though, her insight could not bind those crimes to Declan. They felt… wrong.

Easing back against the pillows, she stared hard at the phone in her hand, digesting this new revelation and recalling all she had learned about him the last few months. Pursing her lips, she opened his contacts list and added her phone number.

A sudden violent jerk of the bed startled Lorelei awake. A ball of translucent energy formed in each hand as she bolted upright, looking wildly around the room. Moonlight spilled in through the bay window, illuminating the room in a pale silvery glow. An incoherent mumble came from beside her, pulling her gaze down to Declan. Though his face was cast in shadow, Lorelei could see the deep crease between his brows. His eyes darted back and forth at a rapid pace behind his closed eyelids. She extinguished the roiling spheres of magic and reached for him.

"Declan?" she whispered loudly, placing a hand on his shoulder. For a moment, his mumbling quietened, and the furrow of his brows eased. The reprieve from his nightmare was short-lived, and his body gave a convulsing shudder, muscles coiled tight. A blood-curdling sound spilled from him that could only be described as a low, mournful, groaning howl.

Getting out from under the comforter, Lorelei scrambled to her knees beside him. Grabbing his shoulders, she shook him roughly and called his name, but he was too deep in the nightmare. His lips pulled back, baring his teeth as another terrifying howl groaned.

Shaking him again, Lorelei yelled louder, desperately trying to wake him. He suddenly sat up, forcing her to jerk back as his arms extended out on either side of her. She tried to move out of his embrace but his arm wrapped around her middle, holding her in place.

"*Why?*" he muttered, sweat trickling down his temple. His other hand hung suspended in mid-air, reaching for something unseen to Lorelei. She laced an arm around his shoulders, and for a moment, he calmed, his outstretched arm slowly lowering to his side.

Placing a hand on his cheek, she coaxed his head to turn. His eyes were even more frenzied behind his lids. She racked her brain, sifting through a mental catalog of information. Slowly, Declan bared his teeth to her, menace and hatred contorting his handsome features. An idea struck her just as he lunged for her throat. Using her magic to halt his advance, she leaned against him and pressed her cheek to his.

"Declan, it's Lorelei. You're safe," she whispered, lips brushing against his ear. His reaction was instantaneous and he stilled, tension easing from his muscles. Pulling back to look at him, she saw his features had softened. Still, he was muttering incoherently with his brows drawn tightly together. Laying a hand on the side of his face, she caressed his cheek and repeated the soothing words.

"Lorelei," his voice was soft and raw, breath fluttering the loosely hanging curls at her nape. Goosebumps erupted across her skin, making her shiver. She breathed a sigh of relief when his body fully relaxed into her touch. Declan slumped back to the mattress, pulling her down on top of him, his arm still anchored around her waist.

"Oof!" she grunted as the air whooshed from her lungs. Breathing a heavy sigh of relief, she rested her forehead against his shoulder.

Unsure of how long she lay there with him, Lorelei carefully unwound his arm from around her and sat up. She gazed at his now peaceful features for several minutes, brushing a few sweat-soaked strands from his forehead. Easing back to her side of the bed, she sat cross-legged, watching the slow, steady rise and fall of his chest until the alarm sounded on her phone.

Rushing from the bed, she silenced the incessant chiming before it could wake the whole inn and grabbed her preselected garments from the settee. Pausing in the doorway, her gaze drifted to the bed just as Declan rolled to his side, facing her. Taking a moment, Lorelei sent up a silent request to the Lunar Goddess, praying that the man was truly innocent of all that had been levied against him.

Chapter 10

"You want anything?"

Declan inserted the gas pump nozzle into the tank, stealing a look at Lorelai – his gaze lingering longer than he expected. She stood on the passenger side step, arms propped on the open-door frame and the roof. Her auburn curls hung wild past her shoulders, caressing the sides of her plump breasts. She wore a semi-loose white tank top, showing off her figure, and a pair of navy-blue sweatpants. She was absolutely mouthwatering, and he had to shove a hand into the pocket of his joggers to adjust his throbbing erection. He shrugged a shoulder and gave her a crooked grin, notching his chin up.

"Surprise me, darlin'," Her cheeks turned pink and he saw her nipples harden beneath her tank as she rolled her eyes, returning his crooked smile. She dropped from the sideboard, pushing the passenger door shut, and Declan watched her walk across the small parking lot. His eyes glued to her perfect backside until she disappeared into the convenience store.

'I like her,' his wolf said suddenly, and he chuckled at the admission. His beast had never liked anyone except their family. For a moment, grief tore through his heart when he remembered that most of his family was

gone. All of them, except Wyatt. Blinking away the moisture in his eyes, he leaned back against the side panel, absently watching the ticker roll over, pushing the thoughts from his mind.

"Hey baby," an irritatingly high-pitched voice called out, "where ya headed?" Declan looked around to the only other car in the parking lot, a candy-apple red Porsche. A woman with platinum blonde hair sauntered towards him, leering harder with each step. He cringed inwardly as he took in her appearance. Though the woman was not *un*attractive, she wore heavy makeup, a too-tight spaghetti strap that exposed her ample cleavage, black leather pants and four-inch red stilettos. Her bright red lips pulled into a coquettish smile as she came around the Wagoneer to stand near him.

"Road trip," he said gruffly, a thin smile on his lips.

"Oh, that sounds fun!" she purred, sliding a manicured hand along his arm, "Wouldn't it be so much better with some company though?" The suggestiveness was not lost on Declan as she pressed her breasts against him, clutching his bicep. He gave her a charming smile and stepped away from her as he pried her desperate grip from his arm.

"What makes you think I'm alone?" he asked, his gaze slipping past her. Surprise lifted her too-thin brows and the woman whipped her head in the direction he was looking.

Lorelei leaned casually against the back gate of the Wagoneer, an overstuffed bag filled with snacks and a large styrofoam cup in each hand. Her posture was relaxed but her eyes held a fire in them – one that made his cock twitch and his wolf rumble approvingly in his head. The beast really did like her.

'Mate,' the beast stated, practically panting as Declan allowed his gaze to roam down her body.

"We should get goin', darlin'. We've got some more baby makin' to do," Lorelei said with a wink, biting her bottom lip. Caught off guard by her words, Declan nearly choked trying to contain his laughter. She pushed off the gate with her hip, silver eyes cutting to the wannabe seductress, and a coy grin spread across her lips.

"I think he was raised by wolves. The man is a *beast,*" she told the blonde, moaning her last words. Declan fought to maintain his composure as he busied himself returning the pump nozzle to its cradle and twisting on the gas cap. The woman stood there awkwardly for several moments before rushing off, embarrassment evident on her overdone face.

Chuckling, he ducked into the driver's side and found Lorelei with her bare feet on the dash, happily sipping on her slushie. Her gaze swiveled to him and she smiled brightly, the straw still between her perfect teeth. He shook his head as he turned over the engine and pulled from the gas station.

"Raised by wolves, huh?" He grinned as she shrugged her shoulders, her laughter filling the cabin.

"I mean, technically it's true." She smiled broadly and looked over at him, making his breath hitch. Glancing between her and the road ahead, he could see the distinct pounding of her pulse in her neck.

'*Mate!*' his beast panted urgently, and this time Declan shook his head, roughly pushing the horny wolf to the back of his mind.

"How much longer 'til we hit Atlanta?" he asked, clearing his throat and taking a large gulp of his cherry slushie. She was busy rifling through the junk food and pulled out a bag of cheesy poofs. Holding them out to him, she picked up her phone and opened the GPS.

Pressing his left knee to the bottom of the steering wheel, Declan pried open the bag. Keeping his eyes on the traffic, he tilted back his head and shook a couple of the crunchy spheres into his mouth, returning a hand to the wheel.

"Give it a sec. Signal's terrible right now." She held up the device, watching the spinning indicator. A minute later, the satellite map popped up and she read off the remaining time.

"Little over four hours. Need me to drive for a while?" She looked at him as she popped a chocolate-covered almond into her mouth.

"No, just wonderin'," he said, shaking his head. They slipped into a comfortable silence with Declan glancing her way every few minutes while she munched on her almonds, watching the scenery go by. Suddenly, she twisted her body towards him and hiked a knee up onto the bench seat. Leaning back against the door, she eyed his large frame. He glanced at her a couple of times, fighting the amusement that pressed his lips together.

"What?" The word chuckled from him and Lorelei grinned.

"Truth or dare?" She asked, and he raised his brows at her unexpected question.

"Truth."

"Tell me your most embarrassing moment." He laughed and thought about it as he shook out a few more cheesy poofs, chewing them slowly. Remembering a humbling experience he had when he was younger, he told her about when he was seventeen and thought he was man enough to challenge his father.

They had been arguing about something that he could not remember now, and Declan made a bid for the position of Alpha. Even though he held his own for a good while, he eventually lost the fight. Needless to say, he was beaten to within an inch of his life that day in the arena. When the fight was over, they talked for the rest of the afternoon about discipline and responsibility, and what being an Alpha truly meant. His father had told him he would have let it go, had Declan not challenged him publicly. Several pack members had been present in the house that day and heard the formal challenge, so the fight had to happen.

"All right, truth or dare?" he asked, glancing into the side mirror before merging back into interstate traffic.

"Hmm.. Dare." Lorelei said, grinning.

"I dare you to…" Declan glanced around the cabin, "Moon the next semi-truck we pass."

"All right," she said and clambered to her knees as they came up alongside an eighteen-wheeler. As they passed by the cab, he was shocked to see that Lorelei actually pulled the back of her sweatpants down and flashed her backside to the driver. The man in the cab did a double take and let off several short blasts of his horn, grinning from ear to ear. Though he did not like the idea of another man looking at any naked part of her, Declan had to admit he was impressed with her grit. He was learning very quickly that Lorelei did not back down from a challenge and had more guts than most Deltas he had trained.

Over the next few hours, they exchanged stories about their lives, where they grew up, and their schooling. Anything they could think of became a conversation topic. It was easy to talk to her, and he found himself smiling at the simplest anecdotes that she told. Lorelei was animated with her storytelling, sometimes making it hard to concentrate on the road as he tried to watch her. She was mesmerizing to him. Beautiful, graceful, and had a personality most would kill for. In the middle of a story about her childhood, there was a strange tug in his heart; his gaze bounced between her and the road. A sensation that his chest was suddenly empty and full at the same time.

Chapter 11

Lorelei stepped out of the en-suite shower an hour later, scrunching the water from her hair. She dressed quickly, pulled on the deep green dress and tugged on a pair of soft, brown suede boots. Her stomach churned as she checked her reflection and straightened the loose V-neck. Stepping out of the bathroom, she adjusted the flowing sleeves and tugged at the skirt that billowed around her knees.

She cleared her throat, anxiety making her tremble slightly as she ambled up behind Declan. When he turned to look down at her, they both stared in surprise, eyes roaming and devouring. Arousal shot straight to her core as she appreciated the obscenely sexy man standing in front of her.

Despite the blood stains, he wore the same outfit he had the night of the massacre, and though the blazer and slacks fit a little looser than before, he still wore it well. The top buttons of his black dress shirt had been left undone, just like she had seen in his memory, and the crimson pocket square peeked from the blazer pocket. Lorelei's mouth went dry when her gaze trailed lower; she ogled the bulge at the front of his trousers. Her arousal pooled between her thighs, and she fought the urge to squirm as the wetness became almost uncomfortable. She only looked away when his large hand deliberately adjusted his obvious erection. Blinking, she looked up at him and found Declan's gaze roaming her body. The unmistakable burning desire shone bright in his dark eyes, and her nipples drew taut in response.

"Declan?" she managed to whisper. His focus snapped to her flushed face and she gulped. His eyes were crimson, the beast within barely held at bay.

"You're beautiful," he breathed, his voice was hoarse, and made goosebumps erupt across her skin.

"Thank you. You look incredible, too." Her voice was barely audible, the air stalled in her lungs. Placing a glamor on the suit to temporarily hide the blood, Lorelei realized there was no way that she could stomp out her growing feelings for Declan. She could no longer act as his therapist and would have to figure out what to tell Adam when the time came. Excitement coursed through her briefly until reality set in. They still needed to get through the hearing. Still needed to convince a room full of Elders of his innocence.

Lorelei bounced her knee, watching the tall double doors across from the bench where she and Declan were seated. Any minute now they would be standing before ten Elders with Declan's fate hanging in the balance. Hands clasped loosely in her lap, she barely noticed the

Supernaturals meandering up and down the halls, their glamors wavering in and out of focus.

"Lorelei." Declan settled his hand on her knee, squeezing gently. His warm, tingling touch instantly calmed her and the bouncing slowed to a stop.

"What if I screw this up?" she blurted out suddenly. Declan gave a crooked grin and tipped his head down, lips brushing against her ear. The hand on her knee drifted up her thigh slightly as he leaned toward her, making her breath hitch.

"You're gonna be great. I got all the faith in the world in you." He pulled away and all she could do was stare at him, heart fluttering wildly in her chest. Declan gazed down at her, and she felt herself being drawn to him. Her eyes dropped to his lips, and her tongue darted out to wet her own. Her body had begun to lean in on its own volition when someone nearby cleared their throat loudly. Crashing back to reality, Lorelei looked toward the source of the noise and noticed a smartly dressed secretary standing next to the entryway.

"Doctor McCann, Alpha Wolfe, the Council will see you now," said the man, giving them a stiff inclination of his head.

Lorelei glanced around at the raised singular pulpits, surrounding a circular floor as she and Declan entered the large round chamber. Men and women stood behind podiums, all wearing the same prim white robes with golden trim. The Elders eyed them critically as they stopped in the middle of the open space. Elder Caine stood in the center dais and was the first to speak.

"Doctor Lorelei Katherine McCann, and Declan Elijah Wolfe. Thank you both for coming on such short notice. I understand you are here today because you have new information about the massacre at Crescent Ridge, correct?"

"Yes sir, we do." She stepped forward and took a steadying breath.

"As you all know, I have been tasked with evaluating Declan Wolfe while he was housed at Saint Thaddeus to determine the accuracy of his innocence or guilt. As previously mentioned by my client, he has no recollection of the events that happened at Crescent Ridge the night he was accused, and committed. I would like to preface this testimony by informing the Council that I have the gift of insight. It gives me the ability to know when someone is lying or telling the truth, be it half-truths or white lies. I'm also able to see through glamors, and detect what's hidden from sight." She waited a beat before continuing, "During one of our sessions, I attempted to help Declan with the amnesia he's experienced since the incident. I've been successful in the past with numerous clients who suffered memory loss due to traumatic events. In this case, however, I've learned that Declan does not suffer from amnesia.

Instead, a powerful barrier surrounds his memories of that night, created by dark magic." A low murmur went around the room, "When I began to push against this barrier, it triggered a defense mechanism within the spell that caused excruciating pain in us both. Despite the spell's defenses, I was able to extract a memory fragment of Declan on the evening of the Alpha Ceremony. He was wearing the same clothing when he was admitted to Saint Thaddeus." Lorelei lifted a hand, indicating the suit he had on, "Only memories surrounding that specific incident are blocked." A cacophony of questions was launched at her but Caine held up a hand, silencing them.

"I'm here today to declare to the Council that I do not believe Declan Wolfe is responsible for the crimes he's accused of due to the use of dark magic to conceal only those memories, as well as other contradicting evidence." She took a deep shaky breath, feeling slightly winded after her monologue. Peering around the room, she saw that many were regarding her with curiosity, and she gently cleared her throat under the scrutiny. She stepped back beside Declan, awaiting the inevitable questions that hung in the air.

"Well, this is awfully convenient." Lorelei peered up at the woman who spoke. "A psychologist, who *happens* to possess the gift of insight, is assigned to Declan Wolfe's case." She was beautiful, with long pure white hair, and a light brown complexion, though her tone was one of mocking condescension. Declan went rigid beside her and she brushed her fingers lightly against his thigh, feeling some of the tension leave him at her touch.

"If I may be blunt?" Lorelei directed her question to Caine, who nodded, keeping his features neutral, "My boss was contacted by Elder Caine who then assigned me the case. There was obviously something that unsettled the High Elder for him to seek out someone with my specific talents. Would you prefer to see an innocent man condemned for crimes he did not commit?" Lorelei challenged, earning a searing glare from the woman.

"Of course not. However, there are eyewitness testimonies stating that Declan Wolfe razed his pack," the white-haired female remarked with disdain.

"They could have been lying." Lorelei waved away the glamor concealing Declan's suit. "Do any of you see what I do?" she asked, glancing around the room as the Elders examined the pattern of blood spatter on the blazer. "The saturation of blood only on the left arm, and some splattering over the front here?"

"What's your point?" the woman demanded. Lorelei smiled at her, elated that she asked.

"My point is that there were two-hundred and twenty-eight pack members that died that night.

Mutilated. *Dismembered.*" Understanding bloomed on the faces of the Elders as they considered her words.

"While I agree that there's a possibility of Alpha Wolfe's innocence, I am still wary of your claims in regard to your gift. Perhaps you could demonstrate your talents for us, Doctor McCann?" The smooth voice spoke from the opposite side of the chamber. Lorelei studied the man momentarily before nodding her head. The hidden meaning was clear. Dance monkey, dance.

"There are no glamors, so a question or statement, then. It can be true, false, or half of either."

"My favorite candy is cordial cherries," Elder Caine said, watching her closely.

"Half-truth. You love the chocolate and the filling but hate the cherries." Elder Caine lit up in a hearty laugh.

"Remarkable! Absolutely right! Dreadful things, cherries." Lorelei chuckled softly along with the rest of the Elders when an unnaturally short man spoke up.

"There is a treasure trove hidden beneath Mount Everest." Lorelei tilted her head.

"Half-truth. There is a treasure, but not under that mountain." Everyone looked to him for confirmation, and he nodded in astonishment.

"Correct."

"Declan Wolfe is guilty of all charges against him." Lorelei bristled, whipping her head around to observe the white-haired woman who she now realized was a Witch.

"That- is a lie," she said matter-of-factly, earning curious looks from around the room. "You don't really believe he's guilty." The Witch said nothing in response, only stared daggers from her lofty perch.

"I have never been unfaithful to my mate," a male Vampire stated, forcing her to shift her attention across the room. Lorelei peered up at his polished demeanor, pursing her lips.

"I'm afraid that's a lie, sir." To her surprise, the man let out a booming laugh.

"Apologies, Doctor McCann, my infidelity is no secret. I've long paid for that sin," he explained and Lorelei nodded, unsure if she should smile or not.

"I think that is more than sufficient at this point. Thank you, Doctor McCann," Elder Caine said, and she dipped her head to him.

"I'm curious," said a stunning female Vampire with short platinum hair and pale, flawless skin. "If it is *you* who seeks his innocence, then why does *he* need to be free?" Her tone dripped with contempt, making Lorelei bristle once again with anger.

"Declan wants to prove his innocence more than anyone, so with all due respect, *madame*, your tone is uncalled for." There was a collective murmur at her brazenness, and she felt Declan's fingertips brush against her skin, distracting her momentarily. "To answer your question, the magic that created the barrier is dark, meaning to cut out the roots, he'll have to go to the source."

"*Bullshit.* Caine, you aren't actually buying into this nonsense, are you?" the white-haired Witch said, looking at Elder Caine. Something in her voice paused Lorelei and she glanced over at the last pulpit. She did a double take when she began to look away. There had been a wavering in the woman's visage. Though it only lasted a fraction of a second, she caught a glimpse of something twisted and dark. Blinking several times, Lorelei wondered if what she had seen was true or just a trick of the light. A shadow, maybe. Her stomach knotted at the uncertainty, and she glanced over again, seeing nothing but brown eyes and a cafe-au-lait complexion.

"And if he is guilty?" asked a male to the right of Elder Caine. No one had noticed the infinitesimal moment, so quickly it did not even register to the others around the room.

"Then I deserve to die." Declan's deep voice filled the chamber, and ten sets of eyes snapped to him. He did not waver under the scrutiny as he stood there spine straight, one hand gripping his wrist loosely behind his back.

"Truth," she said, staring up at him. The thought of him dead made her feel numb inside, and her chest constricted, making it difficult to breathe. Some of the elders nodded, while others looked torn.

"Declan Elijah Wolfe, by the power vested in me by the Grand Council, I grant you clemency." The room erupted in a clamor of voices ranging from outraged to concerned. The High Elder lifted both hands, effectively silencing the room.

"Until the *whole* truth is known, I release you into the custody of Doctor Lorelei Katherine McCann. However, there will be conditions. You are both free to go." Caine waved his hand, and the chamber doors swung open. Giving respectful nods, Declan and Lorelei promptly retreated to the less intimidating hallway.

"This is *well* within my authority, Alistair! My decision is *final!*" Caine shouted angrily as the doors banged closed behind them. Pulling her gaze from the muffled arguments, she smiled up at Declan.

"All the faith in the world," he said with a coy, lopsided grin. Lorelei beamed as her cheeks warmed, and they slowly made their way back to the mini apartment.

"I owe you my life, Lorelei." Declan's voice cut through the silence of the deserted wing they had entered, stopping her dead in her tracks.

"Declan, you owe me nothin'," she said incredulously. She shook her head when he opened his mouth to argue, "Let's wait 'til we figure this out before we start makin' lifelong commitments." She blushed at the duality of her statement, averting her eyes from Declan's charged gaze as it danced over her face. He moved with predatory grace as he prowled towards her. Heart pounding, it's tempo increasing with each step, her eyes snapped up to his as her lips parted in anticipation.

*   *   *

Declan lifted a large calloused hand to her cheek, his thumb sweeping gently over her bottom lip. He listened to her heart fluttering wildly as he leaned in and pressed his mouth to hers, skin tingling on contact. His sharp intake of breath mixed with her soft sigh shot straight to his cock. Lorelei's hands slid to his sides, fists gripping his shirt tightly as she leaned into him. A groan pulled from deep in his throat when her softness pressed against the hard planes of his body.

'Take her. Claim. Mate!' his wolf howled. Declan could not deny that was exactly what he wanted, but it would be her choice. Not his. No matter how right this felt. No matter the need he felt to be inside her, ravishing her curves and laying claim to every inch of the

gorgeous woman that set his blood on fire. It would be her decision, always.

Using every ounce of control he possessed, Declan gently broke the kiss, his muscles tense like a bow sting ready to snap as he slowly opened his eyes. When her eyelids fluttered open, he saw the faint shimmer of silver in her irises, knowing then that she was just as lost in him as he was in her. Goddess, she was beautiful.

"You didn't have to, but you did. And I'll be forever grateful for the angel that saved me from a livin' hell. When the time comes, I *will* owe you my life in more ways than one." Lorelei let out a soft groan and his brows knit together in confusion.

Before he could open his mouth, her hand reached up and gripped the back of his neck and pulled him crashing back down to her lips. He growled softly and backed her against the wall, pinning her between his body and the smooth surface behind her. Her breasts flattened against his chest as he pressed against her soft curves, the scent of her arousal a heady drug that clouded his mind. Slipping his hand into her hair, he fisted the curls, angling her head as he deepened their kiss. Lorelei moaned into his mouth, her tongue clashing with his for dominance, her hands drifting over his abdomen. His breath caught when he felt her palm on the bulge of his length, and he pressed against her hand.

Goddess, the things he wanted to do to this woman. *Needed* to do to her.

Declan broke away from her mouth and pressed his lips to her skin, kissing his way down her throat. Tightening his grip on her curls, he controlled her movements as she whispered his name breathlessly. He raked his teeth over her soft skin where a mark would go, eliciting another moan from her as she gripped his shaft through the fabric. Losing himself, his beast urged him to sink his teeth into her flesh where her shoulder met her throat.

'*Claim. Mate,*' his wolf encouraged. Declan's head twitched in a half-shake as he tried to clear his mind. Tried to reign in the beast pressing just beneath the surface, attempting to break free. Lorelei's hand moved to his waistline, and he was vaguely aware when she unfastened his pants, her fingers brushing beneath the band of his boxer briefs.

Feeling his teeth begin to lengthen and his eyes shift, his breath came out in ragged pants as he glared at the wall behind her. He growled as her hand dipped lower brushing over the base of his cock. Desperately grasping at the fraying threads of his control, he shoved away from her just before he sank his teeth into her shoulder, internally cursing his beast.

Lorelei stumbled when he unexpectedly released her, and she gazed at him in concerned confusion. The sight of her did nothing for the throbbing erection still barely contained in his undone trousers. Her hair was a bit disheveled, her lips puffy from their kiss, and his teeth left a trail of red streaks across the column of her throat. He backed away until he hit the opposite wall, breathing hard as he gazed down at her.

"Declan?" The uncertainty in her voice tore at his insides.

"Don't!" he said a little too harshly when she stepped toward him. He blanched at the hurt in her eyes, the silver fading as she looked down at the floor and wrapped her arms around her middle. His teeth had returned to normal the moment he had pulled away from the temptation of claiming her but his eyes still burned crimson. He needed to calm himself before he lost complete control and did something neither of them could come back from. She had to understand that he never wanted to hurt her, and that would have been the outcome if he marked her. Declan took a deep breath, though his voice was gruff with arousal when he spoke.

"I'm sorry, Lore. I was losin' control. I'd never forgive myself-"

"It's fine," she said flatly, cutting him off. She turned away from him without a second glance, leaving him leaning against the wall. He watched her go, the dredges of his control piecing together the farther she got away. However, when she disappeared into the suite, slamming the door behind her, Declan got the sinking feeling that he had just royally fucked up.

Chapter 12

The next morning, Lorelei sat in the passenger seat of the Wagoneer, staring out the open window as the city of Atlanta faded behind them. She absently twirled a lock of hair around her fingers, recalling their conversation with Elder Caine the night before. She had been in the shower trying to soothe the sting of rejection that Declan's words had left her with when he arrived at the suite. Dressing quickly in a tee and leggings, Lorelei joined the two men in a recessed sitting area within the mini apartment and had made a point of sitting in the chair farthest from Declan. Though the tension was palpable, the High Elder ignored the obvious awkwardness between them, explaining that there were no actual conditions to Declan's release. The only requirement was that once they had compiled enough evidence, they were to send it directly to him.

"Keep an eye out for Garridan when you return to Crescent Ridge. He is a trusted and loyal friend, and already knows of your impending arrival." Elder Caine took a long sip of his tea then, "Declan, I fear your return to your home may not be well received, but know that you do have allies, and dare I say, friends who are on your side." He glanced pointedly at Lorelei. "Garridan has maintained the upkeep of the lake house on Juniper

Springs since he joined the pack, residing there on the weekends. I suspect that will do quite nicely for the two of you."

"Who's Garridan?" she and Declan asked in unison. Elder Caine chuckled when they glanced at each other, amused by the heavy air, hanging between them.

"Garridan is a Werewolf. A Delta, in fact. He is highly trained in combat and weapons, and has been with the Crescent Ridge pack for..." the Elder's nose scrunched up, head bobbing side to side, "about three years now. I sent him shortly after the massacre."

"Doin' what, exactly?" Declan had asked dubiously.

"Surveilling," the Elder stated, "we've been suspicious of the Daughtry's for quite some time."

"Wait. Are you sayin' you think two Omegas are responsible for the deaths of two hundred and twenty-eight Werewolves?" Lorelei asked. Elder Caine gave her a pointed look, telling her that was exactly what he thought.

"Why'd you send me to Saint Thaddeus?" Declan asked suddenly. Lorelei looked at him then. His brows lifted together, obvious hurt and anger marring his features.

"I sent you there to save you, son. You would have been *executed* had I not ordered you committed to the asylum," Elder Caine spoke the words softly. "I never believed that you were responsible. I never for a moment considered the tale that Apollo spun that night to be true. However, I had no evidence. Anything I would have said that night would have been disregarded simply because your father was my friend." Regret etched into Caine's wizened features, "I am incredibly sorry that it took me so long to release you. I have been looking all this time for someone with a particular skill set that could help you." Caine pivoted his gaze, "You would be surprised how few have your gift, Lorelei. It is quite uncommon."

"Was Caine tellin' the truth?" Declan's question pulled her back to the present but Lorelei gave no indication that she heard him speak. After what had happened in the hallway, she could barely bring herself to look at him. The rejection hurt, but the things that he had made her feel in that moment, Goddess, she did not think she would ever recover from those overwhelming sensations. The tingles that danced over her skin, and the feeling of his lips and teeth on her throat raised goosebumps all over her body once again. Her stomach clenched remembering the feel of his shaft beneath her fingertips. Lorelei got ready for bed when Declan stalked into the suite. He attempted a bit of small talk but she refused to speak to him. He rejected her. So tit for tat, she went to bed without a word and had not spoken to him all morning either.

"Lorelei," Declan said, his voice holding an edge, a warning. Shifting her body away from his, she rested her chin on the arm propped on the window frame. There was a heavy silence for several minutes until a rumbling growl filled the cabin, and he veered the Wagoneer off the road. Her irritation only grew when she threw out her arm, bracing her hand on the dash as he skidded to a halt. Slamming the shifter into park, he turned on the bench seat, his intense glare making the hair on her nape stand as she looked straight ahead, crossing her arms under her breasts.

"Why're you ignorin' me?" he demanded. She heard the controlled anger in his voice now. Still, she made no attempt to acknowledge him. Maybe it was childish, but she figured it was better than throwing a tantrum.

"Lorelei!" He snarled her name and she whirled on him, eyes alight with silver flames.

"What, Declan? What the fuck do you want?" she bit out, glaring at him while his eyes shifted crimson. Lorelei notched her chin up in defiance of the Alpha next to her, while the muscles bulged in his jaw as he clenched his teeth. Despite her anger and frustration at the man, her mind betrayed her by flashing images of angry sex in her mind. She mentally cursed the man as she glowered at him, trying to calm her erratic heartbeat.

"Why are you ignorin' me?" he ground out the question again.

"I'm sorry, I just don't wanna lose control. I'd never forgive myself." She spat his rejection back at him, and realization fell over his features.

"That's what you're mad about?" he questioned angrily, voice booming in the small space. "You're actin' like this 'cause I stopped myself from markin' you? Would you rather I'd claim you as mine whether you wanted to be or not?" Her face fell at his words, the anger dissipating when she gained insight and realization sank in. Declan's eyes shifted back to their normal beautiful brown as he stared at her. Wishing she could crawl into a hole somewhere, embarrassment colored her cheeks. The blush only deepened when she understood the implications of him fighting to not claim her, and her voice was quiet when she spoke.

"I didn't realize. I didn't think that…" she trailed off, not finishing her sentence as she looked away from him. She did not want to admit that she never thought he would want to be with someone like her. He knew nothing of her past, so it was a bit silly. Still, for a survivor like Lorelei, she always felt like there was a neon sign above her head advertising her trauma.

"Didn't think what?" Declan probed, reaching around to gently cup her chin, and she tried to quickly blink the tears from her eyes before she turned back to him.

"I just wasn't thinkin' about that at the moment. My mind was pretty preoccupied with other things." It technically was not a lie and she gave a one-sided shrug. Declan watched her for another moment longer before he sighed and nodded his head.

"All right." With that, he faced the steering wheel and pulled back onto the road.

"Wanna answer my question now?" he asked, his crooked grin sending her heart into overdrive.

"He was tellin' the truth, Declan," she said, giving him a soft smile.

Elder Caine called not long after they crossed into Louisiana, informing Declan that he was the sole owner of his father's lake house. He explained that the former Alpha had met with him years before his death and drawn up a will, leaving everything to his son. The Elder apologized for not finding it sooner, cursing the filing habits of the Goblins who worked in the archives department before bidding them farewell.

"Well, that's good news," Lorelei said, laying her phone on the seat between them. To her left, Declan only grunted from his slouched position behind the steering wheel. He had been driving for well over seven hours, and if his slow blinking was any indication, it would not be long before he was dozing off.

"Declan, pull over. You're exhausted." Lorelei offered to drive several times throughout the trip, but he refused. This time, he did not argue as he edged the Wagoneer onto the shoulder of the empty road. They clambered from the vehicle and took a moment to stretch their stiff limbs before switching places. Declan input the address to the lake house into her GPS, reclined himself on the bench seat, and went right to sleep.

The sun had long since set as Lorelei navigated the Wagoneer along an overgrown lane deep in the forest, surrounding the Crescent Ridge pack-lands. The headlights bounced high and low with the humps and bumps of the ill-maintained trail. The tall mixture of trees blocked out the moonlight, their canopy as dense as the undergrowth, weaving around their trunks. The road suddenly split off in two directions, each as thick with leafy bushes and tall grass as the other. She looked from the divided trail ahead of her to the sleeping man whose head now rested in her lap. He slumped over halfway across Louisiana and rather than wake him, Lorelei smiled softly and adjusted her thigh that was pinched under his shoulder.

"Declan." She shook his shoulder, slowing to a stop. The only response was a groan and a soft furrowing of his brows. Chuckling softly, she shook him again, harder this time.

"Declan," Lorelei said loudly. He inhaled sharply as his head jerked up, nose narrowly missing the steering wheel.

"Hey, there's a fork in the trail not on the GPS. Which way?" He sat up, blinking the sleep from his eyes before pointing to the right.

They followed the path for another ten minutes before the dark forest around them began to thin. Moonlight finally broke through overhead, and in the distance, Lorelei could see a large two-story house nestled in the age-old trees.

Declan instructed her to stop outside the two-car garage at the front of the house, and she watched as he strode up to a keypad on the wall. The doors rose slowly a moment later and Lorelei drifted into the empty bay with Declan walking in behind her. As the doors slipped shut again, she turned off the vehicle, darkness shrouded the enclosed space.

"Declan?" She could hear him moving around in the darkness as he opened the back gate of the Wagoneer and collected their belongings.

"One sec." His voice echoed slightly around them and she waited, expecting him to turn on the lights.

"Is there a light? I can't see," she asked, startled when the driver's door suddenly opened.

"I can." Lorelei shivered as his deep voice cut through the darkness. He took her hand and guided her through the darkness, telling her when to step and how many. Neon blue light blinded her momentarily as he lifted their joined hands and used his index finger to enter the code on another keypad lock.

"Grab the door," he said, and she quickly turned the handle. Declan shifted beside her and she heard the distinct click of a light switch flicking on. A wash of warm light came to life and Lorelei recognized she was at the threshold of a large living room with the kitchen and dining area.

"Oh wow," she said as her eyes adjusted. The large family room was decorated with beautiful rustic furnishings, all made from rough-hewn wood. Picture windows graced the front wall on either side of a magnificent fireplace made of large smooth river stones. On the mantle, sat several picture frames of different sizes, and though she could not make out who was in each one, the subjects all seemed to be smiling and happy.

Lorelei meandered over to the kitchen, running a hand over the island top. The polished white oak shone under the soft lights, the lines and woodgrain beautifully preserved under a smooth layer of shellac. Birchwood trunks had been attached under the extended counter for support, with several rustic stools lining the eating space. A deep stainless-steel sink sat opposite the seating arrangement, with a high gooseneck faucet. Turning, she caught sight of Declan watching her from where he leaned a shoulder against the doorframe, thick arms crossed over his broad chest.

"This is beautiful," she breathed. The dining area showcased a stout, white-washed farm table complete with a matching bench and several dining chairs.

"I'm glad you like it. This was a really special place for my parents. And me," Declan said, giving her a soft, forlorn smile. Unsure of what to say, Lorelei nodded her head gently and returned his smile. Clearing his throat, he picked up her suitcase and made his way towards the staircase that backed up to the kitchen.

"This way, darlin'," he said over his shoulder, and she hurried to follow him.

"My parents built this place when I was a kid," he told her, "they wanted to have a getaway without bein' too far from the main packhouse. Dad called it our safe haven."

Declan climbed the flight of stairs up to a spacious lofted area that was home to a foosball table, bean bag chairs, and a pinball machine. A stereo system sat under a huge flat-screen television on the wall with several gaming consoles lining the shelves of the entertainment display.

"Could we play sometime?" she asked as she eyed the game systems.

"Whenever you want," he said with a heart-stopping smile, as he opened a door just to the left of the staircase.

"This'll be your room." He stepped inside and hit the switch, setting her suitcase near the door.

The first thing Lorelei noticed was the bed. Crafted in the same rustic style as the furniture downstairs, the wooden frame had been polished and preserved, showcasing its natural beauty. A comforter that looked like suede leather laid over the mattress with two plush pillows covered with tan cotton cases leaning against the headboard. A soft moss-green rug covered most of the hardwood floor beneath the bed, and she noticed another in a little sitting area tucked in the far corner of the room. The cozy spot was complete with a loveseat, a side table and a large bookcase covering the wall beside the small couch. The walls were painted in a soft beige, lined with stark white wainscot. The dresser matched the bed frame, and sat in front of one of the picture frame windows, across from the bed. Two doors on the left stood ajar and she peeked inside each one. The first one was an oversized walk-in closet and the other was the bathroom, complete with a large walk-in shower, and jacuzzi tub.

"Declan this is incredible, but I can't take the master bedroom." She turned to him, suddenly feeling like she was imposing.

"All the bedrooms are masters." He gave her a crooked grin when she raised her brows in surprise.

"Oh," she said quietly, pursing her lips. Relieved, she sat down on the edge of the bed while Declan leaned against the door frame.

"There's a balcony out the door there," he said with a nod at the decorative glass door to the side of the dresser. "The door here in the loft leads out there too."

"Good spot for mornin' coffee." She smiled up at him. "Thank you, for invitin' me to stay here. Sure beats a motel."

"Well, after everything you've done for me, this is the least I could do. It's yours as long as y'like," he said with a shrug and shoved his hands in his pockets. Her stomach clenched with butterflies at the thought of being with him long-term, her heart hammering at the prospect.

"I'm the door across the loft from you. Holler if you need anything." They said good night, and Declan closed the door softly as he left.

Pulling out a change of clothes, she took a quick shower and crawled into bed, sinking into her soft pillow with a contented sigh. Unpacking would have to wait until tomorrow.

Early next morning, Lorelei woke to the smell of fresh coffee and bacon wafting up from the kitchen. Her stomach growled loudly and she flung off the comforter as she quickly tied her messy curls into a bun on the top of her head and made her way downstairs.

"Declan, you didn't have to cook. I could'a done that," she said as she rounded the staircase, stopping short when she saw a man standing at the stove. The stranger turned slowly, looking at her with furrowed brows and a very confused look on his face. He took in her oversized band shirt and athletic shorts then pointed his spatula at her, bits of egg clinging to it. Lorelei noticed he was wearing a frilly, floral patterned apron, cinched tight over his clothes.

"You're not Declan. Declan doesn't have boobs." Lorelei was taken aback momentarily by his blunt statement.

"Depends on what you define as boobs," she said matter-of-factly. The stranger raised a brow at her, and they eyed each other until the man broke out in a broad grin. Pearly white teeth gleamed under the kitchen light, his canines slightly longer than normal. He was a Werewolf.

"Wyatt Leal. Playboy extraordinaire, lover of beautiful women, and rescuer of damsels in distress. Oh, I'm also the handsome cousin to the owner of this here house." He bowed with a flourish of the spatula, slinging egg bits around the kitchen.

"Really sellin' yourself there, huh?" she teased.

"Someone's got to," Wyatt said with a lopsided smile that reminded her of Declan. Unable to hide her amusement any longer, she grinned at Wyatt and inclined her head regally.

"Nice to meet you, Wyatt. I'm Lorelei," she said with an exaggerated curtsey.

"Well, Lorelei, the pleasure's mine," Wyatt said and turned back to the eggs, cursing softly as they started to burn. "We have casualties. Your fault too, ma'am." He grinned as she slid onto one of the stools, leaning her forearms onto the island.

"Hey, don't blame me if you're so easily distracted." She smiled at him and shrugged her shoulders innocently as he set the scorched pan in the sink, fanning at the smoke that had started to swirl up from the char. She watched as he moved over to the wall oven, pulling large platters from the racks. Wyatt deposited plate after plate onto the island. Each one heaped with a mountain of pancakes, bacon, hash browns, and sausage links.

"Lorelei, you didn't have to cook breakfast," Declan called as he descended the stairs, "Is somethin' burnin'?" Turning in his direction, Lorelei watched as he quickly alighted from the stairs and rounded the bannister. He came to a sudden halt when he noticed the man standing in the kitchen.

"Wyatt?" Declan's surprise was evident and he stared at his cousin in disbelief. Lorelei blinked back tears as she watched the two men meet in a rough bear hug, both barely keeping their emotions in check as they clapped each other on the back.

"Goddess, I thought you were dead," he said, voice thick.

"Far from it, Dec. It's good to see you," Wyatt said as he stepped back, sniffing. "We've got a lot to talk about."

Chapter 13

Declan bit into a piece of bacon, looking over his cousin for a moment. His black hair was longer, currently tied up in a short ponytail at the back of his head, but he had the same brown eyes with that mischievous glint. His skin looked darker than he remembered, and the man had bulked up since he had seen him last.

"How the hell did you know we were here?" he asked, chewing slowly. Though he was glad to see his cousin was alive and well, he could not help the suspicion creeping up the back of his neck.

"Correction. I knew *you* were here. Had no clue I'd meet *this* marvelous beauty though." Declan growled softly at Wyatt's flirting, but Lorelei rolled her eyes with a smile.

"I thought you were in here," she said, nodding to Declan, "Instead, I found the *playboy extraordinaire*." He'd never been that kind of man, but with women constantly fawning over him, the nickname stuck years ago.

"I like this woman. Can I keep her if you don't?" The question earned Wyatt a fork aimed at his forehead, which he casually dodged, grinning wide. The thought of Lorelei with another man ignited a streak of possessiveness in Declan that caught him off guard. With some effort, he reigned in the growl rumbling lowly from his chest.

"I mean you'd be a fool not to." He winked at Lorelei, and Declan rolled his eyes, realizing his cousin was trying to rile him up.

It was working.

"Answer the question, cousin," he said a little more bluntly than intended.

"Elder Caine, geez." Wyatt held up his hands. "Down boy."

"Why didn't I hear from you?" he asked, ignoring the jab with a bit of effort.

"No one knew where you were, and if they did, they wouldn't say. I found out a little over a month ago that you were in Saint Thaddeus, but Caine forbade me from goin' to see you. Reassured me that he already found someone that he thought could help you." Wyatt glanced over at Lorelei, and raised his brow.

"Must've been about the same time that Elder Caine emailed Adam. I left for Saint Thaddeus the same day they spoke," she said, answering his cousin's silent question.

"Who?" Declan asked, the mention of another man rekindled the possessiveness he felt seconds ago. Roughly spearing a sausage, Declan tried to stomp down the unfamiliar feeling.

"Adam Dawson? He's my boss at Dawson Therapies. I thought you knew that," she said, giving him a confused look.

"Nope," he said, mouth turning down at the corners as he shook his head. She never once mentioned her boss, Adam Dawson at Dawson Therapies, until now. That *feeling* surged again. Only this time, it was coupled with a stab of jealousy.

"So, you said we had a lot to talk about." Declan cleared his throat and looked at his cousin, clenching his jaw. Wyatt looked between them, his glass of orange juice stalled halfway to his mouth. He groaned inwardly, knowing that the man had tuned into the tension between him and Lorelei. Wyatt had impeccable intuition, a trait they believe branched from their Nan's insight.

"Oh, yeah. So, the night of the massacre, Cormac took over the pack, exiled me, and managed to recruit a ton of Rogues. We've lost allies, business deals, *and* there's a war brewin' with Shadow Paw," Wyatt said, taking another bite of his pancakes.

"You were exiled?" Declan asked with his mouth full, nearly choking.

"Yep, but I made my way over to Silver Moon and asked for refuge. Been there ever since." Guilt made Declan's stomach churn at the thought of his cousin being forced to turn Rogue. It was rare to find a Beta without a pack but even more so to find one living amongst the slums that came with that life.

"How'd Cormac bring in so many Rogues? They're usually hellbent on stayin' *out* of packs," Declan asked as he set down his fork, his appetite slowly dwindling.

"He conned 'em," Wyatt shook his head, "told them he wanted to offer them a better life than slummin' it, waitin' to turn Feral. Made all kinds of promises about wealth, and prosperity without the demands of a sittin' Alpha, though he claims the title. All he's managed to do is fuck it all up."

"How do you know all this if you're not in the pack anymore?" Lorelei asked curiously.

"A Delta named Garridan. He tracked me down a while back in Saint Helena. Don't ask me how though. I've been off-grid since I shacked up with Silver Moon. He put me in touch with Caine, and filled me in on what's been happenin' within the pack," Wyatt explained around bites.

"Caine told us about him. Said we could trust him," Lorelei said, reaching for her coffee mug.

"We can," Wyatt reassured them confidently with a nod. There was another pause as Declan stared at the countertop lost in thought while Lorelei and his cousin finished eating in silence. His mind raced, trying to digest everything Wyatt told him, and Declan wondered what could have brought Crescent Ridge and Shadow

Paw to the brink of war. It was not uncommon for packs to war for one reason or another, but they had a long-standing business deal with the other pack. With Crescent Ridge occupying over half of the Louisiana coastline, Shadow Paw had come up with a commerce agreement and presented it to his father. Trade routes were established, rules and guidelines placed, and marinas were built. Shadow Paw had been the figurehead in this endeavor, and it did not take long for the other territories to see the benefit – not to mention the profit to be made, from such a deal.

"Somethin' else though," Wyatt said as he pushed his plate away. "Cormac claims he was the one to take you down." A fork pointed at him, jolting him from his thoughts.

"How? He's an Omega. No one would believe that," Declan scoffed, leaning forward on his forearms.

"The story goes that you were so lost to the bloodlust of your beast that he was able to sneak up on you and gain the upper hand. Somethin' about you was so absorbed in offin' pack members that one hit was all it took. The details are spotty at best," Wyatt said, finishing his orange juice. Beside him, Lorelei shifted uncomfortably on her stool and he cast a glance in her direction. She looked troubled as she peered across the island at Wyatt.

"Well, apparently father and son didn't get their stories straight. When I woke up the night of the massacre, Apollo was tellin' Caine that I was taken down with a modified tranq," Declan said, earning a look of surprise from Wyatt and Lorelei.

"While neither of those are true, I still don't understand somethin'," Lorelei said, "who would believe that one wolf, even an Alpha as strong as Declan, could massacre over two hundred and twenty wolves *before* being taken down by two Omegas?"

Declan raised his brows at the question. She had a point, and it was something that he never considered.

"Everyone was paralyzed. Well, everyone except me." His cousin had gathered their dishes and piled them in the sink.

"What do you mean?" Lorelei asked, watching him carefully. Declan knew that she was weighing Wyatt's words for any deception.

"I didn't drink the wine." A low ringing began in Declan's ears. "It's the only thing that made sense. Once everyone took a drink for the toast," *Louder*, "they fell like dominoes in seconds. Dad managed to warn me," *Louder*, "right before I downed it," *Louder*, "and when he collapsed–"

"Wyatt, stop!" Lorelei said loudly, just as Declan bent his head, pressing the heels of his hands into his temples, but she was too late. The memory pulled through the block and searing pain ripped through his skull, stealing the breath from his lungs. His beast let out a ferocious snarl at the intensity, writhing beneath his skin. Though as quickly as it started, the ringing and pain were gone. Dropping his chin to his chest, he let out a slow deep breath.

"What the fuck just happened?" Wyatt demanded, standing beside him now with a hand braced on his shoulder.

"That was the spell blockin' Declan's memories." Lorelei canted her head to look up at him, her worry evident, "You okay?" He nodded and rolled his neck and shoulders, trying to ease the tension knotting his muscles.

"How'd you know?" he asked softly.

"Magic calls to magic. I could hear the ringin' once it was loud enough." She shrugged her shoulders. "Do you remember anything?"

"I remember everything that Wyatt was talkin' about." Declan relayed the memory of the moment when everyone drank for the toast, recalling every detail up until his uncle fell to the ground. The mental image of seeing his family sprawled on the ground, paralyzed, would haunt Declan for the rest of his life. Even though he did not know what transpired after the pack fell, he knew the memories would grow far worse the more he remembered.

"So, a Witch fucked with his mind?" Wyatt asked, pulling his attention back to the moment.

"Yes." Lorelei lifted a hand, rubbing her forehead. "And it seems that if Declan even hears somethin' about that night, it sets off the defenses of the spell."

"Well, you can fix it, right? Witches can crack spells that aren't theirs. Similar to codebreakin' or somethin' like that?" Wyatt turned on the sink tap and started washing the dishes. Declan took the hint and stood to help with cleaning up.

"Yes, with time, but this is different. The magic is dark and extremely strong. I can't even begin to try to break it without the source, and there's no promise that I can." She gave him an apologetic look, and he nodded solemnly.

"The only thing I can do for Declan at the moment is try to pull out the memories," she explained, her tone soft as she padded over to the stove. For the next half hour, the trio cleaned the kitchen while Declan recounted the first memory they pulled through the block and how his wolf lunged from his body.

"I didn't even know that was possible. How the hell'd that happen?" Wyatt dropped down in an overstuffed armchair in the living room, rubbing his full belly.

"Tryin' to escape the pain. It's indescribable, it's so bad," Declan explained as he settled on the couch, draping a thick arm across the armrest. His suspicions dissipated once he realized that Lorelei was not catching him in any lies, and he almost felt guilty for suspecting his cousin of any kind of betrayal. Wyatt had never been a liar, and told the truth even if it meant punishment, but Saint Thaddeus taught him one thing during his time there; you could not trust anyone. Other patients would sell you out if it meant they avoided the basement, and some did just that for the fun of it. So, Declan learned quickly to only rely on himself, which turned out to be easier than he thought since he had no one.

Pushing the past to the back of his mind, his gaze followed Lorelei while she drifted around the room examining the many photos that were collected over the years. Every so often she would ask about the places or people in the frames, and he readily gave her their backstories. Wyatt was kicked back in the armchair now, fingers laced behind his head, eyes bouncing between the two of them with that mischievous glint in his eyes.

Declan was in the middle of telling Lorelei about a photo of his parents when buzzing sounded from the chair next to him. He could feel the tension rolling off his cousin as he looked down at the screen.

"What, Wyatt?" he asked, keeping his focus on the woman in front of him. Lorelei half turned to look at the two men, arms crossed and her brow furrowed at the change in his tone.

"It's a text from Cormac," Wyatt said, anger lacing his words.

"What's he sayin'?" he asked, clenching his jaw as he looked at his cousin.

"That he knows you're out." His phone started buzzing incessantly, causing the Beta to curse under his breath.

"Answer it," Declan commanded, and his cousin hit the green button and placed the receiver to his ear with a grimace.

"What?" Wyatt demanded. The next moment he turned on the speakerphone, rolling his eyes. "It's on, Your Majesty."

"Don't tell me you're *hiding*, Wolfe." Cormac's voice grated through the speaker, dripping with an almost laughable false superiority. Lorelei stepped closer, and Declan brought a finger to his lips, urging her to stay quiet.

"You hide from somethin' you fear, Cormac," he said, his deep voice smooth and calm. "You are not that somethin'." There was a long pause on the other end of the line.

"*Always so touchy.* I call in peace, *brother*. I only wish to inform you of the welcome home celebration I have planned tomorrow in your honor. The preparations are taking place as we speak. I do hope you'll come." Though he sounded sincere, there was a sliminess to his words.

"You can count on it," Declan said without hesitation, catching Lorelei staring at him.

"Wonderful! See you there." Cormac ended the call quickly, and Wyatt dropped the phone into his lap with a sigh.

"How the hell did he know? How in the hell did he even know that I was with you?" His cousin demanded, eyes beginning to shift color.

"To answer the first, I don't know. As for the second, he's not an idiot. He knows that if I'm out, you'll be close by," Declan said as he rubbed an index finger under his bottom lip.

"It's not possible that Garridan told him, is it?" Lorelei asked, and he noticed she was swaying gently side to side.

"No," Wyatt said firmly, "Garridan hates 'em both."

"Whatever's goin' on, somethin's not right." Declan paused for a moment, considering, "I think it'd be best for us to stay close for the time bein'. I'd like you to move into your room here," he stated, swiveling his head to Wyatt.

"Done deal, cousin. I'll head back to Silver Moon and pack. Should be back tomorrow night sometime."

They both stood and Declan held out his hand, smiling when Wyatt clasped his forearm tightly.

"It's good to have y'home, Dec. We'll sort this shit out, one way or another." With a final nod to each other, Wyatt turned to Lorelei and offered his hand. When she took it, he bent and placed a quick kiss on her knuckles.

"Keep him in line for me 'til I get back," his cousin said with a wink. Declan growled, eyeing the Beta as he crossed through the kitchen and left out the back door.

"Well, he's one of a kind," Lorelei said, once the back door banged shut. She sidled over to the couch and plopped down, an amused grin brightening her features. Declan gave her a crooked smile and eased down next to her, lounging back against the cushions.

"He's a character for sure. Always been that way too," he chuckled, "he was the ladies' man of us three. Never slept around but c'mon, you met him. Wyatt was funny and outgoin'. Cormac was the grumpy, untouchable type." Declan leaned his head back against the couch, a smile tugging at his lips.

"And what about you?" Lorelei questioned, and he turned his head to look over at her.

"I was the quiet, reserved one that everyone thought was shy. Couldn't'a been further from the truth though. Just didn't have much time for a girlfriend. Most of the time, I would be doin' some kind of trainin'. The free time I got, I'd hang out with Wyatt and Cormac." He hefted a sigh and shrugged.

"Well, I think any girl woulda been lucky to have you, busy or not," she said, picking at an invisible piece of lint on her shorts, her eyes downcast. He could sense her nervousness, hear it in her erratic heartbeat.

"Yeah? Well, if I had my way, I'd be the lucky one," he mused, and her eyes snapped to him. She stared at him for a long moment, and Declan wondered what was racing through her mind at the moment.

"And who would you have if you were lucky?" She held his gaze, a playful challenge flickering in her eyes.

"You," Declan said, the certainty of his tone surprising her. Her eyes dropped to his lips and that was all the invitation he needed. Leaning forward, he captured her mouth in a soft kiss, fingers threading into her hair. Her reaction was immediate as her hand clamped around the back of his neck. Tingles danced on his skin everywhere she touched and he wanted more.

Raising to her knees, Lorelei took control as she leaned over him and their kiss shifted gears instantly. Declan groaned against her lips, breath stalling in his lungs as she swept her tongue seductively over his. Straddling his lap, she settled her core over his rapidly hardening cock, and Declan ran a hand along her thigh to grip her backside. The scent of her arousal hit him like a Mack truck and his fingers dug into her flesh as he pressed her warm center firmly against his shaft.

"I want you," she whispered when she broke the kiss to nip at his bottom lip. A growl rumbled from his chest as the control he was barely holding onto nearly severed. Lorelei trailed soft kisses along his jawline and down his neck, and he groaned at the tingling sensation her lips left on his skin. When her teeth raked over his skin, Declan lifted his hips to press his aching length harder against her core, the pleasure crashing through him like a runaway train.

"You shouldn't've done that," he rasped against her ear, and in one swift motion, flipped their positions. Lorelei gasped in surprise as she landed on her back, and he braced his hands on the cushions, hovering over her body. His teeth began to lengthen as his wolf pushed him to claim her just like he had in the hallway of the Council building.

'Claim! Mate!' The beast howled in his mind. Panting, Declan closed his eyes trying to regain his control as several long moments passed.

"Declan?" she said softly, her hand cupping his cheek.

"I'm sorry." He leaned into her touch, skin tingling beneath her palm. Goddess, he wanted her. Needed her in ways that scared the hell out of him.

'*She is ours!*' his wolf snarled roughly, and Declan shook his head. Not yet, and he would not force anything on her – especially not a claiming that would permanently tie her to him forever.

"I don't wanna hurt you." The small confession was true but not the whole of it and he wondered if she could tell that. Truth be told, he was terrified of the memories that were blocked from him. Jaw clenched, Declan willed himself to pull away from her and sat back on his haunches, bracing his hands on his thighs.

"I know there's more than what you're tellin' me." Her voice was soft, and he opened his eyes, peering down at her, sighing as he clambered from the couch.

"What if I'm guilty?" he questioned her. *Savage. Vengeful.* The words whispered out from the darkness as he moved to the fireplace, attempting to put some distance between them.

"Declan, I've already told you *and* the Elder Council that I think you're innocent," she countered, her shocked gaze following him as she sat up.

"I know you *think* I'm innocent, Lorelei, but what if I'm actually *not*?" He turned to face her, his frustration and fear rising as he waited for an answer.

"Then I think we'll cross that bridge when we get there," she said, and her calmness wormed under his skin. He understood that being a psychologist called for her to keep her composure in certain situations, but in the moment, it set his anger boiling his veins.

"So, you'll fuck me *before* knowin' for sure if I'm a mass murderer or not? Great standards, Doc," he lashed out reproachfully. The words were cutting and crass, and Declan immediately regretted them. Shock and hurt flitted across her face, making his insides churn violently but he refused to back down.

"There's a chance that I've done some messed up shit, Lorelei. You *know* this. And Goddess knows I want you. But I can't with this hangin' over my head. I can't have– I don't want… I just–" Floundering, he let out an exasperated yell as the dam holding his anger and frustration collapsed and he pivoted, striking out at the stone fireplace behind him.

The pictures on the mantle shuddered as several bones broke with a sickening crunch. The skin on his knuckles split open from the impact, but he barely felt the pain through his ire. Immediately, his shattered wrist began to heal, and the wounds on the back of his hand sealed shut before the blood could drip from his fingertips.

"There's darkness in me, Lorelei," he stated, refusing to meet her gaze.

"Declan, we all have some darkness in us. Goddess knows I do," she said with that calm, understanding tone.

"You don't get it." He glared at her, anger rising again, "I've done terrible things in the past. Granted, it was deserved but I loved every fuckin' second of agony I caused. Every bit of pain, theirs or mine. I *crave* it." He needed her to understand, but instead of balking at the honesty of his admission, she stood from the couch and walked over to him. Her hands slid lightly along his forearms, stopping just above his elbows and he had to close his eyes as the sensation from her touch nearly overwhelmed him. He had to get away from her calmness and the heavy scent of her arousal still hanging in the air. Abruptly, Declan pulled away and sidestepped around her.

"I'm goin' for a run."

Chapter 14

Lorelei stood before the mirror the following evening, critiquing her reflection as she brushed her teeth. The sweetheart neckline of the dress she chose showed off a tasteful amount of cleavage while corset-like stitching hugged her torso in an allover sunflower print. The skirt fell beautifully around her knees and featured a slit running up the top of her thigh. The gap in the fabric widened with every other step, exposing her smooth, lightly tanned skin. A quick, two-rap knock sounded at the bedroom door just as she was rinsing toothpaste from the sink basin.

"Come in," she called over her shoulder, drying her hands and adjusting the thin straps nervously. The tension between her and Declan was tangible ever since their make-out session yesterday, and they had not spoken much since then. He was gone the rest of the day, and Lorelei found herself wandering the house, exploring her new home. She found the basement with its separate entertainment room and gym, sat on the balcony outside her room sipping coffee, browsed her bookshelf, and even took a peek in Declan's room. It was identical to hers, except the walls were gray, and he did not have access to the balcony. The comforter on his bed was navy blue with white sheets, and the rugs covering the hardwood flooring were dark gray. She had been too nervous to look around, fearing Declan would think she was snooping if he caught her. Truth be told, she just wanted to know more about him. About the man he was before that horrible night. They talked endlessly about their lives before Saint Thaddeus, but Lorelei wanted to know every nuance. The music he liked, and the books he read. Little things that most people took for granted.

She was already in bed when he finally returned home that night, and she listened to the back door close somewhere beneath her room. Her heart pounded when she heard him trudging up the staircase. Several long moments of silence hung heavy, and she knew that he was standing just outside her door. There was a soft thump against the wood before his footsteps receded across the loft to his room.

She did not see him much today, except for when she stepped out on the covered back porch to get some fresh air. A sharp whacking sound caught her attention, and Lorelei walked to the far side, following the noise. Leaning over the railing beside the steps to peer down the side of the house, her breath stalled in her lungs when she caught sight of him. He was shirtless, torso slick with sweat as he stared down at a chunk of wood with a long handle balanced in his grip.

Lorelei watched in appreciation when he swung the heavy ax over his head, muscles rippling as he brought it down in a smooth, powerful arc. The resulting *thwack* echoed around the property as the block of wood split cleanly in two. Resetting his target, he swung again, repeating the process until he had a pile on either side of him. She leaned against the railing, mesmerized by the sureness of his movements while he sunk the blade into the chopping block and gathered the pieces. His skin glistened in the sunlight, muscles bulging with the heavy load as he carried the firewood to a small lean-to against the side of the house. Catching sight of her from the corner of his eye, Declan did a double take when he realized he was not alone. She smiled sheepishly having been caught ogling him, and lifted her hand in a small wave. He gave her a soft crooked grin and swiped the sweat from his nose with the back of his hand before returning to his work.

"You about ready?" Declan asked, jerking her back to the present. Her stomach flip flopped, hearing his booted feet drawing closer to the bathroom.

"Yeah, just finishin'. . ." Lorelei trailed off as he appeared in the mirror, stopping short when he saw her. Her heart rate skyrocketed as she watched his eyes roam over her body.

". . . up," she finished quietly as she brushed a few loose curls from her eyes, momentarily stunned by the sight of him. He wore a navy-blue button up, faded bootcut blue jeans that did nothing to hide his swift erection, and a pair of scuffed matte black combat boots. His scruffy stubble had been trimmed to a five o'clock shadow, and his hair was still a bit damp, hanging shaggily over his forehead.

"You look great," she said quietly. His gaze found hers in the mirror and she saw his hard swallow, the muscles of his jaw flex.

"Goddess, you're a beautiful woman." His voice was rough when he spoke and it sent a shiver down her spine. She turned to face him when he took a hesitant step forward. Lifting a hand to her cheek, Declan brushed the rebellious curls from her eyes again as he moved closer, stopping only when his chest brushed against hers. Lorelei stared up into his dark eyes, the masculine scent of him invading her senses, filling her mind with images of summer nights in the mountains.

"Lucy, I'm home!" Wyatt suddenly called from downstairs, and Declan visibly willed himself to step away from her, his hand lingering a moment longer on her cheek.

"I'm ready when you are, darlin'," he said, letting his arm drop to his side as he backed away and left her room. She heard his booted feet thumping down the staircase a few seconds later.

Lorelei took a deep breath as she listened to the murmur of the men speaking somewhere beneath her. She was certain at this point they could both hear her heart pounding in her chest and groaned inwardly as she trudged out of her room. She paused at the top of the stairs for a moment, glancing from the couch to the fireplace. The chimney above the mantle bore the scar from yesterday's frustration, the impact of Declan's fist leaving a stark chalky discoloration on the dark river stone.

As she descended the stairs, his words drifted through her head, her stomach clenching with butterflies all over again. He wanted her but could not be with her. Not without knowing the truth. Though his statement in the bathroom only moments ago left her confused by its duality. She wondered whether he meant that he was 'ready when she was' to leave the house, or something else entirely.

Pushing the thought to the back of her mind, she realized she was probably overthinking the whole scenario. There was an undeniable attraction, a connection, between them, but Declan pulled away every time any intimacy further than kissing came into play. If she were honest with herself, Lorelei could not care less about the accusations against him. She knew the man was incapable of committing the crimes that landed him in Saint Thaddeus. Was he capable of terrible things? Absolutely. He was an Alpha with a pack to protect. Would he murder innocents? Mutilate them? Absolutely not.

Declan never had an incident at the asylum outside of mouthing off to the guards, or being attacked first. She requested all reports since he arrived at the asylum from the security office after finding him badly injured that second day. Her numerous requests either fell on deaf ears or were outright denied, despite orders from Elder Caine. Luckily, with a tiny bribe of sheep's gallbladder, Officer Strickland printed them out for her a week before Declan was released. Her insight revealed fact from fiction within each one as she read over them every night when she returned to the bed and breakfast.

"All set?" Declan was asking Wyatt as she dropped from the bottom stair.

"Yep, got everything I needed from the cabin, and told Alpha Jared to do with it as he saw fit." Wyatt did a double take and let out a soft whistle when he saw her, which earned him a cutting glare from his cousin.

"We ready?" she asked, grabbing her keys from the counter, avoiding looking both men in the eye. The tension still hung heavy between her and Declan, and she was unsure if it was emotional, sexual or a combination of both.

"We're takin' mine tonight," Declan said and led the way into the large garage, flipping on the light switch at the top of the steps.

"Y'all have fun. Be home by curfew," Wyatt called after them.

Following several steps behind, Lorelei peered around, noting that the space was much larger than she originally thought. A pair of ATVs were parked near the steps and a dirt bike stood propped on its kickstand nearby. There was another vehicle beneath a thin, soft sheet in the bay beside her Wagoneer. Declan grabbed a handful of the beige fabric covering the hood and yanked it back, revealing a matte black 1970 Chevelle.

"She's beautiful," Lorelei said as she alighted from the steps. Sliding into the passenger side, she watched as he pressed a button on the wall lifting the garage doors, and ducked in behind the steering wheel.

"Yes, she is." His gaze drifted over her face, and she knew he was not talking about the car. Declan leaned across the bench seat and opened the glovebox, dropping his wallet into the compartment. As the engine growled to life, he gave her a wink before guiding the muscle car from the bay.

An hour later, Lorelei stepped out onto the wide driveway of the Crescent Ridge packhouse and smoothed down her skirt. The estate was enormous and she stared in amazement at the sheer size of it all. A three-story Antebellum style mansion with pillars every twenty feet or so created an elegant but imposing facade. Black shuttered windows were spaced evenly across each floor, some of them lit with a warm inviting glow. There was a wraparound balcony on the second floor, the railings stained a deep red, with spiraled wrought iron balusters. Wide steps led up to the massive front porch, all crafted from the same dark gray flagstone shining dully in the pale entryway light.

Declan explained the layout of the packhouse to her on the way over, informing her that the main floor was mostly a common area including a massive living room, conference room, dining area, and kitchen. The second floor was home to the offices of the Luna, and Beta, and also where some of the higher-ranking pack members stayed if they chose, with a few extra rooms for overnight guests. Finally, the top floor was reserved for the Alpha and his mate, and included the master bedroom, a library, and a shared personal office.

"I think this is bigger than that producer's hundred-million-dollar mansion in Atlanta," she said to him as they climbed the steps, feeling incredibly small compared to the enormous home.

"It is," Declan said with a wink. Scoffing, Lorelei reached out for the doorbell and was surprised when his hand latched gently around her wrist. She looked up at him and her brows drew together when he shook his head.

"I'm not ringin' the doorbell to get into my own home," he said as he turned the knob and pushed, swinging the heavy oak door open wide.

"Shall we?" Giving her a crooked grin, he offered her his arm.

"I suppose it's too late to turn around now." Lorelei placed her hand in the crook of his elbow, and they stepped over the threshold. For the moment, it seemed, the tension between them eased.

Following the sounds of the party, Declan guided her through the mostly empty estate and out to an expansive veranda. Soft white lights were strung around the edge of the roof in graceful swoops creating a beautifully lit atmosphere. Multiple buffet tables sat off to one side piled high with various meats, hor d'oeuvres, and desserts, and a bar had been set up close by serving chilled champagne in black and red ombre flutes. Several long tables lined the outskirts of the main gathering area where many pack members had settled in to eat or talk, away from the larger crowd.

"Well, if it isn't the *big, bad Wolfe*, himself." A grating voice rang out that she instantly recognized as Cormac. Declan let out a grunt of disdain at the terrible wordplay. Schooling her features, Lorelei fought the smile tugging at the corners of her lips as she glanced in the direction of the voice. She found him rising from a wooden chaise made of thick planks, and an unsettling feeling crept up her spine as Cormac leered in her direction. Declan tensed beside her seeing the look in the man's eyes, a soft growl beginning to rumble in his chest. Lorelei nudged him gently with her elbow, relieved when he quieted with a huff.

"How in the hell did you manage to get out of Saint Thaddeus?" asked Cormac incredulously, eyes narrowed in suspicion.

"Good behavior." Declan gruffed, leveling his former friend with a hard stare, who scoffed at the statement.

"Was there anyone left alive when you left?" he sneered as he came to a halt in front of them before adding, "And who is this *exquisite* creature?" Giving Lorelei his full attention, cutting off any response Declan might have. Cormac offered his hand to her, and she hesitantly took it. When he leaned down to kiss her knuckles, she gripped Declan's bicep in a vice, desperately fighting the urge to recoil, unsettled by the small touch.

"Lorelei," she managed to say, plastering on a smile and gently prying her fingers from his hold.

"What a beautiful name. Declan, you should have told me you were bringing a friend." His gaze was lecherous, and it made her skin crawl.

"Must'a slipped my mind." Declan's voice was smooth, but there was a tense edge to his tone. Cormac fought a grin, fingers lazily covering his strangely full lips.

"I'm *Alpha* Cormac, and it is a pleasure to meet you, Lorelei," he crooned.

"Pleasure's all mine," she said politely. The effort it took to hide her grimace at the foul taste of his words was substantial, making her hands ball into fists. Lies tasted awful.

"You know, he's always been so perverse." Cormac chuckled, leaning closer to her and she resisted the urge to step back into Declan's protective presence. "So easy to provoke, this one. Dangerous, even, at times."

"Huh, maybe he just likes me more," she joked, though her statement was met with a soft squeeze of her hand in agreement from the man beside her. Oblivious, Cormac nodded his head, chuckling at her quip.

"I suppose, that's fair. We did leave off on bad terms the last time we saw each other. Do you remember, Declan?" There was a gleam in his eye as his attention returned to the man next to her, who gave a stiff nod, and she took the opportunity to observe the unsettling man. He was a few inches shorter than Declan, lean but well built. He wore a black long-sleeved button-up tucked into the waistline of his trousers. The silken fabric was snug over the muscles in his arms, and showed off the taper of his waist. His trim black slacks advertised a pair of toned legs, with black loafers covering his feet. Overall, he was an attractive man, but something about him made Lorelei uneasy.

"Well, are you going to tell Lorelei, or should I?" His tone was a mixture of malice and amusement. She realized that the crowd around them was still watching and listening to the conversation of the trio, captivated by the exchange that was happening.

"We fought, and I lost," Declan stated simply, looking down at her with a shrug of his shoulders. A moment later, there was a sudden, acutely shrill ping, and Lorelei saw him wince just as she did. His jaw muscles bulged as he clenched his teeth, bearing down so hard she swore she heard one or two cracks. She stared up at him in shock, watching his features, and he gave her an infinitesimal nod, assuring her that he was all right.

"I suppose every dog has his day." She patted his arm comfortingly, carrying on as if nothing happened.

"Yes, the better man won." Declan's statement made Cormac stiffen, giving a knowing smirk. Lorelei shifted her gaze to look at the other man. His body was rigid with tension as he nervously cleared his throat.

"I should think so," Cormac muttered indignantly before he snapped his attention back to Lorelei, "Could I tempt you to join me for a little stroll in the moonlight?" Declan tensed again, his whole body going rigid at the suggestion, and she lifted her hand, placing it on his chest.

"Actually, I was just about to see if my date wanted to dance with me. Maybe later, *Alpha*," she said, both of them sidestepping around Cormac as Declan led her out onto the dancefloor, amusement sparkling in his dark eyes. Taking her hand in his and placing the other on the small of her back, Lorelei slid a hand to his shoulder as he took the lead. Notching her chin up a fraction, she subtly pulled against his shoulder, and smiled when he took the hint, leaning down as if to whisper in her ear.

"Why did the spell's defense go off?" she asked, her voice barely audible as she leaned her cheek against his. He made a show of wrapping his arms around her waist, pulling her flush against his hard body before he responded.

"My wolf helped me remember the fight with Cormac." She shivered as he breathed the words against her ear, gently nipping her lobe as he straightened.

"How?" she gasped, lacing her arms over his shoulders. Declan bent his head, his lips within a hairbreadth of hers, and she found it difficult to breathe for a moment – heat radiated from him, their breaths mingling. He still smelled of his minty toothpaste and it took every ounce of willpower she had to not lean in and taste him.

"He always refused to believe an Omega could beat us. Tonight, seein' Cormac face to face, I realized my wolf was right. He said one word, 'won'," he explained, causing her to strain to hear him over the music. An idea struck Lorelei like lightning as his words registered, and she suddenly clasped his face in her hands, barely able to contain her excitement.

"What?" he asked, amusement lacing his voice.

"I've got an idea. A theory," she explained, lips brushing against his as she spoke, her quick words nearly silent even to her, "I think that if you're told single words, spaced out over several minutes, it might bypass the defenses of the spell. *Hopefully*, you can piece the memory together yourself." Declan inclined his head, brushing his nose against hers, a coy smile pulling his lips into a wicked smile as if she had just said something incredibly naughty to him.

"Try," he said, dropping his lips to hers as if he meant to kiss her, but pulled away teasingly instead. Lorelei released a shuddering breath, trying to think past the arousal swimming in her veins.

"Alaric," she said and nipped at his bottom lip, her stomach clenching as his groan vibrated against her skin.

"Mhmm." Was all he managed as he placed soft kisses along her jawline. Closing her eyes, her head fell back as she let herself get lost in the feel of his lips on her skin.

"Decapitated." Declan straightened, gazing down at her with crimson eyes. His brow creased as he tried to piece the two words together with the blocked memory.

Suddenly, his body went rigid and the shrill ping reverberated in her ears again. He surged forward, fisting a hand in her hair and captured her mouth in a ravaging kiss as the pain ripped through him. Muscles trembling in effort to avoid raising suspicion that something was amiss. His thick arm around her torso was like an iron band, but he never tightened his grip.

As quickly as it started, the ringing was gone and Declan's body relaxed in her arms, the tension leaving his strained muscles. He kissed her thoroughly, his tongue dancing sensually with hers as the world faded into the background. Lorelei's heart stuttered, feeling as if a million butterflies erupted suddenly within her chest. Gently breaking the kiss, he leaned back to gaze down at her with what looked like wonder in his eyes.

"I remembered," he breathed, so only she could hear.

"What did you-?" Her whisper was cut off, the nearby voice making her startle slightly.

"I'm afraid I have to cut in, *brother*," Cormac said from a few feet away. Lorelei felt the rumblings start in his chest, and pressed her lips gently to his, effectively silencing the building growl. Her knees felt like jell-o as Declan loosened his hold, and the wetness between her thighs bordered on uncomfortable with the ache throbbing there.

"You don't *have* to do anything. Except walk away," he said low and dangerous, his eyes never leaving hers, arms protectively around her waist.

"Oh my, are you giving orders to the Alpha, Wolfe?" The man tutted in disapproval, shoving his hands into his pockets.

"I see no Alpha here." Declan cut his crimson gaze to Cormac, his voice rough and graveled with his beast. Lorelei sucked in a breath, realizing a challenge would soon be declared, and she swiveled her head to peer at the false Alpha.

"*Alpha* Cormac," she said, giving him her best attempt at a smile, and pulling his attention away from the brewing fight, "I believe I owe you a stroll in the moonlight, yes?" she added, hoping to diffuse the hostile tension between them. Declan remained silent as Cormac gave her that oily smile and she took the arm he offered. Slipping from the protective embrace, she allowed herself to be led away across the veranda. She could feel Declan's gaze branding her skin, and she fought the urge to look back.

"How do you know Declan?" Cormac asked, making small talk as they strolled along the edge of the party.

"I met him at Saint Thaddeus," she stated, forcing a smile. As they ambled through the crowd, she noticed that several groups had split off around the lawn, conversing amongst themselves as eyes bounced between Declan and Cormac.

"My my, were you committed as well?" he inquired, stopping short to let a woman carrying a stack of plates pass by.

"Not this time," she said, earning a chuckle from him. "No, I was a psychologist at the asylum. Declan happened to be one of the patients that I saw there." Technically, not a lie.

"Ah, so you specialize in supernaturals? Admirable. I'm afraid the ones sent to Saint Thaddeus are a bit beyond saving though, wouldn't you agree?" Lorelei seethed at the insinuation in his tone.

"There are some hard cases, but I believe therapies should still be tried. It's not so much about tryin' to cure them as it is helpin' them. Many just need the strategies, medications and resources to process and cope with the trauma that led them there in the first place. I'm not sayin' that it's a cure-all, but it certainly does help in most cases." Cormac nodded as she spoke, considering her words.

"And do you know what led Declan Wolfe there?" he asked, probing for how much she actually knew.

"Yes. I've read his patient file," she said matter-of-factly, realizing they were treading into dangerous territory.

"How do *you* know Declan?" Lorelei countered, veering the conversation away from her as they rounded the corner of the packhouse. The hair on the nape of her neck prickled suddenly and she casually looked around the lawn, taking in her surroundings as the sensation worsened with every step. In the distance, she noticed what looked like a headstone, large and black, glinting faintly in the moonlight. A short distance behind the marker, a large weeping willow sat motionless among the other trees dotting the area, its long vine-like branches so dense that you could barely make out its trunk underneath. A heavy sense of foreboding settled in her chest, and she tried to maintain a calm demeanor as they drifted closer.

"His father, Alpha Kai, rescued my father and me from a horrible situation when I was a child," Cormac said vaguely, and she wondered what sort of 'horrible situation' he meant.

"I'm so sorry. That must've been hard at such a young age," Lorelei said gently. She was not expecting his sardonic laugh and glanced at his expressionless features.

"My father believes it built character, experiencing a massacre." Cormac seemed to catch himself, glancing in her direction. She wanted to question him further, but the sensation crawling down her nape was becoming impossible to ignore as he drew her to a stop in front of the large marker. She felt as if millions of insects were skittering over her skin, and she suppressed the shudder threatening to streak down her spine.

Lorelei realized she was standing before a large chunk of obsidian, shaped into a perfect circle with the tree of life carved into its surface, the branches and interconnecting roots expanding beautifully around the edge of the stone. A list had been written in place of the tree trunk, filling in the circular gap with painstakingly detailed script that she had to lean closer to read.

Her stomach dropped when she realized she was looking at a memorial. She would not need to count them to know that there would be two hundred and twenty-eight victims listed. However, she still read the top names, Alpha Mordecai Wolfe, Luna Alora Wolfe, and Beta Alaric Leal. The list seemed to go on forever, listing the rest of the massacre victims according to their hierarchical ranks within the pack.

"You know, Lorelei, I had a bit of an ulterior motive in bringing you here," Cormac spoke again after several moments.

"Oh?" she asked, trying to sound casual while his words left an ominous weight in the pit of her stomach.

The hairs on the nape of her neck stood up more as she gently removed her hand from his arm.

"I feel it necessary to enlighten you about the man who brought you here tonight," Cormac said with a sense of duty, his gaze still focused on the willow tree.

"I'm sorry, I don't understand." He gave a mirthless laugh.

"You're fucking him, and you obviously don't know what an atrocity that man is, despite his file." Rage flared through her at the scathing remarks, and she tried to control the emotion.

"Whether I'm *fuckin'* him or not, is none of your damn business, Cormac," Lorelei snapped.

"*Alpha* Cormac," he grated, shifting his gaze now to glare at her, and she leaned away at the ferocity shining in his hazel eyes.

"My apologies, *Alpha* Cormac." Lorelei tipped her head, showing a modicum of respect.

"None needed." He gave her that oily smile again, ire gone as quickly as it came. "I only wish to educate you on the horrendous things that Declan Wolfe is capable of. Did you know that he raped his mother, as well as another seventeen helpless women?" Queasiness rolled through her stomach, and she closed her eyes, swallowing hard against the feeling.

"Oh, I've upset you. I'm so sorry," he said silkily, but the giddiness in his tone told her that he relished the distress he was causing her.

"No, I need to know. Continue, please." Her voice was husky when she spoke.

"As you wish. He crushed her skull clean to the back of her head with the heel of his boot, coming back later to 'have his way with her', so to speak." His statement was so matter-of-fact it was disturbing. "Goddess be with her. He then turned on his father, who lay paralyzed, and ripped his heart from his chest– Are you all right?" She must have looked green even in the moonlight because the concern in his voice sounded genuine.

"This information is startlin', is all. Did you say Mordecai was paralyzed?" she asked as she placed a shaky hand on her knotting stomach, breathing deeply through her nose.

"He was. Unable to make a single move against the attack. *Then* Declan murdered his uncle, Alaric. Picked him up with his maw and crushed his skull before he ripped the man's head clean off and beat his corpse until the man was unrecognizable. He picked off every single pack member, dancing through the bodies as he went. Such a tragedy. Though jealousy often ends that way." Lorelei could not hold her stomach anymore as it clenched painfully, and she turned away, vomiting its contents into the grass below.

"Such a sensitive woman, you are," he crooned, stroking between her shoulder blades with the back of his hand. Lorelei wanted to recoil from that slimy touch, it felt vile for reasons she could not explain.

"Thank you for tellin' me, but I think I need a moment. Excuse me," she said once she recovered, needing to get away from the memorial and Cormac. Something was terribly wrong.

"There's a small bench just beyond the branches of the willow. It is the perfect place to clear your mind, Lorelei," Cormac offered.

"I'd rather go back to the party, find Declan. Maybe another time." She gave a small apologetic smile, trying to politely decline as she turned to leave.

"I insist." His voice growled from him gravely and darkly. Debating only a second, she decided it was best to not provoke him, and turned back to the beautiful willow tree.

Swallowing hard as she trudged across the lawn, each step heightened the prickles on her nape, until it felt as if pins and needles were being pressed along her spine. Brushing the spindly branches aside, she stepped into the small open space they created around the trunk and sat down stiffly on the bench. The cold concrete on the backs of her thighs barely registered as the minutes ticked by. In the dark, eerie silence, the intense sensation along her spine was slowly becoming painful, and she shifted her weight on the bench.

"Tell me something." Lorelei was startled as Cormac's voice cut through the quiet from behind her. "How did Declan *really* manage to get out of Saint Thaddeus?" She leaned slightly away from the hand he placed on her bare shoulder, as her fight or flight response kicked into high gear.

"From what I understand, he kept petitioning the Elders until they agreed to hear him out." She swallowed the foul bitter taste that came with the lie.

"And what's your role in all of this, hm? Why are *you* here, Lorelei?" Cormac leaned against the tree trunk beside her, the fingers on her shoulder running along the thin strap of her dress.

"Oh, I'm just fuckin' him, remember?" She shrugged as she parodied his earlier insult back at him and slapped his hand away from her. "I think I'll go back to the party now. Thanks for the walk." Lorelei stood abruptly, managing to take a single step before Cormac's hand snaked out and latched onto her wrist, his grip far too tight.

"Why not share the love, gorgeous? Hmm? If you'll fuck an abomination like him, why not me too?" Cormac yanked her to him, forcefully rubbing her palm against the front of his pants. Her reaction was immediate and she grabbed a handful of his crotch and squeezed as hard as she could. Averting her gaze, she pumped magic into her hold, increasing the force of her grip. He released her the next second with an agonized, inhuman scream as he dropped to the ground in the fetal position, holding his crushed testicles.

Diving headlong through willow branches, Lorelei raced across the lawn in the opposite direction that they came, getting as far away from the Cormac and the memorial as possible. Fearing he would chase, she glanced over her shoulder just before rounding the corner to the front of the packhouse and slammed into a hard, muscled wall. The air punched from her lungs and the man grunted from the impact as she stumbled backwards. Right before she hit the ground, a strong arm wrapped tightly around her torso, pulling her upright. Her skin tingled where his palm was splayed over the exposed skin of her back, and she looked up at him, breath heaving from her lungs.

"Lorelei! What's wrong?" Declan demanded, his concern evident as he quickly looked her over.

"You bitch!" Cormac shouted from the darkness. Lorelei felt every muscle in Declan's body tense, and his eyes shifted crimson in a blink.

"Declan, I want to leave. Now!" She gripped his bicep tightly, pulling his attention back to her. With a resolute nod, he quickly ushered her back to the car, and

she slid into the passenger seat with a shuddering sigh
of relief.

Chapter 15

Lorelei did not speak the whole ride back to the cabin, replaying the latter part of the evening in her mind. She could not figure out what was so off-putting about the memorial and Cormac. He was a creep, for sure, but aside from that she could not figure out the aversion she felt towards him. From the corner of her eye, she could see Declan glancing over at her every couple of minutes but he never questioned her about what happened. Not yet, anyway.

"I'm gonna go shower," she said quietly as she slipped past him through the garage door and hurried upstairs to her bedroom. Kicking off her boots, she unzipped the side of her dress and let it slide from her body in a heap on the floor. A flick of her finger had the water turning on in the shower and she quickly brushed her teeth.

Under the hot spray, Lorelei washed her body twice, trying to scrub away the trepidation she still felt crawling on her skin while Cormac's nauseating words echoed in her mind. She never gained insight once in her conversation with the false Alpha. Everything he said to her was muddied, impossible to discern truth from lies, and the more she thought about the things he told her, the more her stomach churned.

"Hey." Lorelei was startled when Declan's voice sounded softly from the balcony doorway. She looked up from her perch on the railing and smiled softly.

Even in her worry, she admired the gorgeous man leaning against the doorframe. He changed into a pair of gray sweatpants and a white tee shirt, a combination she now realized was a form of kryptonite as dirty thoughts swirled in her mind.

"Wanna tell me what happened?" he asked, his voice gentle and calming as he closed the door leading to the loft.

"I don't even know how to explain it, Declan," she said quietly, exasperation creeping into her tone.

"So, start from the top. I'll ask if I don't understand." Heaving a sigh, she gazed up at him as he stopped beside her, leaning against the post she rested her head on.

Lorelei carefully recounted the walk with Cormac, the unnerving sensations she felt, and the memorial. An angry snarl ripped from him when she told him the man touched her, and forced her to touch him. His eyes were crimson as he stepped in front of her, and cupped her face.

"I'll rip him apart if he touches you again. *No one* lays a hand on you without your okay," Declan vowed, and she nodded, knowing he meant it. Stepping between her legs to pull her flush against his body, he wrapped his arms around her and gently kissed her forehead. She liked his protectiveness, it made her feel safe and valued.

Lorelei fisted the sides of his shirt in her hands, feeling the muscles bunch at her touch. She buried her face against his chest, breathing in the masculine scent of him. Declan's hands trailed down her back and she shivered at the sensation she felt through the fabric.

"What if I want *your* hands on me?" she asked quietly, squirming slightly as wetness pooled between her thighs.

"Lorelei." His voice was husky with desire, and she knew he could smell her arousal when he drew in a deep breath. His cock immediately bulged in his sweatpants and she thought how easy it would be to push her loose-legged shorts to the side and slip him deep inside her. The thought had her biting her bottom lip to suppress a moan, and a growl rumbled from deep within his chest.

"Goddess, I can almost taste you." He leaned back to peer down at her, and lifted a hand to her cheek. Using his thumb to gently pull her lip from between her teeth, he leaned forward and captured her mouth in a slow, sensual kiss, making her toes curl. Declan fisted a hand in her hair as their kiss deepened and her hand trailed down to the hemline of his shirt. Her fingers delved beneath the material, drifting over the hard planes of his abdomen, eliciting a sharp inhale from him.

"Stop," Declan said softly as he broke the kiss, "We gotta stop. I can't–."

The abruptness of his departure left Lorelei grasping for the post next to her as she fumbled to regain her balance. Looking over her shoulder at the ground below, she huffed out a sigh of relief and slid from the railing just as a howl sounded from the forest beyond. She gazed out at the dark trees surrounding the house and took in a deep breath, trying to calm the arousal and discontent Declan left her with again.

As she turned to go back to her room, a flash of color in the distance caught her eye. Crimson eyes practically glowed up at her in the moonlight from the treeline and she paused, watching him just as he watched her. The hair on her nape stood on end as the beast stepped from the shadows. The predatory grace of Declan's wolf sent a shiver racing down her spine. He paced along the edge of the property line, his large head turning in her direction every few steps.

Suddenly, the beast let out a snarl and shook his head roughly before darting off into the trees, vanishing into the shadows. Lorelei stared after him from the balcony, torn between anticipation and frustration, hoping his wolf would reappear from the darkness.

He did not come back that night.

The next morning, Lorelei sat in the kitchen with a steaming mug of coffee clasped between her hands. She opted for the rustic farm table this morning instead of her usual perch at the island. Sitting cross-legged on the bench against the wall, she stared sleepily at the white-washed table top while Wyatt drifted around the space making breakfast.

"Y'know I could always eat cereal," Lorelei said when a string of curses rang out from the direction of the stove.

"Where's the fun in that?" Wyatt said over his shoulder. "I can't burn nine out of ten fingers pourin' milk." This morning he was attempting a new all-in-one recipe they found online. He mostly succeeded except for managing to burn every finger on both hands.

"Besides," he continued, "This was somethin' we both wanted to try, so I'm gonna see it through." Lorelei could hear the smile in his voice, and decided it was best to let the man in the frilly floral print apron have his way.

The aroma of eggs, bacon, and cheese filled the space as muffin tin after muffin tin clattered onto the stovetop and nearby cooling racks. Lorelei stood from the bench and sidled over to take a look at Wyatt's handiwork, setting her cup beside the coffee maker as she passed by.

"Not too shabby, Leal," she praised, cuffing his arm gently with her elbow as he carefully dug the breakfast bites from the pans. "Just three for now. I don't have the metabolism of a Wolf, y'know." Lorelei chuckled as she took the plate he offered her and poured herself another cup of coffee.

She was just sitting back down at the table when she heard booted feet marching heavily up the back-porch steps. Glancing out the window, she spied Declan trudging across the deck, wiping his hands on a scrap of dirty red material.

"Where the hell's he been?" Wyatt wondered aloud, piling more of the breakfast cups onto a plate he pulled down from the cabinet. Lorelei shrugged just as the back door swung open and Declan strolled in, heading straight for the sink.

The heavy smell of motor oil and sweat assaulted her senses, and her mouth went dry as she took in the grease smudged tee shirt hugging his torso. Equally dirty blue jeans were slung low on his hips making him look even more rugged than usual. The brown leather belt that played peekaboo as he leaned over to wash his hands was scratched and scuffed from years of wear and tear. There was something irrevocably manly and downright sexy about him at that moment. Declan was always those things, but it seemed to have increased tenfold seeing him now. Lorelei carefully swiped up her mug and took a sip of coffee, trying to clear the hunk of egg lodged in her throat as her eyes roamed over the man across the room from her.

"Been tryin' to get that old generator workin'," he said, answering his cousin's question as he continued to scrub the grease from his skin.

"Did you sleep at all last night?" Lorelei asked quietly, finally managing to free the food from her esophagus. She saw the muscles in his shoulders tense at the sound of her voice. He must not have noticed her at the farm table when he came in. Not entirely surprising since she never sat there before, having always been perched on her stool at the island when they gathered in the kitchen.

"No," Declan said, spearing her with a heated glance, and even though his tone was calm, gentle even, there was an edge to it. Averting her eyes, Lorelei focused on finishing her breakfast as the two men bantered back and forth about what could be done about the stubborn generator.

Tuning out their talk of mechanical parts that sounded like Greek to her, she pushed the remaining bites of her breakfast around idly on her plate. Her mind wandered to the events of last night and the way Declan jumped from the balcony to get away from her. She hoped the words she gave him at the party would help him remember what happened to his uncle, ultimately relieving some of his self-doubt, so they could figure things out.

"See ya later, Lorelei," Wyatt called as the back door banged shut, making her jump. She peered around the empty kitchen and sighed. She was so lost in her thoughts that she did not realize they had eaten breakfast already and washed their dishes.

The guys were gone for the better part of the day, so Lorelei kept herself busy by cleaning up the kitchen before tossing a load of clothes into the washing machine that started to pile up in the laundry room. She was nearly finished folding the last dryer full of sheets when she heard the muffled voices of Wyatt and Declan near the back porch.

"--her how you feel," Wyatt was saying. Lorelei froze in the middle of folding a fitted sheet as she strained her ears to listen.

"I *can't*, Wyatt. Not with all this shit hangin' over my head," Declan said, frustration creeping into his voice. Apparently, they had been talking about this for a while.

"Who gives a shit? D'you really think she'd still be here, *livin' with you*, if she thought you were actually guilty?" Wyatt demanded, and she could almost see the expressions on either man's face through the brick separating her from them.

"You– that's actually a good point," Declan admitted. He was quiet for a long moment, "Truth is, I figured she's here because of her job. Caine released me into her custody at the hearin'. So, I just assumed that she stayed out of obligation."

"I didn't know that." She could barely make out the words over the hammering of her heart. "You *really* think she's just here because it's her job?"

"Why else would she be?" Declan let out a mirthless laugh.

"Oh, I dunno, Dec. 'Cause she's got feelin's for you?" Wyatt stated bluntly. "You've been in each other's company *every day* for *weeks* now. You can't tell me there's nothin' there 'cause I've seen the way you look at each other when you think no one's payin' attention. Is it so hard to believe she cares about you?"

"Yes, it is!" Declan shouted angrily. There was a long pause before he continued, "I've been accused of mass murder, Wyatt. Of killin' my parents, and your dad. Of fuckin' *rape*. Who in the Goddess damned universe would have feelin's for someone that could be guilty of that?"

"You were paralyzed like the rest of them!" Wyatt yelled back at his cousin. Lorelei heard the shrill ping of a memory pulling through the barrier, followed by a string of curses.

"Why didn't you say somethin'?" Declan said, sounding a bit breathless.

"I wanted to, but after I saw what that spell did to you– You've been through enough, Dec. I just couldn't bring myself to cause you more pain," Wyatt said after a long silence, "You're capable of many things, but killin' our family, our pack, isn't one of 'em."

There was a barely audible sniff followed by Declan muttering something incoherently, and Lorelei nearly climbed on top of the dryer to press her ear against the bricks just to hear what he was saying. Shame be damned. Before she could do just that, the sound of their boots clomping up the steps sent her into a frenzy of dropping the sheet and hurriedly switching the washing machine and dryer on, noisily humming the first song that came to mind.

She quickly knelt to retrieve the linen just as the men poked their heads into the laundry room. Confused amusement was evident on their faces as they observed her for a long moment in the doorway.

"Are you hummin' the teapot song?" Wyatt asked while Declan watched her carefully. She saw the ghost of a smile tugging at the corners of his mouth.

"Yeah, it's been stuck in my head for days." The lie was bitter and she barely concealed her grimace at the foul taste.

"Maybe next time you should listen to Edgar Allen Poe," Declan said, his signature crooked smile making her weak at the knees.

"Why Poe?" Lorelei asked innocently, maneuvering the corners of the sheet so she could fold it properly.

"A Tell-Tale Heart," He gave her a knowing look when she blinked up at him, swallowing hard. Declan could hear her heartbeat through the wall, she realized. They both had.

"One of my favorites," she said and gave them a feeble smile, feeling like she had been caught with her hand in the cookie jar. Technically, she had but she was not about to admit to it now.

Declan let out a soft huff of a laugh before he turned from the laundry room, calling out that he was going to shower. Lorelei stared at the space a moment longer until Wyatt's hearty laugh made her cheeks burn with embarrassment.

"Shut up, Wyatt," Lorelei threw the sheet at him as she started to chuckle along with him.

"Oh, that was gold. I wish I'd recorded that." The Beta was nearly doubled over, one hand holding his abdomen and the other gripping the doorframe, when she marched by him and back into the kitchen.

"You can finish the damned laundry yourself," she shouted over her shoulder and hurried up the stairs to her room, the sounds of Wyatt's laughter following her every step of the way.

Chapter 16

That evening, Lorelei sat at the kitchen island while scrolling through an app on her phone looking at pizza options. Wyatt leaned against the counter, bracing his forearms on the polished wood as he gave her part of the order; four extra-large carnivores with extra everything, six orders of breadsticks including cheese and dessert, every flavor of wings the place had, and a couple two-liter bottles of soda, just for him and his cousin. Lorelei ordered a medium pizza for herself and sent in the order just as Declan entered the living room behind them.

"We ordered pizza. Should be here in about an hour and a half," she said with a half-smile, glancing over at him as he prowled through the space.

"All right," Declan said, acknowledging he had heard her, "Have y'all seen my wallet?" he asked, rummaging through the cushions on the couch.

"It's in the glovebox of the Chevelle," she said, remembering that he stashed it there before they left for the party. He inclined his head and disappeared through the door leading to the garage. Wyatt straightened and looked down at Lorelei, a thick brow quirked in silent question.

"What?" she asked, brows furrowing at his scrutiny.

"What's goin' on with you two?" he asked, leaning back against the counter and crossing his arms.

"There's… nothin' goin' on with us," Lorelei said, shrugging a shoulder.

"Let me rephrase my question; why are y'all fightin' this thing between y'all?" Wyatt inquired.

"There've been moments, but Declan is…" She struggled to find the right word.

"Declan's innocent of what the Council's charged him with," Wyatt stated, "but you already knew that. Even before today, you knew."

"I did," Lorelei confirmed, nodding her head. There was no point in denying it, not that she wanted to.

"So, I'll ask it another way; if you have feelin's, and so does Dec– what's the problem?" Wyatt lifted his brows, the challenge clear.

"The problem is it's complicated," she said with a sigh. Wyatt waited for her to elaborate, but when she remained silent. He dug his keys from his pants pocket and headed for the back door.

"Is it actually complicated, or have you both been complicating it?" The Beta asked before quietly exiting the house. Lorelei crossed her arms, glaring at the door as she mulled over Wyatt's words. She supposed it was a bit of both as she propped an elbow on the counter and rested her cheek against her palm. The chiming of her phone interrupted her thoughts and she unlocked the device to see a notification from Adam. Sighing, she opened her email and noticed at least ten messages from her boss that she needed to respond to.

Lorelei just finished clearing her inbox when a notification dropped down from the top of her screen. Wyatt collected the miniature feast from the delivery driver and was heading back home. Glancing around the space, she noticed Declan still had not returned. Sliding from the stool, she strode over to the garage door and swung it open, stepping onto the small landing at the top of the stairs.

"Declan?" she called out when she saw the faint broken outline of him through the windshield of the Chevelle. The door was standing open, one bare foot still on the cold concrete, and his hands propped on the steering wheel, staring at the piece of paper he held.

"Yeah." His voice was raw, full of emotion, and she rushed down the steps.

"What's wrong?" she asked, and he held out the paper to her as she came around the car door, swiping the back of his hand across his nose.

"It's from my dad," he said when she took the letter, and her heart clenched seeing the wetness clinging to his lashes. Looking down at the stationary, she saw the Crescent Ridge crest stamped at the top left of the page.

Declan,

If you're reading this, it means that your uncle and I are gone. I pray to the Lunar Goddess that Wyatt and your mother are still with you. While I sit here writing this letter, I'm reminded of when you sat at this very same desk, practicing your flags. You never gave up, no matter how frustrated you were until you could identify them at a glance. It was then that I knew you would be a great leader. Your perseverance, and dedication are unmatched, and my biggest regret is that I won't be there to witness all I know you will accomplish in the years to come. I have no doubt, you will be a greater Alpha than I could have ever hoped to be.

I never said it quite enough while you were growing up, but I love you, son. You've made me a very proud father these last 30 years.

Love from beyond,

Dad

P.S. Everything you need, you'll find in a safe haven.

"You know, he told me before the ceremony to go check the ole girl if anything ever happened to him and my uncle." He let out a mirthless laugh, bumping the side of his fist on the steering wheel. "Meet the ole girl." Grabbing his wallet from the bench seat, he leaned out of the car and stood, taking the letter back when she held it out to him.

"He must have known, or at least suspected that somethin' would happen. Why would he say that otherwise?" she questioned. Declan shrugged his shoulders, slipping the letter back into its black envelope.

"Ever since the massacre at Silvertooth, my dad was always on edge when the Summer and Winter solstice rolled around. Always worried that somethin' would happen during those two events," he said, shutting the car door.

"Why those two?" she asked, following him through the garage.

"The Silvertooth massacre happened durin' the Winter Solstice gala. If the Alphas keep with tradition, which Desmond did– the entire pack attends to celebrate," Declan explained as they made their way back into the house. Lorelei heard about the slaughter of Alpha Desmond's pack, but she did not realize the gravity of *when* the massacre took place.

"Ya know, I don't remember ever sittin' at dad's desk learnin' flags. I mean, I learned them, just not in his office." Declan set the envelope onto the counter and stared at it for a long moment. Like it would reveal the answer to the somewhat cryptic letter that lay within.

"What flags?" she asked, leaning against the kitchen island.

"Nautical. We had an old catboat dad restored that I wanted to learn how to captain. Before he'd let me anywhere near it, I had to learn all the flags and their codes." Despite his sadness, a smile softened his features at the memory.

"Is the boat still around?" she asked, holding out her hand. He passed the letter back to her and she slipped it from the envelope.

"No, it was destroyed. Hurricane in New Orleans where she was docked." Regret tinged his voice, and she nodded, rereading the letter.

"'Safe haven'… Didn't you say that's what your dad called this place?" He nodded and stepped up beside her, craning his neck to read over it again.

"Yeah, no one else knew about this place except Uncle Ric and Wyatt. Dad's work didn't usually allow him to travel very far unless it was for business," Declan explained. When she lifted her gaze from the letter, she found herself almost nose to nose with him. His eyes dropped to her lips, and her breath hitched as she stared up at him. Thinking he would more than likely bail again despite knowing he was innocent, Lorelei cleared her throat and returned her attention to the letter. She really did not feel up to another round of rejection, no matter what Wyatt confirmed earlier.

"Everything you need, you'll find in a safe haven..." she reread the postscript aloud. "So, there's gotta be somethin' here," she stated, looking up from the paper.

"It sounds like it, but I don't know of any secret levers or hidden rooms where he could'a hid somethin'." Declan straightened, spreading his arms wide with a dry chuckle.

"Okay, well, let's just wait on the food for now. It's been a long day and I think we need a break. Maybe Wyatt'll have some idea about all this." She folded the letter and set it on the counter under her keys as a faint honk pulled their attention to the garage door. Declan half smiled as he hurried out to help his cousin.

"If you drop somethin', Dec, I'm gonna be pissed." She heard Wyatt grumble from the back door as they shuffled into the kitchen. Both of them were loaded down with boxes and bags. As they situated the feast, Lorelei slipped over to the cup cabinet.

"Want a glass or do y'all prefer it straight from the bottle?" Both of them grabbed their two-liter and lifted it. She stared at them, amazed at how much alike they really were. Polar opposites but their mannerisms were identical in many ways. She plucked a tumbler from the shelf, filled it with ice water, and rejoined them at the kitchen island.

"Yesterday evenin' at the party, Lorelei figured out a loophole with the spell," Declan said, flipping open his box.

"What? How?" Wyatt asked through a bulging cheek of pizza.

"Well, his wolf helped him remember by sayin' one word. It gave me the idea that we could feed him single words of things that we knew about the ceremony, and hopefully, he could piece it together on his own," she said, taking a sip of her water, "it worked."

"I thought the spell would hurt him if anything was mentioned about that night." Wyatt's brows lifted together in concern.

"It will if you try to tell him what happened. But, spells are specific. They don't deviate from what they're created to do. The loophole is givin' him specific words that can help him connect the dots and pull the memory from behind the block by himself. It doesn't bypass it completely, but it reduces the pain to a fraction of what it was," she explained, glancing between the two men. She knew they did not have much knowledge about Witches or spells, and waited patiently to see if they had questions.

"Wyatt, did you see who killed your father?" Lorelei asked when neither of them spoke, and he nodded his head, glancing at Declan.

"One word, cousin. Make it count," Declan said as he rolled his neck, readying himself for the coming pain.

"Werewolf," Wyatt said after some thought. She wasn't sure any of them were breathing while they waited for a reaction, as he leaned back in his stool, brows furrowed.

"Werewolf, Alaric, decapitated... How could a werewo–" The ear-splitting ping rang out in her ears as he put the pieces together. His large hand slammed into the edge of the island top, rattling the piece of heavy furniture as the pain wrenched through his mind. His features contorted in a silent scream, and Lorelei saw his teeth lengthen momentarily before returning to normal.

"Fuck!" he shouted, still gripping the countertop. Once again, it was over as soon as it started, and she placed a tentative hand on his bicep. His muscles jumped beneath her palm and he glanced at her, giving her a grateful nod of his head.

"So, he can just piece it back together with the right words?" Wyatt asked as he gawked.

"Yeah. The spell can only block him from remembering what happened, and hurt him and the speaker if anything from that night is mentioned. If he figures out the truth on his own, there's nothin' the spell can do to stop it. So, it briefly triggers the defense when the fragment breaks through." The men were silent as they digested the information. "Knowin' that though, worries the hell outta me. It means that whoever did this, didn't count on Declan ever gettin' out of Saint Thaddeus, or havin' anyone on his side."

"That means we're all potential targets if whoever did this finds out I'm rememberin'," Declan said, realizing her train of thought.

"Exactly," she nodded, taking another bite of her pizza.

"Well, who would wanna do that?" Wyatt asked, looking at them questioningly before chomping into a breadstick.

"Cormac," Lorelei and Declan said in unison, and the Betas brows raised in consideration before nodding.

"Yeah, that tracks." He chewed slowly, lost in thought for a moment.

"You never suspected him?" Declan asked as he leaned around her, and tossed his second empty pizza box on top of the first.

"Of course, I did, but I couldn't see anyone other than you and dad. I couldn't go to the Elders with no witnesses other than the two I suspected. Not to mention I was exiled that night, and had no fuckin' way to get any proof." Wyatt took a long chug, finishing off his bottle of soda. "It's not just what happened at the ceremony, though. It was how he acted at the arena beforehand too. All the little spats and tussles before that. Lookin' back, it's easy to see how jealous Cor was."

"The memory my wolf helped me pull at the party was about that last fight. For the last two years, I thought I'd lost." Wyatt looked at Declan like he had grown three heads. "I know, but when I was face to face with him, my wolf finally convinced me that it wasn't possible."

"Why didn't you say somethin'? I recorded that fight, Declan." Wyatt whipped out his phone and after scrolling through two years' worth of photos and videos, pulled up the recording of that day.

"Sure, you wanna watch that, Lorelei?" Wyatt asked her, suddenly serious. Declan took his cousin's phone and waited for her response, only hitting play when she nodded.

She was soon completely absorbed in the video as her eyes followed the lethal grace of Declan's movements. Wyatt followed them like an expert, circling the fight, filming the action from all sides, ensuring he captured every movement the two men made. There was little talking done between them, but the emotions that played over both of their faces needed no words. Pure, unadulterated hate fueled Cormac while betrayal and rage shone in Declan's eyes. The other man never managed to land a blow until the very end when he wrapped his hand around Declan's throat. She saw the grin that only widened when he snapped Cormac's arm, the undeniable satisfaction relaxing his features into a savagely beautiful calm. A shiver ran up her spine when Declan vowed to kill the man, causing him to glance over at her as he handed the device back to Wyatt, clearing his throat.

"Wait, there's more." Declan snatched the phone back as the video panned away from a metal door that was swinging closed and focused on Cormac, who still sat on his knees, cradling his broken arm. The angle was low and swung back and forth, making her a bit dizzy, and she could see the toe of Wyatt's sneaker peeking into the bottom of the screen every other step. Popping sounds could be heard as tendons and bone reconnected themselves, the wounds quickly healed over the next few moments.

"Learn your lesson this time?" Wyatt's voice echoed slightly from above the camera.

"I'll destroy him. I will fucking decimate *everything* that is Declan Wolfe. Wait and see, asshole," Cormac spat, obviously unaware that he was still being recorded.

"Good luck with that, princess." The video ended with a scoff from Wyatt, and Declan stared at the screen until it faded black. He slid the phone across the countertop and his gaze lifted slowly up to Wyatt.

"You never said anything." The accusation was clear but the man did not flinch as if he expected his cousin to question his loyalty. Lorelei watched the two men, her gaze bouncing from one to the other as the tension grew.

"Declan, you know how he was. Always spoutin' off at the mouth about one thing or another. Lookin' back, I shoulda said somethin' but I honestly didn't think he'd do anything," Wyatt explained, food momentarily forgotten. Declan rested his forearms on the counter, leaning forward as she looked over at Lorelei.

"He's tellin' you the truth, Declan," she assured him, smiling at his soft sigh of relief.

"Oh no. Is she a walkin' lie detector like Nan was?" The breadstick Wyatt had half way to his mouth froze and a look of dismay twisted his features.

"She's actually better than Nan was, so I'd always tell the truth if I were you, cousin." Declan grinned as he nodded his head.

"Do lies really taste bad?" Wyatt asked suddenly.

"They do, but only if I tell them. So, I don't lie, unless I have to." Lorelei gave him a small smile and finished off her water.

The mood lifted significantly, as they bantered back and forth while cleaning up the kitchen together. As they cleared away the boxes, Wyatt noticed the letter and picked up the black envelope while Declan retreated out the garage door to toss the cardboard. Lorelei wiped the crumbs from the island, as Wyatt read the letter, muttering the words softly.

"Have y'all checked the dock?" he asked when Declan returned.

"We have a dock?" Lorelei glared at them when they both nodded and Declan gestured for her to follow him. He and Wyatt led her from the back porch just outside the kitchen to a footpath cutting through a dense swath of trees.

"I didn't check cause dad never put flags out here. No one knows about this place and there's no access to the springs except ours." They emerged on a sandy, moonlit shore, with a long plank walkway leading out to the large dock. Lorelei could just make out the silvery outline of a boathouse.

"What the hell?" Declan muttered, stunned to see a flag pole standing proud over the roof of the structure with two square pieces of fabric fluttering in the gentle wind.

"Can you tell which flags they are?" she asked, folding her arms against the chilly breeze.

"No, they must be pretty faded. I can't make out the colors right now. We'll check them out in the mornin' though," he assured her, bracing his hands on his hips.

"This is turnin' into a regular murder mystery," Wyatt said from behind them, and both she and Declan twisted around to look at him.

"What?" The Beta asked, his gaze bouncing between them. Lorelei snorted softly, trying to cover the chuckle that escaped her as she turned back to the lake house.

Chapter 17

The following morning, Declan shuffled from his bedroom, half exhausted, and made his way downstairs where Wyatt was in his usual spot cooking breakfast.

"Mornin'," he gruffed to his cousin, rounding the island.

"Mornin', Dec," Wyatt said, keeping his attention on the food he was preparing. Looked like a quick feast of pancakes and bacon was on the menu as he poured himself a large cup of coffee and leaned back against the counter, taking a long sip. As the grogginess began to slowly dissipate, his ears picked up the sound of the shower upstairs turning on, and his mind conjured the image of Lorelei naked, stepping under the warm spray of water. Soap lathering her gorgeous body, hands sliding tantalizingly over her perfect breasts, and trailing lower to the apex between her thighs. Letting out a stout growl of frustration, he set down the coffee mug a little harder than he intended and strode to the door, yanking it open.

"Gonna go check the boathouse," Declan said over his shoulder, not waiting for a response.

As he crossed the back porch, the sounds from upstairs slowly began to fade and he forced himself to think of anything other than Lorelei. Heaving a sigh,

Declan adjusted the front of his sweatpants and set off at a jog towards the dock.

'How long are you going to deny yourself and her?' The question was a borderline snarl, reverberating around his mind. He growled in response, pushing the wolf to the edge of his consciousness where he had been for days. The beast knew damn well how long. Goddess knew he wanted her. *Craved* her on a level that was nearly maddening at times. She haunted him in his dreams – the ones he could remember anyway – with her soft curves and delectable mouth. But he refused to take her to bed until there was no doubt of his innocence. There was an echoing huff of annoyance but nothing else.

Declan broke from the dense treeline a minute later and slowed to a walk, nearing the plank walkway jutting from the side of their little private beach. His bare feet were silent except for the occasional creak of the wood beneath his weight. Glancing up at the flagpole, he thought to recall the square flags' meanings, and realized there would be nothing in the structure itself. Still, with all the mystery that seemed to be centered around the letter his father left him, Declan figured it best to double check the larger vessels.

Entering the boathouse, he was hit with a sense of nostalgia and melancholy as his gaze landed on the pontoon that was tied off in the farthest boat slip. A soft smile tugged at his lips as he read the faded name painted along the large aluminum tube. *The Alora.*

There was a soft whine from his wolf, and Declan was surprised by the vulnerable sound. However, that quickly turned into a disapproving growl at being seen as anything but a beast. He wondered if he would continue to get the silent treatment, and the lack of response confirmed it well enough. Other than the question minutes ago, his wolf had not spoken to him since he leapt from the balcony to get away from Lorelei. Honestly, he could not blame him. Especially when the beast tried to return to her moments later and claim her himself. Declan nearly lost the internal battle that night. Only when he threatened to set Lorelei up in a secondary packhouse did his wolf finally relent and take off into the forest.

Heaving a sigh, he quickly checked the pontoon and its many cubby holes and storage compartments, then the runabout. There was nothing. He did not bother checking the jet skis and instead checked around the boathouse for anything remotely out of place. Again, he did not find anything.

"If there's anything out there, it's in the water. There wasn't anything in the boathouse," Declan said as he took a seat beside Lorelei on the couch, tucking a hand behind his head to obscure the vision sitting on the middle cushion. Her curls were loose and wild this morning, and she put on an oversized sweater hanging loosely off one shoulder. She was currently tugging the legs of her black sweatpants up, settling the elastic just below her knees. He had to casually drape an arm over his lap to hide the growing bulge in his own sweatpants. It still caught him off guard that no matter what she wore, whether it was a dress or pajamas, he found her absolutely stunning every time.

"*The Alora*?" Wyatt questioned, pulling his thoughts back to the moment.

"Pontoon, jet skis, and the runabout," he confirmed with a nod.

"Runabout?" Lorelei looked at him in confusion over the rim of her coffee cup.

"It's a blanket term for boats with'a an outboard motor that's twenty feet or less," Declan explained, reaching for his cup. "We used it for wakeboardin', and tubin' mostly."

"Hey, are those wetsuits still lyin' around? We might need 'em with how cold the water's gonna be," his cousin asked as he stood and walked up to the window looking out at the glittering lake. From this distance, the water was merely a thick, shimmering line, nearly blinding to look at in the mid-morning sunlight.

"Wyatt, we had those when we were ten. Besides, it's only mid-fall, it won't be that bad." He chuckled at the mental image of his six-foot-one cousin in a preteen's scuba suit.

"Laugh it up, Dec, but you know as well as I do how cold it's gonna be," his cousin said with a grin.

"What do you think the coffee's for?" Lorelei asked, smiling brightly, though a glint of mischief danced in her soft gray eyes at her teasing. Wyatt grumbled something about waking up and downed the rest of his cup before setting it on the coffee table.

"Ready when y'all are," he said, and Declan nodded, setting his mug down as he stood from the couch.

They walked single file down the half-overgrown path leading to the water's edge in silence. Each step clawed a pit of anxiety in Declan's stomach over what they would find beneath the shimmering surface of the lake. He could not understand why his father did not just tell him what was going on instead of all the smoke and mirrors. Thinking back to the morning of the Alpha Ceremony, he recalled part of their conversation in his father's office and the pieces fell into place.

'We'll discuss it tonight at the lake house, so try not to worry until then.'

His dad was going to tell him. They just never made it to that point.

Declan stopped directly across from the nautical flags flapping lazily in the breeze. The top flag was colored red and yellow meeting in the middle diagonally, red on top, and yellow on bottom. The second flag was solid white, with a red X crossing in the middle and ending at each corner.

"'Man overboard', 'requires assistance'." Declan pointed to each as he named them.

"So, it's probably under the flagpole, or near it under the dock," Wyatt said as he shaded his eyes against the bright sunshine, scanning the water's surface. The dock was built directly on top of the water with no gaps, making coming up for air tricky since they would have to swim out from under the structure and lose their progress. Or find the slips and risk being crushed when the boats shift.

"I might be able to help, but it'd probably stir up the bed pretty bad," Lorelei offered.

"Show me what you're talkin' about." Declan gestured in the opposite direction of the dock. She nodded and stepped down to the small sandy beach, her eyes already shining like mercury. Nothing happened for several long seconds and Declan could see Wyatt glance at him from the corner of his eye. As his cousin opened his mouth, magic shot from Lorelei like a cannon, splitting the water down to the lake bed from the shore to the end of the dock.

Wyatt jerked back a step and let out a curse as the force of the blast exposed the waterlogged sand beneath.

Chuckling at his cousin, Declan watched the water hang suspended for a moment before crashing back in on itself. Lorelei turned back to him just as her eyes returned to normal, and gave him a sheepish smile, shrugging her shoulders.

"Can you keep the water apart?" Declan asked her and she shook her head.

"Maybe if I practiced, but right now, I'd drain faster than I could pull." He raised his brows, confused, and she grinned at him, "I can pull energy from nature but to keep the water back would drain me of energy faster than I could replace it from…" She extended her arm in a sweeping motion at the wilderness around them.

"Looks like it's all brute force today, ladies." Wyatt clapped his hands together, grinning as he and Declan pulled off their tee shirts and handed them over to Lorelei.

The temperature of the water was not so bad until he was deep enough for it to slosh up his thighs. Taking a few quick, cheek-puffing breaths, Declan pushed off the sandy bottom and dove into the freezing water. The sensation of a million pins pricking his body nearly overwhelmed him as his breath stalled in his lungs. Kicking against the numbing cold threatening to lock up his muscles, Declan broke the surface with stammered, huffing breaths.

"I f-fuckin' told ya it was gon-na be c-c-cold, ya p-prick!" Wyatt shouted when his head broke the surface next to him, and Declan let out a stuttering laugh, panting roughly from his tight chest.

"C-c'mon, let's m-make this qui-ick," he said as he swam swiftly towards the dock where Lorelei now stood, watching from the railing. He and Wyatt dove again, trying to make out the blurred shapes around them as they searched for anything out of place. Not finding anything, they resurfaced and dove again.

And again.

And again.

His arms were starting to go numb from the cold when Wyatt suddenly grabbed his ankle and pointed to the surface.

"It's un-der the p-planking, betw-tween the p-pontoon and the runa-runabout, s-s-strapped." Wyatt was slightly breathless as he spoke, teeth chattering violently. "It's p-pretty bi-big."

"L-Lore, po-po-pontoon fr-front seat, c-c-coil of ro-ope," he said, his speech clipped, and she disappeared, her hurried steps creaking over the planks. She quickly returned with a thick coil of rope and handed it down to him. He and Wyatt dove down again and tied off the large watertight storage box, using their claws to cut the straps keeping it secured to the underside of the dock. Without its tethers, the box sank quickly to the lake bed, jerking them both roughly down with it. Planting their feet in the sand, they hauled the heavy locker slowly toward the shore. They resurfaced for air only a few feet from the dock.

"G-gonna ta-take a wh-while," Declan called up to Lorelei as she stood on the walkway, following their slow progress. Worry marred her brow and she bit her bottom lip as they dove back down to resume tugging the line. Before their feet could touch the bottom again, a sudden rushing undertow surged in the water around them like they were caught in the path of a ship's propeller. The locker surged forward, dragging them along the bed with it. A second push quickly followed, forcing them closer to shore. Declan's knee dug into the sand just as his head broke the surface. Shaking the water from his hair, he staggered momentarily through the rough current, his gaze searching for Lorelei. She was stepping from the walkway onto the miniature beach, her eyes shimmering silver in the sunlight. Her brow was furrowed in concentration as the locker slid quickly up onto the shore while he and Wyatt clambered out of the lake, both of them shaking uncontrollably.

Running over to them, she took their hands and Declan could immediately feel the cold being pulled from his body. He watched her intently as she gazed up at him, noticing that she was shivering. When her lips suddenly turned blue, and her breath left her in shuddering puffs of steam, Declan pried his hand from hers. Fear stabbed him in the heart when tremors wracked her body, and her teeth chattered so hard he thought they might break.

"Lore, stop!" he ordered and went to wrap his arms around her but she held up her hand, taking a step back.

"W-w-wait," she huffed softly and closed her eyes. Declan could hear a cracking sound and his gaze trailed lower. Lorelei stood motionless as the ground beneath her bare feet frosted over, turning the damp sand into thick, gritty ice. Slowly, her shivering lessened, and her lips returned to their natural dusty pink.

"What the hell was that?" Wyatt asked once she finally stopped shaking, and opened her eyes again. As they faded, she swayed gently, taking a step to steady herself. Instinctively, Declan reached out, gripping her shoulders.

"I took the energy away. I'm fine, just a bit light-headed." She smiled, placing a hand on her forehead as his gaze roamed her face. "I'm okay, Declan, I promise." He stared another moment longer before he nodded, and cupped her face, bending down to bring himself to eye level with her.

"I'll freeze to death before you do that again." Pressing his lips to hers, he cut off any protest she might have had. Lorelei gasped in surprise, and he had to admit it surprised him too, but seeing her in that state did something to him. The sheer terror that gripped him in a chokehold when he thought she would freeze to death on this sunny mid-autumn shore nearly sent him to his knees.

'*You love her,*' his wolf spoke from the corner of his mind, and as he pulled away; he could not deny his beast's statement.

Chapter 18

With a grunt, Declan and Wyatt hefted the locker onto the back porch while Lorelei grabbed a roll of paper towels from the kitchen to wipe away the excess water. They made sure the outside and any seams were bone dry before they lugged the box inside, and set it on the counter.

"Ready?" Declan asked, looking from Wyatt to Lorelei. They both nodded and he released the latches securing the lid, carefully lifting it away. The inner compartment of the locker was shallower than the outside walls but still held a tremendous amount of papers consisting of stacks of photos bound by rubber bands, documents, and manila folders. His eyes fell on another black envelope lying on top of the files, and a heavy feeling settled in the pit of his stomach. He reached in and picked up the thick stationery. Swallowing hard, he tore it open and propped his forearms on the edge of the locker, reading it aloud for Lorelei and Wyatt.

Declan,

I sincerely hope that you are never going to read this, but if you are, then Alaric and I were not able to hand over the evidence to Caine in time. I should have told you long ago of our suspicions regarding the Daughtry's. While we cannot undo the past, Uncle Ric and I hope to aid you in the future.

As you know, nearly 25 years ago we brought Apollo and Cormac into the pack after finding them the only survivors of the Silvertooth massacre. Many things did not add up that night, most of which are documented in the files you now possess. However, we uncovered a long and bloody trail going back nearly three decades. Be careful, son. The Daughtry's are cunning and extremely dangerous.

Goddess be with you,

Dad.

"I think before we get too involved with all of this, we should move it to the basement," Declan said, trying not to let his emotions get the better of him. Clearing his throat, he folded the letter and returned it to the envelope.

"I'll help you get it down, then I'm gonna go grab us lunch. Subs all right with y'all?" Wyatt asked, walking over to grip the handle and they slid it from the counter. Maneuvering the locker around the island, Declan opened the basement door situated at the back of the living room staircase and flipped on the light.

"Lore, could you give me a hand down here?" he called up the stairs when they reached the bottom.

"Yep, be right down."

An hour later, the basement, which originally was a gaming spot with a huge projector and comfy chairs, was rearranged into their investigation headquarters. Several long tables were stacked with documents near a stretch of empty wall space, and the desk that Lorelei would use sat opposite the staircase in the corner. Now Declan was sifting through one of the stacks, while Lorelei looked over some of the pictures.

"Oh, that makes more sense," she muttered and he peered up at her over the paper he was reading. She flipped over one of the photos, and read an adhesive label stuck to the back aloud.

"'New Orleans; Meeting unknown female; Tense conversation.' Is this Alaric's handwritin'? Cause it isn't your dad's," she said, handing him the photo.

"It's mine," stated an unfamiliar voice.

Declan spun quickly at the stranger's words coming from the top of the basement stairs. Stepping protectively in front of Lorelei, he noticed the air around them warble slightly. She placed a barrier between him and the newcomer meaning to protect him. A conversation they had during one of the sessions at the asylum floated through his mind.

"I protect what I care about, and who I love. No matter the cost."

"Who the fuck're you?" he demanded as the man descended the stairs, trying to ignore the feelings the brief memory ignited, "And how in the hell'd you get in my house?" The man pulled his hands from his jacket showing he was unarmed, and Declan took a moment to glance over the stranger. His straight blonde hair was balled into a loose man bun and shaved close to his scalp on both sides. He was tan with dark green eyes, a prominent brow, and a straight Romanesque nose. His lips were pressed into a thin line and surrounded by a well-kept beard that was a shade darker than the knot on his head. The man was well built and wore a dark gray jacket made of canvas, a burgundy shirt underneath, and a pair of black tactical cargo pants settled over scuffed combat boots.

"I'm Garridan. I believe Elder Caine told you about me?" His voice was deep and held traces of an accent Declan did not recognize.

"Lore?" Declan inquired softly over his shoulder, eyeing Garridan as he dropped from the bottom step.

"It's true," she said, stepping from behind him and the gentle warbling disappeared.

"How did you get in here?" he asked again, less aggressive this time.

"I have a code," Garridan stated simply and took a cautious step forward. Declan eyed him warily but did not protest when he ambled further into the basement.

"Your father gave it to me before he died. He knew that if anything happened to him and Beta Ric you'd need an ally, and I'd need access to the house. Kai figured you would see that he trusted me, and reciprocate. But I see now your time away has made you distrustful." He gave Declan a pointed look. "Saint Thaddeus will do that, no matter how strong we think we are." The grim realization hit him that Garridan had experienced the horror show that went on in the asylum, just as he had.

"It's good to finally meet you, Declan, despite the circumstances." He clapped his hand to Garridan's extended forearm, their grips firm as they both finally relaxed. "And you must be Doctor McCann. Elder Caine speaks very highly of you. Both of you, actually." He shook Lorelei's hand gently and offered her a kind smile.

"Just Lorelei is fine, and thank you. For helpin' us." Garridan nodded and stepped up to the locker. He dug around for a moment before pulling out a jump-drive, holding it between his thumb and forefinger.

"This is going to be the most critical piece of evidence we have. It's video surveillance of the night of the massacre in Silvertooth, *and* Crescent Ridge. The footage I managed to get from Desmond's backup drive doesn't show the event itself, but Apollo and Cormac make an appearance. The Crescent Ridge feed was tampered with, and no amount of reconstruction, tweaking, or manipulation has been able to restore it."

"I'll take a look," Lorelei said quickly and swiped up the storage device.

"We'll need you to comb through everything we have as well. I know it's asking a lot but your gift is invaluable here, and you're the only one who can discern fact from fiction," Garridan said, and Lorelei nodded, stepping around them to her desk and connecting the drive to her laptop to download.

"Food's here. Get it while it's hot!" Wyatt called from the main floor, and the swish of multiple plastic bags could be heard as he ambled through the kitchen.

As Lorelei and Garridan headed upstairs, Declan hung back a moment to straighten the papers he had scattered. For over two years he begged for someone to give answers. He petitioned the Council, wrote letters to anyone he could think of that might help him, and received nothing, time and time again. Just when he had given up hope, an auburn-haired angel swooped in, doing her damndest to try and save him. She broke through the wall he had built, trusted him, and in return he trusted her. With his life, he realized.

However, now they had hard evidence of the massacre, video footage at that, and he truly feared what they would find on that jump-drive. He knew now that he was innocent, he knew that he would never hurt his family or his pack, but still, that nagging doubt crept out of the darkness to whisper in his ear. *Savage. Vengeful.* What if Wyatt's memories had been tampered with too?

Declan understood then, that he feared the truth as much as he craved to know it. Even more so, he was terrified that he might lose the woman he had fallen in love with.

Chapter 19

Over the course of the next few weeks, Lorelei spent most of every day removing the dark magic used to alter the surveillance footage of the Crescent Ridge ceremony. She discovered the issue when the recording finished downloading to her laptop and was currently removing the spell one frame at a time. It was a painstaking process that had to be done, otherwise the magic could destroy the entire file.

Declan, Wyatt, and Garridan sifted through the stacks of the documents and were working on establishing a timeline over the last thirty years for Apollo and Cormac. It was tedious to say the least, but they made good progress in such a short time, unveiling that the father son duo left a messy trail in their wake over the years.

Before losing his wife, Apollo was a fairly stable man. Active within the pack that he and his growing family were part of, respected in their community, and overall seemed to be an upstanding member. However, after his mate, who was human, died under mysterious circumstances when Cormac was four and things took a dark turn. There were reports from Cormac's school of suspected abuse, and though it was investigated, no charges were ever filed. Only adding to the suspicion that things at home were volatile, they had moved after that incident, joining a new pack across the country.

Again, reports of suspected abuse were filed, but no charges were ever made. One after another the pattern continued until murders, suicides, abductions, and even rapes in and outside of the packs began following the pair. Countless territories from North America to New Zealand, everywhere they went some form of tragedy struck, tainting the illusions they had built to stay under the radar. At this point, they both were experts in manipulation and keeping up appearances in the public eye, making it all the more difficult to pin anything specifically on them.

Taking a moment to stretch, Lorelei's gaze drifted over to the three men who currently had their heads bent over several documents, muttering about dates. Garridan moved into the house the week prior, and would stay for the duration of their investigation, or until it proved too dangerous for all of them to be together under one roof.

They learned that Cormac and his father knew Lorelei was a Witch and had the gift of insight after Garridan overheard a rather tense discussion earlier in the week. Exactly how much the father son duo knew about the extent of her abilities, no one knew for sure.

"Oh Goddess…" Lorelei breathed after tapping to the next frame. The software was state of the art, thanks to their new friend, and the image on her screen currently showed the pack collapsed on the ground.

"What is it?" Declan asked as he and the other two men looked over. Declan kept his distance, not wanting to trigger the spell's defenses. He made that mistake already and ended up on the floor writhing in pain. It took nearly an hour to pull the fragments through the barrier with Wyatt and Garridan holding him down, and Lorelei using her magic to wheedle the memories though. He now could remember a large chunk of the ceremony that involved a portion of a speech that Apollo gave. A speech that Lorelei had recently played back, the dark magic removed, and a shiver ran along her spine at Apollo's final words.

'To Declan! May your legacy far outshine your fathers.' The manic grin that distorted Apollo's features after everyone drank the wine left no doubt in her mind that he had orchestrated the coup d'état.

Lorelei blinked the tears from her eyes, and shook her head, indicating that she could not tell him what she was seeing. He had been suffering from a terrible headache following the incident a few days ago but he still would not rest longer than a few hours. Looking at him now, she could see the dark circles under his eyes, and the slight slouch to his shoulders. His insomnia was getting the better of him, and the nightmares had doubled down since they began sifting through the evidence and pulling memories from the mental block.

"Declan, you're exhausted. Go get some sleep." she said gently, worrying he would collapse if he stayed up much longer.

"I'm fine." His tone was clipped, and he turned stiffly back to the documents.

"Go to bed, ple–" Declan spun on her with a snarl, eyes shifting red.

"Do *not* command me again, Lorelei." The tone of his voice was low and dangerous. "There's enough shit goin' on without you naggin' me like a fuckin' motherhen." His words struck like a slap to the face, and she stared at him wide-eyed for several long moments.

He did not know it, but every night she had heard him yelling out or thrashing in a nightmare, she ran to his bedroom to soothe him. Only Wyatt knew the truth. They had nearly crashed into each other at the top of the stairs on a particularly violent night, and he had helped by shielding her from Declan's mindless, blind strikes.

A single swing had made it past Wyatt when his cousin had knocked him off balance. Declan had landed a devastating blow to her thigh, breaking the bone on impact. She was sure that her agonized scream would have woken the dead, and Declan had only thrashed more at the sound of her pain. So she had grit her teeth and sobbed silently as she soothed him. Only taking care of her own injury once she was sure he was free from the unknown terrors that plagued his dreams. Afterwards, she and Wyatt had sat in the kitchen for hours talking about everything that had happened before, and since Saint Thaddeus.

Glancing at Wyatt now, she saw that his eyes glowed a brilliant icy blue. Ever since that night, he had taken on the role of protective big brother, and did not care who he had to defend her from. Even if it was his own cousin. He had seen firsthand what she was willing to endure, what she *could* endure, for the sake of helping someone she cared about.

"You got it, Wolfe." she snapped, cutting her eyes back to him. She hated that her voice cracked, hated the tears stinging her eyes. Shutting her laptop roughly, she shoved from the chair at her desk, and rushed up the stairs, refusing to look back. As she stepped into the kitchen, a resounding crack followed by a string of curses and snarls told her that Wyatt had just landed a bone shattering blow to Declan's jaw.

"What the fuck, Dec? You don't know *half* the shit she's done for you–" She closed the door on the altercation, and walked around the island to make a cup of coffee, angrily swiping away the tear that rolled down her cheek. Spooning some sugar and creamer into the mug, she tried to ignore the rumbling growls that continued to reverberate through the floorboards.

As the men argued louder, she picked up her cup and trudged up the stairs and across the loft. Lorelei padded out onto the balcony and curled up on one of the armchairs where she finally broke down. The stress and chaos of the last couple months finally boiling over as the last warm rays of the sun dipped past the treetops on the other side of the lake. The air quickly turned cold in the twilight and she shivered slightly as shadows finally took over, expanding out before starting to slink away in the slowly brightening moonlight.

The sound of the door suddenly slamming open beneath the balcony made her jump. Warm light spilled from the kitchen, illuminating the lawn several yards out and she peered over the railing in time to watch Declan leap from the back porch and shift into the biggest wolf she had ever seen. Despite his hulking size, he landed gracefully on long, powerful legs and launched into a full run. She caught a glimpse of his dark gray pelt just before he disappeared from sight, and marveled at how massive his true form was. The thought of Declan in his Werewolf form and the unbelievable size he must be sent goosebumps prickling over her skin. As an Alpha, he would be bigger than the lower wolf ranks, but Lorelei never realized how incredibly large they were. It had been too dark on the night she had seen his true form slink from the trees weeks ago. At best, she had seen a rough outline and the glow of his crimson eyes.

It was not long before the cold night air forced Lorelei back inside, and she traipsed back down to the kitchen. She was surprised to look up and see Garridan standing at the stove, stirring a large pot of fragrant liquid. Curious, she sidled over to take a peek and saw several different flower petals and herbs she could not identify tumbling in the rolling boil.

"It's a special remedy that'll help with Declan's nightmares. Family recipe, top secret," Garridan said with a sly grin, trying to lighten the thundercloud that obviously hung over her.

"That's really kind of you. This a hobby of yours?" Lorelei asked as she rinsed out her coffee mug and set it in the drainboard.

"Somewhat. My gran taught me when I was young. She'd always say, 'You never know when you'll need a *poțiune medicală, lupul mic,* best to be prepared,'" Garridan said, strengthening his accent and heightening his voice to imitate his grandmother.

Lorelei chuckled at the unexpected humor from him, "I suppose that's true. I've never needed potions personally, but I can imagine they do come in handy."

"I'll teach you this one another time. This batch should last him quite a while since he only needs a tablespoon, and make sure he's in bed before he takes it, or at least within falling distance," he warned.

"Powerful stuff, huh?" Lorelei noticed she was getting drowsy just from the vapors, as Garridan nodded.

"I'll have to take a break once I reduce the heat, otherwise, you'll find me here on the floor in the morning," he said, stirring the concoction before turning down the heat.

"We definitely don't want that, so mind your nose." She smiled and bid him good night.

Lorelei was vaguely aware of her mattress sagging as Declan climbed into her bed smelling faintly of the fragrant mixture Garridan cooked up earlier. Slipping his arm around her middle, he pulled her flush against him and pressed a kiss to the back of her neck. Finding his large hand in the dark, Lorelei laced their fingers and gave him a gentle squeeze. Declan let out a relieved sigh as he relaxed against her, and in the next moment, he was snoring softly. His warm breaths fluttered over her skin, leaving goosebumps on her goosebumps that still had not gone away from his kiss.

Wide awake now, she was surprised to see the world brightening outside her window with the first light of dawn and carefully slipped from Declan's embrace. Heaving a sigh, she walked into the bathroom and took a long, hot shower trying to clear her mind and get ready for the long day ahead. Throwing on a hoodie and a pair of leggings, she made her way down to the kitchen, following the sweet smell of cinnamon and sugar.

"Good mornin', you beautiful ray of sunshine!" Wyatt said in a singsong voice that was slightly off-key but made her smile all the same.

"G'mornin' to you, frilly floral apron man," Lorelei sang back to him as she poured herself some coffee.

"Declan probably won't be up today," he said from his post in front of the stove. He was making stacks of French toast and a mountain of bacon this morning, thanks to Garridan restocking the previous afternoon.

"I know. I was outside when he took off last night. I don't think he knew I was out on the balcony." She sipped her coffee, feeling as if she had witnessed something she should not have.

"Well, that's probably 'cause we can't actually scent you very well," Wyatt explained over his shoulder.

"And that's odd?" she asked, a bit confused.

"Yeah, real odd. Every species has a distinct scent, but yours is pretty faint compared to other Witches we've met." He sprinkled more cinnamon and sugar over a fresh stack of toast with a shrug of his shoulders.

"Could it be that Lorelei is a rare one herself?" Garridan said as he walked from his room to the left of the kitchen, wearing only a pair of plaid sleep pants.

"What d'you mean?" she and Wyatt asked in unison.

"Well, unless you've intentionally masked your scent." She shook her head when he looked at her. "It's quite possible that you're a Chimera. As far as I know, they're the only, and I say this with love, mutant species who don't produce a strong scent if they do at all." He pulled his mug from the cabinet and poured himself some coffee.

"What the hell's a Chimera?" Wyatt asked, sliding a plate over to her.

"They're pretty rare, but they're supernaturals who're born with only half of their genetics. Well, no. They have all of their genetics and are complete, but there's another completely blank side, like a mirror image. Any species that can turn another has the potential to fill in those blanks," she explained it the best she could without getting too technical or complicated.

"So lemme get this straight. You're sayin' that if- oh I dunno- Declan marked you? You'd become a witchy-wolfy hybrid?" he asked, smacking Garridan's hand with the fork he was using when the Delta reached for a plate stacked with toast.

"Yes. I would need to get some testin' done to make sure, though. I guess the pack hospital could do a genetic workup on me?" Wyatt glanced over his shoulder, nodding hesitantly.

"Wait, do you *want* Declan to mark you?" he asked, only mildly surprised, and she shrugged, focusing intently on her breakfast. "Well, I think you'd be a badass wolf," he added, making a smile tug at her lips.

Chapter 20

A few days later, Lorelei quietly made her way up the stairs to Declan's room to check on him. He had been sleeping for twelve or more hours every night since he started taking the tonic Garridan made him. So far, the nightmares had subsided and it seemed he did not have nearly as much trouble falling asleep now. Though she missed his presence, Lorelei was just happy that he was finally getting the rest that he needed. It was astonishing to think that he had gone nearly three years without a decent night's sleep and remained able to function normally. Werewolves had three basic needs that all species relied on; food, rest, and sex. Only their consumption of each was elevated to the highest degree, and he had been denied all three while being housed in Saint Thaddeus. She honestly did not know how he, an Alpha, survived.

Lorelei could hear noises through the door of the bedroom as she approached, and she twisted the knob. Easing it open just enough to poke her head in, she sucked in a breath when her eyes fell on the man lying tangled in a flat sheet on his side, facing away from her. The corner of the rumpled material just covered his bare backside. Biting her bottom lip, she padded over to the bedside, admiring the muscles of his back, and shook his shoulder gently.

"Declan?" Lorelei whispered loudly. He turned toward her voice, rolling onto his back and she suddenly realized what all his groaning was about. The sheet momentarily bulged with his erection before sliding away as he drew one knee up along the bed, exposing his shaft to her in all its glory.

"Lore…" His words were a mumbled whisper, and she saw his cock twitch just before her eyes snapped up, finding him still sleeping soundly. She felt the wetness pooling between her thighs seeping through her athletic shorts at the thought of Declan having an erotic dream about her.

"I can smell your arousal, darlin'." The words growled from him deep and gravelly, making the air stall in her lungs, and he slowly opened his eyes to gaze up at her.

"What're you gonna do about it?" she shot back, breathless with her bold words, and honestly terrified he might reject her again. But she was so tired of fighting this. So, done with denying herself, and him, what they wanted. Declan's eyes flashed crimson at the challenge, and in the next instant, she found herself pinned beneath his hard body.

"You're sure about this?" His voice was a rough whisper as he stared down at her with an intensity that made her stomach flip.

"Yes." Her breathless reply was all she could manage as she gripped the hem of her hoodie, and lifted the material over her head. Declan swallowed hard, eyes glazing like he was in a trance as he cupped her breasts, teasing her tight buds with the callused pads of his thumbs. She gasped at the sensation, the pleasure shooting straight to her throbbing core and Lorelei delved her fingers through his hair, urging him closer as she arched against him. She did not think it was possible to be any more turned on than she already was, but when he leaned down and suckled her nipples, she felt the wetness between her thighs trickle from her in anticipation. Lorelei panted, moaning and writhing against his mouth as he moved from one nipple to the other, swirling his tongue around the tight peaks.

"Declan, please," she gasped, begging. She felt as if she would lose her mind if he continued to tease her like this.

Declan released her nipple with a soft pop, a sinful grin pulling up the corners of his perfect lips. Lorelei stared as he slowly kissed his way down her ribcage, hands trailing down her sides, teasing and caressing. He planted an open mouth kiss against her hip that had her legs parting with a moan as if on command. When he hooked his fingers in the waistband of her shorts, Declan paused for a long moment, and she gazed down into his crimson eyes.

"Tell me to stop, or I won't be able to." Declan's voice was hoarse as he looked up at her, pupils dilated. She wondered how she must look to him with her auburn curls loose from her hair tie, disheveled around her, flushed skin, and her breasts rising and falling with her heavy breaths.

Lorelei gave him an answer by lifting her hips, her sex a hairbreadth from his nose as she lay her hands over his, and pushed her shorts down. An almost feral growl ripped from his chest as he snatched the shorts from her legs, and leaned close inhaling her scent as she opened herself for him again. Slipping his hands around the tops of her thighs Declan yanked her to his mouth, tongue laving viciously over her clit.

Lorelei saw stars as the air was punched from her lungs at the overwhelming pleasure she felt as he devoured her like a man starved. Over her moans of pleasure, she could hear soft grunts of satisfaction coming from him as he lashed her one moment, and softly licked and kissed her the next. Hands gripping the sheets beneath her, Lorelei arched off of the bed when he released his hold on one of her hips. Declan groaned against her sensitive skin as he slid two fingers into her, praising the tightness of her core. With every stroke,

Lorelei moaned louder, her body clenching around his invading fingers while her hips undulated against him.

Declan's groan vibrated along the sensitive bundle of nerves, and a wanton cry of pleasure pulled from her lips as she pressed into the onslaught of his tongue and fingering. All too quickly she felt her orgasm building low in her belly and she tried to pull away, needing to prolong the ecstasy. A growl rumbled from deep in Declan's chest and the hand still gripping her thigh snaked across her body as he wrapped his arm around her hips, anchoring her to his mouth. Declan increased his speed, hooking into her g-spot just as her orgasm exploded, gushing around his fingers. Lorelei's voice cracked as she crashed over the edge, hips bucking roughly against him. Muscles tense and shaking from the intensity of her climax, she pushed at the iron band of his arm around her waist. Lifting his head from between her thighs, Declan peered up at her while she fought weakly against the intense pleasure. He slowed the pace of his fingers, still buried deep, massaging over her pleasure point.

"Never pull away from me when I've got my mouth on you," he said, and she gazed down at him with hooded eyes. Lorelei could only nod, and he gave her a crooked grin, his skin glistening from the tip of his nose to his scruff-covered chin, before dipping his head back between her legs.

Declan withdrew his fingers from her sex completely before slipping slowly back in while he tongued her clit with languid strokes. She slid her fingers lazily through his hair, guiding him as she lifted herself on one elbow. Her head fell back, each breath a mewling moan as every slow swipe of his tongue brought her pleasure beyond anything she had ever experienced. All too quickly, Lorelei felt another orgasm blooming, and she could not decide if she wanted to clamp her legs shut or part them further. Before she could make up her mind, Declan gave her bud a final open mouth kiss and withdrew his fingers. She let out a sound of frustration and lifted her head to glare at him as he prowled up her body.

When he hovered above her, he dragged a hand over her breast, teasing her nipple before his fingers wrapped around the column of her throat, both gentle and firm. Dipping his head, he captured her lips in a deliciously sensual kiss. Between the hand at her throat and the way his tongue danced over hers, a whole new level of arousal threatened to ignite the blood in her veins. She could taste herself on him and she laced her arms around his shoulders as he claimed her mouth, making her toes curl. Lorelei delighted in the growl rumbling up from his chest. She hiked one leg up over his hip and pressed him into her, his stiff erection cradled against the valley of her sex.

When he gently broke the kiss, Declan was panting and he braced his hands on either side of her, caging her body beneath his. Lorelei could see he was trying to calm the carnality threatening to break loose, and he gave a subtle, half-jerk of his head. The control barely clung to its tethers, close to severing, and she secretly wanted exactly that. She wanted him wild and savage. Needed him to take her. To claim her as his. Lorelei pressed her hips up against his at the thought, his length sliding tantalizingly against her core. Jaw clenched, the muscles bulging, Declan gazed down at her, and the desire in his eyes matched her flame.

"Lore. Tell me. We can stop." His voice was rough, and breathless as he struggled to maintain his control. She slid a hand to the back of his neck, and met him halfway in a soul-searing kiss, moaning in satisfaction when his hand fisted in her curls. He pulled his hips back, the head of his shaft nestling against her entrance as he awaited her answer.

"You." She gasped against his mouth with an intensity, surging him forward. Lorelei cried out as he buried himself deep inside her, filling and stretching her with a groan of pleasure.

"Yours. Mine," he rasped out as he slid out of her slowly. His body was taut, muscles straining as he clung to the control he had left. He leaned down and kissed her as he pushed back into her fully, moans tangling as their tongues clashed. Lorelei wrapped her arms around his shoulders pulling his chest to hers, and Declan lifted her, sitting back on his knees as the last shreds of his control snapped. Hands gripping her backside, he spread her open to him as he pistoned into her roughly, the predator within finally unleashed. Lorelei gasped against his lips as she bounced mercilessly against him; his thrusts morphed into pure primal need. Goosebumps erupted over her body as she let out gasping moans with each plunge of his cock, head falling back in pure ecstasy.

"Declan." His name groaned out of her, and she felt her body tensing.

"That's it, darlin', come for me." His voice was gravelly, and Lorelei unraveled at his words. Her hips bucked violently against him, nails digging into his shoulders as she let out a deafening scream.

"Look at me," Declan commanded, and as she lifted her head, her shimmering silver gaze locked on his. Their bodies came together in rough arousal-soaked slaps as he pounded into her, and a moment later, the intensity of his orgasm punched a ragged yell sounding part man, part beast from his lungs. Bodies shaking and slick with sweat, he leaned forward and captured her lips in a slow, rapturous kiss branding her completely, and she knew in her soul that it branded him too.

"Lore," Declan said a little while later as he idly trailed a hand along her back, leaving goosebumps on her tingling skin. "I wanna apologize for what I said to you the other day. There's no excuse for how I treated you." She lifted her head from his chest, peering up at him for a long moment, and nodded.

"Apology accepted," she said softly and pressed her lips to his. "But if you act like that again, you're gonna see *my* dark side." She was not surprised when she felt him harden against the thigh she draped over his hips.

"As much as I'd like to stay in bed with you all day, I've got to go work on the surveillance footage, and you need to sleep." Lorelei clambered off of his chest, and scooping up her leggings, sat on the edge of the bed to pull them on. She soon realized her mistake when Declan sat up and his hand snaked under her arm, cupping her mound. Unable, and unwilling to resist him, her head tipped back with a moan as his fingers gently circled her overly sensitive clit. She could not have fought her desire for him if she tried, and she realized that she did not want to anymore.

"Goddess, you're gorgeous. I could watch me pleasurin' you all day, darlin'." Moaning with each deliciously slick rub against the bundle of nerves, she turned her body slightly, and wrapped her fingers around his erection, pumping him in time with his swirling fingers.

They were soon panting, stealing kisses as they silently dared the other to come first, working each other up with barely controlled desire. The sounds of their mutual pleasure grew louder, echoing around the bedroom as their arousal morphed into a desperate, all-consuming need.

Declan's control finally snapped, and in a blink, he lifted Lorelei from the mattress and stood behind her, driving his cock into her core with such ferocity, that she came with his first thrust. He pulled her body flush against him while he continued to rub her clit with firm, intentional strokes. His free hand slid to her throat, holding her in place. Her hips bucked wildly against his punishing thrusts and she cried out as the wet sounds of their joined bodies only drove Declan harder and he slammed home with each thrust. Lorelei gasped for air as she felt her third orgasm building to a fever pitch when Declan tensed behind her, the distinct sound of his teeth snapping together near her shoulder as he unloaded deep in her core. A mixture of him and his beast filled the room with a guttural rumbling growl of pleasure as he relentlessly pulled one more orgasm from her. She gushed once again over his pulsing shaft, her muscles seizing from the intensity of her orgasm, and he helped her to ride it out. Holding her body upright when her knees gave out, the uncontrolled undulation of her hips forced her to thrust along his length.

Lorelei finally sucked air into her lungs and leaned her head against his shoulder, trying to catch her breath. She slipped her fingers up the back of his neck and into his hair, deliriously content. Declan placed soft kisses against her neck as large hands roamed her body leisurely, fondling and caressing every inch of her. Nothing had ever felt so right as it did in this moment. Here with Declan, she was where she was meant to be. She was home.

"I almost marked you, again," he murmured against her shoulder when he eased them onto the edge of the bed, his fingers rubbing lazily over her tight nipples.

"You could have," she moaned quietly, leaning back against his chest, and Declan slowly lifted his head.

"Happy as that makes me to hear you say it, this is somethin' we need to discuss, Lore. It's permanent, and there's no going back once it's done." He kissed her skin softly where he would bite her to make his claim. She shivered as they sat joined in contented silence for several minutes.

"I don't need to discuss it, Declan. I want this. With you," she said, feeling his shaft stiffen deep in her core. His calloused hand cupped her chin and gently urged her to turn to him. Though his expression was serious, desire smoldered in his crimson eyes.

"We will discuss it. It's more than just your decision we need to talk about." Declan kissed her then, effectively silencing any protest she thought to voice.

"Garridan thinks I might be a Chimera," she said when they came up for air. Lorelei stood slowly and they both groaned with pleasure and loss as his cock slipped heavily from her. Ambling to the bathroom on trembling legs, she pulled her sex-mussed curls into a messy bun with an elastic from around her wrist.

"Really? How can you find out for sure if you are?" he asked as he leaned back on his elbows.

"Genetic testin'. I'm gonna call the pack hospital and see if I can get in this week. Whatever the results are though, I've made my decision." She padded over to him and leaned down to give him a long, languid kiss that she knew teased them both.

Chapter 21

Two days later, Lorelei pulled into the parking garage of Crescent Ridge Memorial Hospital and made her way into the state-of-the-art building, following the signs pointing her to the on-site laboratory. After speaking with the receptionist and filling out the necessary paperwork, she took a seat in the waiting area, anxiously bouncing her knee. Her phone buzzed just as a nurse stepped into the small lobby, calling her name. Silencing the call, she followed the woman down a short hallway to a collection of small cubicles and sat in the chair the nurse gestured to while reading off the order form.

"Name and date of birth?" The nurse asked, and Lorelei told her the information as the woman tied a tourniquet around her arm and felt for a vein. "So, the only test that's been ordered is to check you for Chimerism. We'll have the results in about thirty minutes, if you'd like to wait?" She swallowed hard and nodded, smiling as she thanked the nurse.

She barely felt the needle stick and watched as the small vial filled halfway with blood. The nurse was quick and efficient as she released the tight elastic band from around her bicep, removed the needle tossed it into a Sharps container, and pressed a cotton ball to the tiny puncture mark. A length of self-adhesive bandage was wrapped around her elbow, and she was pointed to another waiting area as the nurse hurried off with the blood sample.

The thirty-minute drive back home seemed to take forever and Lorelei kept glancing over at the envelope that contained her test results. She had not looked at them yet, convincing herself that she wanted to read them with Declan. Parking around by the back door, she trudged into the house and headed straight for the basement. As she was booting up her laptop, her phone buzzed again.

"Hi, Nana," she said as she answered the call.

"Hello, Sunflower! How're you doin'?" Her grandmother's slightly shaky voice blasted through the speaker and she quickly lowered the volume. Apparently, their last conversation had long been forgiven.

"I'm great. How're you and Mama?"

"Oh, I'm doin' all right, but you know your mother. Nutty as a squirrel's nest."

"Nana…" Lorelei warned.

"All right, I'm sorry, Sunflower. Truth be told, she's doin' pretty well right now. She's done some paintin' the last few weeks, this time of Blue Ridge, and the lake near the house. I believe she's working on another wind chime at the moment. Silly girl took all my damn spoons, too." Lorelei chuckled, her heart suddenly homesick for the little cabin tucked away from the world against the Blue Ridge Mountain range.

"Nana, just let her have the spoons, you can get new ones," she said and the old woman scoffed.

"I swear if I could undo the past-"

"We can't. Mama found that out the hard way." Lorelei cut her off, voice hard.

"Yes, Sunflower, I know. I only meant if there was a safer way," the old woman insisted, trying to backpedal.

"Well, there's not. So, can we please stop bringin' it up, and move on with our lives?" she demanded, glaring at the laptop screen.

"Lorelei, what's goin' on?" Nana asked softly.

"Nothin'. Everything's fine, but every time we talk you wanna dredge up the past in some way, and I have enough to think about without being forced down a memory lane that nearly killed me and landed me in a fuckin' psych ward for six months." She rarely snapped at her grandmother, and though she felt bad, she did not regret what she said because it was true. The elderly woman always found a way to bring up the past no matter what the conversation topic happened to be.

"Lorelei Katherin McCann, don't you think for one moment that I ever intentionally bring up what Markus and those me-"

"I gotta go. Bye, Nana." She hung up the phone and propped her elbows on the tabletop, dropping her head into her hands. Several minutes passed by as she just sat and breathed through the anxiety starting to build in her chest.

"Lorelei, you down here already?" Wyatt called from the doorway, and she jerked her head up in surprise, watching his booted feet march down the stairs.

"Yeah. Haven't been here long though," she said loudly, worried he might have heard the conversation with her grandmother.

"How'd the test go?" he asked when he dropped from the last step, and she shrugged, noticing the way he glanced at her with concern. He had heard everything.

"I haven't looked at the results yet. I wanted to wait for Declan," she said almost sheepishly.

"Fair enough. Nervous?" Wyatt ambled around one of the tables and picked several pages up, looking back and forth from the documents to the timeline wall.

"A bit, yeah." The video popped up on her screen and opened to the last frame she had been working on, her stomach clenched when she recognized Declan and Wyatt lying on the ground near the middle of the screen. There was a slight gap surrounding them and three others, creating an irregular circle grouping them separately from the other pack members. She knew the three figures were Alaric, Mordecai, and Alora, and she took note of how they were lying. Declan was furthest to the left on his side, facing toward his family. He was next to his uncle who lay face down in the grass, and Wyatt beside him halfway on his stomach and side. Mordecai lay to the right of his nephew on his stomach, head toward his son, and Alora lay half-curled on her side, the skirt of her dress still billowing above her in the frame. Dread settled in her stomach while she gently broke the dark magic weaving throughout the footage, knowing that the scene was only going to get much, much worse.

A few hours later, Lorelei sat alone in the basement while Declan still caught up on some much-needed sleep upstairs. Wyatt had left to go pick up Garridan and grab lunch for all of them about an hour before. As she worked through the next several frames, a pair of slender, tanned legs slowly walked onto the screen. Pulling the magic, she tapped to the next frame, eyes flitting over the screen and she tried to quickly remove the spell as the figure stepped further into the view of the camera. As she moved to the next frame, she clenched her jaw when she realized their face was obscured by the hood of a dark cloak.

"Shit," she hissed and leaned back in her chair, staring at the screen. Sighing, her cheeks puffing out with force, she tapped over to the next frame and saw Cormac's striking hair come into the frame. A wave of revulsion swept through her as she broke through the magic. Over the next several frames, she saw the man walk over to Declan, and kneel to hover over him. More frames restored, she watched in horror as Cormac stood over the late Luna and brought his foot down on her upturned face. The details the Omega told her about the night of the massacre drifted through her mind, *"He crushed her skull clean to the back of her head with the heel of his boot, coming back later to 'have his way with her', so to speak."*

Another hour passed as she cleared away the dark magic, her anxiety mounting with each frame she cleared. She witnessed a massive Werewolf dismember Alaric, followed closely by Apollo removing the former Alpha's heart. There was a long break in the brutality until Cormac re-entered the frame placing a harrowing kick to Declan's abdomen, and then proceeded to attack him over and over again. Lorelei blinked back the tears threatening to spill down her cheeks as she watched the beating in agonizing slow motion.

Finally satisfied, Cormac's head turned in the direction of Declan's dead mother, and he sauntered over to her lifeless body. Though his back was to the camera there was no mistaking what he was doing, and Lorelei's stomach flipped over violently with nausea as the memories she barely held at bay flooded to the front of her mind. Feeling her panic rising, she shoved away from the desk and hurried up the stairs from the basement. As she shoved open the door, she nearly collided with Wyatt and Garridan who stopped short as she sidestepped around them without so much as a glance.

"You okay?" Wyatt asked as she breezed by.

"Fine." She did not look back as she strode through the kitchen, and out onto the back porch. Memories of a past she longed to forget invaded her senses as she paced back and forth along the plank flooring. Lorelei closed her eyes and tried to breathe through the flashbacks. The fear she still felt down to her bones, etched forever on her soul. Their faces flashed behind her closed eyelids and her skin crawled as if their hands were still touching her body. Fondling and caressing, invading and violating. Her eyes popped open, blazing with liquid silver as the memories collided and swirled.

She could still smell their hot breath, soured with the rank stench of the cheap beer they had been drinking all day and night. Still remembered the searing pain she felt as they forced themselves on her over and over again as she screamed for help. How they struck her when she called out for her mother, clammy hands covering her mouth as she sobbed. Could still feel their disgusting lips brushing her ear as they tried to convince her she would enjoy it if she just relaxed and calmed down. The fear and panic twisted through her and she cradled her head in her hands, bending over at the waist. She vaguely heard Declan calling her name as rough hands settled on her shoulders and she lashed out in her terror. Firing a ball of magical energy from her open palm, she sent her assailant flying across the back porch and out onto the grassy lawn beyond.

"Lorelei, you're safe! It's Declan!" His shout broke through the fog of her flashback and she shook her head, blinking rapidly as she focused on him. Wyatt must have told him about the words she would speak to him during his nightmares.

Declan clambered back up the steps, slumped to one side with an arm wrapped around his torso. Face contorted in a grimace of pain, she could hear the distinct sound of bones popping beneath his skin. He straightened a moment later with a sigh of relief, and Lorelei realized she had broken his ribs when she attacked him. She glanced at Wyatt and Garridan, looking at her with a mixture of surprise and concern.

"You're safe, darlin'," Declan said softly and cupped her face in his hands as he came to stand in front of her. "What's goin' on?" he asked her gently, leaning down to look her in the eye.

"I'm so sorry," she said, her voice trembling. "I thought you were–I thought they…" Lorelei took a deep shuddering breath and closed her eyes, hot tears spilling down her cheeks. Without a word, Declan gathered her in his arms as she broke down in front of all three of them, her sobs echoing around them through the trees.

"I was raped," Lorelei blurted out sometime later, grimacing at the bluntness of her confession. Declan tensed, his arms tightening around her, and his heavy breaths came out in a rumbling growl as he tried to calm the beast within him. To the side of them, Wyatt and Garridan's growls merged with Declan's, all matching in their ferocity at her admission.

"Go on, darlin', I've got you," he said gently after several moments, though there was a strain to his voice.

"I was thirteen. My mom had a boyfriend named Markus at the time, and one night he and a couple of his buddies were at our house. Mama was there too, but she'd gotten blackout drunk from drinkin' most of the day with them. Well, they started wonderin' what it'd be like to fuck a little girl as pretty as me, at least, that's what they said after they'd snuck into my bedroom. I screamed for help, begged them to stop, and prayed to the Lunar Goddess to save me. No one came though." Her voice broke at the reminder of the abandonment she felt at that moment. "They took turns over and over again, and would hit me. Cover my nose and mouth to shut me up when they got tired of me beggin'. I eventually lost my voice from screamin' and passed out a couple of times from not bein' able to breathe. They tried to convince me that I'd enjoy it if I just relaxed. Said that if I just let them take care of my sweet little pus-"

"Stop!" Declan said loudly, interrupting her. Wyatt and Garridan snarled wildly behind her, and she jumped at the sudden sound, having forgotten they were there. "Please stop, Lore," he said again, his voice a hoarse whisper. Lorelei tipped her head up to him, tears rolling down her cheeks, and she saw that his eyes were closed tightly, and a muscle ticked in his jaw.

"I'm sorry. I-"

"You're sorry?" His eyes popped open as he tipped his crimson gaze down to her. "For what, darlin'? You did nothin' wrong." His large calloused hands cupped her cheeks.

"Where are they?" Garridan asked, and when she looked around her she saw three sets of vibrant, angry eyes. Crimson, icy blue, and fiery orange gazes trained on her, beasts barely contained in their rage.

"Dead," she said flatly, "I killed them after I'd healed enough to walk. It's the only time in my life I've used dark magic." Declan kissed her forehead and pulled her tight against his chest.

"Goddess, I was so rough with you," he exclaimed suddenly, and she swore her cheeks would burst into flames. Wyatt and Garridan's booted feet quickly retreated into the house, and Lorelei waited until the door was firmly closed before she spoke.

"Declan, I like it when you're rough. There's a chasm of differences between it being pleasurable with you, and it bein' a violent assault from three scumbags." She felt him relax at her words, but she still worried about how he felt about her.

"I'm not sure if I would have ever told you if this hadn't happened today. I didn't want you to think differently of me. To see me as damaged or made of glass." She did not look at him when he held her at arm's length.

"I could never see you as anything other than an angel and a warrior, Lorelei. You saved me from a living hell, you've survived one of the worst experiences anyone could have, and you're still here." His brows furrowed at her mirthless laugh. She had already told him this much.

"I tried to kill myself when I was sixteen, and it landed me in a psych facility for six months. The therapies helped me, sure, but I'll always be a rape victim. I'll always carry that with me. I'm not a warrior, not strong. If I were, this wouldn't have happened today." Her anger was not directed at him. She was angry with *herself*. Angry at the three whose bones could be found buried in the Shenandoah Valley. Angry for the opportunities the bastards stole from her.

"You're angry," he said softly, and she stepped out of his embrace.

"Yes! Because I'm weak, Declan. I can't fight, I can't defend myself! If Cormac hadn't led me right to the target at the party, I'd've had to rely on fuckin' screamin' for help again! I'm angry for what those bastards took from me! I'm angry that… '" Her raised voice echoed around them as she stared at him, tears prickling her eyes again.

"That what?" he asked, gently encouraging her.

"That I'll never have children, Declan," she whispered as new tears slipped from her eyes. "I can never have a family because of how savagely those bastards hurt me." His eyes slowly closed, and she somehow knew he grieved with her. He pulled her against him again, and she wrapped her arms tight around his torso afraid that he would disappear now that he knew the whole truth.

"I'll train you," Declan said quietly after several minutes. Emotion clamped her throat closed painfully and all she could do was nod against his chest.

"You sent me flyin' fifty feet or more earlier, and snapped at least two ribs with one hit, Lore." She felt his chest thump gently as he chuckled, and she could not help but feel a bit proud of herself.

"I'm so sor–" Her words were cut off as Declan stepped back abruptly and leaned down to capture her lips. Emotions swirled in her chest, making her heart clench as tears pricked behind her closed eyelids. Despite knowing the truth about what happened, he still wanted her. Still kissed her like he was leaving his own personal brand on her lips, and he was.

He did not know it, but she fought from the moment they met to guard her heart from him. To resist the electric connection she felt when their skin touched. She failed, and she had never been happier too. Butterflies erupted in her stomach at the thought, and she knew, without a doubt, that she had fallen in love with Declan Wolfe.

Chapter 22

"Again," Declan commanded, earning a groan from Wyatt as he dropped from the dock railing.

"Goddess be with you," Garridan said sympathetically, wringing out his soaking wet shirt. It took every ounce of restraint Declan possessed to not tackle his cousin when he leapt for Lorelei. He did not know how she managed to track the man running toward her at supernatural speed, but her magic caught him mid-jump. He hung suspended for a moment before a wall of energy slammed into the Beta and sent him sailing out over the water. Declan schooled his features, trying not to laugh when his cousin landed gracelessly, limbs flailing, nearly one hundred feet out in the icy lake. They had been working with Lorelei most of the morning on defensive techniques and maneuvers. Her only goal was to keep him, Wyatt, and Garridan as far away from her as possible. They were taking turns as her living targets, giving her something tangible to focus on.

"You okay?" Lorelei called across the water, and his cousin gave her a thumbs up. He knew the man had a few broken bones. They all had this morning. Declan leaned over the rail, holding out a hand to Wyatt as he neared the dock. Gripping his cousin under the bicep, he and Garridan hauled him back onto the deck.

"Your turn, cousin," A wet and freezing hand slapped against his chest, making his breath hiss through his teeth.

"This'll be the last round," he said as he stepped in front of Lorelei, "but I'm fightin' back." He lunged without warning, earning shouts from the other two men sitting on the sidelines. Razor sharp claws erupted from his nail beds as he swiped at Lorelei. Her eyes blazed silver as her magic erupted around her, forming a wall of energy to block his attack. His nails glanced off of the barrier near her shoulder, sending a ripple through the warbling magic. Electric tingles shot from his fingertips to his shoulder causing a shiver to snake along his spine.

"Woah! Seriously, Declan?" She looked up at him, though the invisible shield did not falter.

"Don't hold back," he told her, lunging again. A ball of energy collided with his abdomen, knocking the wind out of him. Staggering back several steps, Declan dropped to one knee, gasping for breath, his hand braced on the deck.

"This isn't a good idea," she said, hurrying over to him and placing a hand on his shoulder.

"Lore, don't-" Wyatt's warning came too late as Declan whipped his leg out in a low spinning kick knocking Lorelei's feet out from under her. He caught her just before she hit the rough planks, giving her a crooked smile.

"Never let your guard down in a fight, darlin'," he instructed, and she nodded. Her attack was so quick he had no time to react before he was struck under the chin, the force snapping his head back with a grunt. Lorelei scrambled from his arms, and backed away, eyeing him warily. Declan wiped the back of his hand over his lips when he felt the trickle of blood ooze from the corner of his mouth.

"Good girl," he smiled broadly as his eyes shifted crimson and rose to his feet, "don't hold back." The order was soft but firm as he went on the offensive again. Lorelei blocked and dodged, huffing with exertion. He was continuously checked by her shield no matter what he did, pulling his punches when he was unsure if she would block him in time. She was quick though and always managed to place a barrier of magic between them.

"Don't hold back, Lorelei! Attack me!" Declan said loudly, panting now.

"I'm not!" she grated through clenched teeth as she sent out a blast of magic, and he felt the bones shatter in the arm he lifted to shield himself, forcing him to take a step back. Pushing through the pain, he circled her, allowing his body to heal before he dove for her again.

"You are!" he yelled, slamming his elbow against the solid barrier. The impact caused her to stumble, and her anger only made her eyes shine brighter.

"I. Am. Not!" she screamed, and something shifted in her magic. He *felt* it shift, wild and dangerous. The energy crackled along his skin, raising the hair on his arms. Then it solidified, morphing into semi-translucent projectiles, their ends narrowing to lethal points. They hung suspended in the air, shimmering faintly as Declan was lifted from the planks and thrown across the dock. A roar of pain ripped from his chest as the slender missiles slammed into his body, nailing him to the shingled wall of the boathouse. The attack took a matter of seconds, and he smiled faintly seeing the spikes jutting crudely from his body. There was one in each shoulder and near both wrists, his thighs were skewered clean through, and one just off center in his abdomen. His eyes found hers, and he smiled down at her, pride making his chest tighten.

"That's my girl," he growled softly, holding her gaze as searing pain began to radiate from his wounds. The silver faded from her eyes as she stared at him in horror, tears threatening to spill over onto her cheeks. Wyatt and Garridan let out a string of curses as they rushed over to him, making to remove the spikes, but in a blink, they were gone. Blood flowed freely from the gaping wounds as he dropped to the deck with a pained groan.

"I'm so sorry–" Lorelei covered her mouth with her hands as a quiet sob spilled from her.

"You have nothin' to be sorry about," he said, clambering to his feet, eyes returning to normal. "I knew you would possibly draw blood if I pushed you."

"You're a damned fool, Declan Wolfe," Lorelei breathed, "What if I'd killed you?" She looked at him like he was crazy when he chuckled softly, shaking his head.

"You wouldn't have, darlin'. Even in your frustration, your anger, *you* were still in control." He pointed a bloody finger at her. "You may not have noticed, but I did. When you formed those spikes, they were all aimed directly at my chest, but look where they hit." He pointed to the spots that were now healed over.

"She's right, Dec. One slip-up and you'd've been dead," Wyatt said, backhanding his newly healed shoulder.

"It was worth the risk. She needed to know what she was capable of," Declan said, daring his cousin to argue as he cut his eyes to him. Movement in his peripheral caught his attention, and he turned toward Lorelei just in time to feel the hard, stinging slap she lashed across his cheek. The crack of her palm connecting with his face echoed across the smooth surface of the lake and he felt the inside of his cheek split open. She used her magic to intensify the strike.

'*That was deserved,*' the beast within huffed with approval.

"Don't you *ever* do anything that fucking stupid again!" Tears streaked down her cheeks as she glared at him. Everything around them seemed to still, holding its breath after Lorelei gave him the command. Even Wyatt and Garridan stood immobile, only their eyes shifted as they looked on. Declan walked over to the railing and leaned over to scoop up a handful of water, rinsing the blood from his mouth. He turned to face the angry Witch and gave her a soft, lopsided smile.

"I can't promise I'll *never* do anything stupid, but I'll do my best," he nodded, reaching out for her. Lorelei stepped into his embrace with a heavy sigh and leaned into him, resting her forehead against his chest.

"From now on, I practice with non-livin' targets," she said, wrapping her arms around his torso.

"I'm proud of you," Declan said as he and Lorelei shuffled into his bedroom later that afternoon. She insisted on training until summoning the spikes became second nature to her, and she could now form them suspended or in her hands. Once she had mastered both variations, they moved on to target practice, with him, Wyatt, and Garridan tossing rocks, pine cones, and chunks of wood into the air. The woman had deadly aim, and he knew that she would be a walking force of nature the more she practiced.

"I'm proud of myself too. I've never used my magic in that way. Never knew I *could*," she said, following him into the bathroom. Declan smiled over his shoulder as he turned on the shower. He could already see her confidence growing, a new light shining in her beautiful eyes.

"You should be. I'm surprised that you were never trained." He stripped out of his ruined clothes and tossed them in the sink to throw away later. Declan saw the ghosts of her past flicker in her eyes as he stepped in front of her, and lifted his hands to smooth away her wild curls.

"I wish I had been," she said softly, and his heart clenched in his chest knowing exactly where her mind had taken her. "Thank you."

"For what, darlin'?" he asked with a soft smile, lifting her shirt over her head. She braced her hands on his shoulders as he knelt to tug off her leggings, and stepped free of the material. Declan gazed up at her, his calloused hands sliding up the backs of her smooth thighs.

"For pushin' me today." Lorelei stared down at him, goosebumps forming over her skin. Declan watched her body respond to his touch, his shaft instantly hard, and he reigned in his control on a tight leash.

"Sometimes, we all need a little nudge." Leaning forward, he planted an open mouth kiss on her hip and stood. Taking her hand, they stepped into the large shower stall together where they washed the blood and sweat from each other before Declan claimed her body over and over again.

The next few days were filled with training sessions, and combing through the evidence his father and uncle collected. Declan was glad to see Lorelei managing the surveillance footage with little issue now. She had told him that a phone call from her grandmother combined with what she had seen on the video set off her flashback. He begged her to tell him, but she had refused, only promising that she would once the evidence was turned over to Elder Caine.

Declan blinked, shaking his head when he realized Lorelei was speaking as she marched down to the basement, phone clutched in her hand.

"What?" he asked, looking up from the document he leaned over as she alighted from the stairs.

"Cormac's invited us to the Halloween party at the packhouse tonight." She held out her phone as he stalked over. He read the text that came in a moment before from the unsaved number, a low growl rumbling from him.

'Hello, little witch. There will be a celebration at the mansion tonight in honor of All Hallow's Eve. I do hope you

and Declan will join us for the festivities. Costumes are strongly encouraged.'

"How the hell did he get your number?" he fumed, handing the device back to her.

"He could have looked me up on the internet. A small fee is the only thing keepin' your information private." His eyes shifted to crimson at her words.

"Wasn't either of you, was it?" Declan cut a glare to Wyatt and Garridan and both men gave him a reproachful look.

"C'mon, Dec, really?"

"Are you serious?"

Their incredulous responses overlapped as they brushed him off and went back to their stacks of documents. He knew that they would never betray her, or him for that matter, but still had to ask for his peace of mind. Though he had not been there long, his time in the asylum forced him to question everything. This, Lorelei explained, stemmed from his questions, and the letters he had written, never being answered. From not knowing why he was there, or what he had done to be sent away and forgotten.

"Well, however, he got it, I don't like it," Declan grumbled, looking back down at Lorelei.

"Do we have to go?" she asked softly, and he shook his head, crossing his arms.

"No. But… It might give us a chance to poke around a bit. The Halloween parties have always been held out in the forest, so the mansion should be fairly empty. If Cormac's kept in line with that tradition, that is," he said, mind mulling over the possibilities.

"He has," Garridan assured, adding a file to the timeline wall.

"Wyatt," Declan said firmly, "You're on the mansion. Garridan, you'll be with us at the party. Keep a distance though. We don't want Cormac and Apollo to realize you're with us."

Chapter 23

The sun just set when Declan parked beside the front steps of the mansion with Wyatt curled up in the cargo space of the Wagoneer. Lorelei placed a simple charm on his cousin to hide his scent before leaving the lake house. They could not risk him being scented out by Apollo or Cormac, or any guards that may be roaming the estate. Garridan arrived hours ago and kept them in the loop of what Cormac and his father were up to. So far, the father and son berated a few members over decorations, seating arrangements, and a jack-o-lantern that they decided looked too 'happy'. Declan parked near the front steps of the mansion as Lorelei read the newest message aloud. Apparently, they were screaming about the makeshift throne that was erected at the party, causing Declan to roll his eyes. Without turning, he told Wyatt they were near the front door and stepped from the vehicle.

Walking around the Wagoneer, his gaze devoured the vision that stood on the passenger side waiting for him. She wore a sleeveless jade green overdress of a thick linen material hanging just to her knees. Wide straps laid over her shoulders exposing the graceful curve of her throat before dropping into a square neckline. Leather string lacing ran from the hem of the bodice and over her breasts, continuing down the length of the skirt. Her gorgeous auburn hair hung loose down her back, and she wore her brown suede slouchy boots to complete the outfit.

"Have I told you yet how stunnin' you are?" he asked as he slipped a hand to her waist and captured her mouth before she could respond. Lorelei moaned softly against his lips, making his shaft harden instantly. Groaning as he remembered where they were, Declan gently pulled away, reigning in his desire before he threw her in the nearby bushes and fucked her senseless.

"You look great too," she said with a smile. He had foregone a costume, and instead wore a dark heather gray button up, left undone, over a black tee shirt, faded acid wash blue jeans, and his old battle-scarred combat boots. His hair was as unruly as ever and there was a fair amount of stubble covering his cheeks.

"Let's get this over with, darlin'." He held out his hand, skin tingling when she laced her fingers with his and led her across the lawn toward a lantern-lit path. Lights of all different colors strobed from somewhere overhead, and the thumping bass of music could be heard in the distance. Along the trail, there were decorations scattered along in various macabre displays with the occasional tarp-wrapped body hanging from the branches above. Large spider egg sacks made of fake webbing littered the ground as they rounded a bend, stepping under a massive tarantula serving as the entryway into the clearing beyond.

A hundred or more Rogues crowded the center of the space, dancing, and drinking while heavy rock music blasted from speakers hidden somewhere in the trees. Beside him, Lorelei tilted her head side to side and rolled her shoulders when the next song kicked off, the bass vibrating the ground beneath their feet. She huffed out a breath and Declan could see that her eyes shifted to silver, making him frown down at her in concern.

"What's wrong?" he asked, shouting over the music.

"There's so much energy here. The music, the people." Lorelei glanced around at the crowd that was now jumping up and down in a frenzy.

"What's that mean, Lore?" Declan leaned closer to her when she stood on her tiptoes, hand grasping his shoulder.

"I'll have to cast soon." His eyes met hers and he nodded seeing the mild fear shining in her silver orbs. He did not need to ask what would happen if she took in too much energy, the look on her face told him it was not anything good.

"We'll figure it out, darlin'." She mouthed the words 'I know', and he squeezed her hand gently. They stared out at the dancefloor until the next song kicked off with a slow, seductive beat, and Declan looked down at her with a sly smile.

"What?" Lorelei said, grinning. Keeping his eyes on her, he tugged her into the sea of writhing bodies. He stopped near the edge of the crowd and pulled her body flush against him, dipping his head to capture her lips. Declan smiled against her mouth as her arms laced around his shoulders, and they began to sway to the music, singing the lyrics in between kisses. Lorelei pulled back and stared at him with a mix of surprise and arousal. It was a little-known fact that he could sing, and though he was far from being stadium-worthy, he could carry a tune well enough.

"Y'know, if Alpha doesn't work out for you, you might consider rockstar," she said loudly over the music. He tipped his head back, laughing, and even over the pulsing speakers, Declan could hear her heart pounding in her chest.

"I'm not that good, darlin'," he said as the song came to an end.

"Then you'll just have to be my rockstar in your time off." Her coy smile had him hardening against her, and he pressed his hips against hers, making her gasp. Lorelei tightened her arms around his neck, drawing him in closer, and they danced the next several songs pressed against each other, stealing kisses and whispering their desires in each other's ear. Neither of them cared if the Rogues could hear them.

The music suddenly cut out mid-song, and Declan lifted his eyes, peering around at the confused crowd. At the back of the clearing, he spotted the raised dais that Garridan mentioned. Cormac was lounging on the blackened throne, his hand raised high in the air. He wore all black and donned a half mask for the festivities. Declan glared as the false Alpha stood and descended an absurd number of steps ending at the edge of the partygoers. The Rogues parted, leaving Cormac a direct path to where he and Lorelei stood. As his former friend drew nearer, the mask he wore became more distinguished. It was the face of a demon cast in burnished gold, splattered with red paint over one side, and large black ram horns curling over the top of his head.

'*Appropriate,*' his wolf huffed, followed by a low growl. Declan agreed.

"I am exultant that you could make it tonight," Cormac said, coming to a stop beside them. "Though I am a little disappointed you chose to not dress up, Declan." His mouth pulled down into a mocking pout. "I believe there's a clown suit lying around somewhere if you wish to partake." The man sneered from behind his mask, making Declan laugh aloud at the irony of his insult.

"I don't think I could play the part of court jester better than you have for the last two years, Cormac." Declan's grinning remark caused the other man's eyes to shift with a soft snarl.

"Yes, well, I suppose that would make you the executioner then." The comeback only made his smile twist from the darkness within him. Images of all the ways he wished to inflict pain on the man swirled to life in devastating detail within his mind.

"Would you like to find out, *Alpha*?" Declan's tone was lethal, eyes crimson in a blink, and he felt Lorelei shiver next to him. Fear flashed in that sickly green gaze before they returned to their normal hazel, his inner wolf having tucked his tail and run at the challenge.

"Actually, I intended to invite Doctor McCann to join me for a drink. I have something rather important I'd like to discuss with her." He was about to protest when movement over Cormac's shoulder caught his eye. The crowd all turned to look in their direction and a myriad of glowing eyes focused on him. Glancing around, he clenched his jaw realizing the Rogues had surrounded them. He foolishly let his guard down while dancing with Lorelei, focusing only on her and her body pressed against his.

"It's fine," Lorelei said quietly to him, tightening her grip on his hand momentarily. The smile she plastered on did not quite meet her eyes as she stepped away from him. As the music resumed at a lower volume, Declan glanced over the Rogues still staring at him and his eyes shifted crimson once again. Baring his teeth, he took a step towards the edge of the haphazard circle they formed. The first several rows took an instinctive step back from him at the challenge, recognizing him as a true Alpha.

'They will abandon him,' his beast gruffed. Declan considered this and thought the wolf might be right though he was given no response.

"Don't fuckin' touch me." Lorelei's voice drifted back to him, snapping his attention to the drink table they were meandering away from. Cormac's hand hovered over the small of her back and a low growl rumbled from his chest. The cell phone in his front pocket buzzed at that moment and he dug it out, glancing down at the screen. Wyatt already managed to get into the office of the former Beta and was now in the process of combing through the late Luna's. Unfortunately, he had not found anything yet and Declan quickly tapped out a reply to check the Alpha's office, and Apollo and Cormac's bedrooms. If he did not find anything there, he was to leave the mansion and return to the Wagoneer.

Looking up from the phone, panic lanced through him when he found Lorelei and Cormac were nowhere to be seen. He frantically scanned the crowd around him looking for any sign of her in the sea of bodies dancing to the music. Movement across the clearing drew his attention and he saw a group of Rogues surrounding a lone figure. A snarl ripped from his throat when he realized it was Garridan. He was hemmed up near the throne by a swarm of pack members. The Delta's bright orange eyes flashed in the moonlight as he tried to shove his way through them. As Declan took a step in the direction of his friend, the Rogues around him suddenly converged, blocking the way.

"The forest!" Garridan shouted across the clearing, unable to break through the group surrounding him. Rage swelled in Declan's chest and his beast burst from within, shifting him from human to Werewolf in a matter of seconds. The rapid transformation tore his clothing to shreds and sent the Rogues scattering in all directions. Yelping and screaming, they cleared a path as he barreled across the field. As he neared the tree line, a terrified scream echoed around them, and Declan slid to a halt when Cormac's body ejected violently from the dense forest. Tumbling head over heels, the man careened through the crowd, knocking over several members until he came to a stop halfway across the large clearing.

Turning his head toward the sound of soft footfalls, Lorelei strode from the darkness, silver eyes practically glowing. Her arm was held out in front of her, fingers bent like she was clutching the Omega by the throat. He could see the faint warbling of her magic through the air as she strode toward Cormac's prone form. Huffing with pride, Declan lumbered over to her and caught the heavy scent of fresh blood. When she came to a stop near Cormac's feet, he prowled around her body, sniffing out the location of her injury.

"How fucking dare you try to force your mark on me!" she screamed as she pinned him to the ground. His jaws snapped together viciously when he saw the trail of blood seeping into the bodice of her dress, at her outraged words. White hot fury blinded him and he lunged, smashing a massive clawed hand over the bastard's chest. Declan was going to rip him apart limb by limb, and he wondered how long the Omega could last after being disemboweled. Hovering above the false Alpha, he snapped his jaws again, baring his teeth.

"Declan," Lorelei's voice cut through his fury as her fingers delved into the soft fur on his shoulder. His large head whipped around in her direction, crimson gaze softening as she peered up at him without fear, "He didn't."

Relief hit him like a tsunami and he reached for her, gathering her in his arms with a soft whine. Keeping her flush against him, Declan shifted back into his human form. The thought of Cormac marking her made him want to vomit, and the knowledge that she could be a

Chimera on top of it only amplified the queasiness rolling in his stomach. The only comfort that he could glean from the moment was that they trained with her to wield her magic. Her arms wrapped tightly around his naked torso, and he heard her take a deep, steadying breath.

"I'm so sorry, darlin'," he whispered, kissing her forehead. Lifting a hand to move her blood-soaked curls aside, Declan was surprised when his fingertips brushed against a barrier of magic. For only a moment her arms tightened around him, and he took the hint. Leave it be, for now. Placing a kiss against her temple, he grunted softly in acknowledgment.

There was absolute silence until the sound of someone clearing their throat pulled Declan's attention to a male Rogue. The stranger was holding a pair of athletic shorts in his outstretched hand. The unexpected gesture caught him off guard but he thanked the man, who only nodded and backed away with his head bowed.

'It has already begun,' growled his wolf softly. Declan did not have a response as he quickly tugged on the garment, keeping his eyes on those around him. A heavy silence filled the clearing, broken only by the groans of pain coming from Cormac who was trying to stagger to his feet. None of the Rogues moved to help

their 'Alpha' as the man slowly healed and struggled to right himself.

"Let's not let a young man's misbehavior spoil the festivities." Declan tensed and his wolf growled in his mind as Apollo sauntered toward them through the parted crowd.

"I wouldn't call tryin' to force a mark on someone *'misbehavior',*" Lorelei shot back with a mirthless laugh.

"And I believe that if there's no harm, there's no foul," Apollo growled, trying to brush off what his son had tried to do.

"Right, cause claws and fangs out mean no harm is intended," she snapped, swiping her hair to the side to reveal the long gash into the meat of her left shoulder. "Does that look like no fuckin' harm to you?" Declan realized she had not healed herself intentionally, wanting everyone to know and see what Cormac attempted to do to her. Anger bubbled up within him again and his eyes shifted crimson as he cut a withering glare to the Omega.

'Clever little Witch,' his beast rumbled with pride, and even though Declan hated seeing her injured, he admired her quick thinking.

"I *will* kill you if you ever touch her again, Cormac," he promised as Lorelei slipped her hand into his.

"Are you openly threatening the Alpha, Wolfe?" Apollo demanded, reaching down to pull his son the rest of the way to his feet. There was a barely concealed look of disgust on the older man's face as Cormac grunted in pain.

"No, Apollo. I'm makin' him a Goddess damned promise," Declan said, his voice was a mixture of man and beast. Fear flickered over the faces of those around them, and many averted their gazes.

"Take me home, please," Lorelei said softly, and he gave her fingers a gentle squeeze as he turned to lead her out of the crowd. Despite the situation, his heart stuttered. She considered the lake house home. With him.

"How the mighty have fallen; An *Alpha* that follows orders," Apollo sneered, cutting through his momentary elation.

"Make no mistake, Daughtry. Only she is free to give them," he warned loudly, not sparing any of them a backward glance.

"I really can't wait to see those two get taken down," Wyatt said, his voice sounding strained. Declan glanced in the rearview mirror at his cousin as he clambered over the back seat, and their eyes met briefly. They were pulling up the driveway to the house and just finished telling him everything that happened while he was poking around the mansion. Though she healed herself when they left the clearing, Wyatt smelled the blood on

Lorelei when she slid into the passenger seat and immediately went into big brother mode.

"I think we all feel that way, cousin," Declan said as he slipped into the garage bay and hit the sensor he put in Lorelei's vehicle. His phone buzzed with a text from Garridan letting him know he was ten minutes out as they trudged into the house.

"We'll talk in a bit," Declan said to Wyatt, and gently took Lorelei's hand, leading her up the stairs to his room. He slipped into the closet and grabbed a change of clothes. When he rejoined her, she was stepping into his bathroom and he followed, grabbing a washcloth from the linen closet.

"I'd like to have that conversation now," she said gazing at him in the reflection of the mirror, withdrawing a folded envelope from her dress pocket.

"Are those the results?" he asked as he moved to the sink beside her and turned on the tap. She nodded as he swept her hair from her shoulder and gently scrubbed the dried blood from her skin while she read the short letter aloud.

"Miss Lorelei McCann, your test results have confirmed that you are positive for Chimerism. Please see page two for your simplified genetic profile. If you would like to seek further treatment– I don't." She laid the document down on the counter and sighed.

"So, you'll turn into a hybrid if I mark you. Is that somethin' you think you'd want?" Declan asked as he rinsed the blood from the cloth.

"Yes," she stated without hesitation. He was slightly taken aback at the quickness of her response, and he cupped her face gently, pressing his lips to hers.

"Like I said, it's permanent. You're sure?" She nodded her head, "All right, well. You should gain a wolf, but with your Chimerism, I'm not too sure how this is gonna work. Our wolves tend to match our personalities but from what I've heard, they're all mostly quiet. So, you won't have a constant voice in your head. A matebond will snap into place but only mates, fated or chosen, are able to open a mind link with each other to communicate. We'll be able to speak freely, share thoughts and memories, and sense how the other is feelin'." She listened quietly while he continued to explain how the transformation would work.

"Whatever you do, no matter how much pain you feel, don't fight it when you shift. It'll get easier, and eventually, it'll become second nature. You'll have your first shift on the next full moon." Declan held nothing back as he told her the good, the bad, and everything in between. By the time he was done explaining, she lifted herself onto the sink counter, a thoughtful look on her face.

"What's it like havin' a wolf?" Lorelei asked, leaning back against the mirror, swinging her feet gently.

"I've had mine since I turned eighteen so it's hard to describe. He feels a part of me, and I couldn't imagine not havin' him. He's quiet, gruff," Declan chuckled, leaning a hip against the counter and crossing his arms.

"Does he have a name?" His brows shot up in surprise at the question.

"Y'know, I've never asked, and he never mentioned it when I gained him," Declan confessed.

'Amarok. Rok,' His wolf huffed softly in his mind, and felt a surge of guilt for never having asked.

'I never offered either.' Nodding his head, he smiled softly at Lorelei who was watching the silent conversation curiously.

"His name's Amarok. Rok, for short." He stepped between her thighs and leaned forward, bracing his hands on the counter.

"Do you have questions?" Declan asked, tilting his head.

"Only one," she said, and he saw silver brightening her eyes.

"What's that, darlin'?" Declan could scent her arousal, and it quickly invaded his senses like a delicious drug.

"Will you mark me now?" Lorelei's come-hither grin had him hardening and he hooked his hands behind her knees and pulled her to the edge of the counter. Gripping her hips, he gently set her on the floor and took her hand, leading her into the bedroom. Stopping at the foot of the bed, he turned her to face the large mirror situated on his dresser directly across from them. Her gaze met his in the reflection and he lifted her dress up and over her head.

Declan's breath hitched at the sight of her, with her shimmering silver eyes, and her nipples peaking into tight little buds. He shoved the borrowed shorts to the floor, as he pulled her flush against his body, leaning down to kiss her neck softly. He reached around to cup one of her breasts as his other hand trailed down her stomach and dipped teasingly into her slick folds.

"You're always so wet for me, darlin'." She gasped, reaching behind her and wrapping her fingers around him, pumping him slowly. Declan's hips pressed forward, groaning against the nape of her neck while his fingers dipped into her core before sliding back up to tease her clit.

"Declan, please," Lorelei begged breathlessly, and a growl rumbled from him.

"Tell me, Lore," he commanded softly, increasing the speed of his fingers, while the hand on her breast plucked at her hard nipple. Her head dropped back against his shoulder as she lost herself momentarily in the pleasure, moaning loud and long.

"Claim me," her whispered order set Declan's eyes blazing crimson as she turned her head and captured his lips, her body twisting to face him. Bending his knees, he lifted her from the floor, and she wrapped her legs around his waist with a gasp. His tongue delved between her parted lips and they fought for dominance as their kiss turned desperate. Easing them down to the mattress, he plunged into her core with a groan. The moan of pleasure spilling from her lips nearly had him coming undone on the spot.

"You were made for me," Declan rasped against her ear. Nothing ever felt so right then it did when he was with her. *In* her. This woman was his home, his life, and now she was going to be his mate. Emotion tightened his chest to the point he could barely breathe.

Slipping his hands to her hips, he gripped the tops of her thighs, pulling her down roughly as he thrust his hips forward, holding nothing back. She gasped and moaned out his name as she locked her ankles behind him, her breasts bouncing with each powerful stroke. Desperate needs took precedence over everything else. He needed to mark her, needed her tethered to him forever. More than that, he needed *her*. Everything about her intoxicated him challenged him, and he could not dream of a life without her by his side. He was in love with her, and the thought both thrilled and terrified him.

Surging forward, Declan sank his teeth into the sensitive flesh between her shoulder and her throat, branding her with his mark. Their mate bond instantly snapped into place, doubling down on the pleasure he and Lorelei were experiencing with an explosion of heightened sensations. Declan was vaguely aware that Rok was howling in his head, repeating the same two words over and over again with unabashed excitement.

'Fated mate.' His crimson eyes snapped open when the words finally registered and he felt like the wind was knocked out of him. At that same moment, Lorelei came undone beneath him, her moans morphing into deafening screams threatening to burst his eardrums. Her nails raked down his back as her orgasm tore through her body. The violent bucking of her hips against his, the wet sounds of their joined bodies, only added to the intense pleasure threatening to explode from the base of his shaft. The pressure of his bite increased, and the erotically wanton sound from Lorelei sent him over the edge, the intensity bowing him over. The pleasure from his climax ripped through him, and Declan feared he might die from the unfiltered euphoria pumping through his veins. He had heard stories of marking during sex, but nothing in the world could have prepared him for this. Lorelei's voice crackled and broke as unfettered screams of pleasure tore from her throat, her core clenching and unclenching around him

at a frenzied pace. He groaned against her skin as he emptied into her, hips jerking involuntarily with each pulsing ejaculation that seemed to never end.

Slowly, his teeth returned to normal, retreating from the numerous puncture marks now curving over her shoulder in a long oval. The small wounds did not bleed much as he lifted his head and gazed down at her, body buzzing in its high. Lorelei's curls were wild around her head and shoulders and her lips were parted slightly as she tried to catch her breath. Her cheeks were rosy and there was a glittering sheen on her forehead. She trailed her hands along his back and grasped him at the nape of his neck, pulling him down to her.

"Yours. Mine," Declan said against her lips, his shaft still buried deep in her core.

"Mine. Yours," Lorelei echoed back the vow and met him with a slow and sensual kiss. When he pulled back, her eyes were still shimmering a pale silver, and she had a soft, satisfied smile on her lips.

"Are you feelin' okay?" he asked, watching her closely. He knew the virus that all Werewolves carried in them could cause varied reactions, but with her Chimerism, no one knew what to expect.

"I'm a little lightheaded– a bit hot," she confessed as her eyes began flickering dully from gray to silver. Bracing his weight on one elbow, Declan lifted his hand to her forehead. Her skin was fevered and clammy. His brows knit together in concern when he noticed a splotchy redness spreading over her skin, blooming from the mark. Fevers usually did not happen until the night of a new wolf's first transformation. He had never seen a reaction like the one she was having.

"I need to go to the bathroom," she chuckled softly. Giving her a soft smile, Declan withdrew from her center, eliciting a groan from them both. As Lorelei clambered from the bed, he watched her traipse the short distance on unsteady legs. Moving to the edge of the mattress, he kept his full attention on her as she disappeared into the bathroom.

"Lore?" Declan stood when he heard a shuffling sound, and her hand appeared, gripping the door frame before she stepped into view.

"Declan, I don't-" Lorelei's knees gave out and he dashed to her with supernatural speed, scooping her up just before she hit the floor. He rushed her to the bed and, coaxing her up into a sitting position, wrapped his bed sheet around her body.

"Wyatt!" he shouted once she was covered. Only a moment later, the bedroom door burst open, nearly rending the hinges from the frame.

"Hospital. Now," Declan commanded as he rushed into the bathroom and yanked on the clothes he grabbed earlier before stomping into a pair of boots. Wyatt strode over without a word scooped up a now shuddering

Lorelei and hurried from the room. He quickly followed his cousin, snagging his wallet and keys as he passed by the dresser.

Garridan came up from the basement just as they rushed by and fell in behind him without hesitation. The unquestioning loyalty the man displayed made Declan's chest tighten as they marched out of the house and piled into Wyatt's Jeep.

"What the hell happened?" Wyatt demanded once they made it to the pavement. The trip through the woods had been so jarring that they were unable to speak with Declan clutching Lorelei to his chest to keep her from being jostled around.

"I marked her. She was fine the first few minutes, then collapsed." Declan cradled Lorelei in his arms, pressing a soft kiss to her sweat slicked temple.

"Goddess. You know there's a chance she's a Chimera, right?" His cousin demanded, glaring in the rearview mirror.

"Yes, Wyatt. And she is. I'm assumin' that's why she's reactin' this way," Declan stated before whispering in her ear when she whimpered from her perch in his lap.

The drive that normally took thirty minutes, barely lasted fifteen as Wyatt squealed to a halt at the emergency room entrance. Garridan was out and opening the back door before the vehicle came to a complete stop, helping to maneuver Lorelei from the backseat. His cousin was already striding into the hospital, shouting for assistance, by the time he exited the Jeep.

The staff descended on them in a flurry while Declan laid his mate down on the gurney sitting to the side of a pair of double doors. Lorelei gripped his forearm when he cupped her cheek, and he leaned down to press his lips to hers. When she broke the kiss, she looked up at him with tears in her eyes.

"I love you, Declan," she whispered, her irises quickly flickering between silver and gray. He opened his mouth to tell her that he loved her too but her eyes slid shut and her head lolled to the side, suddenly heavy against his palm.

"Lore?" he said softly as the grip on his arm loosened and her hand dropped to the mattress. Panic gripped his chest in a vice as he gazed down at her, eyes wide.

"Lorelei." Saying her name louder this time, he gave her a gentle shake trying to wake her but there was no response. Declan could hear the faint beating of her heart, the sound not nearly as strong as it was before the claiming. Her chest rose and fell in quick, short breaths, beads of sweat trickling over the pulse fluttering near his mark.

"Sir, I need you to answer some questions for us so we can treat her accordingly." Declan slowly straightened and stared at the nurse blankly for a long moment, "Can you tell me what happened?"

When her words finally registered he gave her the details of Lorelei's Chimerism and the claiming that happened less than an hour before as the nurse nodded, taking down quick notes. Several quick questions later, the nurse took down his cellphone number and directed him to a window across the lobby where he would sign off on the paperwork.

"We'll let you know when she's been settled into a room." She turned on her heel and hurried after the small team too the woman he loved, his mate, away down the stark white hallway.

Chapter 24

Several hours later, Declan sat beside the hospital bed, leaning against the arm of the reclining chair he had claimed. He stared at Lorelei, rubbing his index finger beneath his bottom lip, waiting for the smallest sign that she was awake. She looked almost ethereal in the soft moonlight filtering into the room, except for the IV line jutting from the back of her hand. On the outside, he appeared calm and collected. Just a man staying by his woman's side. But on the inside, a whirlwind of emotions threatened to crack his chest in two. He did this. All of it. It was his fault that she was forced from her family and her home. Everything that happened to her from the moment they met had been his fucking fault, and now he put her in a coma. Unable to sit still any longer, Declan stood and began pacing the room. Anxiety wracked him to his core. Fury, hatred, and despair roiled through him until he thought he might lose his sanity.

'Enough! You are not to blame!' Rok snarled, prowling his mind. Anger and frustration got the better of him and Declan pivoted, slamming his fist into the solid wall to his left. Blood smeared against the dented plaster and he welcomed the pain exploding through his knuckles.

"This is all my fault," he muttered, staring at the wall, "I did this to her."

"*Did you mark her against her will?*" his beast demands angrily, "*Did you talk at length about the consequences? Did she agree, without hesitation, that this was what she wanted? With you?*" He had never heard Rok say so much at one time, and though the beast was not wrong, guilt still twisted his stomach painfully.

"*You both made a choice,*" his wolf said, the gruff voice far calmer than it was a moment ago. Declan sighed as his gaze traveled the length of the hospital bed. He could have said no- *should* have. There were still too many unknowns when it came to her Chimerism. It was reckless to take the gamble.

"*Yes. But you are not that kind of a man.*" No, he was not. Though he was willing to become a version of himself that he hated- that Lorelei hated- if it meant she lived.

'*You speak as if she is dying,*' Rok growled loudly, causing Declan to flinch at the final word. He did not want to think about what would happen if Lorelei did come back to him. Refused to consider a life without her because deep in his soul, he knew that it would be the death of *him*.

Four days. Four agonizing days passed without the slightest hint that Lorelei would wake. Four days of sitting by her side, praying to the Lunar Goddess that today would be the day. Declan barely moved in that time, only leaving her side in short intervals when Wyatt or Garridan would come to check on them. They made sure he showered and ate, and brought him clean clothes each day. Today was no exception when a soft knock on the door was followed by Garridan easing into the room.

"How is she?" the Delta asked, settling the duffle bag on the floor by Declan's chair.

"No change," he muttered, voice thick, "Physically, metabolically, molecularly– there's nothin' wrong. They've run every test they can." Tears welled in his eyes as he stared at his mate. Blinking several times, he stood and snatched up the duffle, heading for the en-suite bathroom.

"This isn't your fault, Dec," Garridan said for the hundredth time as he passed, stopping him in his tracks.

"Y'all keep sayin' that, but she wouldn't be *here* if not for me," he glanced sidelong at his friend, "They're releasin' her today since there's nothin' more they can do. It's all up to her now."

Chapter 25

Perfect, blissful silence.

Weightless in a sea of darkness, Lorelei drifted in and out of consciousness. The inky blackness surrounding her felt as if she were cocooned in a swath of liquid silk. Peaceful and warm in the depths of her mind, she slowly became aware of a presence, shifting in the shadows, whispering to her, coaxing her from the divine calm enveloping her.

'Do not be afraid.' She was not. The only thing she wanted was to return to the slumber she had been in moments ago. She did not want to wake up. Not yet.

'You must wake. Our mate worries.' Mate? The moment Declan claimed her flashed in her mind, making her shiver. The memory of the piercing pain quickly gave way to bone-numbing ecstasy causing the presence to rumble with delight. A moment of silence had her drifting back into her dreamless sleep, and she groaned as another nudge roused her to consciousness. She tried to ignore the presence, wishing whatever it was would leave her alone. A huff echoed softly in the back of her mind, the sound was serene and somewhat amused, nudging her again.

'Look at me, Lorelei.' The whispering voice was louder now, feminine and husky. She slowly opened her

eyes a crack, blinking against the bright form in front of her. Taking shape after several moments, she was momentarily dumbstruck to see a pure white wolf sitting on its haunches near her feet.

'*I am Catori, your wolf spirit. We must wake now.*' Sitting up and crisscrossing her legs, Lorelei reached out a hand to run her fingers through the snow-white fur hanging thick near the beast's shoulders. Catori stretched out her neck, allowing her to briefly indulge in the softness of her coat before pressing a warm nose to her chest, over her heart.

'*WAKE UP!*' A howling scream reverberated in her mind and a surge of magic coursed through Lorelei. She jerked awake with a gasp. Sunlight filtered into the room, casting faded shadows across the smooth, white ceiling. She blinked several times, trying to get her bearings. A blur of movement startled her as a calloused hand cupped her face. Tingles erupted across her skin, now feeling more like electrical sparks, and a shiver skittered up her spine. Lorelei suddenly became aware of the heady scent of him, nearly overwhelming her senses. Summer rain in the mountains with a hint of sandalwood. Earthy and masculine. She had never smelled anything more delicious and breathed deeply, taking in the intoxicating mixture.

'*Mate! Fated mate!*' Catori yipped loudly and her mind practically vibrated with excitement. Her gaze found his, and her chest constricted when she saw the tears welling in his dark brown eyes. Lorelei stared up at him, a bit in awe of how gorgeous he truly was, heart hammering against her ribcage. He was kneeling on the bed beside her wearing only a pair of gray sweatpants, and it was all she could do to not throw herself on him. The feel of his hand on her cheek did little to settle the overwhelming need to have his body against hers, skin to skin.

"Hey, darlin'," Declan said softly. Leaning down, he pressed his lips to hers and kissed her like he never would again. Lorelei slid her hand to the nape of his neck, holding him tightly to her as she parted her lips, welcoming his sweeping tongue with a satisfied moan.

"How're you feelin'?" he asked once he finally pulled away, brows drawn together in concern while he eased down on the mattress facing her.

"A little groggy but I feel great, I think," she said, her voice curiously raspy. She lifted onto one elbow when he offered her a glass of water and quickly downed the entire thing.

"What about your senses? They can be overwhelmin' when you first gain your wolf," he asked once she was finished. Taking the cup from her, he smiled ruefully as if remembering his own experience. She inhaled tentatively, sniffing the air but found there was not much to smell in the bedroom.

"Well, all I can smell right now is you, and-," Lorelei's brow furrowed, "There's something bitter but it's faint. Fear, or sadness, I think." She was unsure how she knew which emotion she was scenting. Honestly, she was unsure about a lot of things right now.

"Sadness. Fear *is* bitter but also has a sweaty odor to it." Declan watched her closely as she processed his words. "What about your hearin'? It's fairly quiet so you might not pick up much of anything."

"Wyatt and Garridan are havin' a *very* in-depth conversation about Dungeons & Dice in the basement," she said, smiling. Declan gave her a puzzled look and glanced toward the door, his head tilting to the side slightly. When a grin pulled up one corner of his lips, she knew he had picked up on their excited banter.

"I think your hearin' is better than mine. I can barely hear them," he said, blinking at her with pleasant surprise.

"So, I'm all right?" Lorelei asked, tucking her hair behind her ear.

"You're in perfect health but you've had some changes." Mildly confused, she waited patiently as Declan fished his phone from his pocket and activated the front camera. Taking the offered device, Lorelei's jaw dropped as she stared at the screen in shock. Her right iris had turned a dark midnight blue. The color was so deep that her pupil was nearly indiscernible.

Realizing her hair had changed as well, she stretched out her arm, turning her head this way and that, admiring the color. Crimson. Her hair had darkened to a rich blood red nearly identical to the color of Declan's eyes.

"A side effect of your Chimerism and my Lycanthropy. The scars on your wrists are gone too," Declan said, watching her examine her arms in disbelief. Brushing her fingers over the now smooth skin, tears welled in her eyes. Of everything she had experienced since meeting Declan, this was one of the happiest moments so far. Though through their bond, she felt guilt creep over her.

"Do you feel guilty?" She blurted out the question as she peered up at him, and a look of surprise passed over his features. He averted his eyes, jaw clenching.

"I just don't want you to regret this, Lore," Declan confessed after a long pause, "I'm afraid that you're gonna wake up tomorrow and wish you'd never said yes." Truth. She stared at him for a long moment before placing a hand on his cheek, coaxing him to look at her.

"I love you," Lorelei said when he faced her. "You're my *fated* mate. I will never regret you, or your mark." Declan leaned toward her and, delving his fingers into her curls, claimed her mouth in a heart-stopping kiss.

"Roll it back one more time," Declan said as he stood in the middle of the basement, Wyatt and Garridan on either side of him. Lorelei pulled the slider of the media player back and hit play as he crossed his arms over his chest and watched the large projector screen. There was a crease between his lowered brows as he concentrated on the recording, and she could not help thinking how sexy he looked at the moment. His eyes cut to her and that panty-dropping smile pulled on one corner of his lips. Blinking back to the screen, his voice echoed in her mind, startling her slightly.

'Keep it up, darlin', and we'll have to take another break,' Declan said through their mindlink. They had spent more time in bed in the last two weeks since she had woken in his – their – room than working on the investigation. Something she learned was completely normal for newly mated Wolves.

'It's your own fault you look so damn good in everything you do. Seriously, no one should get turned on watchin' someone brush their teeth.' Lorelei bit her bottom lip at the memory. Declan took her hard and fast against the sink counter, one hand cupping her breast while the other mercilessly circled her clit. He whispered the filthiest things against the shell of her ear as they watched each other come undone in the mirror. Her stomach clenched almost painfully recalling the overwhelming sensations ricocheting throughout her body.

'If you're gonna think about me fuckin' you senseless, y'might wanna close the mindlink. Otherwise, I'll one up myself right here.' Lorelei bit her lips gently to stifle the grin at his crude words. She crossed her legs as heat pooled between her thighs, knowing that if her scent reached him, he would make good on that promise. They needed to finish sorting out the remaining evidence so they could send it to Elder Caine. Wyatt and Garridan finished sifting through the documents while she was in the hospital which only left the task of organizing everything and reviewing the security footage. Unfortunately, their trip to the packhouse on Halloween was in vain as far as evidence went but what the former Alpha and Beta managed to collect over the last two decades proved more than enough.

"Will you two quit mind fuckin' each other and pay attention?" Wyatt said and shoved Declan's shoulder, forcing him to take a step forward.

"It looks like the massacre happened around 8:15 that night." Declan chuckled, cuffing his cousin with the side of his forearm and stepping back between the two men.

"No shit, Sherlock. We can see that from the timestamp," Wyatt bantered, jabbing a finger towards the screen, kicking out his leg to maintain his balance.

"Well, then, Watson, what else do you see?" They all watched the recording, and at 8:20 a very young

Cormac came strolling into view. Exactly seven minutes later, Apollo could be seen walking calmly towards his son, kneeling to speak to him. When he stood, the boy took off towards the house, disappearing from view. Shouting something to Cormac, he waited before turning towards the forest and, just as before, ambled casually across the lawn and vanished in the shadows.

"Pause it, please." Lorelei did as requested, staring at the large screen as possible explanations tumbled through her mind. Catori huffed in her mind at the thought of a single Omega possibly taking out a pack of wolves.

'Impossible,' she growled softly. Lorelei tilted her head, considering, as she propped her chin in her hand. Maybe Cormac and his father had gifts no one knew about. Recruited Rogues or the same Witch that messed with Declan's memories.

"No one ran," Garridan said suddenly.

"Exactly. Can't you see the pavilion just past the corner of the house there?" Declan asked, pointing at the grainy black-and-white image.

"Accordin' to Dad's notes, it was just out of view from the camera, yeah," Wyatt said, turning to rifle through some documents on the table behind him.

"If that's the case, then no one made it off the pavilion. They couldn't have been surrounded either since we don't see anyone around the edge," Declan stated, placing his hands on his hips.

"You think that Apollo did this on his own?" Garridan inquired skeptically, glancing at Declan.

"No. I think he had help. Maybe the Witch or Rogues?" The men fell into silence as they were lost in their thoughts.

"Found it... Yeah, Dad said that the camera placement had been a poor decision on the installer's part, no idea who though, and that the edge of the pavilion was just beyond the corner. Dad and Uncle Kai also thought that it was either an inside job or someone unknown helped them."

"So, we've still got nothing," Garridan said, frustration making his nostrils flare.

"Not necessarily," Lorelei said, "I haven't finished restoring the Crescent Ridge footage yet."

"Wonder why that is," Wyatt said under his breath, giving her a cheeky grin as he casually ducked under Declan's hand aimed at the back of his head.

"Could we visit Silvertooth?" Lorelei inquired, ignoring their antics.

"It's Silver Moon now. The territory was renamed after Alpha Jared relocated his pack there several years ago, but I don't think it'll be a problem," Declan explained, glancing at his cousin.

"I'll make the call," Wyatt said, pulling his phone from his pocket.

"Sure, you feel up to this?" Declan asked her as he walked over to stand beside her desk. It had been two weeks since she returned home from the hospital, and despite the rigorous lovemaking, she was treated like a glass doll. Wyatt told her the day before that seeing her collapse and lose consciousness took a toll on Declan, and the week that followed her hospitalization was even worse. He found his fated mate, then immediately feared he would lose her, and it would have been his fault. Declan never left her side, staying day and night at the hospital, waiting and praying that she would wake up.

"I do. It'll be good for us to get out of the house for a bit." She reached out, taking his hand and he smiled down at her, squeezing her fingers gently.

"We're set," Wyatt said, slipping his phone back into his pocket. "We wanna take anything with us?"

"D.T.L. Bronson's debrief. Lore, can you send a still shot of that frame to my phone?" Garridan asked, and a moment later, his phone buzzed with the photo.

"Let's hit the road then," Wyatt said, leading the way up the stairs.

Chapter 26

Four hours later, Lorelei slid from the backseat near the front entrance of the former Silvertooth packhouse. Though over two decades passed since that tragic night, the mansion was in pristine condition, the lawn was well-manicured. In the back corner of the property, an enormous pavilion stood near the dense treeline. Lorelei stared across the lawn at the structure. There was a distinct hum, much like the buzzing of cicadas, and her brow furrowed slightly as she listened. There was something beyond the low roar. Something roiled in a higher octave that she was unable to make out. In the back of her mind, Catori growled, and she felt her beast's hackles rise at the unusual sound.

"Lorelei!" Declan said her name loudly as his fingers wrapped around her upper arm, jolting her from the trance-like state. She whipped around to look up at him, unaware that she was moving in the direction of the pavilion and now stood several yards away from the vehicle. She glanced at Wyatt and Garridan who were watching carefully, both wearing the same frown as they looked her over. The discordant static was gone.

"Sorry. I thought I heard somethin'." He gave her a look of concern, opening his mouth to speak when a friendly voice called out to them from the mansion entryway. The small group turned to see a tall, well-built man with ginger hair and fair complexion smiling down at them.

"Alpha Jared," Wyatt greeted him with a slight inclination of his head, and the group joined their host at the bottom of the steps.

"Wyatt," Jared said with a nod, holding out his hand. The two men clasped forearms, both grinning broadly.

"This is Garridan, Declan and Lorelei. Delta, Alpha, and Hybrid," Wyatt introduced them, giving her a wink at her new 'title'.

"Pleasure to meet you all," The Silver Moon Alpha said with a smile, giving Garridan and Declan the usual forearm grip. However, when he took Lorelei's hand in his, he bowed, pressing his forehead to her knuckles.

'He greets you as a Luna,' Catori huffed with pride. Lorelei was momentarily dumbfounded at her wolf's statement.

"So, I guess, I'll jump right in. I'm sure you all know about the massacre here twenty-four years ago. Unfortunately, I know about as much as you do. Razed pack, only two survivors, investigation that followed didn't turn up much. You're free to look around the property, the mansion too. Everything was left untouched after we relocated here." Alpha Jared gestured to the estate behind him.

"I'd like to take a look at the pavilion, if that's okay," Lorelei said, glancing again at the structure.

"Of course," The man said with a nod.

"Why didn't your pack claim this estate when you moved here?" Garridan asked, curious.

Jared gave them a wry half smile, "The main reason was out of respect for the victims, and leaving a kind of memorial for them. It's why these lands were left untouched, except for maintenance or repairs." Half-truth. There was something else that kept the pack from moving to these lands.

"And the second?" Lorelei asked, trying to keep the trepidation she felt from crossing the mate bond. Declan's glance and the uneasy shifting of his weight told her that she failed.

"We have a Magus in our pack who came here to bless the land before we moved onto it. When he returned to us, he wouldn't speak of what happened. Only informed us that the land was cursed and unfit to live on. So, we opted for Saint Helena." Alpha Jared let out a sigh as he looked around the property. "Something dark hangs over this land." Lorelei shivered at the ominous words, causing Declan to rub his thumb over the back of her hand.

"Think you two could try to find the Daughtry's old place?" Declan asked his cousin.

"They were in the last house on the left down there." Jared pointed in the opposite direction of the pavilion, "I did some digging into Desmond's files here and found a roster he kept of members living on the estate. Apollo and Cormac joined the pack about a year prior to the massacre," The Alpha said as he pulled a folded document from his back pocket and handed it over to Wyatt.

"See y'all in a bit," Declan said with a nod. Lorelei followed a step behind, her fingers gripping his calloused hand tightly. Walking in silence, her mate continued to rub gentle circles over her skin as the rumbling hum started up again.

"Don't let go," Lorelei breathed, as she focused on the pavilion looming closer with each step. Declan's fingers tightened around hers while the sound grew louder, the higher pitch sang beneath the static – a cacophony of what sounded like disembodied voices. The air warbled in front of them as near invisible shadows danced about the enormous structure.

"There's dark magic here," she whispered, and felt a whirlwind of emotions flooding over the mate bond.

"I can feel it," Declan said in disbelief, "Through the bond. I can feel the magic."

The dissonance grew louder as Lorelei and Declan stepped onto the weather-beaten step, surrounding the pavilion, drowning out any sounds from outside the perimeter of the structure. As the roar in her ears reached its peak, the higher sounds within became clear.

They were screams.

Someone yelled her name far in the distance, their voice muffled as if they were speaking through a wad of cotton. As she ambled toward the center of the platform, a jagged tear flickered in and out of the shadows, dancing over the crumbling fire pit, white and translucent. Lorelei blinked slowly as she reached out a hand, the screaming now an endless symphony ringing in her ears. There was little resistance as her fingers passed through the scar and connected with something ragged and broken.

The shrieks and bellows cut out like a light switch flicking off, replaced by soft, lilting Christmas music playing from somewhere overhead. People she did not recognize milled about sipping on champagne, chatting in small groups. The murmur of conversations and laughter drifting through the wintry night air. Lorelei called out for Declan but it was hopeless. No one could hear her, it seemed. Gazing around the scene, she tried to reign in her panic and take in the details surrounding her.

Strings of lights swung gracefully from the rafters in a frigid breeze before snaking around the pavilion's thick poles, bathing the scenery in a warm buttery glow. A massive fire blazed in the sunken pit marking the center of the structure, keeping the cold night air at bay. Children played with wooden toys, sparklers, and garland as they chased each other nearby on the lawn. Tables covered in white linens with their poinsettia centerpieces sat empty, though some were still laden with untouched food. At one of the smaller tables, Lorelei spotted Cormac eating alone, his bizarre black and white hair making him easily identifiable. Goddess, he could not have been more than ten years old.

Beyond what Lorelei now recognized as the Winter Solstice gala, a fine dusting of frost began to settle over the landscape. Dread prickled along the nape of her neck as she took in the tranquility of it all. The calm before the storm. Everyone here was about to die, and she would be standing in the middle of it when it happened.

The chiming of silverware on crystal pulled her attention to the far side of the pavilion as a younger Apollo Daughtry stepped onto a small stage. Parents all around called for their children, and one by one they charged headlong into the crowd, searching for their mothers and fathers. Tears brimmed in her eyes, knowing there was nothing she could do as she waited for the inevitable.

"A toast!" The Omega bellowed merrily, a wide grin pulling his features out of proportion. "To Alpha Desmond, whose steadfast leadership has brought us yet another fruitful year alongside our allies in the Crescent Ridge pack. In celebration, I would like to share a bit of my culture with you all tonight. Every Winter Solstice in my homelands, we would burn sacred herbs to harbor fortune, prosperity, and goodwill *for the following year." A small satchel was tossed into the roaring fire filling the sunken pit. "To a better year, and finding our true places in this world." The flames in the pit suddenly sputtered and leapt into the rafters of the pavilion, and Lorelei witnessed Apollo slink off the edge of the platform, backing away from the partygoers. The air around the perimeter of the structure warbled and she realized a barrier had been placed to keep the dark magic contained. The pack could not have escaped even if they wanted to. A black haze erupted beneath the logs and quickly filled the area in thick fog choking and gagging the Silvertooth members.*

Gaze darting around in the darkness, Lorelei felt the shift in the air, recoiling as the oily snares of dark magic slithered past her. She shook off the invisible tendrils wrapping around her and trying to back away from the foulness surrounding the pavilion. Panic lanced through her as the magic wrapped itself around her body tightly and a scream ripped from her chest. She struggled against the vice-like hold wrapping around her, fighting wildly until it let her go.

Trying to catch her breath, her momentary relief was replaced by stone cold fear freezing her in place. All around her the snarls and growls that whispered in the clearing fog were quickly replaced by roars and bellows reverberating across the property. Screams of agony rang out as the pack began to turn on each other, slicing and ripping. Lorelei covered her mouth to stifle her screams as the Silvertooth pack members tore each other to pieces. All around her, husbands mutilated their wives, mothers ripped apart their children, and lifelong friends attacked without mercy. Beneath the swirling cloud of dark magic, the plank floor was drenched in a thick layer of blood. Littered with body parts and organs. Slipping and sliding, clawing and biting, they continued to fight.

Tears streamed down her cheeks as she watched the horror that was the Silvertooth massacre. Near the stage, Alpha Desmond let out an enraged yell as his own Delta team swarmed him before turning on each other. Lorelei stared wide eyed at the carnage that took less than five minutes and left over one hundred and twenty bodies lying in an unidentifiable tangled mess of limbs and organs and blood.

"Lorelei!" yelled Declan, and she let out a chest-caving sob of relief.

"--come back to me!" Rough hands gripped her shoulders and a solid figure loomed blurrily in front of her. Lorelei gasped as the carnage suddenly disappeared and she met his terrified gaze. Fresh tears streamed down her cheeks, her hands clasped his face, and she blinked several times, focusing on her mate. On the lines of panic creasing his brow, the stubble rough and coarse beneath her palms. His scent.

"It's okay," she assured him hoarsely, breathing deep, "I'm okay." Relief washed over Declan's tight features, knees buckling as the emotion overwhelmed him, and he sat heavily on a nearby bench. Silently, he pulled her into his embrace and she rested her head against his chest, sobbing. The sound of thundering footfalls reached her ears, and she looked up to see Wyatt, Garridan, and Alpha Jared tearing across the lawn in their direction.

"How?" Wyatt asked gently when she finally stopped crying long enough to recount what she witnessed at the pavilion. Declan refused to answer the questions they lobbed at him as he carried her back to the vehicle, only informing them that she was okay. Now, Lorelei leaned back against Declan who had his arm draped loosely across her chest, bracing them against the hood of the Jeep. The weight of his fingers gently gripping her shoulder centered her, and brought her a level of comfort she had not realized she needed.

"My insight," she said softly, "Becoming a Hybrid must have heightened my gift as well, allowing me to see what caused the scar."

"Scar?" Garridan gruffed, tilting his head.

"From using dark magic. It can leave a scar on wherever or whatever it's used," she explained, "Dark magic can even scar people, supernatural or otherwise." Sadness gripped her heart as she thought of her mother, causing Declan to hold her a little tighter. After Lorelei's assault, Katherine McCann's guilt became so great that she resorted to dark magic to try and avenge the violence committed against her daughter. Though, rather than bringing justice to the men guilty, her mother wanted to prevent the incident from happening all together. The spell failed, leaving Katherine with a severe brain injury that altered her life forever."

"Did you two find anything at the house?" Declan's voice pulled her from her memories as it rumbled near her ear, making a shiver skitter up her spine. His grip on her shoulder tightened briefly in response and he leaned in to kiss the nape of her neck.

"Oh yeah. You're gonna want to see this," Wyatt said and led the way down the lane.

"I'm almost afraid to see what Cormac's life was like given what we've found out," Lorelei said quietly. Garridan and Wyatt exchanged a look before peering over their shoulders at her.

"I won't lie, it's hard to stomach. Especially knowing he was just a kid," Garridan confessed as they turned onto the walkway of a quaint little cottage. The home looked as if it were frozen in time. There was a child's bicycle lying on the small lawn near the front steps, the chain rusted and broken. A pair of work boots had been left by the screened door, and the sparse furniture near the railing was moldy and weather-beaten. Wyatt pushed open the warped front door and disappeared into the dimly lit front room. Garridan stepped aside and gestured for Lorelei and Declan to enter, propping one of the dry rotted boots against the base of the door to keep it from swinging shut.

As Lorelei's eyes adjusted to the poorly lit room, she took in the peeling wallpaper, stained carpets, and twenty years' worth of dust coating the interior. A musty, metallic tinged scent hung heavy in the air as they meandered around the small space. Dark mold crept up the wall behind a worn leather loveseat with a broken coffee table sitting in front of it. Two ripped and faded wingback chairs sat near a picture window looking out onto the small front yard. Through an archway across from them, lay a cramped kitchen that was home to a rickety two-person bistro style table, mismatching chairs, and an ancient gas stove. Roaches scurried to their hiding places over numerous stains and thick, fuzzy mold.

"Apollo was on the left, Cormac near the stove there, and the bathroom is on the right." Lorelei followed Wyatt's finger as he pointed to each room, and she noticed something odd about the room near the stove.

"You're sure that one was Cormac's?" she inquired, swallowing hard.

"It's a child's room, if you can call it that," Garridan said, staring at the door frame. There were numerous rusted bolt latches anchored to the wall, all of them currently unlocked. Taking a deep breath Lorelei pushed into the room, wincing at the shrill whine of the rusted hinges.

The room was bare except for a small, rough cut pad with a threadbare sheet in the far corner of the room. A small dresser with most of the drawers too small for their respective cubbyholes sat nearby. The walls were covered in drawings, some of them on paper, as high as a nine-year-old Cormac could have reached. Each one depicting some form of violence, the next always more gruesome than the last. Blood stains streaked over the worn floorboards and long gouges looked to be claw marks criss-crossed over the planking.

Seeing the scarring on the floor, Lorelei's heightened insight activated, and a piercing scream reverberated around the small space. The vision of a terrified and bloodied Cormac sliding roughly across the floor as his father dragged across the floor flashed in front of her.

She jerked back with a shriek, clapping her hands over her mouth. Snarls and curses spilled from the men as they whirled around, looking for the source of her terror. As the last echoes of the boy's terror faded, Lorelei turned and leaned her forehead against Declan's chest, squeezing her eyes tight against the image that was burned into her memory.

"What happened?" Declan asked against her ear, his tone tense but calm as he held her close.

"My insight. Cormac was bloody and screaming, Apollo draggin' him across the floor," she said, body trembling slightly.

"Do we need to leave?" he asked softly, rubbing her back comfortingly.

"No, I'm okay. It just scared the shit outta me," Lorelei huffed out a breath. This new version of her gift was beginning to remind her of the jump scare videos that became popular a decade or so prior.

"Say the word and we'll go, darlin'," he vowed, and she nodded, giving him a grateful smile. Stepping from his embrace, Lorelei glanced around the room once more before moving back to the kitchen. Garridan and Wyatt wandered into Apollo's room while she moved to the bathroom. Pushing open the door that was splattered with Goddess knows what with the toe of her boot, she stepped cautiously into the filthy, mold covered room. It was cramped like the kitchen with a freestanding sink, and a rust stained bathtub looking worse than the fetid toilet sitting beside it.

Once again, her insight activated and the vision of a bruised Cormac sat in the tub, head bowed as he cried softly. The water lapped gently around his thin little body tinged red and she wondered if the discoloration was from blood or rust.

Lorelei's question was soon answered when the boy lifted his head, and she saw a thin line of blood trickling from his nose. Tears welled in her eyes, her heart breaking for him at the obvious abuse the was suffering at the hands of his father. The ghostly sound of shattering glass echoed from somewhere behind her, and a raging Apollo stormed into the bathroom, a thick leather strap dangling from his fist. Cormac cowered at the sight of his father, fear shining bright in his dull hazel eyes. He opened his mouth to scream when–.

"Come back to me, Lore," Declan said softly against the shell of her ear. She stared at the now empty bathtub and dragged in a shuddering breath, tears staining her cheeks.

"I'd like to leave now," she whispered, and Declan wrapped an arm around her shoulders and ushered her outside, calling to the other two men they were leaving.

"You all right?" he asked once they returned to the packhouse.

"Yeah, I'm good," she said with a small smile, taking a seat on the front steps of the mansion. Declan eased down beside her, an unreadable expression on his face as he propped his forearms on his knees. Their mate bond was silent. None of his emotions played across the link between them and she realized he had closed off his mind to her. Biting her bottom lip gently, she stared down at the toes of her boots, willing herself to not dwell on what that could mean.

"Could you show me?" he asked softly, turning his head to look at her. Lorelei nodded and opened her mind to him, allowing him to see the massacre through the scar as she had. Declan sat quiet and unmoving until the moment her scream cut sharply down the mate bond, and he flinched at the sound. Without a word, he reached over and easily scooped her into his lap.

'I'm sorry for all of this, Lore,' Declan said after several minutes, his voice soft in her mind before he closed himself off again. Silent tears streamed down her cheeks having relived the sheer brutality of the massacre, at Cormac's abuse. Fear that Declan would regret marking her settled like a boulder on her chest, and she wrapped her arms tightly around his shoulders.

"Is she okay?" Lorelei heard Wyatt ask quietly from where she lay curled in the back seat, her head resting on Declan's thigh. They moved to the Jeep not long after returning to the vehicle, exhaustion creeping its way into Lorelei's bones. The back-passenger door was propped open and she heard the soft groan of the hinges as the Beta leaned against it.

"She is. This extreme version of her insight is just gonna take some gettin' used too," Declan said, his fingers combing gently through her curls. "Did you find anything else in the house?"

"More evidence of abuse and neglect, and a box full of documents that Garridan grabbed. We'll go over it all when we get home." As if on cue, the back gate was pulled open and she heard the box of files slide in behind the bench seat.

The men said their goodbyes to Alpha Jared, thanking him for allowing them to visit, and clambered into the front seats with Wyatt sliding in behind the steering wheel.

Chapter 27

Late that night, Declan stood in the basement gym glaring at another destroyed punching bag, his breaths heaving from the exertion. Blood stained the wraps around his hands and wrists, smearing across his skin. The heavy rock music blasting through the overhead speakers did little to quell the rage of emotions swirling within him. He wiped the sweat from his brow and glanced at the clock on the wall. It was nearly three in the morning. Removing the remnants of the old bag, he tossed it into the growing pile in a nearby corner. Hefting the new one by its chain onto the hook above, he stepped back into a fighting stance. His mind wandered to his mate sleeping soundly upstairs in their bed, and the cruel path she was forced down since meeting him.

Flipping her life on its head by being assigned his case. Jab, jab, kick. Her first encounter with Cormac. He grunted with effort, his muscles burning, straining as he pushed himself harder with every swing. Kick, kick, strike. How he hurt her. Broken her leg, lashed out at her. A sheen covered his bare torso as sweat rolled between his shoulder blades, and dripped from the tip of his nose. Cormac trying to force his mark on her. Declan landed a brutal spinning kick to the bag, his heel caving in one side of the heavy material, and the impact made the chain above groan in protest.

'*You are not to blame,*' Rok gruffed in his mind, making him grit his teeth. He was though. Jab, jab, kick. Everything that happened to Lorelei since they met had been because of him. Truth be told, Declan had never wanted to find his mate. Never thought that he would. The level of devotion that seemed to take precedence over everything else, the intensity of every positive and negative emotion was something that he had feared for a long time.

Until he found Lorelei. Or rather, she found him.

He felt his wolf push against him at his thoughts. The beast growled out a warning to him.

'*Lorelei is our* fated *mate. Do not push her away because you feel the need to bear the burden of things beyond your control.*' It was Declan's turn to growl as he lashed out with a roundhouse kick causing the chain to snap, sending the punching bag careening into the corner with its fallen brethren. He glared at the far wall for a long moment, panting hard, then stalked over to the supply closet and yanked out another bag. Securing the chain, Declan eyed his target, debating on whether he should rip it to shreds or go for a run since pummeling the worthless sacks did no good. Deciding a breather was better than making a mess, or running from the problem, he turned away from the equipment.

Striding over to the mini fridge they kept stocked with water, he snatched out a bottle and chugged its contents. He was tossing the trash when he felt her presence, a gentle tug on the mate bond connecting them. Taking a deep breath, his body went rigid when her scent filled his lungs. She smelled of honeysuckle and sweet apples, the aroma making his mouth water, and his shaft jerk with arousal.

'Declan?' Lorelei asked quietly through their link, her voice hesitant. His heart ached at the sound of her uncertainty. *'Could we talk?'*

'Sure, darlin'. What's on your mind?' He kept his back to her, not wanting her to see the guilt etched into his features.

'Are you all right?' The concern in her tone made his gut clench. After everything she had been through because of him, she still worried about his welfare.

'Yeah, I'm fine. Why?' Declan knew that she would sense the lie, but he told it anyway.

'Wyatt told me about the week I was in the hospital,' she stated, ignoring his falsehood for now. He could hear her soft footsteps padding up behind him as he took a deep breath and sighed, dropping his chin to his chest.

'The last thing you needed was to worry about me when you were tryin' to recover,' he replied, finally turning to look at her. His breath hitched, air stalling in his lungs at the sight of her. Her sleep-mussed curls were flipped

to one side, and the boatneck sweater hung loose over her body, exposing one shoulder.

'*Declan…*' Lorelei warned as her gaze narrowed, daring him to continue lying to her as she crossed her arms beneath her breasts.

Averting his eyes, he glared at the pile of discarded punching bags, and, propping his hands on his hips, Declan opened his mind to her. His emotions from the last three weeks crashed down on her through their bond. Despair, fear, anger, and overwhelming guilt. Lorelei jolted and lifted a hand to cover her mouth as if she were fighting the urge to vomit. Tears brimmed in her eyes, her other hand clutching the fabric of her sweater over her heart as he held nothing back. She held his gaze, never wavering, because, under all the turmoil raging within him, another emotion grew stronger, surpassing all of the others. Love. Pure, undeniable love for her.

'*I was terrified, Lore. So scared that I'd lose you. I felt guilty that I'd done that to you, that I'd caused it all.*' The pain he felt radiated over the bond.

'*Declan, don't. Neither of us knew that would happen.*' Lorelei brushed the tears from her cheeks before placing a hand on his bicep, squeezing gently trying to comfort him.

'*It's not just the claiming,*' he stated, turning from her, '*Everything that's happened to you since we met is because of me. It's my fault that Cormac tried to assault you. Twice! My fault that you collapsed into a coma for a week. Your life was flipped upside down and sent headlong into a shitshow, all because of me.'* As he turned back to face her, Lorelei's hand lashed out, striking him across the face.

In an instant, Declan pinned her against the wall with his body, her wrists caged in one large hand with the other braced on the smooth surface behind her. He stared down into her defiant mismatched eyes, the crimson of his own reflecting at him. Even in his shock and irritation from her biting slap, he was impressed by her boldness. Lorelei never ceased to surprise him, and that made him love her all the more.

"What the fuck was that for?!" he demanded aloud as the heat rose on his stinging cheek, surprised when Rok howled in amused approval.

"You're such an idiot sometimes, Declan. I chose this. I wanted this life with you. You can't blame yourself for the actions of other people." She matched the intensity of his gaze, mercury and midnight blue shimmering to life. Rok huffed his agreement.

"I can if it means I wasn't there to protect you." The words choked from him, voice breaking with the admission, and some of the anger faded from her eyes.

"You have always been there to protect me, Declan. From the moment I stepped into that conference room, you've protected me. From Rok, the guards, Cormac, and Apollo, my gift. You endured broken ribs tryin' to pull me from a flashback. Were literally nailed to a wall to test my magic, only for the sake of knowin' what I was capable of. And yet, you still think that you haven't protected me." She shifted her weight, and the friction of her body on his had him hardening against her belly. "There are more ways to protect me than with your fists or body, Declan, and you've done that."

'She is right. You know it,' Rok huffed. He knew that she was right, but still was not able to let go of the guilt. Lorelei seemed to realize his struggle and tugged free from his grasp. Cradling his face in her palms, she lifted onto her toes and brought her lips to his just as she opened her mind to him.

Declan jolted as if he was struck by lightning, eyes drifting closed as he reveled in the tidal wave of sensations pouring over their bond. The love and gratitude she felt for him practically sang in his blood, and he wrapped his arms around her torso, lifting her off her feet. Deepening the kiss, her emotions threatened to overwhelm him as everything that she felt over the last months made the breath cease in his lungs. She trusted him, knew that she was safe with him, that he would never hurt her, wanted and needed him, but most of all, she loved him unconditionally. Not once did she feel regret or shame, or blame him for her circumstances. She was happy with him.

"I love you, Lorelei McCann," he panted against her lips when he finally broke the kiss, easing her back down to the floor. Her gray and blue gaze met his and she gave him the most brilliant, heart-stopping smile he had ever seen.

"And I love you, Declan Wolfe," she said softly, pressing her lips to his again. He was vaguely aware of the thumping bass pounding from the overhead speakers as he bent and gripped her thighs, lifting her in his arms again. His fingers splayed over her backside and he realized she was not wearing underwear.

"Did you come down here with expectations, darlin'?" Declan growled in her ear, holding her firmly against the wall with one hand while shoving his athletic shorts down with the other.

"'Cause I fully intend to live up to them." Declan adjusted their position and hooked one arm under her thigh and then the other, leaving her open and at his mercy.

"Less talk, more action," she goaded him, breathless in her anticipation while she laced her arms around his neck.

Their gazes never left each other as he surged forward at the same time he dropped Lorelei onto his length, burying himself fully with a low groan. Her nails dug into his bare shoulders, gasping his name and he repeated the action, holding her suspended, back braced against the wall. Declan did not bother trying to remain in control as carnal desire took over both of them, his hips pistoning relentlessly. Lorelei slid a hand up the back of his neck, fisting her fingers in his hair, and dragged him down to her lips. Declan groaned against her mouth as she sucked and nipped at his bottom lip, biting hard enough to draw blood. The pain and pleasure sent him careening over the edge with a bellow filled with the sound of his beast.

A moment later, he felt a sharp, piercing pain just below his throat. Bone-numbing ecstasy quickly followed and he realized Lorelei had sunk her teeth into the flesh between his neck and shoulder, claiming him. The bond between them intensified tenfold, and Declan was not sure one person could endure the amount of pleasure that swept through every cell in his body. For a moment, his vision faded and stars flashed in the darkness, silver, blue, and red.

Lorelei's euphoric orgasm ripped through her seconds later and the power of her bite increased, nearly sending him to his knees. Her screams of pleasure were muffled against his skin as her core clenched around his shaft, hips undulating against him roughly. Sheer willpower kept Declan upright while they rode out their climax together. He pressed his lips to her throat, groaning her name against her skin before sinking his teeth into her existing mark, claiming her again.

Lorelei chose him. Claimed him as hers. The guilt eating away at him since she collapsed in his arms the night when he first marked her disappeared. He felt calm, complete. Like a missing puzzle piece had finally fallen into place. His chest swelled with emotion, making it hard to breathe when he realized that his heart, and his soul, were no longer his own. He belonged to her completely, and she to him.

Hours later, Declan lay on his back, staring up at the ceiling with Lorelei pressed tightly against his side. Her head rested on his newly marked shoulder while his fingers trailed idly along the thigh draped across his hips. Every surface in the room had been christened over the last few hours, and a lazy, sinful smile pulled at his lips. He would never be able to work out in the gym again without thinking of taking her from behind in front of the wall of mirrors, or how she rode him at a torturously slow pace as he lay on the bench press. His favorite session though, was when they stumbled into the sauna intending to relax. The image of Lorelei with her back arching, lifting her from the bench as he pleasured her replayed in his mind. Her hands buried in her hair, fisting the wild curls while she moaned his name. He could still taste her on his tongue. Still see how her breasts, with their peaked nipples, rose and fell with her heavy breaths.

His erection throbbed painfully at the memory, and he nudged Lorelei's thigh higher up his hips. The head of his cock nestled into the warm, still-wet folds of her center and Declan pushed his hips forward, fingers digging gently into the swell of her backside. A soft breathy moan fanned over his skin as he pressed deeper, burying himself to the hilt before pulling his length out again. Repeating the action, his arousal reached new heights as he listened to the wet sound of his cock filling her over and over. Lorelei moaned, her breathy kitten-like mewls growing louder with each stroke until her leg locked around his hip and she cried out as her orgasm barreled through her. Declan gritted his teeth as her core undulated around his shaft, forcing his climax to rip from him as her body milked his length. Grunting, his hips jerked with each pulsing ejaculation as he emptied himself deep inside of his mate. With a final groan of satisfaction, he left himself buried deep in her womb and opened his eyes. Lorelei was peering up at him with a satisfied grin on her lips.

"You should surprise me like that more often," she said, her voice heavy with sleep and desire. Declan chuckled as he leaned down and kissed her thoroughly, teasing her tongue with his. He was not sure when they drifted off but when he woke up, the first rays of morning light brightened the dark windows that sat high on the far wall.

Detangling their limbs, and finally slipping his length from her swollen core with a groan, Declan carried her upstairs to their room. Easing Lorelei down onto their bed, he gazed at her upturned face, feeling his chest constrict once again. Her expression was calm and peaceful with her perfect lips parted slightly. The smattering of freckles over her nose and cheeks was a subtle contrast against her lightly tanned skin. Her hair was a crimson halo of wild curls fanning over the pillows and her shoulders, caressing her skin. This woman could burn the world, and he would proudly stand by her side in the ashes.

His queen. His Luna.

Chapter 28

The day after she and Declan thoroughly broke into the basement, Lorelei woke early and made breakfast as a way to apologize to Wyatt and Garridan. She donned the frilly floral apron as she worked her way around the kitchen, making enough pancakes, bacon, and eggs to feed a small army.

"Well, good mornin', sunshine," Wyatt said when he shuffled around the base of the stairs from his room.

"Mornin', Wyatt," she said over her shoulder, smiling brightly at him.

"What're you doin', stealin' my job?" He teased as he grabbed a mug from the cabinet and poured himself a steaming cup of coffee.

"Figured it was the least I could do since Declan and I slept all yesterday," Lorelei said, her cheeks heating several degrees.

"Thank you, but it wasn't a big deal. We may not know what it's like yet, but we understand," the Beta said with a grin of his own, taking a seat on the island. Lorelei felt as if her cheeks would burst into flames, so she hastily changed the subject, clearing her throat.

"Did y'all find anything in the box from the Daughtry's?" she asked as she walked over to Garridan's room and knocked, calling out that breakfast was ready. Hearing his gruff response and the ruffling of his bed linens, she returned to the stove and set out the heavy dishes filled with their breakfast.

"No, not really. We found what we think is a name scribbled on the back of a receipt but that's about it," Wyatt said, digging into the piles of food set out in buffet-style.

"Whose name?" she inquired, grabbing the full carafe from the coffee maker and setting it atop a stone pot pad on the island.

"Mary Good." Wyatt shrugged his broad shoulders, "There was a time and date under the name. Garridan's gonna cross reference it with the photos he took and the timeline."

"Maybe I can find somethin' about the name online," Lorelei said, taking a seat at the island and digging into the breakfast. The name Wyatt mentioned tumbled around in her head, sounding both familiar and new at the same time but she could not place where she heard either. Her attention was pulled to the bedroom door off the kitchen as it swung open and Garridan padded into the room, heading straight for the pot of coffee.

"I just woke up to an interesting text," The Delta said, grabbing a mug from the cabinet. Lorelei and Wyatt waited for him to continue as he dumped some cream and sugar into his cup.

"Well, don't keep us in suspense, Gar," Wyatt said, shoving a fork full of pancakes into his mouth.

"A couple of Rogues want to meet with Declan. Say they have information and need to speak with him about some things," Garridan said, leaning against the counter as he lifted his mug.

"Who're the Rogues?" Declan asked from behind them as he alighted from the stairs.

"Balor, and Eris," The Delta stated, looking up from his cup.

"Know anything about 'em?" Her mate inquired as he stepped up behind her and placed a kiss on her temple. She leaned into his touch, eyes drifting closed at the affection.

"Not much. They're Deltas, who joined the pack not long after the massacre with several others. Balor has a twin brother named Bullard. Eris joined with her friends, Mazzikim, and Wiley. They've all been relatively decent pack members. The twins want to try out for D.T. and have been training for months." Garridan took a slug of his coffee, "I don't deal with them directly, but have seen them in the arena."

"Set up the meetin' at the Rapides packhouse. If there's anyone there, run 'em out, and let the leader at Red Night know we'll be there. Otherwise, we'll have an entire Vampire coven breathin' down our necks,"

Declan stated, not quite an order, but it was clear enough.

"See if you can arrange for Balor and Eris to meet us this evenin', please," Lorelei said as she chewed on a piece of bacon, and the Delta glanced at Declan for confirmation.

"She's gonna be your Luna if you decide to stay. Her words hold as much authority as mine," Declan said, and Garridan gave him a wide grin, nodding as he pulled out his phone.

Lorelei stared blankly at the countertop as Declan added a mountain of food to his plate and settled onto the stool beside her. She sat in silence, her mind reeling. She would be Luna of the Crescent Ridge pack. The idea of leading an entire community of wolves made her stomach flip with nerves and she swallowed hard at the prospect.

'You'll be perfect,' Declan's voice echoed in her mind softly. Catori huffed in proud agreement and a smile pulled at the corners of her mouth.

'You can't possibly know that, but thank you for the vote of confidence,' she replied, stabbing another short stack of pancakes and dropping them on her plate.

'The full moon is tonight. We'll need to make this meetin' with Balor and Eris quick so we can get back home and get ready,' he said, and another wave of nerves sent her stomach into somersaults.

'You'll be with me, right?' Lorelei felt ridiculous asking, like a child fearing something silly and harmless.

'Of course, darlin',' Declan reassured her, leaning over to kiss her cheek, leaving a splotch of sticky syrup on her skin.

The rest of the day was filled with training and combing through the remaining evidence. Lorelei discovered that she could now remove the dark magic in small batches, making the removal process much quicker. Apparently, being a hybrid strengthened all of her abilities, magic included.

By the late afternoon, she was finally able to finish restoring the Crescent Ridge footage, and she, Wyatt, and Garridan had to force Declan to leave the basement, insisting that watching the video was not worth the pain it would cause him. He only agreed when Lorelei promised to help him pull the memories the next day, then left to go on a run.

"Lore, I want you to save a copy of this to your laptop, and send it to both of us," Garridan said, gesturing between him and Wyatt, "We need to get this to Elder Caine, immediately. This alone is enough to send Apollo and Cormac to trial." There was a sense of urgency in his voice, and she immediately did as he instructed.

"All right. Done," she said, sending the file to them before emailing the High Elder, "Would they really get a trial even with the surveillance footage?" Lorelei asked quietly, crossing her arms over her middle. She did not think she could stomach the idea of the two of them getting away with their crimes again.

"At this point, the trial would be a formality. They'll be executed for this. Caine won't let them live," Wyatt said, staring up at the frozen image of the decimated pack. His face was unusually pale as he stared at the carnage lying all around him and his cousin on the large screen.

"When Declan sees this, he's gonna rip those two to shreds," Wyatt said, turning away from the grizzly image, "*If* he sees it."

Lorelei glanced at the muttered afterthought, weighing her options. Declan desperately wanted to know the truth, no matter the pain it caused him to remember. However, knowing the truth would likely send him on a rampage to end the two responsible for murdering his family and pack, and setting him up to take the fall.

'It would be justified,' Catori huffed, and Lorelei was inclined to agree.

"So, that's the Witch who put the spell on Declan?" Garridan asked, pointing up at the screen.

"I would assume so," Lorelei said as she lifted her gaze to the cloaked figure strolling through the remains of the pack. Catori growled low and menacing at the

Witch on the screen. Above them, they heard the back door open and gently close, and Garridan immediately cut the feed from her laptop.

"Y'all ready?" Declan called from the top of the basement stairs.

"Waitin' on you, love," Lorelei answered, leaning over to look up at him in the doorway. He gave her a soft crooked grin before disappearing from view, and she hurried up the stairs with Wyatt and Garridan following closely behind.

"They're late," Garridan said, checking the rugged watch strapped to his wrist. Lorelei glanced over at the men as they stood waiting or pacing around the cozy living room. The secondary packhouse was more of a sizable cabin boasting a rustic elegance similar to that of the lake house. Declan explained that the cabin was more of a sentry outpost to keep an eye on the territory borders. There were several situated across the outer parishes of Crescent Ridge and she understood now why Declan wanted the meeting here, rather than closer to the main house. The cabin was centered on a sprawling lawn surrounded by thick trees and dense underbrush, making sneaking around the property impossible. Not that they anticipated an ambush, but when it came to Cormac and the Rogues that he had taken in over the last few years, it was better to err on the side of caution.

"Declan," Lorelei said when she returned her attention to the window facing the mile-long driveway. He straightened from the doorframe he was leaning against and sidled up beside her, his large hand brushing over her lower back to settle on her hip.

A two-toned pick-up truck was rumbling slowly down the drive towards the cabin, headlights dim in the remaining light as the sun sank lower behind the trees. Garridan and Wyatt stepped up beside them, watching the vehicle draw nearer. As the driver slowed to a stop several yards from the front porch, the silhouettes of two figures could be seen in the cab.

"Stay inside," Declan said quietly against her ear, hand squeezing her hip as he walked over to the front door and opened it wide. She kept her gaze on the pick-up as the doors opened and a male and female stepped out.

"Alpha Declan?" The man asked, his voice muffled through the window.

"That's right. You're Balor, and Eris, correct?" Declan asked, stepping out onto the front porch.

"Yes, sir," Eris said, staring intently toward the cabin as the pair moved closer. She noticed the female incline her head, sniffing at the air.

'Truth,' she told Declan through the mate bond, and some of the tension she felt within him eased.

"Come on in. Garridan said you had some things you wanted to talk about." Declan stepped aside, allowing the two newcomers to enter first. From the corner of her eye, she saw Wyatt notch his head up and his broad chest expand as he took in a deep breath.

"*Mate.*" The woman named Eris said at the same time as Wyatt, surprise evident on both of their faces. The two stared at each other for a long moment as all around the room, eyes bounced back and forth between them.

'*Not the best time, but it is what it is,*' Declan said over the bond, his chuckle reverberating throughout her mind, and the living room.

"Meetin' first, then you two can talk," Declan said aloud, glancing between Wyatt and Eris, then Balor. "Don't I know you?" he asked, giving the man a curious onceover.

"Yes, sir. We met very briefly at the Halloween party," Balor said with an apologetic smile, "I gave you a pair of shorts after you shifted."

Lorelei did not recognize him and she took a moment to look over him and Eris in the well-lit living room. Balor was very attractive with bright blue eyes, a straight nose, and full lips. His brown hair was swept back with a short full beard covering the lower half of his face. The sherpa-lined canvas jacket, and faded cargo pants that covered a well-built physique exuded the ruggedness of its wearer.

Eris, however, was stunning with pale, wavy blonde hair cropped just above her shoulders. Dark angular brows framed her pale green similar to peridot, and she had a petite button nose over full cupid's bow lips, the color of rose. She was slim and toned, and her attire was more casual with a thick linen button-up, and well-worn blue jeans. Both of them wore a set of boots that looked as if they had seen better days.

"I really appreciated your kindness," Declan said as he settled on the couch. The rest of the members of their group found seats around the living room, while she opted for the armrest beside her mate. He smiled up at her, looping an arm around her when she perched next to him.

"It was the right thing to do," Balor said, brushing off the small bit of praise, "That night is what we wanted to speak to you about actually. Before the party, Cormac said that he needed everyone to help him get Lorelei away from you. That she was his mate and you were holding her hostage, refusing to allow them to be together out of jealousy." Balor gave them an apologetic look, "We started to doubt those claims after we saw the two of you dancing together. After she shot Cormac from the forest and came out screaming about him trying to force his mark on her, we realized we'd been deceived."

"We never wanted anyone to get hurt. We were all manipulated into believing we were doing right by Lorelei," Eris said, her voice soft and earnest as she glanced at her newfound mate. Lorelei followed her gaze, seeing Wyatt visibly tensed at the sound of her voice.

'Those two are gonna tear the house down,' Declan said, amusement evident in his tone.

'Oh, you mean like us?' Lorelei teased as she flashed memories of their time in the gym, specifically the sauna, down the mate bond. Her teasing earned her a warning in the form of a hearty growl that nearly sent Catori into a frenzy.

"Lorelei?" Garridan said, clearing his throat, and she snapped her head around, fighting the grin on her lips as her cheeks blazed.

"Sorry. They're tellin' the truth," she said, giving herself a mental shake. Balor and Eris looked at her in confusion, and she quickly explained her gift to them.

"Don't let Cormac know about all that you can do. He knows that you can sense lies, but nothing detailed. He'd go straight to *her* if he found out," Eris warned, looking at her earnestly.

"Who?" Wyatt asked, sitting up straighter.

"All we know is that she's a Witch, and has been with the Daughtry's for a while." Lorelei's brow furrowed as she digested this new information.

"Do either of you know Mary Good, maybe heard the name around the packhouse?" she asked, watching them closely.

"No, I'm sorry," Balor said and looked to Eris who shook her head. Truth.

"Was worth a shot, she sighed, and Declan gave her thigh a gentle squeeze.

"We can ask around if you like." Eris smiled softly at her but Lorelei shook her head.

"Thank you, but the less people know that name, the better. It could be dangerous, so please keep it to yourselves," she warned them, and they nodded in understanding.

"Every day is dangerous when you have Cormac as your *Alpha*," Balor stated contemptuously.

"What do you mean?" Declan inquired as he slipped his arm from around her, leaning forward to give the pair his full attention. Balor glanced at his friend who gave him an encouraging nod and he stood, removing his jacket. As the material slid away, Lorelei could see that his forearms were marred by several scars that crisscrossed over his tanned skin. Eris averted her eyes, looking anywhere but at her friend's arms as he reclaimed his seat.

"Who did this to you?" Lorelei asked as she left her perch beside Declan and crossed the small living room.

"Apollo," Eris answered for her friend.

"May I?" she asked, kneeling in front of Balor. He gave her a soft nod and she brushed a thumb over the knotted scar tissue, shaking her head in disgust.

"Why?" she demanded softly, looking between their two new acquaintances.

"Because I helped Alpha Declan," Balor said quietly, "Cormac took it personally. So, he ordered I be punished for my 'betrayal'. Apollo used a blade dipped in liquid silver. He wanted to make sure I never forgot my insolence."

"Lore," Declan said, and she already knew what he was going to ask her.

"I can heal this," she said, and disbelief creased the brow of the man in front of her.

"You would do that?" he inquired softly, making Lorelei tilt her head in confusion.

"Of course, I would, Balor. What makes you think otherwise?" she asked him, thinking that she might know the answer.

"Because I'm a Rogue," he stated, not quite meeting her eyes, though she smiled softly at him anyway.

"Well, maybe we can change that in the future. In the meantime, Rogue or not, no one deserves this." Lorelei positioned his forearms onto his knees facing up and settled her palms over the scars. Closing her eyes, she focused on her magic and almost immediately she could feel the skin beneath her hands smoothing over.

"Thank you." That was all Balor managed to say when she finished and saw his unmarred skin. Lorelei inclined her head to him with a gentle smile and returned to her place beside Declan.

"I appreciate you both comin' out to speak with us. Is there anything else that either of you needs?" her mate asked, glancing between them.

"I'd like to speak with Wyatt now if that's all right," Eris said, her eyes falling to the Beta. Declan chuckled softly and gestured for his cousin to go and the two of them practically leaped from their seats as they made their way outside.

"I imagine that Eris will be movin' in with Wyatt, so my question is for you, Balor. Would you like to join us for Thanksgiving?" Lorelei asked, and the man's shocked expression made her heart ache briefly. She wondered how long it had been since the man had been shown simple kindness.

"I'd be honored, Luna," he said with a slight bow of his head. Catori pranced around the edge of her mind, huffing with pride.

"I look forward to seeing you there," she said, smiling at him.

'I need to speak to you,' Lorelei said over the mate bond.

"Excuse us for a minute," Declan said, and stood from the couch, gesturing for Lorelei to follow him as he held out his hand to her. Lacing her fingers with his, she let loose a sigh of relief when she heard Garridan strike up a conversation with Balor.

Leading her into the kitchen at the other end of the house, Declan leaned back against the counter and tugged her into his embrace. They stood there for a long moment in silence, content just being in each other's presence.

'You need to challenge, Cormac,' Lorelei said resolutely. She looked up at her mate when he shifted his weight to peer down at her.

'I'll challenge him at Winter Solstice,' he said, making her brow furrow, *'We know what he and Apollo have done. The evidence has been sent to Caine. Is it wrong that I want a little time with my mate before I have to fight for what's already mine?'*

'No, of course not,' Lorelei shook her head, a soft smile on her lips.

'Why though?' he asked, making the corners of her mouth drop into a frown.

'Because I can't tell you what's on that surveillance video,' she said softly and he went completely still.

'You can't, or you won't?' he asked, tone tense and she grimaced, knowing that he would not like the answer.

'Both. At least not until you've challenged Cormac.' She prayed to the Lunar Goddess that he would understand. Declan was silent for a long time and she could feel the internal battle raging in his mind over the bond.

'It's that bad?' he asked finally.

'It's so much worse. Please, just trust me,' she said ardently and felt him release his hold on her. Calloused hands cupped her cheeks and tilted her head up, and she was a bit surprised when his lips crashed down onto hers.

'I trust you with my life.' His voice was a soft caress in her mind as his tongue swept over hers, dominating her senses. Lorelei felt heat blooming from her chest, and a light sheen broke out on her skin as the warmth spread through her torso and down her limbs. She and Declan pulled apart at the same moment as searing pain ricocheted throughout her body, stealing her voice and the air from her lungs.

It felt as if liquid fire was pumped into her veins as another wave of agony speared through her, and her knees gave out. Strong arms scooped her up, and she knew that Declan caught her. Clinging to his solid frame, Lorelei dug her nails into his shoulder as she tried to drag in a breath but even that felt like razors in her chest. From somewhere in her mind, Catori howled, beautiful and haunting, and she could feel the wolf writhing just beneath her skin.

Her first shift began.

Chapter 29

"Shit!" Declan exclaimed, steeling himself against the pain radiating over the mate bond. Scooping up Lorelei when her knees buckled, he hurried to the living room. Glancing at the clock over the mantle, he swore again. She should not be shifting yet, it was too early. However, he thought of her Chimerism and the loops it continued to throw them since day one.

"Garridan, get the door. Lore's shiftin'," he ordered as he paused briefly by the entryway. The Delta surged from the armchair he was reclining in and yanked open the door. Balor followed closely behind them as Declan led the way down the front steps, and lowered Lorelei gently to the grassy lawn.

"Declan..." she groaned, clutching at her abdomen. The sounds of bones and tendons popping could be heard beneath her skin as the shift took over. The agonized scream ripped from her lungs, chilling the blood in Declan's veins, and he knelt by her side, whispering words of encouragement in her ear.

"She's never shifted before?" Eris asked, kneeling beside them.

"No, she was turned," Declan said, earning surprised looks from their new friends, "It's a long story for another time."

Tears slipped over Lorelei's temples into her hair as she let out a groan. Declan felt as if his heart was being ripped from his chest. The pain was nothing like he remembered, but he was born a Werewolf, not a Witch or Chimera. He leaned over, bracing a white-knuckled fist on the ground as his body mirrored the anguish his mate was enduring.

"Don't fight, darlin'. Give Catori control," he urged through gritted teeth, brushing damp strands of her wild curls from her face with trembling hands. Her back suddenly bowed, and another shriek pierced the cool night air as her body twisted, forcing a gasping breath from Declan's lungs. Muscles strained as he forced himself to remain upright, laying a gentle hand over Lorelei's abdomen.

"Lore, you've got to stop fightin'." Declan could feel Rok's panic, the beast lurking just below the surface. A pained yell skinned the back of his throat as another excruciating wave racked his body, nearly forcing him to the ground below.

Just when he thought his insides would surely rip to shreds, the pain suddenly vanished. Sweat slicked and panting, Declan sat back on the ground staring as the woman who lay before him shifted into a massive snow-white wolf. Lorelei, or rather Catori, rose on all fours, shaking her head to settle the new fur growth that now covered her lithe form. She was smaller than his wolf, but not by much, he realized, and that surprised him. The males were considerably larger than She-Wolves but Lorelei– Catori– was the largest true-form female he had ever seen.

As she turned to look at her friends, her ears perked up at seeing their smiling faces. He was in awe of her beauty, the color of her coat, and he reached out a hand to run it through the soft fur hanging heavy at her shoulders. Lorelei let out a soft whine of affection as she turned her head in his direction and her ears lowered as she stepped over to him, bumping her snout against his chest.

"We'll meet y'all at home," Declan said, removing his clothing as he stood, and tossed the garments to Wyatt. He took off in a sprint, wearing only his boxer briefs with Catori nipping playfully at his heels as she chased after him. His eyes blazed crimson as Rok pushed just beneath the surface, eager to break free and run with his mate.

Nearing the treeline, Declan leaped into the air, giving control over his beast as they dove into the underbrush of the surrounding forest. He was a mass of dark gray fur when he landed, and Catori let out an excited yip as they disappeared into the darkness.

Hours later, the first rays of morning sunlight broke over the treetops, bathing the forest in a pale light. Overhead, a mockingbird sang from somewhere in the canopy, and the sounds of animals could be heard all around as they ventured from their dens. Declan placed a hand behind his head, still half asleep in the growing daylight while the tall grass surrounding him and Lorelei tickled his skin. As he lay there, memories of the night drifted through his mind.

In their true forms, Catori and Rok quickly made their way home, then ran for hours in the forest surrounding the lake house. They made it back to the hidden property within a couple of hours and spent the night hunting, playing, and mating. A slow grin spread over his lips as he recalled Lorelei's surprise when his beast mounted hers and sank his teeth into her shoulder, claiming them both. Catori eventually did the same after she pinned Rok while playing, clamping down near the scruff of his neck and marking him as her mate. Only when the wolves exhausted themselves did they find a patch of tall grass near the lake and retreat to the back of their minds, finally sated.

"What're you thinkin' about?" Lorelei asked quietly, and he opened one eye to peer at her. She looked like a wild heathen goddess with the rising sun creating a halo of sunlight behind her mass of curls. Leaves and small debris were tangled in her blood-red tresses, and there were several smudges of mud and dirt from her cheeks to her toes. She sat cross-legged beside him, elbows resting on her knees as she gazed down at him with an amused grin tugging at the corners of her mouth.

"Last night," Declan said, eyes roaming her naked body until they settled on her shoulder and recalled Rok's claiming. Rising into a sitting position, he brushed her hair from her shoulder revealing the new scar beneath smears of dried blood.

"That's somethin' you don't see every day." he mused, brushing his fingertips over her skin.

"What?" Lorelei asked, furrowing her brows. Reaching up, Declan felt the sticky smudges of dried blood and his new mark nestled just below his throat.

"Two marks. One from man." He touched her left shoulder where he claimed her, "And one from beast." His fingers grazed over her collarbone as he moved to her right, making her shiver.

'Mates. Fated, and soul,' Rok gruffed from the shadows of his mind. Lorelei startled, quickly glancing around their surroundings before pinning him with her gaze.

"Was… was that Rok?" she asked, laughing nervously.

'It was,' A husky feminine voice resonated through his mind, and Declan stared in disbelief.

"We can hear each other's wolves," Lorelei stated in a hushed voice, somehow knowing that he heard Catori's words.

"How?" he asked, still in awe as he tried to wrap his head around what was happening.

'We are fated and *soul mates,'* Catori huffed happily, *'We have a greater bond than most.'*

A shrill whistle cut across the property, and echoed across the water as the sound bounced back and forth between the surrounding trees. Declan swiveled his head in the direction of the lake house and let out his whistle, signaling to his cousin they were nearby.

"So, when Catori and Rok marked each other," he said as he rose to his feet and offered Lorelei his hands, pulling her up when she took them.

'Yes. Both sides of each were made for the other. Destined,' Rok spoke, and Declan noticed a faint echoing of the beast's voice as it traveled across the bond. Gently detangling the bits of debris from her curls, he mulled over this newest surprise.

"What do you think about all this?" Lorelei asked, standing patiently in front of him as he removed the last of the leaves from her hair. Warm hands settled on his sides, causing the muscles to flex under her touch as the electric tingles radiated over his skin.

"Well," Declan began as he reached up to remove a small twig he had missed, "It'll make plannin' a surprise party impossible now." Lorelei grinned up at him, laughing softly at his dry humor and he gave her a crooked smile.

"I'm sure you'll find a way," she mused, rising on her tiptoes to kiss him. Declan scooped her up, eliciting a delighted peal of laughter from her as he carried her to the house.

"Your phone's been ringin' nonstop, Lore," Wyatt said when they entered the basement later that morning. Declan gave a nod to Eris as he stopped near the table, looking at the few remaining documents strewn across the tables and then up to the timeline wall.

"I take it you'll be movin' in, Eris?" he asked, his attention on placing the document.

"Yes, Alpha. If that's all right with you, of course." He glanced at her and then Wyatt, who was failing to suppress the grin pressing his lips into a thin line. His cousin was one of the best men he had ever known, but his mischievousness made him a dick sometimes. Judging by the amusement he was trying to hide now, he was already messing with his newfound mate.

"It's perfectly fine." He tacked the page to the wall and braced his hands on his hips, "My family doesn't call me Alpha, though. At least not when we're home." He met her surprised gaze and winked as a slow smile softened his features. Tears pooled in Eris' eyes as she gave him a bright smile, nodding her head vigorously. Wyatt slipped an arm around her waist and kissed her temple.

"Thank you, Alp– Declan," Eris said with a slight dip of her head.

"Oh, don't thank me yet. You're mated to my cousin after all." He laughed, earning him a look of mock insult from Wyatt, making Eris chuckle.

"Shit," Lorelei hissed, causing Declan to peer over his shoulder at her just as she tapped the phone screen and placed the device to her ear, grimacing. "Hey, Adam."

"Lorelei, where the hell have you been? I've been tryin' to reach you for weeks!" Declan heard a male voice demand through the earpiece, and a low growl rumbled from him as their gazes met.

"I'm fine, thanks for askin'," she said snarkily, "I'm still in Louisiana with Declan."

"Why's it takin' you this long to establish–"

"Listen, Adam, I've been meanin' to call you about this, but I haven't had time. It's been a bit chaotic. A lot has changed since I left and I'm sorry but– I'm unable to work for Dawson Therapies anymore," Lorelei said, choosing her words carefully. There was a long pause on the other end of the line and Declan thought the man might have hung up until he heard a soft chuckle.

"You're jokin', right?" Her boss asked softly, though there was a warning in the man's voice that immediately raised his hackles.

"I'm afraid not. Like I said, things've changed, and I can't ethically–"

"'*Ethically*'? You've gotta be fuckin' kiddin' me, Lorelei. You *slept* with him?" Adam demanded angrily, "What the hell's wrong with you?" Before Declan could stop himself, he strode over and gently took the device from her. Lorelei stared up at him with wide eyes, lips parted in shock as he lifted the phone to his ear.

"She doesn't have to explain anything to you," he said, opening his mouth to continue when Adam tried to cut him off.

"Who the fuck do you thin–?" Lorelei's former boss began to demand.

"I'm the man who's gonna remove your head from your shoulders if you speak to my mate like that again. In fact, consider this Lorelei's immediate resignation." He ended the call and handed the phone back to her.

"I was tryin' to be delicate," she said, amusement lighting up her eyes. Declan chuckled and pressed a quick kiss to her lips.

"How was that workin' out for you?" he teased, as he backed away from her.

"Thank you," she said, shaking her head, but he could see her smile falter as she peered back down at the screen. "Now the *real* challenge."

His brows drew together slightly as he tilted his head, watching her locate the next number. Sighing heavily, Lorelei pressed the button and raised the receiver to her ear once again, nervously biting her bottom lip. Turning back to the documents, Declan pushed the image from his mind and picked up a few pages before ambling over to the timeline.

"Lorelei Katherine McCann! I've been worried sick about you!" He turned again to look at Lorelei.

"Nana, I'm fine. Everything's great actually," she said, trying to smooth the elderly woman's obviously ruffled feathers.

"That's no excuse for makin' me worry like you did, what with you off with that deranged Werewolf and all." Declan felt her fury coil down the mate bond, but when she spoke her voice was a deadly calm.

"First off, Declan is not deranged. He's kind and smart, and you would be lucky to know him. Secondly, he's my mate, so I'd appreciate it if you showed him the respect that he deserves."

"Your *what*?!" her grandmother screeched. Beside him Wyatt snorted, causing Eris to elbow him in the ribs, and he cut his cousin a withering glare.

"He's my mate," she repeated, voice still calm like she was speaking to a child.

"I will not allow–" the woman began but Lorelei quickly cut her off, speaking over her.

"You have no say in the matter, Wilhelmina, so you can either accept it or lose your *only* granddaughter. Tell

Mama I love her." With that, she ended the call with a tenuous sigh and dropped her phone onto the desk. She pinched the bridge of her nose between her thumb and forefinger and closed her eyes.

"Are you okay, Luna?" Eris asked softly, breaking the heavy silence hanging in the air.

"Please, just call me Lorelei," she said with a soft smile, "I'm all right though, thank you."

"If you ever need to talk, I'd be happy to listen." A sheepish smile tugged on Eris' lips and she nodded.

'You and Eris don't have to stay down here,' Declan said through the bond.

'She just found Wyatt. I'd have probably killed someone if they had tried to pull me away from you.' Her response was soft, and he understood exactly what she meant. He would have raged if someone tried to take her attention from him when their bond snapped into place and the weeks following. He still hated when they were apart, even if they were only across the house from each other. His only solace when she was not with him, was knowing the strength of their bond, that they were bound to each other by fate and souls.

'I love you,' she said, and he felt it. Unconditional love vibrated across the bond, causing his chest to constrict from the emotion.

'*And I love you,*' Declan said, casting his own emotions to her, and he heard a nearly imperceptible gasp come from her.

"Are you two mind fuckin' again?" Wyatt's question cut through the moment as a wide grin lit up his handsome face. Grabbing a pen from the table, Declan hurled it at his cousin who casually sidestepped the mini projectile.

Chapter 30

Days quickly bled into weeks, and the trees surrounding the lake house long lost their leaves, leaving a barren but beautiful view. Glittering frost-covered grass crunched under Lorelei's booted feet as she walked along the edge of the lake, watching the first rays of sunlight break over the treetops. A small gaggle of Canadian geese was waddling along the grassy shore nearby, and a few wood ducks paddled out on the water's smooth surface. Her breaths billowed in front of her in large puffs, and she stopped to take in the scenery around her.

Tugging Declan's heavy coat tighter around her body, Lorelei pondered over the last month, and what they were leading up to. Burying her nose into the collar, she inhaled her mate's scent, immediately feeling at peace wrapped in the warmth of the too-large jacket. Memories of Thanksgiving floated through her mind as she recalled the laughter and good food she shared with Declan, Wyatt and Eris, Garridan, and Balor. The family that she stumbled into filled her with more love and joy than she could have ever imagined having. She laughed out loud when she remembered Eris flicking peas at Wyatt from across the table, and the Beta thinking it had been his cousin or Garridan. A food fight would have erupted had it not been for Balor's quick thinking when he lifted his glass in a toast.

The next couple of weeks following the holiday were less happy with endless phone calls from her grandmother, who had finally de-escalated from irate and ranting to desperate and pleading. Lorelei still had not told Wilhelmina that she was now part Werewolf, or of her diagnosis with Chimerism. Pushing the thought aside to worry about it for another day, she stepped down onto a patch of sandy beach with a sigh.

Taking a moment, she pulled out her phone and snapped a picture of the sunrise before checking her email. Their group finally finished compiling all of the paper evidence chronologically and sent everything to Elder Caine. Though she had not heard from him, Garridan assured her that the old Warlock had received the files and was nearly finished preparing the summons for the Daughtry's trial.

'Where're you at, darlin'?' Declan's groggy voice rasped down the mate bond, causing goosebumps to erupt over her skin.

'I'm out takin' a walk. You were sleepin' so well I didn't want to wake you,' she said, stopping near a group of cypress trees standing proud in the icy lake. Though his nightmares eased off considerably since they mated, he still dealt with insomnia most nights. Tossing and turning until exhaustion forced him to sleep.

'*Lore, you don't have a jacket,*' he said and she felt his worry. She ordered some winter clothes, but they had not arrived yet to the local post office so she understood his concern thinking she was outside in nothing but a band tee and a pair of thin leggings.

'*I grabbed your heavy camo jacket from the closet before I came out. I promise I'm nice and warm.*' He calmed at her soft reassurance, '*There's fresh coffee made. I'll be in soon, love.*'

Lorelei just settled onto the trunk of a fallen tree near the water's edge when the sound of a snapping twig caught her attention. She swiveled her head in the direction of the sound when something hard connected with the back of her skull. Stars exploded in her vision as she was sent sprawling into the icy shallows. The water was just deep enough to cover her completely and it felt as if thousands of needles were lancing through her body.

Between the numbing cold of the lake and the pounding in her skull, Lorelei struggled to get her bearings. Two sets of strong hands clamped around her upper arms, hauling her from the water. A hood or bag was forced over her head and drawn tight around her throat before she could even think of looking to see who attacked her. A pair of cold handcuffs were clamped around her wrists, burning her skin, and within seconds of being struck, Lorelei was being forced blindly through the dense underbrush of the forest. Stumbling in her blindness and the pain drumming in her skull, she tried to attack with her magic to force whoever they were away from her.

Panic gripped her in a vice when she realized she could not draw on the energy. She opened her mouth to scream for Declan and the others but no sound came out. Desperation began to take over and she called over the mate bond but there was only silence. The cuffs she realized, burning the flesh around her wrists, were laced with iron and salt. Separate, neither would do much harm, but together they worked well at subduing magic of all forms.

The sound of an idling engine grew louder as her captors dragged her quickly through the brambles and briars, lying thick on the forest floor. Lorelei struggled against the two holding her, digging her heels into the dirt in an attempt to slow them down. Her actions earned her another blow, landing near the base of her skull, almost knocking her unconscious. Knees buckling, she cried out in pain as she landed hard on the cold ground.

"Let's go! Do you *want* Wolfe to find us?" a voice demanded as she was lifted into the air. Only a moment later, Lorelei was shoved into what felt like a truck and covered with a heavy blanket. As she slipped into unconsciousness, she felt it.

The putrid oily snares of dark magic.

Chapter 31

'Declan!'

He jolted awake with a growl, the voice echoing in his mind as he peered wildly around the bedroom. It was empty. Sunlight was streaming through the windows, their curtains thrown wide like they always were. Taking note of the state of the room, everything seemed in order. There were no strange scents, nothing out of place except for the panic Declan felt deep in his chest, making his heart hammer against his ribcage.

'Something is wrong,' Rok growled, sending him into motion. Throwing back the comforter, Declan dressed quickly before rushing down the stairs.

"Lore?" he called as he dropped from the bottom step. Glancing around the open space, he quickly realized she was not there. Opening the basement door, he called out again, but there was still no answer.

'Lorelei, where are you?' Declan asked over the bond, but his question was met with silence. *'Catori?'* Rok whined softly.

"Dec, what's goin' on?" Wyatt asked from the hallway that led to his room. A moment later, he and Eris padded into the living room, looking concerned.

"I can't find Lore. She went for a walk this mornin' and now… Somethin's wrong. I can *feel* her, but I can't hear her," he said, brushing past Garridan as the Delta stepped into the kitchen, pulling a sweater over his head. Yanking open the back door, Declan caught the faint scent of honeysuckle and sweet apples on the gentle breeze and took off toward the dock. Yelling for his mate, his bare feet thundered over the wooden planks as he neared the boathouse. She was not there, though she had been at some point recently. Retracing his steps back to the house, dread overriding his emotions, he called out over the mate bond again. There was still no response.

"Eris, hang here in case she comes back," Declan said, "Y'all are with me." Wyatt and Garridan only nodded before they set off, following Lorelei's scent across the lawn and down to the lakeshore. They followed her trail for nearly an hour until it ended at a small cluster of weathered cypress trees, growing near the edge of the water.

"Someone was here," Wyatt said, his eyes shifting icy blue, "Several someones."

"Recognize their scent?" Declan asked, and Garridan grunted in response.

"Devlin Erickson, James Merrick, and the Williams twins," the Delta said through gritted teeth. Fury ignited Declan's blood at the revelation that Balor had a hand in whatever happened to Lorelei. He struck one of the nearby tree trunks, his roar echoing loudly across the surface of the lake. The wood splintered, and the ancient cypress groaned in protest. Barely feeling the pain of his broken hand, Declan turned and strode angrily back to the house.

"They're dead. All of them," he shouted, eyes glowing crimson as he barged through the back door into the kitchen, though he stopped short when he recognized the man standing at the island with Eris.

"Balor," he growled. Declan was on him instantly, hand at his throat as he lifted the man off his feet and slammed him down onto the countertop.

"Where's Lorelei?" he demanded, feeling Rok writhe beneath his skin.

"Declan, stop! Just listen to what he has to say!" Eris shouted, gripping his wrist to try and remove his hold on their friend's neck.

"Why would I listen to a man that betrayed me and my family?" he spat out the word betrayed, his fingers tightening to cut off Balor's air supply. Though the man flinched at the accusation, he did not struggle against the hand choking him.

"I- didn't know..." Balor forced out, his face turning bright red, "Came- soon as... could."

"Dec," Wyatt said from behind him, "I know you're worried, but give the man a chance. He deserves that much." Clenching his jaw, Declan stared down at the man he had in his grip for a long moment before releasing him abruptly and stalking across the room. Balor drew in a deep, gasping breath, quickly followed by a hard cough as he pushed himself into a sitting position on the island's top. Rubbing at his bruised throat, he held up a hand to Eris when she tried to examine the damage that would soon be healed.

"I know how it looks," the man said hoarsely, sliding to the floor, "but I had no idea that they were going to take Lorelei. She's at the main packhouse. I came as soon as we got back."

"Why didn't you call or text one of us?" Garridan demanded, his thick arms crossed over his chest.

"Cormac forbade us from taking our cell phones. Said that there couldn't be any distractions when pickin' up the 'package'." Declan met the man's gaze, lips pressed into a thin line.

"Tell me everything," he ground out, eyes crimson. Balor did not hesitate as he explained the plan to obtain the package, his suspicions when they headed in the direction of the lake house, or how they handled Lorelei once they located her.

"How did Cormac know she was goin' to be away from the house, alone?" he asked, thinking that he might know the answer already.

"The Witch. Somehow she knew," Balor stated.

"And the location of the lake house? Did the Witch *somehow* know that, too?" Declan was not sure if he believed the man, but he could find no sign that he was being deceitful. His body language was relaxed, given the assault he had just experienced and the interrogation he was being put through now. Lorelei gave him tips on spotting lies in case she was not around for one reason or another. Body language and lack of eye contact were the biggest tells of anyone who was lying, and Balor was maintaining both. He was being truthful.

"Devlin, he notices things. It's part of his job being a tracker. He saw Garridan's reaction at the Halloween party and his warning to you. When he left shortly after y'all, Devlin shifted and followed, keeping to the treeline so he wasn't spotted." Balor glanced at Garridan as the Delta let out a growl, though who it was directed at, Declan was not sure.

'I do not think it could have been changed,' Rok gruffed, and though he did not like the situation, Declan had to agree. As many times as Cormac tried to get to Lorelei, they should have anticipated the possibility of the Omega discovering the location of the lake house.

"They've been planning, waiting for an opportunity ever since then," Balor said, his voice finally back to normal.

"What's Cormac want with her?" Eris questioned, and Declan shook his head, not knowing the answer.

"I'm going to assume he still wants her for himself. If he didn't know she and I are mates, he does now." At that moment, his cell phone chimed in his pocket. Digging out the device, he suppressed the snarl rising in his throat.

"You know you're a dead man, right?" Declan said almost casually, despite the white-hot rage burning through him.

"I highly doubt that, Wolfe," Cormac stated confidently, "seeing as how I have your *mate* here with me." The threat was not lost on him, and a low growl rumbled from deep within his chest. The Omega tutted at the sound like he was admonishing a small child.

"Now, now, none of that. I've called with a proposition for you. A treaty, if you will." The man paused before continuing, "You will leave Louisiana, forfeiting the pack, and agree to never return. In exchange, I will return Lorelei to you unharmed. Well, mostly unharmed. My retrieval team was a little… rough, so to speak." Cormac did not bother to hide the amusement in his voice.

"Exile? That's your *treaty*?" Declan asked, even though he would agree to it without hesitation if it got Lorelei back to him, but he did not trust the Omega. The bastard relished in the pain of others, which Declan supposed made them not all that different.

'You need a reason to cause pain. You do not do it for fun,' Rok rumbled in his mind.

"Either you agree, or I kill her, and then send my pack after you and the remainder of your pathetic little family," Cormac threatened, and for a moment, Declan wondered if they could win that fight. Glancing around at the family he found, they watched him, waiting for his decision. Only Balor shook his head subtly, a knowing look in his eye.

"Fine," he ground out, earning him surprised looks from Wyatt and Garridan. Eris only glanced at Balor, who gave him a nod before beckoning the other three down to the basement.

"Wise choice, *brother*," Cormac sneered, obviously pleased with the outcome. "Join me for dinner to discuss the terms of the contract. I'll expect you at 6 o'clock, sharp." Glancing at the clock on the stove, he calculated the time they would have to come up with a plan and hung up the phone.

Declan sat at the ridiculously long dining table just over an hour later, looking almost casual as he leaned to one side, elbow propped on the armrest. Though he appeared relaxed on the outside, his mind was in chaos. He still could not reach Lorelei over the matebond, though shortly after he arrived, a feeling of panic once again gripped him in a vice. This time, however, fear wormed its way in, cold and hard. He realized that it was not his own emotion he was feeling, but his mate's instead. Rok confirmed that he could now sense Catori, though he too could not communicate with her. He and the beast surmised that some kind of block was the cause, something possibly similar to the cages in the basement of Saint Thaddeus.

Glancing around the familiar dining room, with its polished wood panels and elaborate chandelier, Declan was hit with a sense of nostalgia as memories of holidays and formal gatherings filtered through his mind. Of his parents hosting a visiting Alpha and their family for various business meetings or special gatherings. The feast the Alpha and Luna would provide for their pack on Thanksgiving and Christmas Day. His heart squeezed with grief at the reminder that they were gone. Though the emotion was swiftly replaced with something else, something much darker, when the reason for their deaths strolled casually into the room.

"I would apologize for my tardiness, but I had some… unfinished business to attend to." Cormac sat at the head of the table across from him, keeping a healthy twenty feet between them. Snapping his fingers, several servants hurried in and placed silver platters on the table, all in front of the false Alpha.

'He thinks himself dominant,' Rok growled, hackles rising at the silent challenge. Declan crossed an ankle over his knee and continued lounging calmly in his chair. Though he would not have eaten given the

opportunity, the message was clear. Cormac believed he was in control of the situation. Of him.

"Where's Lorelei?" he asked, keeping his gaze on the man across from him.

"Safe. For now," the Omega replied, tossing a bone over his shoulder.

"Don't play games with me, Cormac," Declan warned as his eyes turned crimson, "You're gonna get your treaty. I just want my mate returned to me. Do that, and I'll leave."

"Do you take me for a fool?" Sickly green eyes flashed as they blinked at him, and it took everything not to give the man his honest answer. Instead, he half rolled his eyes, subtly glancing out the window to the treeline in the distance with a heavy sigh.

"You've made your demands, and I'm willin' to agree to them as long as you return Lorelei to me. Now." Declan leveled his gaze at the Omega.

"Demands are not met with demands, Mister Wolfe," said a feminine voice from the archway. Adjusting his position, Declan looked over his shoulder to the woman who stood in the entryway, Apollo a step behind her. He immediately recognized her as one of the members of the Elder Council. The Witch who insisted on his guilt gave him a wicked smile as she sauntered toward him.

"Surely, your father taught you that," she added, extending her hand, "We were never properly introduced– I'm Mercy Good." Declan turned away from the woman, surprised when she let out an almost charming laugh at his rejection. The Witch and Apollo moved away, down the length of the table, taking their seats on either side of Cormac. A sudden wash of relief overtook Declan, and he knew if he were not sitting already, he would have dropped to the floor from the strength of the emotion.

"I didn't realize this was a meetin' of traitors," Declan said coolly as he stood from his chair. Ambling casually over to the window, he leaned against the frame just as his phone buzzed. Digging the device from his pocket, he held up his finger when Cormac opened his mouth to protest. The two Omegas fumed, their faces turning red as they glared at him.

'Safe.' The one-word message from Wyatt sent his heart hammering in his chest. They found her. Willing himself to remain calm, Declan tapped out a response, absently strolling along the length of the table.

"Are you quite finished?" Apollo demanded over his shoulder. He cut his eyes to the older Omega as he slipped the phone back into his pocket. Without warning, Declan lunged for the back of his chair with supernatural speed. His claws erupted as he punched through the upholstery and sank his fingers into

Apollo's back, burrowing straight to his heart. There was a sharp exhale followed by a strangled gurgle as Declan's fist erupted from the Omega's chest, clutching the still-beating heart.

"Oh, I'm just gettin' started," he said with a low growl.

"That's one down." Yanking his arm from the ruined chair, he tossed the organ onto Cormac's plate. As the false Alpha watched his father's heart fall, Declan lunged for him, swiping at the man's throat, but was halted by an invisible barrier mere inches from the false Alpha's face. He turned his head to glare at the Witch, and he could see the subtle warbling of the air around her.

"You'll find you're going to have a hard time getting to him." Knowing she protected herself, he kicked out his leg and sent the table careening into her barrier. "Or me," she added, but the force jarred her backward, causing her chair to teeter on two legs, and she stared at Declan wide-eyed.

An agonizing shot of pain lanced through his skull as a memory flashed in his mind of Apollo holding a heart above his head, blood raining down over him. A snarl ripped from his throat as he doubled over, and he was vaguely aware of the sound of chairs scraping over the hardwood floor. Pounding footsteps followed, and Declan knew the remaining two made a run for it.

'*Good,*' Rok growled excitedly. He followed the scent of their fear down the hallway, through the kitchen, and out to the grassy lawn surrounding the packhouse. His breath billowed from him in large puffs of steam as he rounded the corner of his home and let out a shrill whistle that echoed for miles out into the forest.

Cormac and Mercy were half way across the massive stretch of land when a symphony of howls rose up from the trees surrounding the property, causing them to skid to a halt. The underbrush near the edge of the forest trembled as hundreds of bodies moved through the brambles, flattening the vegetation as they marched forward. Group after group, row upon row of Werewolves stepped from the treeline, some shifted into their preferred form, and some still human. Declan took stock of the Alpha's that were leading their packs forward. Surprised to see that Ironhide, and Gray River came after all, with Shadow Paw, and Silver Moon standing front and center. Only adding to his shock, he saw the Vampire, and Witch coven leaders standing amongst them. The sound of footsteps pulled his attention away from the gathered packs and covens, and he looked over his shoulder to see the Rogues coming towards him, Balor leading. The Delta gestured for them to join the others as he stopped beside Declan, watching them march across the lawn and take their places with the other Werewolves.

"Thanks, Dec," Balor said after a minute.

"For what?" he said, glancing over at the man.

"For trustin' me." With that, Balor gave him a nod and crossed the distance to stand with the rest of their family. Shoving his hands into the pockets of his jacket, Declan ambled past the gathered allies.

"I think you'll find gettin' away this time is gonna be harder than before," he said, stopping several feet from the traitors. With his words, hundreds moved to encircle them, hemming Cormac and Mercy into a makeshift arena.

"Let's just talk about this, Declan," the false Alpha pleaded, fear shining bright in his hazel eyes. "We can come to some agreement, I'm sure."

"The moment you ordered your men to take Lorelei, you signed your death warrant," he said, meandering around the three of them.

"She was never meant to be hurt. We only took her as insurance," Mercy stated matter-of-factly. Rok writhed beneath his skin, the beast begging to be unleashed.

"You say that like it makes it better," he growled, stalking towards the Witch.

"I can kill you with a snap of my fingers," Mercy spat out, stepping between Cormac and Declan. His crimson gaze found hers, causing the vehemence in her expression to falter.

"If you could, you would've by now," he stated calmly, "But seein' as I'm still alive, I gotta call bullshit." Mercy's nostrils flared, but she remained silent, glaring as he began to prowl around them.

"There's a reason you can't use your magic right now, Mercy." She glanced nervously around the circle, settling on Cormac who stared in disbelief. "It's 'cause my mate's blocked you."

"That's not possible," The Witch muttered, shaking her head in denial.

"Oh, it's very possible," Lorelei called from the outer edges of the assembly.

To his right, the crowd parted briefly, and Declan watched as she made her way over to him. There were smears of blood under her nose and lip, and a greenish tint discolored the skin high over her cheekbone. She had a slight limp as she came to a stop beside him, sliding her hand into his. A melting pot of emotions stormed through him as he stared down at her, taking note of the injuries. Bones healing in her leg, broken nose, busted lip, and the remnants of a black eye that was nearly healed.

"Name them," he said, his voice a blend of man and beast.

"Devlin Erickson, James Merrick, Bullard Williams, Cormac Daughtry, Apollo Daughtry, and Mercy Good," Lorelei said, cutting her eyes to the pair in front of them. The Rogues she named quickly tried to tuck tail and run but were each caught within seconds and shoved into the circle.

"Cormac Daughtry, I challenge you for the title of Alpha to the Crescent Ridge pack," Declan stated as he led his mate over to the sidelines where she joined Wyatt and Eris. Garridan and Balor were positioned on either side of the three Rogues, making sure they did not interfere.

"I accept, on one condition," he said, with a sly grin, "No magical interference."

"Fine," Declan said after a moment of consideration, and nodded to Lorelei. He could feel her magic withdraw as the block over Mercy was lifted.

'I don't like this. She's goin' to– Look out!' Her warning came a second too late, and in the next moment, he felt the pain ricochet through his mind as a fist connected with the side of his face, sending him stumbling backwards.

Chapter 32

Declan glared up at Cormac from where he dropped to one knee, the echo of the spell's defenses still ringing in his ears. The pain caught him completely off guard and the Omega took full advantage of it by waylaying a brutal right hook into Declan's nose. Though he healed quickly, blood still trickled over his lips. Cormac stood arrogantly above him, grinning like a Cheshire cat.

"You will not take this from me, Wolfe," Cormac said, "But I will take everything from you. *Again.*" Cormac lifted his pale green gaze at his last word, and Declan knew what– who– he was looking at. Lorelei.

Fury that could have rivaled the might of a god erupted in his veins, and he let out a teeth baring snarl. Using the arm he braced on the grass as leverage, Declan lunged, sweeping out the opposite leg with supernatural speed. He let the momentum of the spin pull his body around as he stood, righting himself into a defensive stance as Cormac crashed to the ground in a heap. Without waiting for the man to recover, Declan brought his heel down hard on Cormac's throat.

Another shot of pain rattled Declan's skull as a heavy kick connected with his spine and he staggered forward. The new memory flickered in and out as he struggled to regain his bearings. For a brief moment, he remembered his mother and father milling around the Alpha ceremony, speaking with their guests. The smiles on their faces as they greeted each pack member made his heart ache.

"Does it hurt?" Cormac sneered with an uppercut. The blow snapped Declan's head back and he staggered again. Jolt after jolt of excruciating pain ripped through his mind as the memories were dragged through the barrier, each simultaneously followed by an attack from Cormac. An inhuman groan echoed across the lawn as he fought through the pain, barely blocking another blow from Cormac.

Something warm slid down his cheek, the metallic scent of blood overwhelming as he swiped at his skin. Declan had been in so much pain he had not even noticed when Cormac raked his claws across the side of his face. Panting, he tried to regain his bearings and focus on the man in front of him.

Another violent stab of pain. Another vicious strike.

'Why are memories coming through the barrier?' Rok howled, writhing in pain.

'I don't–' Declan faltered as the pattern became obvious. *'The Witch.'* Declan understood their game now. The Witch would pull a memory leaving him momentarily blind with pain, and Cormac would strike. Giving the illusion that the Omega could indeed beat a true Alpha.

For a brief moment, the onslaught stopped as the air around them suddenly vibrated with energy. The hair on the nape of Declan's neck stood on end and electric tingles crackled pleasantly along his skin. His gaze immediately found Lorelei. She was staring at Mercy, a translucent spike forming in her hand. He noticed that none of their friends, their allies, moved. Eris seemed to be watching Lorelei, while Wyatt, Garridan and Balor peered in various directions, monitoring the Rogues.

'Why do they not move?' Rok gruffed, his voice filled with worry.

'Because they can't. They've been spelled,' Lorelei stated grimly, and he felt the trepidation skitter down the mate bond. In a swift, almost imperceptible motion, Lorelei slung out her arm toward Mercy. A resounding boom shook the ground beneath their feet as the projectile collided with an invisible wall. Dazzling sparks erupted from the point of impact and the barrier rippled. Jagged cracks formed, seeming to float in the air as they quickly fluttered outward in all directions. Within seconds, the barrier shattered, its shards evaporating in wisps of black smoke.

"Well done, Doctor McCann," Mercy said, a wicked smile pulling her lips up sharply, "Who knew a Witch so young could harness such power. I wonder what other secrets you've been keeping? Perhaps the knowledge that you've known what I was since the hearing?" Declan felt as if he could have been knocked over by a feather at that moment. His gaze flicked to his mate, muscles rigid with near painful tension. Rok and Catori issued a warning growl. Not at Lorelei, but at him for doubting his mate for even the briefest moment.

"I wasn't sure what I saw that day," Lorelei said softly, and he felt regret pulse from her. "Whatever it was, it wasn't significant enough to think you posed a threat."

Declan saw Cormac beginning to shuffle nervously from the corner of his eye as the grin on Mercy's face became strained, slowly turning downward as Lorelei's words sank in.

"I'm the greatest threat you'll ever face, little Witch," Mercy spat out vehemently. With a flick of her wrist, a large ball of black swirling energy formed in the span of a blink and launched across the gap separating her and Lorelei.

"Lore!" Declan bellowed, but the energy already swallowed her. It exploded into a swath of thick black fog obscuring his view. Lurching toward his mate, he only managed to take a single step before a granite-like forearm slammed into his throat. Cormac might be an Omega, but thanks to his training, he was toned and stronger than others of his rank. Struggling to pull in a breath as his crushed trachea mended itself, Declan barely avoided another kick to his abdomen as he called out over the mate bond.

'I'm fine, love,' Lorelei said as a barrage of razor-sharp spikes and glowing orbs shot from the haze. Mercy managed to deflect most of the projectiles, but two of the spikes embedded themselves deep into her chest, and one of the orbs collided with the side of her face. The resulting screech was near feral and caused every hair on Declan's body to stand on end. Even the trees around them seemed to shudder.

Risking a glance at Lorelei as the darkness dissipated from around her, his relief nearly overwhelmed him when he saw the faint warble of her shield. A blur of movement out of the corner of his eye caught his attention, and Declan barely dodged the spinning kick, aimed for his head. Feinting to the left, he spun around Cormac and landed a powerful blow to the man's spine with his elbow. The muffled crack of vertebrae told him that he had broken the Omega's back, giving him the few precious seconds he needed for his trachea to fully heal. As he finally drew in a ragged breath, Declan stared in disbelief at the other woman.

'Did your magic do that to her?' He asked over the bond, trying to process what he was seeing.

'No,' Lorelei said, a hint of pity in her voice, *'My magic shattered the glamor she was using. That's the real Mercy.'*

There was a gaping hole on the side of Mercy's face. She looked like a broken porcelain doll as cracks splintered across her skin. The shards of her glamor crumbled before disappearing into wisps of black smoke, leaving the true visage of Mercy standing before them. Her skin was sallow and heavily wrinkled. It clung to her bones, creating severe hollows in her cheeks. Eyes the color of putrid swamp muck glared at Lorelei from black, impossibly sunken sockets. Thin ashen lips pulled back to in a snarl revealed a mouth full of broken, rotting teeth. The only thing that remained similar to the glamor she had worn before was her hair. Though now it was a thin, wiry tangle of silver strands.

"Your death will be a slow and painful one," Mercy said, her voice harsh and rasping, and there was an underlying echo to the sound. As if hundreds of voices were speaking all at once.

At his feet, Cormac groaned as he rolled over to his back. Declan almost forgot about the man until that moment, and he bent down to seize the Omega by the throat. He lifted the man, fingers digging into his flesh. Panic flashed over Cormac's rapidly reddening face as he clawed at the arm holding him aloft, legs flailing weakly.

"Mercy!" Cormac choked out weakly. Glancing over at Lorelei and then the Witch, both women extended a hand in his direction, but Mercy was faster. Barely.

Pain shot through Declan like a wrecking ball. He was wrenched off his feet as the writhing dark orb slammed into his torso, knocking the wind out of him. Fingers slipping from the Omega's throat, he crashed to the cold, hard ground. Gasping for air, he blindly fumbled to his knees as the memories flooded his mind. White-hot agony threatened to split his skull in two and Declan released a roar of pain that tore at his throat, burning his chest.

"Ladies and gentlemen, could I have your attention, please? There's been a request to give a speech in honor of tonight's celebration." Alaric's voice boomed over the property, as Apollo took the stage, and gestured to someone beyond the party. Several carts carrying hundreds of wine glasses were wheeled out with a rich black liquid sloshing gently in the crystal vessels.

"Thank you, Beta Leal. You're all probably wondering what this is about. Well, the black wine in your glasses is the direct result of the unmatched generosity of our Alpha, Mordecai Wolfe." Apollo said smoothly and murmurs erupt as everyone examined their glasses with new curiosity. "It is because of Alpha Kai that we were given a second chance. We have had the privilege of being a part of this pack for over twenty years now and I am finally able to give back some of that generosity. The vineyard I was able to procure and turn

into a successful business is all thanks to him!" As the last of the wine glasses were handed out to the few remaining empty hands, he grabbed one in passing. Picking his way through the crowd to his family, he peered down at the wine. It was opaque with a soft shimmer that roiled around gracefully in the darkness.

'What is that?' his beast questioned, wary of the miniscule particles that continued to undulate throughout the wine. He wondered the same, giving his glass a gentle swirl before lifting it to his nose and taking a cautious sniff.

"Thank you, Alpha. And now, a toast!" Apollo said almost gleefully, as he stepped up beside his uncle, "To Declan! May your legacy far outshine your fathers." Apollo lifted his glass, watching as they all drank. However, the Omega looked down at his watch, and then back at the gathered crowd. Watch. Crowd. Watch. Crowd.

Suddenly, the din of conversation died out and an eerie silence descended over the party. Everyone was staring straight ahead and slack jawed. A strange sensation blossomed throughout his chest. Warmth spread along his limbs, relaxing his muscles, and he struggled to speak. Knees wobbling under the power of the paralytic, understanding struck him like a freight train.

Uncle Alaric dropped first, slamming face first onto the lawn. Wyatt hit the ground hard a second later. He toppled onto his side, pain radiating through his skull. His mother and father soon followed.

A shadow loomed over him, and he knew the scent of the man, did not need to see his face to know there was a sneering grin tugging at his lips.

"My only regret, brother,*" Cormac said softly, squatting beside him, "is that I don't get to kill you myself." Giving his cheek a hard smack, Cormac straightened and strolled over to his mother.*

"However, I do take great comfort knowing it is you who will take the fall." Without warning, Cormac lifted his foot high and brought it down on the side of her head. With a forceful shove through the last bit of resistance, Cormac's shiny dress shoe disappeared as her skull caved in. He tried to scream, to rise and put an end to the bastard but his body would not cooperate. Cormac wiped the sole of his shoe on the grass as if he stepped in something foul and vanished from his line of sight. Tears trickled from his deadened eyes as he stared unblinking at the lifeless body of his mother, and a hatred he would surely carry with him in death sparked to life.

The metallic scent of blood was so thick in the air that it coated his tongue. The sounds of bones crunching, and the squish of flesh could be heard from somewhere behind him. A Werewolf crouched between him and his uncle, causing his stomach to feel as if it dropped through the earth. He recognized Apollo's scent as the beast leaned over and clamped down on his uncle's head. Alaric was silent as the Omega's sharp teeth pierced his skin. Blood lashed across his face, dripping from his nose as some body part splattered to the ground nearby. Bile burned the back of his throat hearing the slow, deliberate crunching of his uncle's bones. Droplets of warm blood splashing over his skin instantly cooled before trickling to the grass below. When Apollo was finally satisfied with the Betas dismemberment, the traitor shifted back into human form and knelt beside his father. Rolling the Alpha onto his back, the Omega surged forward, claws extended and plunged a hand into his father's chest.

"You sealed your fate twenty-two years ago when you welcomed me and my son into your pack. You made this all possible, Kai." Apollo's grin was malevolent as he tore the Alpha's heart from his chest with a sickening squelch and popping of arteries.

As pack members were picked off one by one, he prayed to the Lunar Goddess. Begged her to help them or end their misery. Anything would be better than what was taking place around him. The response he received was a ruthless kick to the abdomen that cleaved the air from his lungs. A muffled wheeze issued from somewhere in his chest as he was shoved onto his back. The stars above twinkled mockingly down at him from the safety of their inky night sky. The sucker punch came out of nowhere, careening into his nose. Cartilage popped and blood oozed from his nostrils, choking him as it poured down the back of his throat. With his wolf unconscious, his healing was slowed, and the pain was immeasurable. Cormac struck again, this time cracking his eye socket. Over and over, he was struck. He had never experienced so much pain in his life, and the adrenaline coursing through him turned his stomach. As his vision *blurred, the last thing he saw was Cormac's bloodied fist swinging down. The final blow landed like a cannonball, fracturing his skull on impact, and sent his world fading into blackness.*

"Why?" Declan rasped the demand quietly through gritted teeth.

"Power, of course. Why else?" Cormac offered nonchalantly, "Power and fear are a dangerous, yet heady, combination. You can make anyone bend to your will if you just know how."

"What power? You're as intimidatin' as a *pup*," Declan stated, chuckling despite the throbbing pain, still lingering in his skull. A fist connected with his chin, snapping his head to the side. The force of the punch made him rare back, and he had to drop a hand to the ground to remain upright.

"Seems I struck a nerve." Declan could taste the blood coating his teeth as he grinned broadly and straightened. At that moment, he picked up the sound of a rapid thrumming, and his brows briefly drew together. Declan strained his ringing ears to listen, eyes drifting up to look at his mate who was locked in a battle of her own with Mercy. Time seemed to stop, and for a moment he forgot to breathe when he understood what he was hearing. A pulse. Alternating from stable to erratic as the quick heart beats fell out of sync.

Cormac lunged to deliver another blow, and the time bomb within Declan finally detonated. Eyes still on Lorelei, he caught the incoming fist and squeezed it tightly. He wanted Cormac to scream. To beg for his life. Wanted him to feel every ounce of pain that he caused tenfold. The agony he would inflict on this traitor would be unmatched. He would take his time, savor the torture, and the pain, and the revenge.

"You *will* die here," Declan said, only it was Rok's voice that grated from him, harsh and deep. His grip tightened further, shattering the bones in Cormac's hand. The Omega let out a guttural scream that was quickly silenced when Declan slashed his claws across the man's throat. Blood sprayed from the gaping wound, and it took a moment for Cormac to realize what happened. Eyes bulging, the false Alpha gripped the mangled flesh with his good hand trying to staunch the flow enough to heal.

Releasing the ruined hand, claws erupted from his nail beds as Declan buried his fingers in Cormac's chest. Bone and cartilage sliced at his skin, but he did not stop. He could not stop despite the pain that raked up his arm. All the suffering and misery this bastard brought to so many people over the course of his miserable life would be dealt right back to him. Wrapping his fingers around the Omega's heart, he grinned much like Apollo had when murdering Declan's father.

A gentle caress along the bond brought him back to the present, instantly calming the savage that raged within him. Eyes drifting closed, Declan took a deep breath. When he opened them again, he found Cormac's hazel stare reflecting the crimson of his own back at him. Blood burbled from his mouth, dripping down the Omega's chin as he tried to speak.

"For everyone," Declan rasped out, squeezing the frantically beating heart. Cormac emitted a strangled cry of pain as the organ collapsed into a tangled mass of muscle in his fist.

Chapter 33

One week later, Lorelei stood over the sink of her and Declan's en-suite bathroom, hands braced on the counter. Sighing impatiently, she lifted her head, peering at her reflection in the mirror. So much had changed in just a few short months. Was *still* changing.

'What if he's wrong?' Lorelei asked anxiously.

'He is not wrong,' Catori gruffed softly in her mind. Declan told her the day after their confrontation with Mercy and the Daughtry's of the heartbeats he heard during the fight. Even though he had not heard them since, he encouraged her to take a pregnancy test. He only kissed her forehead when she insisted that it could not possibly be true. The corners of her mouth pulled up ever so slightly, recalling his words to her,

'The scars on your wrists healed. Why couldn't the same be for the others, too?'

Despite his logic being perfectly sound, she was positive it had been another female nearby, not her. It was only when Catori said something that she allowed herself to hope. A soft beep sounded from the slender test that lay beside the sink. Closing her eyes against the sting of her tears, she picked up the slender pregnancy test with a trembling hand. Taking a deep, steadying breath, she peeked down at the tiny window.

POSITIVE

Lorelei stared in disbelief as silent tears rolled down her cheeks. She was pregnant. Catori practically vibrated with excitement, and she nearly lost her hold on the mindlink block she had in place all day.

"Lore! We're gonna be late," Eris called from downstairs.

"I'm comin', I'm comin'." Wiping the tears from her cheeks, she adjusted her sweater and hurried to meet her best friend.

"Wyatt said they're almost here," Eris said as they wound their way into the packhouse living room.

"Is everything ready?" she asked, looking around at the simple but many decorations. A banner proudly declaring, 'Welcome Home, Alpha!' had been strung from the ceiling, and hundreds of black and red balloons rolled lazily above their heads.

"Yep. We just need our Alpha to get here," Balor said as he sidled up to her. Lorelei wrapped her arms around the man in a tight hug.

"Thank you. I couldn't've pulled any of this off without y'all," she said, stepping back. The Delta gave a bright smile and a gentle nod of his head.

"Was my pleasure, Luna."

"Oh, don't start that again," Lorelei warned as the weight of the title settled on her shoulders. She still had no idea what being a Luna meant and grew anxious every time someone addressed her by the title. Looking around, she wondered if there would even be a pack left to lead. Most of the Rogues left the day after the Daughtry's death for various reasons, however, each one thanked Declan before leaving.

"They're here!" Eris called out, nearly as excited to see her mate as Lorelei. Wyatt and Declan had been gone for two days to Atlanta to meet with Elder Caine and the rest of the Council. That morning, he had officially been exonerated of all charges relating to the Crescent Ridge massacre. Lorelei insisted that Wyatt go with him since she decided to finally take the pregnancy test and throw him a *proper* welcome home party.

"-really want to go home and see Lore. I haven't been able to reach her all day, and with Mercy still out there-"

"Dec. I promise you, Lorelei is fine," Wyatt said, his voice muffled through the wood. A moment later, the heavy oak door swung open, and Declan froze, seeing the crowded living room.

He blinked in confused amusement until his gaze found her. In an instant, Declan was standing before her, strong arms wrapping around her waist to pull her against him. Lacing her arms around his neck, Lorelei met him in a world-stopping kiss that had her toes curling in her boots. Around them, their guests hooted and hollered at the display.

"Welcome home, Alpha," Lorelei said, smiling against his lips.

443

444

Character Gallery

Declan Wolfe, 34

- Date of Birth- 2/14/1989
- Species- Werewolf (Alpha)
- Mate- Lorelei McCann
- Parents- Mordecai Wolfe (Father, Deceased) & Alora Wolfe (Mother, Deceased)
- Extended Family- Wyatt Leal (Cousin), Alaric Leal (Uncle, Deceased)
- Factoid- Declan secretly loves Christmas and had planned to carry on his father's tradition of dressing up as Santa for the children in the pack.

Lorelei McCann, 32

- Date of Birth- 10/23/1991
- Species- Witch (Light)
- Parents- Katherine McCann (Witch, Disabled due to dark magic) & Issac Rafferty (Deceased)
- Factoid- Lorelei gave her grandmother a pig nose by accident when she was a toddler. She would also be found sitting on the roof of the cabin every night, staring at the moon.

Hybrid Lorelai

Wyatt Leal, 31

- Date of Birth- 4/29/1992
- Species- Werewolf (Beta)
- Parents- Alaric Leal (Deceased) & Hannah Leal (Deceased)
- Factoid- Wyatt accidentally set the packhouse kitchen on fire while trying to set up a prank when he was a teenager. Unsurprisingly, he was trying to boil eggs.

Garridan Kemp, 35

- Date of Birth- 3/16/89
- Species- Werewolf (Delta)
- Mate- None
- Parents- Redacted
- Extended Family- Redacted
- Factoid- Garridan is Romanian. He was once a member of a traveling circus with his family before moving to America when he was still a child. His act was juggling on the unicycle.

Mordecai 'Kai' Wolfe, 63

- Date of Birth- 1/19/1960 (Deceased)
- Species- Werewolf (Alpha)
- Mate- Alora Wolfe (Deceased)
- Parents- Redacted
- Extended Family- Alaric Leal (Brother-in-law, Deceased) Wyatt Leal (Nephew)
- Date of Death- 6/24/2021
- Factoid- Kai would dress up as Santa Claus, and the Easter Bunny every year for the pack children.

Alora Wolfe, 59

- Date of Birth- 7/27/1964 (Deceased)
- Species- Werewolf (Delta)
- Mate- Mordecai 'Kai' Wolfe (Deceased)
- Parents- Redacted
- Extended Family- Wyatt Leal (Nephew)
- Date of Death- 6/24/2021
- Factoid- She was the Hula Hoop Champion during her senior year of high school with a record setting 33 minutes that has not been beaten to this day.

Alaric Leal, 59

- Date of Birth- 7/27/1964 (Deceased)
- Species- Werewolf (Beta)
- Mate- Hannah Leal (Deceased, Rogue attack)
- Parents- Redacted
- Extended Family- Mordecai 'Kai' Wolfe (Brother-in-law, Deceased), Declan Wolfe (Nephew)
- Factoid- Alaric never had a 'second chance' mate, and he preferred it that way. He raised Wyatt, who was 4 at the time of Hannah's death, with the help of Alora and Kai.

Apollo Daughtry, 57

- Date of Birth- 11/13/1966
- Species- Werewolf (Omega)
- Mate- Celeste Daughtry (Deceased, Died in Childbirth)
- Parents- Redacted
- Extended Family- Redacted
- Factoid- Apollo grew up as a Rogue, which plays a large part of why he hates being forced to submit.

Cormac Daughtry, 33

- Date of Birth- 6/6/1990
- Species- Werewolf (Omega)
- Mate- None
- Parents- Apollo Daughtry (Father) & Celeste Daughtry (Deceased)
- Extended Family- Redacted
- Factoid- Cormac was so incredibly close to Declan and Wyatt at one point that he nearly exposed his father's plans to take over the pack. However, his loyalty to his father prevented him from warning his 'brothers'.

Balor

Elder Council Witch, Mercy

Eris

Elder Caine

Real Mercy Good

www.ingramcontent.com/pod-product-compliance
Lightning Source LLC
Chambersburg PA
CBHW060604300726
48975CB00005B/1443